DEATH IN THE AIR

He turned and noticed a handful of nails embedded in the wall near his head, the sight of it tightening the springs of his tension. He crawled back toward the open doorway, pressure building in his ears. If they ever got out of this thing alive, he'd put up a storm shelter. Say the Lord's Prayer every single night. Quit swearing. *Please, God, have mercy on my family.*

Crawling back into the hallway on his hands and knees, Rob swept the flashlight beam across the red and green area rug, a pair of sneakers by the front door . . . Wait a second. *Sneakers?* Brand-new jogging sneakers, white and champagne shelltops. He gaped at those neatly tied laces and the jeans-clad legs attached to them, then gave a squawk as dirt danced into his eyes. He couldn't see.

He took a quick, sobbing breath as the owner of the sneakers stepped boldly into the house . . .

ACCLAIM FOR *THE BREATHTAKER*

The Breathtaker

Also by Alice Blanchard

Darkness Peering
The Stuntman's Daughter: Stories

THE
Breathtaker

ALICE BLANCHARD

WARNER BOOKS

NEW YORK   BOSTON

Copyright © 2003 by Alice Blanchard
Excerpt from new novel copyright © 2003 by Alice Blanchard
All rights reserved. No part of this book may be reproduced in any form or by any electronic or mechanical means, including information storage and retrieval systems, without permission in writing from the publisher, except by a reviewer who may quote brief passages in a review.

Cover design by Mimi Bark
Art by Franco Accornero
Handlettering by David Gatti

Warner Books

Time Warner Book Group
1271 Avenue of the Americas, New York, NY 10020
Visit our Web site at www.twbookmark.com

Printed in the United States of America

Originally published in hardcover by Warner Books
First Paperback Printing: November 2004

10 9 8 7 6 5 4 3 2 1

For Doug,
my light in the darkness

Come from the four winds, O breath,
and breathe upon these slain.

The Book of Ezekiel

PROLOGUE:
DANCING ON AIR

Rob Pepper stepped into the cheery yellow kitchen, ready for a fight. "Hey, Jenna, what's up?" he asked.

Cradling the receiver against her ear, his wife looked at him with a hint of hostility. *On the phone, always on the phone.* Today she was wearing too much champagne-colored lipstick, a thick layer of moss-green eye shadow glopped sluttishly on her lids. "Be right there," she said, tipping her head back and blowing smoke into the room.

He glanced at his watch. She'd been on the phone for fifteen minutes now and had missed the beginning of the movie. Spoiling their daughter's fun. A rainy Saturday afternoon. Popcorn and Jackie Chan. Rob and Jenna had called a truce. They'd promised their daughter, Danielle, that they would stop fighting and just be a family for once. Ha. That was rich. "Who're you talking to?"

"Rita," she said.

"Well, say bye-onara to Rita and come watch the movie with us."

She stared at him blandly. She was using an old cracked cereal bowl for an ashtray and sat on the kitchen chair like a monkey—knees drawn to her chest, those lovely peanut-shaped toes curling over the edges of the red vinyl seat. So sexy-looking in her peach-colored top and vintage jeans with the little holes in them. Rob had fallen in love with Jenna Kulbeck back in the seventh grade. Hopelessly, stupidly in love. She'd been such a slovenly, confused kid; born to poverty. Slutty, even. The school slut—he should've known. A girl so tiny he used to imagine he could carry her around in his pocket. She brought out his protective instincts. Shortly after their high school graduation, they'd gotten married on a grassy knoll surrounded by cottonwoods, and about a month later, Jenna had announced she was pregnant. After Danielle came three miscarriages in a row, *boom, boom, boom*. Three dead little boys named Robert Jr., Victor after her dad and Farley after his favorite uncle.

"So, Your Highness," he said with as much sarcasm as he could muster, the tension in him mounting, "you figure on joining us anytime soon?"

"Yeah," she said. "In a minute."

"You said that fifteen minutes ago."

She played deaf.

"All right, fine. Be that way." He opened the refrigerator door and slid a beer out of the six-pack, pried off the cap. It was warm inside the house, humid. Almost tropical. He glanced out the window. The overcast sky was looking ominous. *Cauliflower tops, good for the crops.* He tossed the beer cap into the wastebasket and left, advertising his disgust with a dismissive wave of his hand. But then, out in the hallway, he stood for a guilty moment and eavesdropped.

". . . you can never . . . that asshole . . ."

Asshole? Had she just called him an asshole? He peered around the corner and wondered if she was deliberately trying to provoke him. Her hair was dark and soft and came to just below her ears. Her glance fixed dully on her cigarette. She knocked the ash off with a moody finger. *Didn't she care? Didn't she care about her daughter's feelings anymore?* Rob was beginning to suspect that his wife might be having an affair. Too many mysterious phone calls lately, too many trips out of the house to buy things they absolutely, positively had to have, like peanut butter or toilet paper or *TV Guide*.

He stood there pawing at the truth. Was it his fault that their marriage was in trouble? Well, yeah . . . maybe. Maybe it was his fault. He wasn't a rich man. In the spring, he had to get up at 4:30 A.M. to plant the crops, repair the combine and execute his fertilizer program. He worked eighteen-hour days, then collapsed in bed at midnight. Slept like a log. Snored. They hadn't had sex in a while. Summers and winters were better for sex. Still, why punish Danielle? Why not punish him and spare their daughter's feelings? With an angry pivot, he walked back into the kitchen.

"Hold on," Jenna hissed into the receiver. "Now what?"

"Well?"

"Well, what?"

"How about it?"

"How about what?"

"The movie."

She closed her eyes. Cold. Contemptuous. "I'm on the phone."

You're on the rag. "With Rita?"

"Please." Her toes wiggled independently of one another like the keys on a player piano. "Go away, Rob."

"Fine. Break your daughter's heart."

He could tell by the stricken look on her face that he'd finally gotten through to her. *Finally, you bitch.*

Back in the living room, he gave his fourteen-year-old daughter an "everything's okay" smile and sat on the floor in front of the bay windows. Danielle preferred the old wicker chair with its flat, woven arms, whereas Jenna liked to curl up on the sofa and clutch herself as if she were in danger. He twisted his beer bottle into the shag to root it, then watched Jackie Chan do some amazing things with a chair. "Did I miss anything?" he asked.

Danielle rolled her eyes. "Bad guy just tried to kick Jackie Chan's butt, but Jackie Chan turned the tables on him."

"Turned the chair, you mean."

"Ha ha. Funny, Dad."

"I'm the coolest dad on Planet Earth."

"Kewl as a ghoul."

"Pass the popcorn, pip-squeak."

"Is Mom coming?"

"In a minute."

She slid him a look. "You guys okay?"

"Yeah, everything's fine."

He'd been so busy lately, so worried about his crops, he hadn't had time to consider his wife's needs. When you drove a tractor for eight hours at a stretch, you didn't feel like doing much of anything afterward. Your ears rang, your back ached. If she'd grown bored with the farm, there wasn't much he could do about it. Many years ago, Jenna in her white one-piece bathing suit used to lie on the carpet in front of him, her tanned back to the cinnamon-colored shag, and point her toes like a horizontal ballerina. She had such slender legs and narrow feet and those flexible toes—long, malleable wraparound toes she would cross and spread apart like the feathers of an opening fan. She would prop her feet on his thighs and fold all ten toes around his penis and work them up and down, stubby and grasping as baby fingers. She could even pick up objects with them—beer bottles and wooden blocks, things as tiny as paper clips.

The wind died suddenly.

Danielle whipped her head around. "What was that?"

He glanced out the window and saw leaves falling out of the sky. He'd developed a Zen-like attitude about the weather. You got what you got. "Thunder and lightning," he said. "Good for the crops."

Danielle steadied the bowl of popcorn on the arm of her chair. "Is that the town siren?"

He hit the Pause button. "Oh. That. Remember what happened last time it went off?"

She looked at him. "Nothing."

"And the time before that?"

"Nothing."

"And the time before that? And the time before that?"

She smiled. "Okay, Dad. You've made your point."

"Good. Now pass the popcorn, little one."

She handed him the bowl, and he glanced around the plant-festooned living room at the worn armchairs, cluttered coffee table, camping gear in the corner, the rumpled sleeping bag on the floor, the soundless clock. It was a little past two in the afternoon, and they had no basement to take shelter in. Another one of his failings, he supposed. Rob Pepper had neglected to provide his family with a basement, right here in the middle of Tornado Alley. What a dope. Maybe that was why Jenna hated him so much. Because of the generations of failure running through his veins. He glanced out the window and noticed that the clouds were moving rapidly across the sky now.

"Hey, Dad?" Danielle's long red hair was done up in ponytails today, and she looked like a little kid in her overalls and candy-apple-red T-shirt. But she had the same curvaceous figure as her mother, the same heart-breaking radiance to her skin and animation to her slender limbs that would torment every male creature she encountered from this point onward. "It's getting positively weird out there."

He touched the lip of the beer bottle to his front teeth and listened to the rush of wind. The air was humming like a tuning fork. Maybe Jenna was right. Maybe his whole problem was that he didn't understand anything. He got up and walked over to the bay window.

Outside, the clouds were whirling and twisting together, and the wheat waved and rippled. He stared at the boarded-up house across the street where nobody had lived for many years. The front door was flapping open and shut, as if a parade of ghosts were heading for the hills. The Peppers lived at the tail end of Shepherd Street in Promise, Oklahoma, just about the loneliest place on earth. There was nothing around for miles but winter wheat and circling hawks, rattlesnakes and a highway sorely in need of repair—a highway that took you either south to El Reno or north into Munchkinland.

"Dad?" Danielle was tugging on his shirtsleeve, a hint of wildness in her eyes. "Holy cow, this is major!"

He followed her gaze and noticed the funnel cloud reeling across the wheat toward them. The hairs on the back of his neck stood up and screamed. The funnel was miles away but rushing toward them fast, heaving surges of dirt into the air. They had to seek shelter immediately. He wouldn't have time to free his livestock.

"Jenna," he yelled. "Get your butt in here!"

"Mom?" Danielle wailed.

She met them in the doorway, looking flustered as hell. "What is it? What's going on?"

"A tornado," Rob said, "and it's coming up fast."

"You're kidding, right?" She headed for the front door, but he yanked her sharply back inside. "Ow!" Her hands groped for him, fingers twitching. She had long, sharp nails, and he let her go. "Don't grab me like that, you asshole!"

"Mom," Danielle pleaded, looking at her parents with the concern of a child whose emotional range and maturity had somehow far outstripped theirs.

Jenna stood rubbing her arm, nursing imagined wounds. Her eyes grew soft in her rigid face. "Let's get in the bathroom, quick!" she said.

"No, wait," Rob told her. "We want to be in the center of the house . . . not the southwest corner."

"You're supposed to get to a small, windowless room on the first floor . . . like a closet or a bathroom."

"Don't argue with me, Jenna. That corner of the house is gonna buckle first."

Her eyes seemed sunken, cautious.

"Front hallway. Now!"

They kept a flashlight in the chest of drawers supporting the TV set, and Rob clicked it on. A clatter of wind blew the window shades into the room. He snatched the cushions off the couch and scooped up the old sleeping bag. Covered in cat hairs, it made him sneeze. He'd read somewhere: *Old blankets, quilts and mattresses can help protect you and your family against flying debris.*

The three of them met in the front hallway, where he made a nest out of the cushions and sleeping bag, then Danielle folded herself down into it with her chin on her chest, while Jenna wrapped her arms protectively around her.

"Be right back," Rob said, bounding up the stairs.

The second floor groaned like a person in pain. Some of the upstairs windows were open, and he found himself trapped in a strange eddy of currents. Rooted to the spot, unable to move. What was that noise? It sounded like a hundred helicopters hovering above their white frame house, banking this way and that. For a few terrifying moments, this strange air current tossed him about like a tree swaying in a gale, and then, abruptly, it released him.

With a burning sensation in his chest, Rob hurried down the hallway into the master bedroom, where he tore the covers off the bed, grasped the polyester mattress by its thin elastic handles and lugged it off of the box spring and onto the floor. Then he paused to rummage through the big oak dresser for his brown billholder with all their credit cards and insurance papers inside. He tucked the billholder into the waistband of his jeans, then dragged the mattress down the stairs.

Back in the narrow front hallway, he propped the mattress diagonally against the wall, and the three of them hunkered together inside the crevice. He wrapped his arms around his wife and child and waited. There was nothing softer in this world, he thought, than his daughter's gentle breathing.

"Shit!" Jenna fiddled with the radio, getting nothing but static across the dial. "C'mon, talk to us . . ."

Rob crouched over them in that pitiful excuse for a hallway and met her angry gaze. Her mouth was stitched shut, as if this were somehow all his fault. *Go ahead, blame me.* He realized he was no prize with his eccentric nose and out-of-date pants, but he was a good provider, dammit. She should be thankful.

"Where's Bullette?" Danielle suddenly asked.

"Shh, honey. Cats are smart. He'll find himself a good hiding place," Rob told her.

As if on cue, above the rattling windowpanes, they could hear a plaintive meow.

"Bullette!" Her eyes filled with hot, terrified tears. "Daddy, go save him!"

"Shh, we have to stay put."

She began to weep convulsively, and Jenna stared at Rob over their daughter's quaking shoulders, a sodium stain from the flashlight playing across her grim features. "Go get the cat," she said.

"What?"

"Bullette!" Danielle screamed, her fist jerking to her mouth. "Daddy, go help him!"

Oh great. Just by doing nothing, he'd drawn the full weight of his wife's displeasure. Before she could get really vehement about it, he gripped the long-handled flashlight and crawled out from underneath their makeshift lean-to.

Almost instantly, a bitter chill engulfed him. Goose bumps prickled his arms as he swung the flashlight in an arc across the thin-legged mahogany mail table his grandfather had built nearly fifty years ago; past the wooden coat stand choked with rain slickers and the old picture frames clattering against the faded wallpaper. All he could hear was the wind, thunderous and cascading.

Get the cat. Ridiculous.

He crawled along the hardwood floor on his hands and

knees, moving like a poorly wired robot toward the kitchen. The thunder sounded strange—no rolling echo, just a thick-throated *boom. Boom.* Abrupt, like bombs dropping. The air was a swift current, hard to maneuver through. *Jesus, help me.* He crawled past the hallway chair with its stout oak legs and shone his light around the corner into the kitchen.

The calico cat was crouched in the crevice between the stove and cabinet. Rob could see its glowing eyes.

"Here, kitty . . ."

The cat tensed and stared at him. *Blink.*

"Here, kitty!"

It shuddered.

"C'mere, you mutt!"

It arched its back and fled.

"Fuck." Rob craned his neck, nerves raw, then heard a crackling sound, distantly sinister, and a thunderous *bang* that made his whole body quake. He covered his head just as glass shattered above him and a violent wind came rushing in. Screaming in his ears. Swirling up into his face. The seconds ticked past heavily. When he finally raised his head again, he could see a massive tree limb sticking in through the kitchen window. "Jesus Christ," he said, watching the tattered curtains dance. It was like being inside a vacuum cleaner, the pressure building in his ears. The wind rocked the refrigerator ever so slightly back and forth, and he aimed his light into the four corners of the room, but the cat had vanished. *Screw the cat.* He turned and noticed a handful of nails embedded in the wall near his head, the sight of it tightening the springs of his tension.

"Rob?" came Jenna's distant cry.

An unraveling roll of toilet paper skittered across the

floor toward him and rose up like a cobra. A long, sinuous strand of it danced in midair above his head, gravity gone. His eyes grew wide as he watched the spectacle. His ears were ready to pop. He crawled back toward the open doorway that led back into the front hall, pressure building in his ears. If they ever got out of this thing alive, he'd put up a storm shelter. Buy one of those "safe rooms" he'd seen advertised. Donate blood. Feed the homeless. Say the Lord's Prayer every single night. Quit swearing. Whatever it took.

Please, God, have mercy on my family . . .

Crawling back into the hallway on his hands and knees, Rob swept the flashlight beam across the mahogany legs of the mail table, the red and green area rug, a pair of sneakers by the front door . . . Wait a second. Back up. *Sneakers?*

Brand-new jogging sneakers, white and champagne shelltops, the kind of blinding white that made you want to step all over them. He gaped at those neatly tied laces and the jeans-clad legs attached to them, then gave a watery squawk as dirt flew into his eyes.

He couldn't see. The front door was open, leaves and shredded debris whipping into the house. "Hello?" He squinted up in anxiety, blinking away the tears. Who was this person? A rescue worker? An intruder? The thought pulled at his stomach.

Blind, he was fucking blind.

He took a quick, sobbing breath as the owner of the sneakers stepped boldly into the house, crunching over broken glass. Then the door slammed shut with a *thunk.*

APRIL IS THE
CRUELEST MONTH

1

POLICE CHIEF Charlie Grover was surprised to find Main Street's stately granite buildings still standing, their dimpled windows and variegated roofs intact. Back at the station house, he'd thought the sky was falling, but now he could see with his own eyes that downtown had withstood nature's fury. The air hung wet and still, and with his high beams on, he could make out the muck and debris the tornado had deposited everywhere like Christmas tinsel — long strands of videotape draped over tree limbs, black cables slithering across the road, insulation dust swirling through the air.

He was shaken up pretty badly and wanted a drink. He hated himself for drinking. He'd promised Maddie on her deathbed that he wouldn't touch the stuff ever again, but he had. Not with a vengeance. He wasn't a full-tilt, fall-down drunk, but he needed a drink now and again. And really, now was as good a time as any. Less than thirty minutes ago, a harmless-looking milky white F-1 on the Fujita scale had dropped down out of the sky over Promise, Oklahoma, and quickly transformed itself into a quivering black F-3 that'd zigzagged over open country south of town, wreaking selective havoc. According to reports just coming in, the damage path was ten miles long and nearly a quarter of a mile wide. Charlie was on his way now to coordinate whatever rescue efforts might be necessary and assess the damage. Through the static and crackle of his police radio, he could hear Patrol Officer Tyler Drumright's hoarse, urgent voice: ". . . the roof is gone . . . we've got a home with no interior walls left standing . . . Chief? Are you there, Chief?"

He picked up the hand mike. "Go ahead, Tyler."

"I'm at the Black Kettle subdivision. We've got a fifty-eight-year-old with chest pains, and no ambulance in sight."

"If he stops breathing, start chest compressions. The paramedics are on their way."

"We've got lots of stunned and bewildered residents suffering only bumps and scrapes."

"Hang in there, buddy, you're doing great. I'll be there in five." He dropped the mike back in its retainer and had a flash of his baby sister, for some reason. His baby sister in her crib. Little Clara Grover had died thirty years ago at the age of two. He remembered her lying in her crib and gazing up at him with those enormous green eyes of hers.

Forget, forget . . .

This tornado had him reeling. A million things to do, and he was the guy in charge. Under the uniform, he was afraid. He tried to reach his daughter again and got the busy signal. The phone lines were jammed. He took a deep breath, confident that sixteen-year-old Sophie was okay. The tornado hadn't traveled that far north, but he needed to be sure. Just needed to hear her sweet voice, her smug indifference. *"Oh Dad, I'm fine. What's wrong?"*

He squeezed the wheel, drawing into himself. Life could take everything from you. So scared, dammit. That anxious fire in the pit of his stomach. Loved ones snatched away in the dead of night. Unfair. He rotated his shoulders, the pain shooting up the left side of his body like a trail of fire ants. It was the ancient miasma of burn scars and skin grafts that was causing all the discomfort. He'd felt that dull throbbing ache on the scarred left-hand side of his body ever since this morning, the cramps in his muscles and aches in his joints that usually portended foul weather. He should've known about the severity of this storm—his joints had never bothered him so bad.

Thirty years ago, Charlie Grover had suffered second- and third-degree burns to the left side of his body—arm, chest, rib cage and leg—a crazy quilt of melted flesh extending from his earlobe down to his ankle, where the scarring ended abruptly, like a tube sock with the foot cut off. Fortunately for him, his genitals and face had been spared *(thank you, God),* but some of the hypertrophic scars with their donor skin grafts had healed improperly, and the resultant lack of elasticity forced him as a matter of lifelong habit to turn around stiffly at the waist, as if his vertebrae were fused together. An odd handicap that'd made the top brass hesitant to promote him. Not that he blamed them, but Charlie Grover could fire a weapon, write a traffic ticket and solve a homicide with the best of them, yet he'd had to work extra hard to prove his worth to Mayor Whitmore and his cronies. He'd never filed a discrimination lawsuit, although he could have many times. It was only through sheer grit and determination on his part that those in charge had eventually come around. If Charlie knew one thing, it was that he was perfectly suited for the job. The bad guys of Promise had something to fear from him.

"Chief?" His police radio squawked again. "Pick up!"

He scooped up the hand mike. "Yeah, Tyler?"

"We have a casualty! An elderly woman got blown out of her house . . . Oh God, she was literally thrown across the street into a barbed-wire fence . . . She's dead at the scene."

"I'm on Willow Road. Almost there."

"Where's the ambulance? Where the hell is everybody?"

"Paramedics are on their way, I promise you that."

"Looks like fifteen homes were destroyed, maybe twenty. There's major damage. Everybody's running around in a panic."

"I'm minutes away. Hang in there, buddy, you're doin' great." Around the next corner, he found himself on the long approach to the Black Kettle subdivision, where he had a sweeping panorama of the plains. As far as the eye could see was an unbroken stretch of winter wheat and wild grass, so much motion in the landscape it dazzled the senses. All those lush green pastures, all those red and orange wildflowers and blooming dogwood trees. A wet spring was essential if the wildflowers were to reach their peak in April.

Now Charlie stepped on the gas, his sense of urgency piqued. Road gravel struck the undercarriage of the police car as he sped past fields bounded by thin belts of trees, their gloves of new growth khaki-colored from the insulation dust. The road he was on crossed a steel bridge, then waved gently up and down the map. April was the month of rebirth, and all week long the grass had kept its promise, growing thick and green in the meadows and crowding out the tassel-headed weeds. The last few pockets of ice in the woods had finally thawed, giving way to a carpet of Indian paintbrush and bluebonnets. Funny how you could watch very carefully for spring and still miss it, he thought as he glanced at the departing storm clouds amassed along the horizon.

He rolled to a stop at a beheaded stop sign, and from this angle he could see down into the path of obliteration. The tornado had swept through like a giant reaper, ripping a spotty but destructive swath across the grasslands and dissecting the subdivision almost in half. Many of the expensive two-story homes had been reduced to one-story homes; some had been swept completely off their slabs. The blue water tower was knocked over, and injured cows and pigs from nearby farms were wandering around aimlessly. Crumpled sheets of corrugated tin were strewn across the landscape like discarded pieces of paper.

Charlie veered the rest of the way down the snaking road, then came to a screeching halt. Two EMT vehicles and a highway patrol car were parked in the middle of the road in front of a tangle of downed power lines.

He got out of his patrol car. "Hello?" All the emergency personnel must've taken off on foot. He climbed onto the trunk of a fallen oak and surveyed the partially destroyed subdivision. The wind was so strong he had to hold on to his hat. Two or three entire blocks of homes had been decimated. It was an awesome sight—exterior walls were missing, garage doors had buckled, roofs had caved in. Front lawns were clogged with waist-deep debris, cars were accordioned into buildings and most of the ash trees that grew especially dense in the Black Kettle subdivision had been stripped of their leaves, their trunks twisted like wrung washcloths.

Mike Rosengard lived on this block, Charlie recalled with a start. Third house down, south side of the street, in a spot that was now Toothpick City. "God," he breathed. Nothing was left standing of Mike's house but the central staircase rising out of the rubble and leading nowhere.

His heart rate accelerated as he picked his way downhill, feet crunching over shattered glass and splintered twigs. The wind at his back made a debris trail in front of him, and Charlie could smell natural gas in the air—or rather, the chemical substance they put in the gas to make it recognizable. Alarmed, he activated his cell phone and dialed the station house.

"Promise P.D.," Hunter Byrd answered in that nasal drawl of his.

"Hunter, I'm at the Black Kettle subdivision. Listen, we desperately need a gas company crew down here right away. And commission as many bulldozers and earthmovers as you can to clear a path for police and fire crews. And call up the National Guard. We're gonna need some sort of heavy rescue extraction unit."

"Okay, boss." A former linebacker gone to fat with curly red hair and a rectangular chin, Sergeant Hunter Byrd was the practical joker of the unit, always pulling crazy stunts, like ordering fifty pizzas at once or making choking sounds over the P.A. system. You never knew whether he was serious or not, but Charlie could tell he was dead serious now.

"We're gonna need a massive emergency response to restore electrical power. And where the hell is the fire department?"

"On their way, Chief."

"Well, light a fire under them. Metaphorically speaking." As if on cue, the sound of screaming sirens reached his ears, and he turned to see two fire trucks and a squad car careening up the road toward him, their red and blue beacons strobing in the hazy air.

Clutching his portable unit, Charlie waded through the muck and debris toward Mike's house—now just a pile of lumber on a concrete foundation. A huge tree was horizontal on the front yard, as if a bulldozer had knocked it over, and a slender woman suddenly appeared from behind it. Jill Rosengard was almost unrecognizable, covered in mud from head to foot.

"Jill?" Charlie called out, but she didn't respond. She was busy filling a trash bag with debris from the yard. "Jill, is that you?"

Now a man popped his head out of the basement. "Chief?"

Charlie recognized the timbre of Mike Rosengard's voice, deep and melodic as the tones of a cello. He was holding two small children in his arms—two little boys so covered in mud they could've been carved out of chocolate.

"Holy shit. D'you believe this?" Mike crossed the debris field of broken glass and downed electrical wires, stumbling shoeless and sockless through the mud. Mud ran down his face and plastered his hair thickly to his skull.

Charlie grabbed him by the arm. "Are you okay?"

"Yeah, things are fine. Considering."

Mike's two boys, Sammy and Jerry, stared at Charlie with surreally wide eyes.

"We made it, guys," their father said, jostling them affectionately on his hips. "Thank God we made it, huh?" He laughed with relief as the boys nodded their heads in unison.

Detective Sergeant Mike Rosengard was a close friend and a seasoned cop with an unassertive chin who had over eleven years on the force—six as a patrol officer, five as a detective handling everything from shoplifting to suicide. He liked to introduce himself as the only Jew in Oklahoma and was the kind of cop who would work a case until it was solved. Of average height and build beneath neatly pressed suits, Mike had a calm confidence that didn't come off as cocky, and Charlie had all kinds of faith in him.

"Hey, my family's fine," he said, jockeying the boys in his arms. "That's the important thing, right?" He pointed at the muddy Bronco parked in the driveway. "Now, isn't that a lovely shade of crap?"

"How's Jill doing?" Charlie asked, genuinely concerned.

"Trying to retrieve pieces of her life," Mike whispered. "You watch. Half of our stuff is in Helena by now."

"She all right?"

"I think so, why?" He seemed suddenly worried.

"Let's get somebody down here to look at her." He got on his portable and directed one of the EMTs over to Mike's residence, then stood staring at the remains of the house, stray plumes of dust wafting up from the ruins. It was a miracle they weren't all dead.

"I heard this high-pitched whistle, really piercing," Mike said. "Then our garbage cans started to blow around. Then the wind slammed the door in my face, and suddenly it grew utterly quiet. Fuckin' eerie, Chief. We ran down to the basement, and I held on to my babies. The house was twisting and heaving, you could hear it creaking at the seams. I kept thinking about my babies getting sucked out of my arms, and I didn't want that to happen, so I hung on extra tight. So tight they could barely breathe. Right, guys?" Tears trembled in the corners of his eyes. "I can honestly say that I have never been so scared in all my life, Chief. There was this irrational movement of the walls and ceiling, then I heard a loud screech . . . as if a hundred cars were rounding a corner too fast. Then everything exploded. I looked up, and there was just a gaping hole where the roof had been. Gone! It was gone. In the blink of an eye, we lost everything. Half our neighborhood's gone," he said with a dumbfounded shake of his head. "It was here this morning. Now it's gone."

To the right of Mike's property, a neighboring house had been pushed forward some twenty-five feet off its foundation; now it slouched like an old man on a long Sunday.

"Are the neighbors okay?" Charlie asked.

"Yeah, everyone in the immediate vicinity."

His portable unit squawked. "Chief? It's Lester. You'd better get over here right away."

He held the unit to his lips. "Over where, Lester? Where are you?"

"The Peppers' house on Shepherd Street." His voice was shaking. "Oh my God . . . You're not gonna believe this . . . I can't describe it, Chief . . . Just hurry, please."

2

THE WIND stiffened as Charlie stepped out of his cruiser, bits of leaves and debris flying into his face. He was way out in the middle of nowhere at the tail end of Shepherd Street, facing Rob Pepper's ruined farmstead. Most of the buildings had been scoured off their slabs—barn, stables, henhouse, toolshed. Huge thirty-foot I-beams were tossed around like straws. The big shady trees that'd once shielded the property from the noontime sun had blown over. The Peppers' pickup truck had rolled across the street and slammed into an overturned clothes dryer. Large areas of winter wheat had been stripped bare, and dead hogs and wind-plucked chickens littered the landscape—Chester White, Berkshire, Spotted Poland China. All blue-ribbon winners.

Only the Peppers' house stood intact amid the chaos. Charlie stepped gingerly over broken tree limbs and a Tupperware bowl twisted wildly out of shape, then paused to study the white frame house beneath the overcast sky. This slab-on-grade farmhouse was similar to many others in the area, without any basement to take shelter in. The tornado had narrowly missed it, coming to within an eighth of a mile. Some of the windows had blown out, the chimney was toppled and part of the roof was gone; but the structure had withstood the kind of pressure that'd knocked almost everything else down. How had that happened? He rubbed his forehead. He'd heard of multivortex tornadoes before, and it made sense. A single tornado might occasionally contain two or more small, intense subvortices orbiting around its center; these vortices, forming and dying within seconds, were the cause of most of the narrow, short swaths of extreme damage that arced through the tornado's tracks.

"Chief?" Assistant Chief Lester Deere said from the front porch. "I think they're dead up there."

"What?"

"The Peppers."

He noticed the mud on Lester's clothes, the blood on his hands. Lester was the kind of guy who had a problem with life's little rules; he was always late for work and full of excuses. Today, on his day off, he wore the flannel shirt and denim jeans of a ranch hand. Now in his post-football years, his stomach pooched out and his big square body was topped off by an unruly mop of sandy blond hair that he gelled almost too carefully in place.

"They're all dead up there," he repeated mindlessly, his bloodshot eyes not quite focusing. "I'm in shock. Look at my hands. I can't stop shaking."

Charlie glanced at Lester's bloody hands. "What d'you mean, they're all dead? The house is still standing. What happened?"

"Go see for yourself." His voice was so constricted you wanted to find the choke control and ease up.

The front door wasn't locked. The interior of the house was so dark it took a few moments for Charlie's eyes to adjust. The hairs on the nape of his neck shivered as he inhaled the sharp, coppery scent of blood. He aimed his flashlight into the chaos of the front hallway. The mail table and coatrack were overturned, pictures were off the walls, broken glass was everywhere.

He proceeded slowly forward, his flashlight beam raking across the rose-covered wallpaper. A few picture frames still clung tenaciously to the walls: innocent candids of the Peppers one Christmas Eve; of Rob Pepper carving the Thanksgiving turkey; of Danielle and her mother dressed as Raggedy Ann and Andy some long-forgotten Halloween. In the center of the hallway was a bundle of couch cushions and a soggy mattress, a bunched-up sleeping bag, a broken radio on the floor and a flashlight whose batteries still worked, light playing off the floorboard. He took a closer look at the mattress and saw bloodstains. He found a pool of blood on the floor, then saw the drag marks leading toward the stairs.

Taking the stairs two at a time, he followed the drag marks down the hallway into the master bedroom, where he paused in the doorway to catch his breath. There was a huge, gaping hole in the ceiling, where the rafters, roof and part of the wall had been torn away. He could see the gray, overcast sky and the backyard from here. The bedroom was a mess—broken glass, overturned furniture, everything covered in mud. One of the tornado's vortices must've ripped through the roof, like a fairy-tale giant taking a bite out of a gingerbread house.

The Peppers' teenage daughter was huddled in a corner behind the queen-size bed, her arms curled protectively around herself. Danielle Pepper had been impaled by flying debris—shattered glass from the broken windows, splintered pieces of wood. Gruesome. Horrific. There was penetrating trauma with what looked like a splintered chair leg and the bloody strut of a picket fence.

Charlie squatted in front of her and felt for a pulse. Her skin was waxy and translucent, at the beginning stages of lividity. Her open eyes did not react to light, although the corneas were clear. He observed in her stiffened jaw the beginning stages of rigor mortis. She reminded him of Sophie, and that made him cringe. Her long red hair was done up in ponytails, and when he wiped the mud off her face, he could see deep bruises over her right eye and cheekbone.

The world swam for an instant as Charlie stood up and took a step backward. He glanced around the master bedroom. The mattress was missing from the bed and the box spring was wet with rain. He heard an odd creaking sound. It was coming from somewhere above him. There was an explosion of splinters as something came crashing through the ruined plaster over his head, and a scream lodged in his throat as he leaped away.

Rob Pepper's torso was dangling from the ceiling like an upside-down jack-in-the-box. He was stuck like a pincushion with flying debris—face, neck, chest. The bottom half of his body remained lodged in the crumbling plaster while the upper half swung hideously back and forth.

Charlie dragged his hand across his mouth, the fear crowding in on him. Everything stood still for a moment. The house was shaking with wind, and he suddenly wondered if the structure was stable. Maybe it had sustained more damage than he'd initially thought. He backed away from the bodies and almost tripped on an overturned rocking chair. He caught his balance and pivoted, then found himself on the edge of a precipice, floorboards jutting into nothingncss.

Jenna Pepper had been flung into a nearby tree by the wind, her body nestled in a bed of tangled branches just a few yards from where he stood. She was a petite woman, five foot two, maybe a hundred pounds soaking wet. Her sleek dark hair was cropped short, and she wore faded Levi's and a peach-colored pullover top, no shoes or socks on her slender feet. Charlie swallowed hard at the sight of the mahogany bedpost protruding like the hilt of a knife from her neck. She had penetrating injuries to her chest with what looked like a staircase baluster, and the bloodstains on her pullover were like scattered red roses. Squinting hard, he thought he could detect defensive wounds to her hands and forearms.

Something stirred in him. The old-fashioned roller shades flapped in the wind as he walked back over to where Rob Pepper dangled from the rafters. Charlie reached for his hands and turned them palms-up. There were defensive wounds to his forearms, standard slash marks from a knife or a blade. *Drag marks in the hallway leading up the stairs . . .*

Charlie got on his portable and said with some urgency, "Lester? I want you to cordon off the area."

"Some of the rescue workers just pulled up, Chief."

"Send them away. Access to the area is being restricted. Post a man at either end of the street. If anybody asks, tell them we're having problems with gas leaks."

He stared into Rob's eyes—unfocused eyes that seemed to be retracted into infinite regret. "Lester? Did you get all that?"

"Are they dead?"

"Yeah," he said with wonder, "they're all dead."

3

THAT NIGHT, military men in green jeeps patrolled the streets, while TV trucks cruised the ruins in search of anything poignant or shocking they could put on the eleven o'clock news. Volunteers with chain saws helped clear the debris from the roads so that the gas company crews could check for damaged lines. Most of the cops on duty that day didn't go home when their shifts were over, and the town's fire crew worked all night long to contain the sporadic fires. Meanwhile, the screams of ambulances and police cars never let up.

Around 8:00 P.M., the temperature dropped and a cold driving rain pummeled the town. A thousand residents left their unheated, unlit homes for the warmth of the Red Cross shelters, where volunteers served up free meals of pork ribs from Babe's Bar-B-Q and the works on Texas toast from the Roadside Diner. At the damage site, people stood around in amazement in the freezing-ass rain, while a pea-soup fog tinted with the fiery glow of the strobing emergency lights settled over everything. Men passed around paper bags, talking softly among themselves, while housewives with no homes to go back to traded drags off cigarettes and prowled through the rubble in an attempt to salvage whatever valuables they could before they were ordered away for good. Prayers were said. Those little bargains you made with God. *Please let it be over with. Let this be the worst of it.*

Local TV anchors shoved microphones in Charlie's face and followed him around relentlessly wherever he went. He tried to answer their questions as best he could while keeping his suspicions about the crime to himself. It was such huge news he didn't want to be wrong about it, didn't want to make a fool of himself on national TV. He would wait until after the autopsies were done to make an announcement, until he knew for certain what they were dealing with.

"Those parts of town with underground electrical lines will regain power first," he told reporters outside the police station, his voice hoarse from reiterating a thousand details. "Those homes and businesses served by aerial lines should take a little longer. Part of the problem is moving huge piles of debris out of the way. We need more volunteers with bulldozers and tractor-trailers, if you could get the word out."

"Chief? Can you confirm the number of dead so far?"

"We have it at six."

"What about financial aid for the victims?"

"A representative from FEMA will be here tomorrow to help with the recovery."

"Chief? Why is Shepherd Street closed off to traffic?" asked a reporter whose darkly challenging looks told you he'd get to the bottom of things, with or without your help.

"We're checking out some damaged gas lines in the area," Charlie lied, referring to a yellow legal pad so covered with notes he could barely read his own writing. "There are nine-hundred-plus people staying in shelters tonight, three dozen National Guard troops requested. We had approximately twenty minutes of warning, which helped keep the death toll low, compared to what it might've been. The fire department has completed its search for bodies and survivors in the Black Kettle subdivision, and the cadaver dogs have been called off. You can reach the courthouse all night long. Somebody'll be there to keep you posted."

He turned to leave, but a well-groomed anchorwoman from KVMX stepped in his path. "What about the rumors, Chief? We keep hearing rumors that one of today's tornado victims has met with foul play."

"I have no comment at this time."

"Chief!" He was pummeled with questions as reporters scrambled after him. "The helicopter cam shows a cordoned-off area on Shepherd Street. Care to comment?"

"I'll have more to say tomorrow morning. G'night, folks."

"Chief? Chief?" News crews surrounded his vehicle, preventing him from leaving until a few of his men chased them off. Charlie stepped on the accelerator, all those ghostly faces in his headlights' glare clamoring for enlightenment. A sudden gust of wind rammed into the car, and the taste of whiskey lingered on his lips. *Bad idea. One of the reporters could've smelled it, and then what?* An hour earlier, he'd changed his shirt at the station house and had taken a few covert swigs from the bottle of Mr. Daniel's the dispatcher kept in his desk drawer. Now he passed through downtown with its rain-slicked streets and flat-faced brick facades, thinking how baffling this case was. Jenna, Rob and Danielle Pepper had sustained defensive wounds to the hands, forearms and face. There were drag marks leading up the stairs from two or more bodies, and Danielle had scrape marks on her arms and mud on the back of her clothes, indicating that her body had been dragged. He wouldn't know about the other two until the medical examiner arrived on the scene and gave them permission to move the bodies. It sent shivers cascading across his scalp. Their last homicide case had been six months ago, a drug killing. The last tornado to hit Promise, Oklahoma, was in 1924.

He took a right onto a poorly paved road, his headlights wrapping across the twisted landscape. Some people came out of their nightmare childhoods to become priests or criminals; Charlie had become a cop. He held a criminology degree from the University of Oklahoma and had done his police training in Tulsa, where he'd walked a beat for several years before returning home. This town of 22,000 had its share of bad guys and a serious drug problem, mostly pot and amphetamines. He'd worked with informants, prostitutes and junkies. He'd taken on three thugs in a gun battle once—a classic check-your-shorts moment. He'd worked robberies, jack-rollings, shootings and cuttings. You carried a big stick, depending on which neighborhood you were in. Charlie had even killed a man once—nothing he was proud of. Five years ago, an unemployed mill worker had taken his own children hostage. Trained in hostage negotiations at the University of Oklahoma, Charlie'd almost talked the distraught man into surrendering, when the perp suddenly turned the gun on his four-year-old daughter and Charlie was forced to shoot him dead. He'd gotten decorated for it, but he still had nightmares over it.

Now he nodded at the National Guard standing post at the entrance to Shepherd Street. He'd stationed as many patrol officers as he could spare around the scene of the crime, stationed even more officers along Main Street and other areas of business in order to discourage civil disobedience. A handful of his men were out canvassing the Peppers' neighborhood, going door-to-door in search of any eyewitnesses who might've seen or heard something suspicious that afternoon.

The crime scene was a virtual dead zone, full of the glow of headlights and the sound of gas generators. Half a dozen detectives and officers in double gloves and protective Tyvek-type shoe covers were inside the house now, processing the scene and collecting trace evidence. Despite the heavy fog, a tireless news helicopter circled overhead, and Charlie hoped they'd run out of fuel soon and leave.

Around midnight, the helicopter finally flew away. Reports were coming back that the town was by all accounts quiet now, most of its citizens holed up in their own homes, if they still had a home. The rain stopped around 3:00 A.M., and the sky blew clear, the stars came out. Exhausted but resolved, Charlie and his men continued to gather physical evidence from the primary scene until around 5:00 A.M., when Roger Duff, the medical examiner, came to take the bodies away. Charlie was about to accompany him over to the morgue when Duff told him, "Go home and hug your daughter, Charlie. These bodies'll keep."

It was 5:30 A.M. by the time he turned down Red Bud Road. The rising sun hit him in the eyes and lit the fine hairs of his knuckles so that they glowed translucent. His throat was hoarse from nonstop talking. His clothes were streaked with mud, his fingernails black with grime. All he wanted to do was lie down and close his scratchy eyes, but he wouldn't be getting any sleep for the next forty-eight hours, at least.

As he parked in the driveway, Charlie was disheartened to discover that the flag had been wrenched from its place by the front door and twisted, pole and all, around the branch of a dogwood tree. The tornado had left its imprint everywhere like a colorless poison. Pink and white bits of insulation littered the front yard, along with a multitude of roofing shingles. Envelopes were scattered everywhere. *Nice to see the mail's being delivered.* The clear blue sky made him feel blotted out. He looked at the peeling white frame house with its dark green shutters and sighed. At least nothing important had blown away. Some of the siding was damaged and tree limbs were scattered over the grass like abandoned croquet mallets, but the house itself remained intact. His daughter was safe and sound. The April air was bracing. As he crossed the yard, a swallow careened in front of him, snapping at invisible bugs.

Charlie half expected to hear Maddie's honeyed voice as he opened the front door. *Sweetie?* But there was no familiar greeting, no hug. Not the warmth of her body, not that ugly flannel robe the color of gravy she'd worn the last few months of life. Beautiful Maddie, smarter than him, better than him. *The doctors had tried every available option, but when all else failed, they suggested implanting irradiated rods in her head. Irradiated rods that would presumably kill off the cancer cells, blast them all to hell along with half her brain. Sophie wasn't allowed*

*to visit Maddie in the hospital during the procedure,
since it was far too dangerous, and Charlie could only
stay for fifteen minutes a day. But Maddie, his lovely
dying wife, had remained inside that specially outfitted
room for over a week, those rods in her head emitting
dangerous doses of radiation. Surely it had done more
harm than good . . .*

The front hallway smelled of burned toast. The polished floorboards creaked in the same places they always
had; only Maddie was gone. He missed her most when he
got home from work. Pictures dusty with neglect lined
the hallway walls, and he paused to straighten one out—
a youthful Maddie smiling down at him, her eyes two
crescents of amusement. He frowned, letting the sadness
and guilt wash over him. If he held perfectly still, it
would be gone soon.

"Charlie?" Peg Morris said, popping out of the kitchen
and cinching her blue kimono shut. "Oh my gosh. You
scared the bejesus out of me!" Peg had swooped in to fill
the void after Maddie's death with her rumpled maternal
instinct and tattered blue silk kimono, cigarettes and God
knows what else bulging from the pockets. She was
Maddie's second cousin and lived across town, but she
spent an occasional night at their place whenever Charlie
had to work late. She had no children of her own and had
taken Sophie under her wing, and for that, Charlie would
be eternally grateful.

"Thanks for looking after her, Peg."

"Oh please, don't even mention it." She had penny-
colored hair and a mole beside her mouth that wasn't
pretty. "You look like you've been through the wringer,
Mr. Man. How about some French toast and bacon?"

"I don't have time to even contemplate breakfast, Peg."

She had a laugh like watered-down Scotch. "What about coffee? You got time to contemplate that?"

"Love a cup."

"Is everything okay?"

"Some major damage. A few people died."

"Mary Jo Crider, Rob and Jenna Pepper, Danielle, John Payne, and Bill Rowley. Oh my gosh, when we first heard about it on the radio, we couldn't believe our ears." She shook her head in shock. "You hear about tornadoes all your life, but you never think it'll happen to you."

"How's Ben?" he asked, remembering Peg's boyfriend.

"Lost a few horses, but we all survived, didn't we?"

He paused on the stairs. "Can you stay tonight?"

"Sorry, Charlie. I promised Ben."

"Yeah, sure. Don't worry about it. I'll figure something out." He took the stairs two at a time, then knocked on the DISASTER AREA sign taped to his daughter's door. "Sofe? You awake?"

"C'mon in," came her groggy voice.

Entering his daughter's room with its peach-colored walls, ivory curtains and vanilla oak floor was like diving into a pale pool. Disaster area was right—there were dirty clothes everywhere you looked, magazines and soda cans, CDs and cosmetics. Her room looked like the inside of a Dumpster, but she knew exactly where everything was. Sophie was curled in a fetal lump beneath her bedcovers. She slept with her fists squeezed shut, as if she were clinging to a thin rope of consciousness.

"Hey there, jelly bean."

"Dad!" She sat up and gave him a hug. "I was so worried about you!" She had her mother's widely spaced eyes and sensual mouth, same mixture of innocence and self-reliance. She had Maddie's long cinnamon-colored hair and porcelain skin with that rich pink color to her cheeks; but make no mistake about it, she was her father's daughter. Stubborn, methodical, same worry line between her eyes. At five foot seven, she was taller than most of her classmates but had fortunately inherited none of her father's innate awkwardness. She was blessed with Maddie's athletic grace and moved like liquid mercury. "Phew, you reek," she said, clamping her pillow over her face.

He ran his fingers over his beard bristle. "I was just about to take a shower, thanks a lot."

"Take a nice long one, okay? With lots and lots of soap," she said with a muffled giggle. "You're staying for breakfast, right?"

"Can't."

She removed the pillow and looked at him, disappointment in her eyes. "Dad . . . I need some face-to-face time with you."

"Yeah, well. I need face-to-face time with you, too."

"So?"

"How's tonight sound? I think I can get away."

She frowned. " 'Think' isn't good enough."

"Lemme see what I can do. C'mere." He wrapped his arms around her again and gave her a lingering hug, needing to know that she was okay. If she'd been left relatively unscathed by yesterday's events, then he could get back to work and quit worrying.

"The whole house was shaking like a leaf," she told him. "You could hear hail bouncing off the metal cellar doors. Peg and I were like, 'What was that? What was that?' We were jumpy as hell. I was so scared at one point I thought my heart was going to burst."

"I'm glad Peg was with you."

She gave him a despairing look. "I tried to call Grandpa, but the lines were down."

He could feel his face tense up. "Don't worry," he said. "That side of town didn't get hit."

"Yeah, but still . . . shouldn't you go check on him?"

"I'm sure he's fine."

"Please?" She fingered the locket at her throat, the heart-shaped locket on its long silver chain that her mother had given her for her tenth birthday. She never took it off. She slept with the damn thing on, probably bathed with it on. Just like all the other sentimental objects she couldn't bear to part with—her cowgirl lamp with its torn shade, the moth-eaten Indian throw rug with the mystical symbols on it. He was sure she'd die of old age with that silver chain clasped around her neck.

"Your grandfather's fine," he insisted.

"Come on, Dad. Please? For me?"

"Get some sleep."

"Yeah, right. He's *only* your father."

He narrowed his eyes at her. "Are you trying to guilt-trip me?"

"Gee, I dunno. Is it working?"

"Fine. I'll go see him," he said. "Happy now?"

"Tell him to call me, okay?"

"I've got a few things I have to do first. But I promise, okay? Now get some sleep, you pain in the butt."

She giggled and said, "You should talk."

4

CHOKING BACK the stench of the autopsy suite, Charlie observed this most indecent scene through narrowed eyes. The three victims lay side by side on identical chrome tables—Jenna Pepper, Rob and their fourteen-year-old daughter, Danielle. The bodies had been X-rayed, weighed and measured, and any identifying marks such as tattoos or old injuries had been recorded. The bloodstained clothing, along with the wrapping sheets, had been bagged and sent off to the state lab for processing, and now the victims lay naked and exposed, miscellaneous debris protruding gruesomely from their bodies.

"Sorry I'm late." Roger Duff secured his lab coat around his stout middle as he swept into the morgue. "How's Sophie?"

"Fine."

"Good. Glad to hear it. Any property damage?"

"Minor. You?"

"I can't find my cat." Duff was a small man with a big attitude, a sour-faced old-timer whose irritating arrogance Charlie had long ago accepted as part of the package. He was the medical examiner for the whole county and was often called out of bed in the middle of the night to drive to a crime scene as far away as Camargo. There was always a push-pull between them. An intellectual tug-of-war.

Duff took the clipboard down from the wall and read the stapled information sheet, then rubbed his chin thoughtfully. "Okay, Charlie. Run it by me again."

"All three victims have defensive cuts to the hands, face and forearms . . ."

"Hold it right there." His eyes narrowed skeptically. "That could easily be attributed to shattered glass. You crouch in a defensive position, arms across your face, when the windows explode. That would explain those cuts."

"We found blood in the downstairs hallway. Blood on the couch cushions and mattress they were using to protect themselves with."

"Again, cuts and abrasions from shattered glass. Flying debris blown into the house through numerous broken windows, open doors and that great big hole in the roof."

"What about the sliding marks on the stairs?"

Duff shrugged. "Maybe Jenna and Danielle got injured, and Rob dragged them upstairs. We do strange things when we're scared. That's why it's called 'scared out of our wits.'"

Charlie wasn't buying it. "What about the scrape marks on Rob's back? If he dragged the other two upstairs, then how'd he get those?"

Duff sighed noisily. "You bring up some good points, Charlie. I'm not saying this isn't a mystery. But tornadoes have been known to do some pretty weird things. For instance, several years ago in Kansas, this tornado picks up a cake inside a house, carries it outside and sets it down so gently on the hood of the car it barely smears the icing. Coffee?"

He shook his head. "Never drink the stuff down here."

"Why not? Because of the smell? Ah, you get used to it. Okay, fine, no coffee." He put the clipboard back on its hook. "Let's see what the autopsies tell us."

Charlie followed him over to Rob's rotatable table, while Duff clipped a tape recorder to his belt and slipped on his headset. "Rob Pepper has sustained an impalement injury to the right side of the chest with a wooden projectile approximately two and a half feet long," he dictated into the machine. "What appears to be a staircase baluster has entered the right side of the chest anteriorly and exited posteriorly. Right lung is lacerated and contused. Internal exam will further assess pulmonary parenchymal damage." He paused a moment and stood tracing the line of his jaw with his fingers. "Remember the Oklahoma City tornado back in '99? Plenty of penetrating trauma due to flying debris. Terrible. The nightmares I had about that one. I'm seeing the same type of injuries here, Charlie, only . . ."

"Only what?"

"Bear with me a moment."

It was getting hot down here in the basement. Charlie shrugged out of his jacket, while Duff slowly circled the table, his breath whistling through his nose. He had nose hairs or adenoids or something. The morgue's narrow transom windows cast brilliant puddles of sunlight over the floor as the day moved into late afternoon. The small dissection tables rolled around on squeaky wheels and were used for cutting up and examining organs. Nearby was the hanging scale for weighing body parts, and a large tank on the floor collected fluids from each of the autopsy tables.

Ripley Funeral Home, two years ago. Maddie lying on a gurney, dead of a brain tumor, the starched white sheets drawn up around her shoulders.

"Maddie?"

There was a long scar like a headband across the top of her head, which had been shaved for the operation; her cinnamon-colored hair had grown back in thick and dark. Strange as the flowers that'd blossomed in the rubble after Hiroshima. Thick and dark and ominous. A grieving cap of hair.

"Maddie?"

She hated people always asking, always thinking about the tumor. She didn't want to discuss it, preferred to be just Charlie's wife, Sophie's mother. A normal person, not her illness.

Charlie leaned over the gurney and for a moment didn't feel connected to her in any way. Instead, he became acutely aware of the man and woman waiting for him out in the hallway. They'd opened the funeral parlor just for him. He stared down at Maddie's arched eyebrows, the delicate curve of her lips, that ski-slope nose. "Jesus, Maddie, I'm so sorry," he said, hoping she'd forgive him and open her eyes. Wake up and relieve him of this awful misery.

Duff stood holding the staircase baluster from Rob's chest in his gloved hands. "This is odd," he said, looking at it.

"What is?" Charlie noticed that one end of the baluster, the penetrating end covered in dried blood, was as sharp as the blade of a knife.

"My father used to make wooden knives," Duff said.

"It's a simple procedure, really. You find a straight-grained piece of hardwood and carve it into the shape of a blade. Then you dry it over an open fire until it's slightly charred. The drier the wood, the harder the point. You make the point of the blade slightly off-center, since the pith is the weakest part."

"So you mean," Charlie said, a stiffness invading his limbs, "this is a weapon we're looking at, Duff?"

He pointed at Rob's chest. "See these multiple stab wounds around the site of penetration, Charlie?"

"Yeah?"

"Those superficial stab wounds indicate to me that the perp was searching for a point of entry. A regular steel knife would require rather low velocity in order to penetrate flesh and muscle, but a wooden knife . . . that would require much higher velocity."

Charlie looked up. "You mean, upper-body strength?"

Duff nodded. "Also, it's easier for a wooden knife to penetrate if you can avoid all the bones."

A chill ran through him.

Duff set the baluster aside. "Hold on a second," he said, his nose whistling like a melancholy wind. "This bruising troubles me." He picked up a magnifying glass and stooped over Rob Pepper's rigored face. "Notice the reddening around the mouth?"

Charlie craned his neck and spotted a flaky white crust in the curl of the dead man's smile.

"Hm." Duff fell uncharacteristically silent.

"What is it, Duff?"

"Sorry, Rob," he said before placing his gloved hands on either side of the victim's face. With one sharp *snap*, he cracked the jaws, breaking the rigor.

Charlie drew back in revulsion.

Duff pried the lips apart and stood staring into Rob's mouth. "There's something wrong with this picture," he said.

Charlie strained to see.

"See that tooth?" he said. "It doesn't belong in there."

5

THE PEPPERS' family dentist, Peter Forgaard, was an ugly brute with a ruined face who smoked unfiltered cigarettes and liked to play the horses when he wasn't drilling and filling. The three of them—Charlie, Duff and Peter Forgaard—stood in a glum semicircle around Rob Pepper's naked body, a stabilizing block placed underneath his head.

"You're right," Peter said, his usually trumpeting voice pitched low. "That tooth doesn't belong in there, Roger."

"I noticed the swelling around the jaw," Duff explained. "Then I saw that the upper right canine was slightly askew in relation to those lateral incisors . . . and the gums were bleeding . . ."

Peter stroked his fleshy lower lip as he mulled over his next thought. His blue sweatshirt and gray sweatpants were soaked from this morning's jog, and his eyes gleamed sharply with speculation. "May I?" he asked Charlie.

"Go ahead."

"Should I remove it?"

"Yes, remove it."

Peter pulled on a pair of unpowdered gloves, selected a

forceps and grasped the unusual-looking tooth. Working his elbow back and forth, he quickly extracted it.

"When a tooth is pulled," he said, "a blood clot will form in the socket. But if the patient is already dead, then no clot will form. In Rob's case, it looks like there was some bleeding involved."

"You mean . . ." Charlie lifted a haggard look toward Peter. "He was alive when it happened?"

Peter nodded.

Shock set in. A vague, annoying numbness.

"Alive," Duff corrected, "but unconscious."

"Most likely," Peter agreed.

Charlie was sweating heavily now, his shirt sticking to his back. He could feel his emotions packed strongly inside his body—revulsion, anger, an overwhelming sense of confusion. He looked into the red porous meat of Peter's face. "What happened? How'd that tooth get in there, Peter? In the plainest language."

"Well, Rob's upper right canine was extracted and a 'replacement' canine was inserted back into the fibrous tissue of the gums. The root of this replacement tooth is long dead." Charlie and Duff followed him over to the drainboard of a large sink against the wall, where Peter plucked a dental X ray off the wall. "He had three crowns and twenty-five teeth in good condition. That's twenty-eight altogether, minus the four wisdom teeth. As you can see from his X rays, this replacement tooth is slightly smaller than the original . . . more curved on the labial surface. Its root is deep and prominent at the place of insertion. The crown is large and spearheaded. The convex labial surface is marked by three longitudinal ridges." He lowered his brooding glance. "Needless to say, these are two entirely different teeth."

Charlie took a deep breath, then let it out slowly, the adrenaline beginning to wear off. Shock setting in. "What about Jenna?" he asked.

"You want me to take a look?"

"Yeah, let's do them all."

They walked in a grim group over to the chrome table where Jenna Pepper lay still as dust. Peter took a hard swallow before he pried her delicate, rigored mouth open and methodically examined her teeth. It didn't take long.

"There." He pointed. "Second upper molar."

"I see it," Charlie said.

After Duff snapped a few pictures, Peter reached for the forceps and extracted the tooth in about five seconds. "As you can see from her X rays," he said, gesturing toward the light board, "there was a large amalgam in her second upper molar, whereas this . . . is in perfect condition." He held it to the light and squinted. "Absolutely flawless."

"And you know for certain it's not hers, because of the filling?"

Peter nodded. "This is definitely not her tooth."

Charlie held himself rigidly upright, afraid to appear even the slightest bit vulnerable. The gravity of it all, the scope of the crime, was beginning to sink in. He could read fear in Duff's taut features, Peter's stern face, and he realized they were all quietly mortified.

"Her teeth are worn down on the lingual surface . . . see how these two don't line up quite right inside the mouth? Notice the different patterns of wear and tear? Even the shape isn't the same. Neck, crown . . ."

"Color's not a match," Duff added.

Peter caught Charlie's eye. "I'm assuming the tornado didn't do this?"

Charlie glanced at Duff, then said, "We need you to keep it confidential, Peter."

"Of course. You can count on my discretion."

"We don't know exactly what happened. We're still piecing it together. But the crime occurred around the same time the tornado struck."

Peter let this sink in. "Can I ask you something, Charlie?"

"Sure."

"What happened to the original teeth?"

Duff jumped in. "It's some kind of ritualistic killing. That's what it is."

"We haven't completed the autopsies yet," Charlie told Peter. "We don't have all the facts."

"We have enough," Duff interrupted, "to assume that whoever did this took the original teeth with him as trophies."

"Hoo boy," Peter said. "Do you keep it hot down here on purpose, Roger? I'm burning up."

Duff turned on the noiseless vent fan, while Peter took out his handkerchief and mopped his dripping face.

"Would you like to take a break?" Charlie asked.

"No, I'm okay. I'm fine. It's these poor people . . ."

"Shall we continue, then?"

He nodded. "If you'll follow me, gentlemen."

Charlie and Roger walked over to Danielle's table and observed in distressed silence.

"The crown is surmounted by two cusps, separated by a groove." Peter's delivery was dry and expressionless, with just the hint of some heaving emotion behind each word. "The neck is oval, the roots laterally compressed. The first bicuspid is the largest of the series, but this *second* bicuspid . . . see where the enamel is worn down? You'd expect a corresponding worn spot here, but there isn't any. You can tell from her X rays, this bicuspid should be chipped, but isn't." He cleared his throat. "Her wisdom teeth haven't been extracted yet. My charts indicate a filling . . ." He looked so drawn and pale that Charlie thought he might pass out and fetched him a chair. "These poor people." Peter sat. "With surprise on their faces, like they didn't understand why they had to die."

"Help me find out who did this," Charlie said. "Anything you can tell me, Peter."

He shrugged. "There isn't a whole lot to tell. Those 'replacement' teeth . . . they're human. They weren't extracted recently, either. Maybe a year ago, maybe longer. I don't know who they belong to, but they don't belong in my patients' mouths, that's for sure." He tugged on his chapped lower lip. "As a general rule, I don't like to extract teeth. It makes people look old before their time, you know? I prefer to save a tooth wherever humanly possible."

"Would you have to be a dentist or have some special knowledge to extract a tooth, Peter? Is it difficult?"

"No, not really." He shook his head. "The tooth is held in its socket by a ligament which physically binds the root to the bone. I prefer an instrument called an elevator. It widens the space between the ligaments and bone and breaks the tiny fibers keeping them attached. But you don't need an elevator for this procedure. In a simple extraction, you merely grasp the tooth with a pair of forceps and rock it back and forth. Rotate left, rotate right . . . then pull. That's all it takes."

"Could you use, say, a pair of pliers?"

"Of course, that would suffice. Especially if you don't care about chipping or breaking the adjoining teeth. Cracks and so forth." He stared glassy-eyed at the bodies. "Can I go now?"

"Yeah, sure."

He got up and shuffled toward the door. "I hope I can forget what I've just seen."

"So long, Peter," Charlie said, his stomach knotting tighter at the fright and bafflement in the older man's eyes. "Thanks for your help."

6

Dakota Road began with a good idea—Pop Okie's Ribs—then meandered for miles past the big white grain elevators and dried-up oil wells into the distended western leg of Promise, where nobody wore designer clothes or locked their doors at night. Parking in the rutted driveway, Charlie paused to study the picture-perfect farmhouse beneath the gradually brightening sky. It was white with red shutters and a gabled roof. The power was still out on this side of town, but for the most part, his father's property had escaped unscathed. The '51 Loadmaster pickup truck—low to the ground and primed the color of sharkskin—was parked in front of the barn, and beyond the barn were the muddy fields where Isaac Grover had spent half his life worrying three hundred fallow acres into productive farmland.

Charlie sat shivering in his police car while the engine ticked and cooled. His arms felt heavy as rotten logs. He was still in shock about it. Triple homicide. Ritualistic murder. Right here in Oklahoma. He closed his eyes and almost instantly felt the flurry of blows, his father's hairy-knuckled fists smashing into his face. He opened his eyes again and watched a squirrel hopping around in the front yard. This was the house they'd moved into right after the old place on Kidwell Road had burned to the ground and claimed the lives of Charlie's mother and baby sister, Adelaide and Clara Grover. Charlie could still feel the old anger, the old sorrow, simmering just under the surface, his burn scars a constant reminder of the past. All he had to do was look down. He'd been marked by God with an enormous cattle brand: thick-ridged hypertrophic scars cascading across his left arm and chest; those raised yellow areas from the skin grafts on one buttock; the contractions in his left leg. He recalled the other kids' taunts. *Burned-All-Over Grover. Charcoal Charlie.* He would come home from school and sit stoically on the edge of his bed, cup his palms over various parts of his body in order to measure the percentages of his third-degree burns: 1 percent for the head, 8 percent for the upper limb, 11 percent for the lower limb, 8 percent for the torso. No matter how many times he did it, it always came out to 28 percent.

Now he stepped out of the car and cautiously approached the house, that perfectly manicured lawn stretching before him like an awkward pause in conversation. The old man was so proud of that yard, always mowing, always weeding—a different man after he'd quit drinking thirty years ago. Quit drinking after their house had burned down. *That was some wake-up call, boy.* Yeah, right. Too late to do anybody else any good, Charlie thought bitterly. Now Isaac's fellow churchgoers liked his putting-green lawn and his repentant demeanor. They'd embraced this sinner, had forgiven him too quickly. Charlie imagined he could hear the roots of all that perfect grass sucking the water out of the ground as he climbed the porch steps and knocked on the rattling screen door. "Pop?"

No answer. The house was dark and quiet. The screen door squealed on its hinges. He scuffed his feet on the doormat and entered. The front hallway smelled of wood polish. A lead weight settled in his stomach as he glanced at the mail table, a week's worth of deliveries gathering dust. Bill after unpaid bill. His father would be asking to borrow money from him again.

"Pop? You home?" he called to a ringing silence, then scanned the dozen or so photographs lining the walls: faded pictures of himself and his family; long-ago stuff, the pain still visible in his mother's eyes. Poor Adelaide. And baby Clara with her large love. And a younger, dark-haired Isaac smiling at the camera lens with boozy indifference, while outside the camera's range, the wildness quickly returned to his eyes.

Forgiven him too easily.

Isaac quit drinking the day after the fire, but he'd merely traded in one addiction for another—drinking for storm-chasing. Now he went storm-chasing every chance he got. He went to church on Sundays and chased extreme weather the rest of the week, and they'd never spoken about that night ever again, father and son.

The house was neat and tidy, everything tucked away. Charlie remembered the messy, cluttered home on Kidwell Road; the fire marshal had come to the conclusion that the fire had started down in the basement where all the rags and newspapers and kerosene lanterns were, perhaps ignited by a spark from the coal furnace. His father used to go down to the basement to stoke the furnace three times a day during the wintertime. Cussing like a madman. *C'mon, you old bitch.* Upstairs in the living room, that *whoosh* of hot air coming up through the wrought-iron grate was like the devil's breath.

"Charlie?" A coarse, familiar voice.

He spun around. "Whoa. Don't shoot."

Isaac lowered the barrel of his rifle, the one he used for deer-hunting. "I thought maybe I had burglars."

"Naw, just me."

"Go on, grab a seat outside. I'll fetch us some root beers." Isaac Grover was a powerfully built sixty-two-year-old with a face mapped by hardship. Tough as over-cooked beef and primed for meanness, he was a notorious insomniac who stayed up late to talk on his ham radio to the only other earthlings still awake at that godless hour—the Germans or the Chinese—speaking pidgin English into the wee morning hours. He farmed three hundred acres, but his return on investment was pretty small. He had a few head of cattle, some chickens, and grew soybeans, but wheat was his main source of income. Needless to say, he wasn't a rich man.

"I saw you yesterday," Isaac said, his powerful hands clasped gently together. "Guess you didn't see me, though."

"Where was this?"

"Black Kettle Road. I was helping with the cleanup."

Charlie frowned. "Why didn't you come over and say hello?"

"You looked like you had your hands full. Go on, grab a seat on the porch."

"I can't stay long, Pop."

"Okay, so go on. Take a load off."

Charlie bit back his irritation. "Five minutes, then I've really gotta run." He went outside and took a seat in one of the ancient wicker chairs that'd always been there, like the pyramids. He could hear the old man rooting around in the kitchen, flipping on the *Farm and Ranch Report* and rummaging through the refrigerator. He remembered his father's long struggle with the farm. The bugs and weeds ate his crops, and the middlemen took his profits. *"If I had any money, I wouldn't be a farmer. I'd buy me a boat and sail around the world."* Now Isaac let the screen door slam shut behind him as he handed Charlie an ice-cold root beer, the old-fashioned glass bottles clinking together.

"Poor Mary Jo," he said, landing in the chair opposite, its tattered wicker protesting as he settled in. He meant Mary Jo Crider, the elderly victim who'd been blown out of her house yesterday afternoon. "She used to baby-sit me and Bo-Bo, I ever tell you? This one time, she let Bo-Bo eat three cans of pork 'n' beans. He was just mad about that ol' gal. She wore a different sweater every day of the week." His eyes widened at the memory. "Thrown twenty yards from her house, all twisted up in barbed wire. You believe that? My gosh. It makes you wonder."

Charlie tasted his root beer with care. "Yesterday," he said. "Feels like months ago."

"Yesterday the sky fell." Isaac gave his son a quick, assessing look. "So how're you holdin' up? You holdin' up okay?"

"I'm wrestling with it, Pop," he admitted.

"Don't just sit on it. Tell me."

His eyes searched his father's face with anxious movements. Little flicks. "It was horrible."

"Death is always horrible."

"Yeah, well . . . this was a particular kind of horrible." *Don't tell him. Don't tell him the truth. They'll all know soon enough.* He was giving a news conference later that morning.

Whenever Isaac blinked, you could track the mileage on his face. He wore a rumpled jacket over a rumpled shirt, since his personal hygiene didn't necessarily match his obsession with domestic cleanliness and a manicured lawn. He wore the same pair of shoes until they fell off, each new pair destined to die a slow, lingering death on his stinky old corn-riddled dogs. He was like some homeless guy who'd wandered into June Cleaver's house and claimed squatter's rights.

"You go chasing yesterday?" Charlie asked, and his father nodded.

"I drifted west on the I-10, headed north for Cradle Rock. First storm split off a left mover, so I swung back down again. Hell, I almost missed it. I went from perfect position, almost under the meso, to out of position in about ten minutes."

"They said it was an F-3."

He squinted at the rising sun. "That cumulus literally exploded skyward. You could see the tower rushing up. Christ, I've known Rob Pepper since he was this high." He wagged his head mutely, wispy white hair shimmering in the early morning light. He grew his hair shoulder-length now, whereas it used to be military style. "I can remember Stretch Pepper tossing red-hot horseshoes into the air and catching them with a pair of tongs. Rob was his firstborn. Stretch handed out Yoo-hoos instead of cigars. That was the day Bob Schul won the five-thousand-meter." He tapped his head. "I keep a lot of trivia up here."

Everybody knew the Peppers were victims of yesterday's tornado. Nobody knew what Charlie knew yet.

Isaac removed his dentures and set them on the broad wicker arm of the chair. His father had been toothless for as long as Charlie could remember. He used to scare the neighborhood kids by flipping his dentures out with his tongue. He liked to joke that his real teeth were waiting for him on the other side, with Adelaide.

"I knew Jenna Pepper's mama, too," Isaac said. "Celine Kulbeck. Real wildcat. Like mother, like daughter."

"Hm?" Charlie glanced up. "What d'you mean?"

"I don't mean nothin'. Just . . . you hear rumors."

"What kind of rumors?"

He shrugged. "This and that."

He wasn't going to tell him. The sweet, cold drink made Charlie's teeth ache. His father was about as tough as an old Texas boot, but today he was looking washed-out—thin and pale, without enough flesh to swell the folds of his cheeks. Charlie wondered if he was getting enough to eat.

A brisk wind blew through the poorly joined wall boards of the screened-in porch. Outside, ravens circled the sky, and the overalls, boxer shorts and skinny bath towels hanging on the line were drenched with morning dew. *What's the sound of nothing?* A knot formed in the pit of Charlie's stomach and wouldn't go away. Suddenly he was propelled back to the good old days, back to those miserable years when his parents were always yelling, always throwing things. *Please make them stop . . .*

Charlie in his attic room, listening to his parents arguing downstairs. Something crashed, and he jumped. The baby was crying. Two-year-old Clara was always bawling. She had the kind of white-blond hair and lizard-green eyes that didn't remind his father of anybody else in the family, and this seemed to drive him crazy. "Is this baby mine? Answer me, woman!" At Charlie's feet were *his broken toys. He'd just turned seven, and there was a storm raging downstairs, a knock-down-drag-out. Please, God, make them stop, I'll be good . . .*

Whenever his father beat up his mother, she'd hide in her room afterward and cry until her mascara ran down her cheeks and she looked like a clown. Now his father was tromping up the attic stairs; coming for him, he knew. Charlie yelped as the stern-looking man with the big callused hands yanked him upright by the scruff of the neck and dragged him down the attic stairs, one bump at a time. Bump, bump, bump, *all the way down to the second-story landing, where he screamed in Charlie's face, "What's the sound of nothing, you little bed wetter?" Over and over again, while Charlie stared, terrified. Losing patience fast, the old man un-buckled his thick leather belt and beat Charlie senseless with it. The boy covered his head and screamed while blow after blow rained down on him, everything snapping and crackling. "What's the sound of nothing, you little bed wetter?"*

Minutes later, Isaac Grover stormed out of the house. They could hear the front door slam shut and the squeal of his tires as he sped out of the driveway, burning rub-ber all the way down Kidwell Road. Charlie sat hunkered in a corner of the hallway, shivering and crying, waiting for comfort and release; but his mother didn't come over and hold him the way she usually did. Instead, she just stared at him with wild, unknowing eyes and walked away.

Later that night, she forgot to kiss him good night. Alone in his attic room, Charlie lay very still in bed, so cold and scared he didn't know what to do. Maybe they'd get lucky and there would be an accident on the way home. Maybe his father would slam headlong into that big oak tree on the corner.

But then, shortly after midnight, his father swaggered home, drunk and disorderly, singing in his big booming voice all the way up the stairs, clomp, clomp, clomp. *Charlie could hear him banging around down there, and his mother's fretful voice. Soon they were arguing. Then his mother screamed, just once . . . and an eerie silence followed. Charlie held his breath while the bedsprings in the room below began to squeak. They squeaked for a very long time, and then there was nothing but silence.*

Charlie lay still as stone, blinking mechanically in the dark, his eyes tracing shadows and jagged silhouettes cast by the half-moon night. Any minute now, he knew, his father would come pounding up the attic stairs to beat him senseless. He just knew it. He could practically hear the creak of the treads every time he closed his eyes.

Eventually he smelled smoke. The air grew thick with it and hard to breathe. Smoke came pouring up the attic stairs like cream poured into coffee. He ran to the top of the landing but couldn't see through all that black billowing smoke. "Mama!" he cried. "Mama!"

He ran to the window and looked out over the peaceful moonlit night, and it suddenly occurred to him that nobody cared. The cows didn't care. The owls didn't care. The half-moon sprinkling the fields with pixie dust didn't care. Soon a fire was roaring up the attic stairs, accompanied by toxic fumes that all but crushed the air out of his lungs. Charlie leaned out the window and cried for help, but when a pale blue sheet of flame flapped across the floor and reached the balls of his feet, he jumped. He jumped in order to save his own skin; but his skin, it turned out, was only two-thirds saved.

Now here they were, the two of them. Father and son. Complete strangers. He wanted to leave. They'd said all there was to say. The only thing left was a bit of awkwardness, his father's hesitant, roundabout request for money. Simply to get it over with, Charlie said, "So you want me to write you a check?"

Isaac grew instantly annoyed. "If I wanted your help, I'd've asked for it."

"Okay, Pop. No big deal."

His father pointed an arthritic finger at him. "Don't you ever do that to me again."

"Do what?"

"Treat me like a charity case. I'll let you know if I need your goddamn help."

"All right already."

"And don't you go flipping me off, either!"

"I'm not flipping anybody off. Jeez, Pop. Forget I even mentioned it."

All gin blossoms and spite, Isaac drained the rest of his root beer in one long swallow. "Six dead. Six dead. That's all they ever talk about. Nobody bothers to mention the fact that hundreds were injured, and sometimes you might as well be dead."

Charlie took a moment to study his father's profile—the long straight nose he'd inherited, those prominent veins in his neck, the height and breadth of that cagey forehead, the poker-player eyes. Would his own eyebrows turn as white as snow and sprout wings? Would he get those sagging jowls? Would his knuckles swell with arthritis? That was when he noticed the expensive-looking wristwatch with the silver sectioned band on his father's wrist.

"Is that new?"

"What, this?" He glanced at the watch face. "I helped a family out yesterday. They were grateful."

"They gave it to you?" He eyed him skeptically. *Picked it up in the mud, you mean.* "Which family was this?"

"Don't remember."

Charlie's mouth grew tight. "You don't remember their names?"

"I don't think they said."

He put his root beer down and stood up. "I've gotta go."

Isaac glared at him as if he were some kind of insect floating in his soup. "Why do you treat me like that?"

"Like what?"

"Like somebody not to be trusted."

"Did I say anything?"

"You don't have to say anything." He shifted in his seat and tugged at the baggy crotch of his pants. "Boy oh boy, you are one slick citizen."

"What's that supposed to mean?"

"You're saying you don't believe me about the watch? That people can't be grateful anymore? That folks can't show a little gratitude?"

"And you don't even remember their names?"

"I said no, maybe it sounded like a yes."

He looked around, disgusted. "Sophie was worried about you, so I dropped by to make sure everything was okay."

Isaac's frown melted at the mention of his granddaughter's name. He shook his head and chuckled softly. "She was? She was worried about her ol' grandpa?"

"Yeah. She tried calling you, but the lines were down."

"My angel."

"She wants to talk to you. Give her a ring."

"Is she okay?"

"See you later, Pop."

He spread his hands palms-down on the chair arms and raised himself up threateningly. "Charlie, is my granddaughter okay?"

"That should've been your first fucking question," he said as he walked away.

7

THE INSTANT he got back in his car, Charlie's police radio sputtered to life. "Yeah?" he answered irritably.

"Chief?" It was Hunter. "We found a phone number written on a napkin tucked inside Jenna Pepper's purse. No name, just a number. Wanna give it a shot who answered?"

"Don't tease me, Hunter. Tell me."

"Jake Wheaton."

"What?"

"You want us to go over there?"

"No, I've got this one," Charlie said, dropping the mike back in its retainer and speeding off.

The Wheatons lived across town on a plot of beaten-down earth littered with automobile carcasses. All the old buildings on the run-down farm were marred with graffiti, and Charlie wasn't sure what they grew there. He only knew that plenty of drug deals took place in the trailer park across the street.

He found Jake Wheaton in the driveway, bent over a chromed-up Chevy pickup truck that looked about ready for the junkyard. The nineteen-year-old held a flashlight in his mouth while he tightened the timing belt with his thin, greasy fingers.

"Jake?"

The flashlight dropped out of his mouth and he caught it one-handed. He gave Charlie a witless grin. "Hey there, Officer Friendly." He was stoned or drunk or both, his eyes two road maps of swollen capillaries.

"Got a minute?"

"What for?"

"Just a few questions."

"Sure, okay." His tongue was pierced by a steel rod, and he was so underweight he was nothing but bones. His tattoos were actually quite beautiful—skinny black bands around his upper arms, mystical symbols decorating those meatless forearms. Jake's long hair was tucked behind his ears, and he wore an oversize black T-shirt and jeans that'd been accidentally-on-purpose splotched with bleach.

"You've heard about the Peppers, right?" Charlie said, and Jake nodded. "Wanna turn your engine off for me?"

The avocado-green pickup truck idled in a puddle of gasoline and racing oil. Jake went to turn it off, then slumped down behind the wheel and lit a cigarette.

"No smoking."

The boy put it out.

Charlie waited for him to crawl back out of the vehicle, but he didn't. "What're you doing?"

"Just chillin'." He tapped his fingers on the padded steering wheel.

"Get out."

The boy obeyed, then stood evasively before him in the driveway.

"You've heard how the Peppers died in the tornado?"

"I saw it on TV, yeah." He dropped his head. Inhaled. Exhaled. "That's a bad way to go."

"You knew them?"

"Sure. Danielle." He nodded. "And my girlfriend has Ms. Pepper for life studies."

"Life studies? Did you know her personally? Ms. Pepper? Or just through your girlfriend?"

He squinted. "What d'you mean?"

"Did you and Jenna Pepper have some kind of personal relationship is what I'm asking."

Jake kept his reaction flat and glanced up the street. "She let us eat whatever her students baked that day. French fries, burritos. Stuff like that."

"So you'd get to sample the goods after class?"

"Yeah, that's right."

"And you'd chat with her a little?"

His eyebrows lifted in unconvincing innocence. "That's right."

"What'd you two talk about?"

"Who, me and Ms. Pepper?"

"Yeah, you and Ms. Pepper."

He shrugged. "Just stuff."

"What kind of stuff?"

"Life and shit . . . and there was this one time when she took me for a ride in her Pontiac."

"Oh, yeah? When was this?"

He squinted, as if it were written on the air between them. "About six months ago."

"Six months? So this was an after-school type of thing?"

"Yeah, after school."

"And?"

"And what?"

They looked at each other significantly.

"Where'd she take you? Ms. Pepper."

"Out to the country. We went looking for pumpkins."

"Pumpkins?" Charlie repeated.

"Yeah, I was helping her buy these pumpkins for school. She was gonna teach her students how to bake pumpkin pie from scratch. We bought a ton of 'em and filled up the trunk."

"Anything else happen while you two were out looking for pumpkins?"

His eyes filled with resentment at being asked such a question. "Like what?"

"Like . . . I dunno. Like how come we found your phone number inside her purse?"

"Okay." He rubbed his eyes and seemed aggravated.

"Why would she have your phone number, Jake?"

He squinted, trying to think. "I dunno."

"No?"

He shook his head.

"Jake . . . you smile an awful lot."

He screwed up his face. "Yeah? So?"

"You like teeth in general?"

"What?"

"It's just a question."

"Do I like teeth?"

"Just tell me why she has your phone number in her purse."

He shrugged, very little going on behind those eyes. At least it seemed that way.

"Might as well spill it," Charlie told him.

After a moment of dogged resistance, the boy's shoulders collapsed and he admitted, "She took me looking for pumpkins, and then we made out."

"You made out?"

"Yeah."

"You and Ms. Pepper? You and the life studies teacher?"

"Yeah. Seriously."

"Did you go all the way?"

"All the what?"

"Did you have sexual relations with her?"

"No, we were . . . no."

"You two made out when you went looking for pumpkins? Did you ever see her again after that?"

"Twice. We saw her twice."

"We who?"

"What?"

"You said 'we.' 'We saw her twice.'"

"I said 'I.' I saw her twice."

"Was there somebody else involved?"

He didn't answer. He just looked down at his shoes, a filthy pair of work boots with the laces trailing in the dirt.

"Jake?"

"I think I've said enough."

"You wanna come down to the station with me?"

"Am I under arrest?"

"Not yet."

He didn't look upset or angry or anything. He just got back in his pickup truck and gunned the engine.

"Where were you yesterday afternoon?" Charlie asked, leaning against the roof and looking at him through the rolled-down window.

Jake switched on the radio. A rap song was playing, and he rocked his head violently to the beat. He'd probably scrambled his brains doing that.

"I might want you to come down to the station house later on and clarify what you just said," Charlie told him.

Jake sat drumming his fingers on the steering wheel. "Okay?"

"Yeah, okay."

"You'll cooperate?"

"I'll think about it." He tapped his hand on the door in farewell.

8

CHARLIE FINISHED out the morning by holding a press conference to announce the homicides and trying to answer reporters' questions as best he could. The news spread like wildfire throughout the reeling community, and Charlie knew there would be a run on dead-bolt locks at the hardware store and bullets at the gun shop.

By noon, hundreds of curiosity-seekers had converged on the area. The Institute for Disaster Studies was mapping out the damage path, while FEMA's assessment team attempted to assign an F-scale rating. Over three dozen homes in the Black Kettle subdivision had been destroyed, another 150 had major damage and five hundred people were still without electric power. The damage path ran across several hundred acres of central-pivot irrigation pipes, where the hopeful green of April had given way to vast expanses of brown.

Back at the morgue, Charlie and Duff extracted the rest of the flying debris from the bodies and carefully examined it before sending it off to the state lab for further testing. There were eight pieces of weaponized debris altogether. "Let's hope we pull a print off one of these," Duff said.

Next Charlie drove to Shepherd Street, where the *rat-a-tat-tat* of the gas-powered generator reached his ears before he even stepped out of his car. He went around back, where part of the roof lay in pieces on the Peppers' backyard and the few trees that remained standing held shredded debris in their upper, leafless branches. Swiping off his sunglasses, he opened the kitchen door.

Mike Rosengard looked up. "Hiya, Chief."

"Mike? What are you doing here?"

"Finding lots of smooth glove prints, for one thing." He leaned over the sink, his features narrowed to a single point of interest as he brushed Chinese-blue fingerprint powder over the faucet and handles. He had a forehead like polished granite and thick dark hair with a streak of premature white, like a worry that emanated from a specific part of his brain. He wore the requisite suit and tie, neatly pressed. "Whoever did this knows crime scene procedure. Fuck. I hate that."

"Sours my already tenuous mood."

"I heard about the teeth. Hunter filled me in."

"Did he tell you about the debris and everything?"

"Debris, teeth, the whole nine yards."

Charlie could hear the melancholy sound of the wind as it whistled through the rafters.

"I know you said to take the week off, Chief, but what am I supposed to do? Sit around and twiddle my thumbs while all this is going down?"

Eleven years ago, Mike had moved here from Boston, where real things happened. Real crimes, not these penny-ante drug busts and B&Es and domestic disputes where people were constantly changing their stories. Charlie often worried that his best detective might become bored with only half a dozen homicides a year; but now it looked as if they had the type of mystery a Boston cop could really sink his teeth into.

"Where are you and Jill staying?" Charlie asked.

"My brother-in-law's house. We had to discuss who parks where, when to take a shower. I feel like I'm living in a dormitory." He scratched his forehead, leaving a daub of blue ash in the center like a third eye. "I tried to keep the boys quiet last night, but Sammy wouldn't stop crying. Still, I can't complain, Chief. We've got a roof over our heads and three hots a day. We're just grateful to be alive."

"Anything I can do," Charlie told him. "Anything at all."

"Thanks, boss." He straightened out his arms, and Charlie noticed that the sleeves of his gray suit were about an inch too short. The tie was blue with green polka dots. Mike smiled. "What can you do? You've gotta laugh."

"I can loan you a few ties. I doubt the suits will fit."

"Ties I'll take," Mike said. "This is about the most conservative one my brother-in-law has."

"So the perp wore gloves?" Charlie said.

"Which means the crime was premeditated."

"Multiple stab wounds, that's rageful. That's personal."

"So he knew the victims?"

"We don't know that yet."

"Premeditation, combined with the viciousness of the attacks, indicate that the perp might've known his victims."

"It's a possibility." Charlie opened the refrigerator and stood inspecting its contents: Tupperware containers with indeterminate leftovers, a plate of hardened hash browns, a slice of lemon meringue pie covered in aluminum foil.

He closed the door, then noticed the refrigerator magnets—Oscar the Grouch, Smiley Face with a bullet through its forehead, a glow-in-the-dark "Earth from Space" magnet. They were symmetrically placed, except for a space in the center where it looked like one was missing. He tucked this bit of information into a corner of his brain. "Soon as you catch your breath," he said, "I want you to call your buddies over at the National Weather Service and get us some pictures of yesterday's storm."

"Good idea," Mike said. "All those storm-chasers with their digital cameras."

"Local TV, too. They had their people out there in droves trying to catch the twister on tape. Maybe we've already got the bad guy's chase car on film, only we don't know it yet."

Mike nodded. "Make and model. License plates."

"At least we can snag some more witnesses."

Sunlight glinted off the broken glass on the windowsill. The tree branch had ripped the curtains, with their simple pattern of forward and backward horses, and the plaster around the window frame had cracked and twisted off. The kitchen countertop was warped from where a wave of mud and rain had crashed through. Charlie could picture Rob Pepper out in the backyard, pruning the trees with his extendable pruner and bow saw. He'd been an easygoing, hardworking guy whose ambition extended no further than his own property line, whereas Jenna seemed to long for more from life, always with that faraway look in her eyes. Charlie wondered: Did Rob know she was cheating on him? With a teenager, no less?

Above the back fields, a red-tailed hawk flapped and

swooped erratically through the air. "You can get to the highway pretty quickly from here," Charlie said.

"From the railroad tracks to the highway, the road passes maybe half a dozen farmsteads, all set back from the road."

"Which explains why nobody saw anything unusual. No suspect vehicle. No suspicious activity." He took a swift breath. "Duff says it isn't all that hard to make a wooden knife. He explained the process to me."

"That was the murder weapon? A wooden knife?"

Wooden knives, daggers, shivs, pikes, spears, stakes . . . a new term would have to be invented. "We found eight pieces of flying debris that'd been weaponized. Staircase balusters, chair legs, fence posts, you name it. These were very skillfully done. If we hadn't carefully examined each piece, we might've missed it."

"Yeah, but . . . can you actually penetrate the human body with a wooden blade?"

"Duff thinks the victims were unconscious first. That would make it easier. Then you just avoid all the bones and keep stabbing away until you find an entry."

Mike put the fingerprint brush down. "What kind of a sick fuck are we dealing with here?"

Charlie pressed his thumbs against his temples. "The X rays showed blunt trauma. Fractures, lacerations, abrasions. We figure he rendered the victims unconscious with a blow to the head . . . but it's the stab wounds that ultimately killed them. Jenna died of airway obstruction, the others bled out."

Mike's eyes grew round with wonder. "What'd he use to knock them out with? A board? A baseball bat?"

"Duff found wood chip fragments with uneven, irregular edges in some of the defensive wounds."

"Wood chips?"

"Maybe from a log."

He frowned thoughtfully. "A log with a knot at one end can act like a weighted club. The knot provides a natural weight to give it better swing."

Charlie nodded. "Could still be on the property."

"Do you realize what this means?" Mike looked at him. "It means he brought the weapons with him. It means he knew that a tornado was going to drop down out of the sky yesterday afternoon. Somehow he fucking knew."

"Do another grid search of the property. Let's look for a log with blood or brain matter adhering to it." Charlie could barely grasp the significance of this statement and sighed heavily, as if he'd been holding his breath. "Where's Lester?" he said.

"Upstairs, vacuuming for hairs and fibers."

"Is Hunter watching him? I don't want a single fiber slipping through our fingertips this time."

"Yeah, boss, he's been riding Lester's ass all morning."

Charlie headed for the stairs. Lester could be sloppy when it came to evidence collection, and Charlie could tell it pissed him off that he didn't have his superior's full and complete confidence, but that was just the way it was when you were a lazy-assed bastard with one foot in your glorious football-hero past. The tension between them had been escalating lately, ever since Lester's promotion a year ago. Mike had been the top contender for the position of assistant chief, but then, wouldn't you know it, politics had reared its ugly head. Turned out Lester was related by blood to the mayor. Charlie wanted Mike for the job; Mayor Whitmore wanted Lester. Guess who won? Charlie didn't like having his arm twisted, and now resentment bloomed on both sides.

Upstairs, the floorboards creaked with oldness. He found Lester in Danielle's bedroom, with its hand-painted cornflower motif and eastern-facing windows. On sunny days, this was probably the cheeriest place in the house. Lester sat slouched on the bed with his back to the door.

"Lester?"

He stood up, minivac in hand. His eyes were blood-shot, as if he hadn't been sleeping very well lately. "Hey," he said.

"Jesus, Lester . . . can I count on you?"

He frowned. "Of course, Chief."

"Just do what Hunter tells you to, okay?"

His face grew resentful. "Why wouldn't I?"

Stuffed animals decorated the unmade bed—the cheap kind, made in Taiwan. Charlie scrutinized the extensive porcelain doll collection, their solemn eyes assessing him in turn. There was a Plexiglas cube of photographs on the messy desktop, pictures of Danielle at Bible camp. She wore a "Jesus Luvs U" T-shirt and squinted into the bright sunshine with a worry-free smile. There was a stack of rock and roll tapes next to a boom box on the bedside table, and Charlie studied these items, his breathing growing shallow. Some presence had been inside this room recently, he was sure of it. A stranger had entered the room and straightened out that stack of tapes. A crazy thought, but one he couldn't shake. The stack was too precise to be the handiwork of a teenage girl.

"Did you touch those tapes, Lester?"

"No, sir."

"Are you sure?"

He greeted this thinly veiled admonition with a strained smile. "No, boss. Why?"

"Vacuum the area very carefully for hairs and fibers. And don't touch the tapes. Tell Mike to dust them for latents. Understood?"

He frowned. "Why don't you trust me, Chief?"

In the silence that followed, you could hear the generator chugging out in the backyard.

"Where'd the blood come from?" Charlie asked him in turn.

"What blood?"

"On your hands yesterday, when I got here. You had mud on your clothes and blood on your hands."

"I must've touched the body . . . the girl, Danielle." He shrugged. "I know you're not supposed to touch anything, but I had to make sure she was dead, Chief. I might've touched the mattress, too."

Charlie nodded slowly.

"Okay, so I fucked up. I know you're not supposed to touch anything, but I didn't know they were all dead at the time."

"But you did by the time I arrived."

"Huh?"

"When I walked into the bedroom, I saw Danielle's body in the corner, but I didn't see Rob. Rob came crashing through the ceiling while I was just standing there."

"I saw him, Chief. The ceiling was gone, and I was looking up at the roof with my flashlight, and I saw a body up there in the rafters. I also saw Jen— . . . Jenna in the tree." His eyes grew hard, as if he'd never laughed a day in his life. "Jesus, it was horrible."

"What were you doing here yesterday, anyway?" Charlie asked. "Wasn't it your day off?"

"I was out chasing," he said defensively. He looked tired. "I was heading north on the interstate, and there were these thunderheads right over me . . . and I remember thinking at one point, 'Wow, look at all those leaves flying around.' Only they weren't leaves, they were tires or tree limbs and shit. Then I saw this car doing doughnuts across a field . . . and I'm thinking, 'Holy fuck. This is it. This is how I'm going to die.' I must've hit a hundred. I took the Shepherd Street exit, that's how I got here."

"So you turned around and drove back here?"

"East on the 412. I got off at the Shepherd Street exit and saw this mess. I stopped and tried to help. Thought I could . . ." He shook his head, his soft-lashed eyes full of regret and of something else. Something Charlie couldn't quite put a finger on.

"You knew the Peppers, right?"

He gave an abrupt nod. "I heard about Jake Wheaton," he said. "I'd like to be in on the interview."

"Mike and I will handle it."

"I'd like to be there," he insisted.

"We'll see." Charlie patted him on the back, deciding to set his questions aside for now. "Make the day count."

"Where're you off to, Chief?"

"To talk to a wind expert."

9

THE WIND Function Facility was nestled in the subbasement of the Environmental Sciences Laboratory at Dryden Technical College in Montoya, Oklahoma. Charlie entered the bulldozer-yellow lobby and took a freight elevator down two flights, then wound his way through a series of gray-carpeted corridors toward the branching test sections—the tow tank facility, the missile launcher chamber, the wind tunnels. The air down here was chilly and dry, a strange hum emanating from the walls due to the building's many generators.

"Watch your step," Rick Kripner said as they entered the wind-tunnel section together. In his early thirties, Rick had the kind of stiffened stride that suggested a disciplined upbringing and a terminally distracted look. Like most science geeks, he collected pens the way a dog attracts fleas. They'd met twice before, and each time, Rick had been exceedingly friendly and knowledgeable about tornado preparedness, but he wasn't the person Charlie was there to see.

"She won't be long," Rick said. "Ten minutes maybe. We're doing a dry run-through." He spoke softly as he

patted his lab coat pockets, searching for something.
"This way, Chief."

They navigated a narrow passageway lined with pipes
and electrical cables toward the back of the facility,
where a huge constructed metal wind tunnel stood on
twenty-foot stilts beneath the sixty-foot ceiling. Charlie
spotted at least two other tunnels inside the warehouse-
sized facility—the place was enormous—before he followed Rick up a white-painted ladder and into a
glass-enclosed control room.

Rick took a seat behind the console and started fid-
dling with the control knobs. "Mind closing the door?"

Charlie shut it, and the hum grew instantly muffled.
He took a seat in one of the cold metal folding chairs and
looked around. The wind tunnel had observation windows all along its side, and he could see Willa Bellman
quite clearly now through the glass. She was standing in
the test section, tinkering with a scaled-down replica of a
high-rise building. She wore an extra-small white T-shirt
beneath the obligatory lab coat, black ballet-type shoes
and khaki trousers with short silver zippers over each
pocket and horizontally down each cuff. Unusual. He
liked her unusual taste.

"Guess who's here?" Rick said.

"Be right with you," Willa answered without looking
up, and Charlie realized that the two-way intercom was
on.

"Take your time," Charlie told her, his voice making a
slap-back echo off the concrete.

Lithe, pretty, in her early thirties with porcelain skin
and curious blue eyes, Willa had a head of coiling black
hair and a bone structure so well defined she reminded
Charlie of some rare breed of cat. Six months ago, they'd

spent an entire afternoon together inside the field laboratory, discussing tornado emergency procedures. The field lab consisted of a 150-foot-high meteorological tower and a data acquisitions room, where they'd worked together in such close quarters he was able to memorize some of her smells—strawberry shampoo, peppermint breath mints, a mothball-tinged sweater so stiff it could probably stand on its own.

"I saw you on TV this morning," Rick said.

Charlie nodded but kept his expression flat.

"Those people were murdered?"

"I can't go into any details."

"Yeah, I hear you." He tilted back in his chair. "I don't know how you do it, Chief, being around dead bodies all the time. I'd get queasy if somebody got a nosebleed."

He shrugged. "Just part of the job."

"Is this part of the job? You coming here?" He leaned forward. "Because I'd be happy to help out. If there's anything you need to know about tornadoes, I'm your guy."

Charlie was used to overeager citizens wanting to help. Glancing at his watch, he said, "So tell me about these wind tunnels."

Rick nodded at the glass. "You're looking at one smooth, sweet machine. Airflow's created by a B-39 aircraft propeller housed inside the drive section there. Wind speeds can reach up to one hundred and twenty miles an hour, and we can replicate all sorts of atmospheric quirks . . . thermal inversions, air stratifications, you name it."

Across the ten-yard divide, Willa was trying to shake the model apart, a growl rising in her throat. "*Arrghh!* Fuck!"

"Easy," Rick told her. "We've got company, remember?"

"How're those pressure taps responding?" she asked.

He typed a command into his computer. "The answer is they're not."

"Nothing?"

"Nada. Zip."

"Jesus loves me," she muttered under her breath.

Charlie smiled, hating the sensation of grease blossoming on his forehead. Six months ago. Why hadn't he called?

"I'm not happy with these taps," she said. "Not happy at all." She made a few adjustments to the northern facade of the model, then heaved a frustrated sigh. "What're we gonna do about this, Rick?"

"I dunno. Have Gordo redo them?"

"I am sick and tired of waiting around for Gordo to get his act together! There's at least a hundred taps missing. I wanted this to be as precise as possible." She picked up the model and shook it.

"Careful. You could lose an eye with that thing."

She released the tower and, kicking off her shoes, crossed the floor in her stocking feet. "This is fucking futile!"

"Temper, temper." He switched off the two-way intercom and leaned back in his seat. "She's a perfectionist. Her data's solid, but it slows the whole process down. It wouldn't matter, except that we're on a tight deadline with this one particular grant. I can just hear Jacobs now. 'Vat d'you mean, she didn't complete ze test?' " He patted his pockets again. "Where are you, keys?"

"Jacobs?" Charlie said, watching Willa exit the test section and descend the metal ladder. She'd left her shoes back inside the wind tunnel.

"Yeah, Professor Jacobs. The guy who runs this zoo."

Willa burst into the control room, eyes alert, cheeks rosy. "Oh, hi," she said. "Hello, Chief." She shook his hand. "Long time no see."

"Charlie," he corrected her.

"Okay, Charlie. Ha. My friend Charlie the policeman." She gave him a wide, wry smile, then tossed a leather briefcase on the console table. "Do me a favor, Rick?" she said, pulling out a messy stack of folders. "Finish these missile impact stats for me? I'm falling so far behind it ain't pretty."

He leaned precariously back in his chair. "Only if you'll cover for me on Friday."

"Yeah, absolutely."

"Deal?"

"Friday."

He took the folders from her—quite a bit of material—and cradled them in the crux of his arm.

"Missile impact stats?" Charlie repeated.

"We're testing a new line of product," she explained. "We get clients coming in here all the time, wanting certification for their aboveground tornado shelters and safe rooms. This one's called Schott Industries . . ."

"More like *Schitt*," Rick muttered.

"Yeah, exactly. You are so witty today." She laughed, then gave Charlie such an earnest look his heart skipped a beat. "Seriously, this product should never go on the market, Charlie. It's supposed to protect consumers from every type of wind hazard known to man, but I swear to God, a mouse could fart on it, and *poof*."

"Feminine, ain't she?" Rick said proudly.

"We're basically the last line of defense."

"There you are, you weasels." Rick scooped his

crowded key chain off the console. "Right in front of me."

"Where're you going?" Willa asked him.

"I'll be in my office, in case anybody's interested. Eating my tuna sandwich, buried under a mountain of paperwork."

"Quit pissing and moaning," she said. "You get Friday off. Oh, I almost forgot! I need those by five, that okay?"

"Yeah, it's doable." He turned to Charlie. "Nice to see you again, Chief."

"You, too, Rick."

Rick left the control room, and suddenly they were alone together. There was a brief but noticeable awkwardness between them, which she handled lightly and he handled heavily. He didn't know what to do with his hands. He stuffed them in his pockets, then tipped back in his chair until it bumped into the wall.

"Want a cola?" She twisted her curly black hair into a French knot, stray tendrils clouding her ears—ears as curved and pearly as the inner wall of a moon shell. "We call it our antisleeping tonic around here."

"Yeah, I could use some of that."

She opened the minifridge, scooped out two aluminum cans, popped the tops and handed him one. Their fingers touched, briefly, and he realized that her eyes were gray, not blue. As gray as dusk, without any specks or highlights. He figured a person could get seriously lost in those dusk-soaked eyes.

"I was there yesterday," she told him. "In Promise."

This nudged him back to reality.

"I was chasing garbage storms up north when I stopped for gas and could barely open my door against the wind." She shivered and cinched her lab coat tighter.

"I could feel that icy chill that told me I was north of the cold front and needed to get south enough to feel that strong southern wind on my face. To see it collide with the cold front. I got there just in time. It had a classic barber-pole appearance. I'd guess it was an F-3. There was F-3 damage, for sure."

"Yeah, it was pretty bad."

"We heard about the murders. What a terrible day you must've had." She nodded with a gentle warmth. "How's your daughter?"

"Fine, thanks," he said. So she remembered their conversation from six months ago? That was promising.

"My mother died when I was twelve," she said. "That can be tough on a girl."

"She's handling it pretty well."

"Trust me, Charlie. She's not." Except for her eyes, her face was still. "So what brings you here this morning?"

"I've got a few weather questions for you."

She frowned and slunk way down in her chair. "Shoot."

"I need to know if a storm-chaser can predict with any accuracy when and where a tornado's going to touch down."

She frowned. "If we could predict exactly where a tornado was going to drop, it wouldn't be half as fun. That's why we're called chasers, Charlie. We love the action. We love the game."

"So it's a guessing game?"

She tilted her head to drink, Adam's apple jutting like the whitened knuckle of a flexed finger. "Meteorology's an imperfect science, but Mother Nature will drop a few clues. For example, the more organized a storm, the more likely it is to become severe. And since tornadoes often accompany severe weather, you make that your first goal. To find yourself an organized storm."

"How would I go about doing that?"

Her face fell into relaxed lines. "You get up early and listen to the weather forecast."

"That's it?"

"No." She smiled. "Next you'd go on-line and check out the computer-model forecasts. You'd study the analysis charts to see how the air patterns have set up. Then you'd check out the satellite pictures and radar images and create your own forecast."

"How, exactly?"

She settled her limbs on the plastic arms of her chair, hands dangling, fingers curled under. Cat's paws. She was relaxed as a cat around him. "Okay, back to basics," she said. "You need three things to create a tornado, Charlie. Sufficient moisture, dynamics to lift the air, and jet streams to help create rotation. Any truck stop nowadays will have a table phone where you can hook up your laptop and download all sorts of weather information. Anybody can go on-line and check out the surface and upper-air patterns, but you have to know enough about weather to make sense of it. So you review the hard data first. Then you assess the sky with your own eyes once the chase begins."

"Okay, so let's say I've got my preliminary forecast. Then what?"

"Then you position yourself under a severe storm and wait."

"Just wait?"

"You stay. You watch."

"And? What am I looking for, exactly?"

She giggled. "You say 'exactly' a lot."

"I do?"

"Yeah."

He smiled.

She smiled. "Wall clouds. Towers. Anvils. You're looking for instability, motion, rotation. Sometimes the sky's so hazy you can't see your own hand in front of your face. Other times, there are so many boundaries out there it's almost impossible to decide which way to go. You could make a case for any direction. But if you get lucky and spot something interesting, then you plot an intercept course."

"That's what Captain Kirk always says."

She laughed. "Am I confusing you?"

"A little."

"You know nothing about this stuff, do you?"

He shrugged. "My father took me chasing once. It was an unmitigated disaster."

"Unmitigated?"

"Fiasco."

"What happened?"

"We painted ourselves into a corner. Floods, lightning, hail. We were critically low on gas with an extremely violent storm approaching."

She smiled. "Sounds like fun."

"Yeah, right. A whole barrel of monkeys."

"What's his chase vehicle?"

"A gray Loadmaster pickup truck, circa 1951."

Her eyes lit up. "Always with the cowboy hat? White hair? One of those die-hard chasers who just dispense with the technology and go on sheer gut?"

"You know him?"

"I've seen him around, yeah." She smiled and caught

her lip between her teeth. "I admire crusty old codgers like him. Some of the best chasers I know forgo all the bells and whistles and just follow their noses."

"What about you?"

"Me? Nah. I like bells and whistles."

Sparks. Definite sparks. It scared the hell out of him. "So what got you started in this field?" he asked, his palms beginning to sweat.

"I grew up in Texas. Red dirt, sandstorms, the whole bit. There wasn't a whole lot to do in our little town. Just church, matinee movies and storm-chasing."

"So you got bit by the bug early on, huh?"

"I admit it. I'm an adrenaline junkie."

"Do you chase often?"

"Every chance I get." She continued to smile warmly at him. "Basically there aren't any hard-and-fast rules, Charlie. Storm-chasing's an art form."

He sloshed his cola around in its can, not wanting to leave just yet. He wanted to ask her out, but he was more than a little nervous about it. Some people were repulsed by his scars. He could see it in their eyes. He didn't want to see it in hers. Back at the station house, he'd occasionally roll up his shirtsleeves and use his scars to intimidate street punks, breach their comfort zones; but with women, you never knew. He'd had a few brief love affairs—if you could call them that—after Maddie had died, drunken encounters with barfly secretaries and middle-aged department store clerks. Stumbling back to their place; a nervous fumbling of buttons; whiskey-soaked breath. And each time, he couldn't wait to get out of there. It bothered him that he hadn't called them back afterward, not even out of common courtesy. He didn't want to be one of those jerks.

"So you've only been storm-chasing once in your entire life?" she asked with a raised eyebrow.

"I don't make any apologies for it."

A wine-colored flush spilled upward from her collarbone. "You'd like it, Charlie. I'm not kidding. It's such a rush when the sky goes from benign to explosive, and the road feels suddenly so small . . . you're chasing the dragon's tail, doing eighty . . . hail bouncing off the pavement . . . bolts of lightning shooting up and down the wall cloud . . ."

"Sounds awesome."

"It is." She glanced at her watch.

"Am I keeping you?"

"Yeah, and in such a pleasant way."

An electric current seemed to run through the room. But Charlie was very good at dropping the ball. "One other thing," he said. "Do you know anyone who's really good at finding tornadoes? I mean, exceptionally good?"

She took a swig of soda and wiped her mouth with the back of her hand. "I don't know anybody who's capable of predicting on a consistent basis when or where a tornado will land."

They watched one another for a moment. Her eyes were wide and curious, letting it all in, and he felt a wave of pleasure. He stood up and set his empty soda can down on the metal chair seat. "Well . . . thanks for your help."

"Thanks? That's all I get?" An odd smile parted her lips. "We're so formal all of a sudden. Listen, Charlie, I'd love to take you chasing one of these days. Show you the ropes. That way, you could see for yourself how unpredictable it is."

"Careful. I might just take you up on that."

"You know where to find me, right?"

He could feel several different sensations passing between them, and it frightened him. It was an awkward moment, but also strangely wonderful. The last time he'd felt
this way was with Maddie. The first time he and Maddie
ever made love, she kept wanting to undress him, and he
kept pushing her hands away. He eased off his shoes—just
the shoes—then lay down fully clothed on top of the bed
and rested his body against hers for a long while, afraid to
let her look at him. His hands were balled into fists, and
she carefully pried them open and kissed his moist open
palms. She took his middle finger into her mouth and
sucked on it very gently, and finally he let her unbutton his
shirt, pull off his jeans, slide down his underwear. He let
her take control while his body burned. She ran her hands,
light as feathers, over his ruined flesh. "It's beautiful," she
whispered, "like a map . . . like a lovely, living map." With
a kind of whacked-out wonder, he let her explore his entire
body until the self-consciousness left him and lust took
over.

Now as he headed for the door, Willa reached out to
stop him. "Charlie?" He noticed that her fingernails were
painted the same Wedgwood blue as her toenails, which
he could see through the cinnamon-colored hose. "This
morning, when I heard about the murders? It reminded
me of something."

He waited.

"Remember that F-3 last March in Texas?"

He shook his head.

"A lot of people got trapped in the rubble. Help wasn't
getting there fast enough, so a few of us formed a search-
and-rescue team. There was this one house . . . it was
conventionally constructed with wooden bottom plates
nailed to the foundation. No straps or anchor bolts. I

mean, a house like that in Tornado Alley? All you've got is a few nails anchoring the frame to the foundation." She shook her head in anger. "I'm talking total collapse."

"The house was in the damage path?"

She nodded. "I forget their last name. A young couple. So sad. Anyway, we went looking for survivors in the voids. Both victims had been impaled with flying debris . . . it was gruesome. The man was DOS, but the woman was semiconscious."

Charlie nodded. "Go on."

"She died of her injuries five hours later. She didn't make it." Willa paused to reflect. "But as I was driving her to the hospital, she said a few things that didn't make any sense. Things that really disturbed me."

"Like what?"

" 'Please don't kill me.' Stuff like that. She sounded terrified. 'Someone's in the house . . . Oh no . . . Please don't hurt us.' Over and over. I just figured she was delirious. I thought she was hallucinating, but now I think maybe there's more to it than that."

He narrowed his eyes at the possibility. "Where was this again?"

10

THAT AFTERNOON, he left wheat-and-sunflower country behind and crossed the border into East Texas, where most of the dirt roads twisting through the surrounding prairie ended in scattered oil wells that coughed up a few precious barrels of crude a day. He could see the birdlike bobbings of the one-cylinder jacks in the distant flint rock hills, where the grass grew wild and untrammeled. A jackrabbit darted in front of the car and bounded across the road, giving him a sudden twinge in the pit of his stomach, and he tightened his grip on the wheel.

Charlie took the next exit to Wink, where dust devils swirled across the stubbled fields and abandoned foundations were spray-painted "Hey, Dorothy!" and "Been there, done that!" Last year's tornado had cut a spotty but destructive sixteen-mile swath through Parson and Cribbs Counties, leaving behind vacant lots and rows of utility poles stripped down to their original pine skin. Downtown Wink consisted of a cluster of one-story buildings beneath a low gray sky. You could tell the town was suffering. Main Street was wide and inviting, with giveaways and balloons tied to the parking meters, and many enticing signs in the plate-glass windows hinting at trouble ahead. WOW! CAN'T BEAT THESE PRICES!!!

Charlie followed directions past the town's only bank with its outdoor ATM down a lone country road, where a pack of dogs ran alongside the car, their tongues flapping like flags. After a few more miles, he pulled into a trailer park, where the sheriff had set up temporary quarters after the tornado had blown the roof off the town hall last March. The Mirador Motor-In was equipped with RV hookups, a communal rest room and a vintage ten-stool diner. Tonight's special was sweet potato pie. The Pepsi thermometer above the doorway read a balmy eighty-two degrees.

Charlie found the trailer without a hitch, a Bluebird Wanderlodge whose retro blue and silver body was peppered with hail dents. Sheriff Jimmy L'Amoureux greeted him at the door. He was one of those Native Americans with the kind of weather-beaten good looks and thick, waist-length hair that made you consider getting hair plugs. Squinting across the dusty fields beyond Charlie's shoulder, L'Amoureux said, "You used to be able to see my house from here. But then Mother Nature got out the wrecking ball."

They shook hands. At six foot five, Charlie was used to being the tallest authority figure in any room, but L'Amoureux beat him by a good couple of inches. They ducked their heads under the doorway as they went inside. "I'm in the middle of something, but I can spare a few minutes," L'Amoureux told him, more polite than friendly.

"I appreciate it." Charlie removed his hat and followed him into a long, narrow space crowded with office furniture. He glanced around at the rich blond-wood interior.

At the far end of the trailer was an efficient-looking kitchen area, dirty dishes stacked high in a chrome sink. On one of the windows, somebody'd scrawled "Clean me!" in the dust with their finger.

"Take a seat," L'Amoureux said, propping his cowboy boots on a desktop so cluttered with old case files and ammunition clips you couldn't see through to the wood.

"Looks like you folks are bouncing back," Charlie said in an upbeat way. The sheriff gave him a bemused expression. "I suppose you think it's progress for a cannibal to use a napkin," he said in a thick Texas drawl.

Charlie frowned. He wasn't expecting sarcasm.

L'Amoureux folded his long arms across his massive chest. "Look, I know what you're thinking. You're thinking, 'The town'll bounce back, we'll be better than ever.' That's what you're thinking to yourself, am I right?"

He gave a reluctant nod.

"Last year, shopkeepers were sweeping up broken glass, everything was in splinters. We had waist-deep debris, twisted cars, battered homes and businesses. And all I kept thinking was, 'We're gonna pull through, it's gonna be better than ever.' Blah, blah, blah." He gave an indifferent shrug. "Just you wait."

"That bad, huh?"

He smiled cagily, his eyes half-closed. "When you find out the factory outlet will not be rebuilt, it kind of puts a kink in your day. They employed seventy-five people. Four other businesses canceled their leases. So you see, we're bouncing back just fine," he said bitterly.

Charlie's spine stiffened. "Look, I'm asshole-deep in worries here, Sheriff. I'm coming to you in a friendly way, trying to get a little cooperation, but all I'm getting is one loud lecture."

L'Amoureux snapped his gaze back inside the room. "So what's this all about, then? To what do I owe the pleasure of your company?"

Charlie cleared his throat. "I'm interested in anything you can tell me about the couple who died last year."

"The Keels?" L'Amoureux licked his lips. "Audra was a housewife. Pretty little thing. Into saving whales and other hippie causes. Matt was a traveling salesman. His pockets were always beeping and buzzing with cell phones and pagers and what-have-you. He was an amateur photographer, and he looked like a ballroom dancer, to tell you the truth. Always so meticulously groomed."

"I heard their house collapsed?"

"Yeah."

"And she was still alive when they pulled her out of the rubble?"

"That's right."

"And she said some things?"

L'Amoureux looked at him sideways. "Where the hell are you going with this, Chief?"

Charlie figured he would have to pitch his cause in order to get a little cooperation. "Look," he said, leaning forward, "you've heard about our triple homicide, right?"

He nodded curtly.

"It happened around the same time the tornado hit. A family was murdered in cold blood, in a ritualistic fashion. They were attacked with weapons made out of wood, but they looked like pieces of flying debris."

"So you're coming to me in a friendly way to let me know that the Keels were murdered, too?"

"That's what I'm here to find out."

L'Amoureux snorted derisively and shook his head, all that long gray hair shimmering down his back like a rope of mercury. "Are you sure about this? Because lemme tell you something. Ain't nobody gonna commit murder in the shadow of an F-3. End of story. Tornadoes are unpredictable. They're indiscriminate and dangerous. Look at us, Grover. We've got badges and guns, but when it comes to a tornado, there's not a damn thing we can do about it. People will die. Buildings will fall. Shit will happen. You can hold your breath longer than it took to destroy all this." He nodded vaguely out the window, his eyes growing remote.

"Whoever killed the Peppers knew a severe storm was headed our way. As the storm progressed, he was able to hone his forecast."

L'Amoureux rolled his eyes.

"We found smooth glove prints and handmade weapons at the crime scene, which means it was premeditated. The crime itself was so well planned and executed I find it hard to believe he hasn't done it before. So I'll ask you again, did Audra Keel make a dying declaration?"

L'Amoureux clasped his big hands together. "Whatever she said that day, it didn't make much sense."

"What'd she say?"

"She just babbled."

Charlie opened the manila folder on his lap. "These autopsies have been sealed by court order. Certain details have been kept confidential. I'd like it to stay that way."

With an impatient grunt, L'Amoureux let his feet drop to the floor. "Hand it over," he said, reaching for the file. After a few minutes of intense concentration, he looked up. "Okay, you've got my attention. Now, just what was it you were hoping to accomplish here?"

"I'd like to exhume the bodies."

He touched the tips of his fingers together. "Look, this

is a bizarre, perplexing case. But you're gonna have to trust me. We examined the bodies at the scene. Cause of death was traumatic injuries due to two-hundred-mile-per-hour winds."

"Did you find any defensive wounds? Did you examine the flying debris? Did your coroner look inside the victims' mouths?"

The sheriff leaned forward, marbled veins showing in his thick bull neck. "Are you questioning my methodology, Chief?"

"No, of course not." Charlie chose his words carefully. "But like you said, you had your hands full that day. There's no reason you should've stopped in the middle of all that chaos and devastation and suspected foul play. Hundreds injured, destruction on a massive scale. You folks were basically on your own. Searching for survivors. Dozers and cranes. Gas leaks. I know the score, I just went through it myself. It knocks you sideways."

L'Amoureaux's voice contained a drop of doubt. "Total of eight dead. That's a lot in a small town like ours. Hundreds injured. No hospital. We were literally in the dark."

Charlie examined his palms, full of the kinds of lines that supposedly foretold your future. "All I'm saying is, if the Keels were victims of the same killer, we'd be able to tell right away by examining their teeth."

"And if you're wrong?"

"Then it's not your problem."

L'Amoureux gazed into some middle distance, his mind turning it over. He had a rough face with broad cheekbones and the kind of steadfast gaze that never seemed to express a moment's hesitation. "Okay," he decided. "I'll have a talk with the next of kin."

"Great."

"But it's up to them. They've been through plenty already. If they say no, then it's over."

"Fair enough."

The minifridge shifted gears, and Charlie's pager went off at the same time, sending tremors of exasperation through his body. He breathed deep, checked the number. It was Mike. "Can I use your phone?"

"Help yourself." L'Amoureux swung the old-fashioned rotary phone around on his desk, then walked down to the far end of the trailer, where he started tackling the dirty dishes, running water in the sink.

"Hey, boss," Mike said. "Good news. Our buddies over at the NWS just FedExed us a bunch of pictures of the Promise tornado. They're up to their eyeballs in the stuff, apparently. It comes flooding in on a regular basis. Weather geeks helping out their fellow weather weenies . . ."

"Great. Put Nick to work on it right away. See if he can get some freeze-frames of vehicles and faces, license plates, you know the drill. Then I want you to send the results over to my house ASAP."

"Your house?"

"Yeah, I'll be working at home tonight. I promised Sophie. She's all alone."

"Say hi for me, wouldja? And listen, Chief, I asked Jake Wheaton to come in for the sole purpose of answering a few questions, but get this. He's threatening to lawyer up."

"Okay, hold off on that. Don't provoke him any further. What about Rob Pepper's brother?"

"He alibied convincingly. We cut him loose with apologies. He didn't provide any significant information."

"Did we get the blood results back yet?"

"Too early, Chief."

"Call Art Danbury. Put a rush on it."

"Okay, boss."

"Go grill a few people." He hung up and dialed his daughter's number.

"It's me," Sophie answered breathlessly, as if she'd been expecting his call.

"Hello, you. This is the other me."

"Dad! I've decided what to make us for dinner tonight. Vegetarian lasagna."

"Mm. Sounds challenging."

"Maybe for you, you meat-eater. You're still coming home tonight, right?"

"Are you kidding? I wouldn't miss it."

"Good, because I'm making us lasagna for dinner."

"I heard you the first time."

"Good, because I wouldn't want to have to throw it all away again."

"Listen, wise guy. Set an extra place at the table. I'm inviting a guest."

"A guest?" Her voice tensed. "What kind of guest?"

"I haven't exactly asked this person yet."

"Jesus, Dad. Are you going through a midlife crisis or something? Who is this mystery person?"

"You'll be nice to her, won't you?"

"Her? It's a she?"

"You'll be nice and polite and not too ironic?"

She sounded deeply offended. "What do you think?"

"I think you're a normal teenage girl. That's what worries me."

"Six o'clock sharp," she said. "Don't be late. You and Ms. Mysterioso."

He hung up and stared at the rotary phone, trying to form the words in his head. *Keep it casual.* He didn't like this jumpy feeling in the pit of his stomach. *C'mon. Thirty-seven and still sweating the dating scene? She told you to call. What more do you want?* He picked up the phone and dialed the wind facility, then asked for Willa's extension.

"Rick Kripner," came the response.

Busted. He could feel the blood rushing from his head. "Hey, Rick, this is Charlie Grover. Is Willa there?"

"I'm not expecting her back today, Chief."

"Oh." He spoke rapidly to mask his embarrassment. "I was going to ask her to take a look at some photographs for me . . . pictures of chase vehicles we received from the NWS. I thought maybe she could identify some of the owners . . ."

"Listen, I've been chasing for years. I know these people. I know what they drive."

He hesitated. "Do you like lasagna?"

"Sure."

"How's six o'clock sound?"

"Great. Where d'you live?"

Feeling like a jackass, he rattled off the address.

11

WOULD YOU like to buy a dog?" Sophie asked Rick, who sat there smiling at her.

"Not especially." He grinned.

"Come on," she said. "Only fifty bucks."

"What dog?" Charlie said, noting that his daughter had lit candles in anticipation of her father's "date," which hadn't materialized. "We don't own any dogs."

They were seated around the dining room table, where the flickering candlelight made their faces glow buttery yellow. Twilight had eroded; darkness had fallen. Charlie and Rick were splitting a bottle of wine between them, and now Charlie was feeling nice and buzzed, albeit a bit confused about all this dog business.

"I'm volunteering for the orphans, Dad."

"Orphans? What orphans?" He didn't have a clue what his lovely daughter was talking about.

"All the stray dogs from the storm," she explained. "Nobody's come forward to claim them yet, and there isn't enough room in the kennels. So we have to find them new owners." She turned to Rick. "A few have respiratory infections, but they're getting better. And they've all been immunized. And they're really, really cute."

He shook his head. "Too much responsibility. You can't drop everything and go chasing when you have a dog. But thanks for asking."

"Lemme know if you change your mind, okay?"

He laughed. "You're good. She's good."

"My daughter," Charlie bragged, "could charm the wig off a drag queen."

Sophie had swept her long chestnut-colored hair off her face and, in the candlelight, was the spitting image of her mother. It moved him deeply, her innocent beauty. So scrub-faced and sincere. It was half past seven, and they'd eaten most of the lasagna. The garlic bread was gone except for the heel, and even the grayish peas were gone.

"What's in the locket?" Rick asked.

"This?" She beamed, her cheeks going rosy. She opened the silver locket at her throat and proudly displayed the picture of herself and Maddie, their smiling faces tipped together. "My mom. Isn't she beautiful?"

"Wow. A total babe."

This seemed to please her. "People used to think we were sisters," she said, then glanced at her father as she clasped the locket shut. "She died two years ago."

"Oh. I'm sorry." Rick's gaze was mellow behind his wire-rim glasses. His dark blue flannel shirt with its mother-of-pearl buttons was tucked into the waistband of his jeans, and his thick brown hair was pressed flat against his skull in the shape of the baseball cap he'd worn into the house.

Sophie yawned just then, and Charlie felt a sudden rush of love for her. She yawned whenever she got nervous or didn't want to talk about something. Her other habits were nail-biting and staying up late to watch *Conan* on weeknights. She excelled in math, biology, English and ballet, and if Charlie believed in anything, he believed in the vast potential of his daughter. Sophie could've been a doctor, lawyer, teacher, ballet dancer, whatever she set her heart on. Funny, she'd been such a fat baby, such a pudge. He remembered the way Maddie used to stand her on her knees and watch as she staggered and swayed and tested her plump little legs, pockets of fat bulging above the kneecaps.

Now Sophie was staring at him. "Hello? Earth to Dad."

He blinked away the memory. "Huh?"

"I said, what were you doing in Texas today?"

"Oh. Just checking on some stuff."

"What kind of stuff?"

"This town got hit by a tornado last year. I was checking out their rebuilding efforts," he lied. She knew about the murders, but he wasn't going to feed her every gory detail.

"I hope they rebuild everything stronger next time," she said, "so it won't come crashing down again."

"You can design a building to withstand three-hundred-mile-per-hour winds if you want to," Rick told them. "But the cost is prohibitive."

"I don't get it." She displayed the wide-eyed earnestness of a Miss Universe desiring to eradicate world hunger. "Why aren't all the schools in Oklahoma built to withstand tornadoes? How come every house doesn't have a basement?"

Rick shrugged. "That's just the way of the world, kiddo."

She glanced at her father and frowned. Sweet. She was sweetness itself, like a fawn in the forest glade staring down the barrel of a hunter's gun and not recognizing danger. Smiling invitingly at strangers, wishing for world peace, firm in her belief that her dear old dad had all the answers. Yeah, right. "Boone says most people don't care about anything until it's too late," she said.

Charlie gave a start. "Boone?"

"Dad . . ."

"Boone Pritchett? Since when do you care what Boone Pritchett thinks?"

Ignoring him, she turned to Rick. "He's a storm-chaser. Do you know him?"

"Yeah, I've seen him around." Rick rolled his eyes. "Now, there's a kid who watches too much NASCAR on TV."

"He doesn't drive that fast," she said defensively, glancing at her father over the rim of her water glass.

Charlie felt a twinge of apprehension. Boone Pritchett was the kind of troubled youth who gave troubled youths a bad name. His biker father worked in a sealant factory and his mother was a whippet-thin alcoholic, and Boone liked to define himself by his misdeeds—shoplifting, truancy, pot-smoking. He was headed for serious trouble, and Charlie didn't want his daughter hanging out with a kid like that.

"He drives an old Ford pickup, right?" Rick said. "Casino pink. This thing is barely street legal . . . one of those 'have title will sell' type of vehicles. He likes to ride low, all the air let out of his air-ride seat, cowboy hat pulled down to his nose . . . how can he possibly see?"

"What's this sudden interest in Boone Pritchett?" Charlie asked his daughter.

"Dad . . . ," she said, blushing. All elegance and self-possession. A modest smile about her lips. "It's no big deal."

"No big deal? That kid is destined to climb a tower one of these days and start gunning down strangers."

"Cut it out," she said, putting on the polite face of a doll. "Besides, nobody's gonna mess with me. I'm the police chief's daughter."

"He'd better not."

She cleared her throat and changed the subject. "So you're a wind engineer?" she asked Rick. "What made you decide to study wind, of all things?"

He answered her question with a question. "You know about the Fujita scale, right?"

She nodded.

"Then you know that an F-1 means moderate, an F-2's considerable, F-3's severe and an F-4 is, well . . . devastating. Real *Wizard of Oz*–type stuff." He shifted slightly in his seat. "You don't want to know about an F-5," he said ominously.

Her eyes lit up. "You've seen one?"

"When I was thirteen." He wiped his mouth on a paper napkin, then folded it neatly across his knee. "This freak hailstorm came out of nowhere and flattened the wheat for miles around our house. It was just me and Dad back then. Mom was long gone, bless her heart. After the hail hit, we went outside to survey the damage, but there was nothing to see. Absolutely nothing. The devastation was that complete. And from the looks of the sky, you could tell it wasn't over yet." He flicked his glance ceilingward. "I remember the wind was roaring in my ears. I couldn't hear a thing my dad was saying, but I could see this terrible force gathering in the sky behind him. I wanted to run away, but he wouldn't listen. His crops were gone. That year's harvest meant just about everything to him. He was heavily in debt. I remember the dogs were yelping, and there was this low, awful rumble, and all of a sudden the sky went black as night. You could see several baby tornadoes sprouting out of the base of this enormous rotating wall cloud . . . like lassos twirling over the ground. Then one of them dropped. First it was rope-sized. Then it was cone-shaped. Eventually it became the biggest wedge I've ever seen. I'm talking two-sixty, two-hundred-and-seventy-mile-per-hour screaming winds headed straight for us." His voice grew hushed. "These storms can close gaps at frightening speeds. The vortex was rushing forward at roughly sixty miles an hour. Unbelievable. Lightning shooting out in all directions. Dad just stood there. I kept tugging on his arm, but he pushed me away and started to scream at the sky. I'll never forget it. He was like a flea cursing out an elephant . . . ranting and raving, shaking his fists. Then he picked up his rifle and shot at the damn thing, as if he could bring it down like a deer.

"I dove for the ground and ate dirt. The wedge was right on top of us by then. I remember it kept making this weird sound . . . shrill . . . almost human. Next thing I knew, I was looking straight up into those screaming innards. She was all hollow and lit up inside, twisting around like a barber pole, first orange, then violet, then neon red, with jagged spikes of lightning ricocheting from side to side." He stopped talking and just looked at them.

"What?" Sophie asked breathlessly.

"She sucked my father right out of his boots. Those old manure-caked shitkickers. Literally right out of his boots. I blinked, and he was gone."

She raised her fingers to her face.

"Then she ripped right over me and slammed into the barn," he continued. "The doors flew off their hinges. The roof peeled away like cardboard. The dogs got swept up yelping. Later on, I had to put three horses down. See this?" He held out his right hand so that they could see the bent tip of his pinkie finger. "A piece of debris nearly tore it off. It never quite healed properly."

"What happened to your father?" Sophie asked with a hesitant politeness Rick seemed to find appealing.

"Sorry," he said. "This isn't exactly dinner conversation."

Charlie cleared his throat. "I think it's time we changed the subject."

"Dad," Sophie said softly, "I can handle it."

"You see," Rick explained, "these aren't just storms to me. They're miniature universes all to themselves. Walls of force sixty to seventy miles wide and over ten miles high. Air and moisture rushing in to build these roiling masses sixty thousand feet thick. They can darken half a state. I mean, think about it . . . Something larger than the Empire State Building should not be able to move like that."

Sophie sat in rapt attention. "Sounds incredible."

Charlie nudged his plate forward and cleared his throat. "The lasagna was a big hit, honey."

"Mm, delicious," Rick agreed.

"Thanks." She smiled shyly at them, the skin of her forehead bunching delicately. "Maybe now you'll stop eating meat, huh?"

"You mean there wasn't any meat in that dish?" Rick said with mock surprise.

She laughed. "I used seitan instead."

"Satan?"

"Sei-tan." She plopped her hands proudly in her lap. "It's a soy product."

Charlie remembered how scared she used to be of the dark, so small and terrified, convinced the bogeyman was lurking somewhere under her bed. He and Maddie would have to coax her through each night with countless bedtime stories and promises of being right next door. She'd been so tiny and afraid of the dark, and now here she was, defending Boone Pritchett, of all people. He longed for the days when she had freckles floating on the surface of her skin and a deep distrust of boys. Couldn't she just stop growing up? The passage of time was like falling down a well—you could claw at the walls all you wanted to, but you couldn't prevent yourself from falling.

"Don't you have homework to do?" he said now.

"Dad . . ."

"Your old man's the boss," Rick said with a friendly, peacekeeping smile. "What he says goes."

"Not when Mom was alive," she muttered.

"Hey," Charlie said.

"Hay is for horses."

"Don't be smart."

"Okay, I'll be dumb." She stood up and started stacking the dinner plates.

"We'll clean up later, honey. Go on upstairs."

Reluctantly she put the plates down. "Nice to meet you," she said, shaking Rick's hand.

"The pleasure's been all mine, Sophie."

Her front teeth caught on her lower lip, then her eyes shifted to her father again. "Peg says to tell you the gutters are clogged, Dad."

"Thanks, honey."

"Well . . . good night."

"G'night." Rick gave her a little wave as she tripped up the stairs.

"C'mon. We can talk in my study." Charlie escorted his guest through the living room, which Maddie had filled with Merimeko throw pillows and decorous rugs, an antique musket over the mantelpiece and lots of American primitive furniture. Since her death, all the exotic plants in the house had died—the African violets and wild indigo, the snow-white amaryllis. No, that wasn't quite true. After her death, wild with grief, Charlie had smashed all the flowerpots in the house, every last one. It wasn't fair that she was dead—why should her plants be allowed to bloom?

"You've got a great kid," Rick said.

"She can be delicately morbid."

Rick smiled as he circled the study, examining the pine shelves crowded with Charlie's medals and commendations. There were photographs of Charlie's great-grandparents standing proud and erect in front of their sod house; of his teenage grandmother selling tomatoes for five cents a bushel during the Great Depression; of distant relatives whose eyes were blurred shut due to double exposure, as if the passage of time had fogged their memories.

Squinting at the old daguerreotypes, Rick said, "My great-grandfather won the family homestead in a poker game. Imagine if you could do that now?"

"Where do you live?" Charlie asked.

"Pixley, embarrassing to report. I come from a long line of the wrong people. I could move anywhere I wanted to now, but I grew up in that house. Pixley's just a church, a post office and a firehouse, but there's still plenty of wide-open space."

"I hear you."

He pointed at a picture of Adelaide. "That your mother?"

"Yes."

"I don't remember mine. They say she was petite as a finch. I got a lot of sympathy dates growing up. Guess some women are drawn to motherless boys. Brings out their maternal instinct." He picked up one of Charlie's track-and-field trophies. "Two-hundred-meter, huh?"

"Back in the Mesozoic era, yeah. It was good therapy."

"Oh. Yeah." Rick acknowledged the burn scars with a glance. "My relationship to sports is confined to the living room sofa, I'm afraid." He put the trophy back on its spot on the shelf. "You've got a lot of medals, Chief."

Charlie sat behind his desk, hands resting on the navy-blue blotter. "That doesn't make me any braver than the next guy."

"Maybe not." Rick took a seat in the armchair in front of him. "But it sure makes you braver than me."

"I haven't looked at these yet." He opened the manila envelope one of his patrol officers had dropped off earlier that afternoon and slid out an inch-thick stack of photographs. Riffling through them quickly, he said, "These were taken by various news crews and storm-chasers yesterday afternoon. See if you recognize any of the—" His breath hitched in his throat as he spotted a photograph of his father's '51 Loadmaster pickup truck. It was just a blur, speeding past the damage site, but Charlie felt the hairs on his scalp bristle like a cold morning. No, wait, it was perfectly innocent; his father had already explained that he'd been on a chase ride yesterday. He'd participated in the cleanup. He'd stolen a watch . . .

"Something wrong?"

"No. Nothing." He tucked the picture into a desk drawer, then handed the rest over to Rick. "See if you recognize any of these vehicles."

Rick accepted the stack. "You know, Chief, this is for the most part an articulate, well-educated bunch. I just want to state that for the record."

"Duly noted."

"Okay, here goes." He started thumbing through them. "Okay, this guy's a hard-core chaser. I've seen him just about everywhere. His name's Paul something or other . . . I'll think of it in a minute. This Ranger belongs to a kid who's truly witless—a rich kid who's got nothing better to do than get in everybody's way. Preston J. Hale, he's from Kansas City. Hm. This vehicle I don't recognize . . . That one, either . . ."

Charlie flicked his ballpoint pen open and shut. "Were you in Promise yesterday?"

"Yeah." He glanced up. "We were out collecting data."

"You and Willa?"

He nodded.

"Did you take any photographs?"

He shook his head. "I don't like having a camera between myself and the storm, Chief. It's like wearing a condom."

Charlie smiled.

"We work as a tag team, but sometimes we split up. Different data has to be collected from the same storm, so we alternate who gets the van. She got the van. I took my GMC Sierra. You need all-wheel drive, since you never know what kind of rough terrain you might find yourself in." Charlie had seen Rick's truck parked in the driveway tonight, a black GMC Sierra virtually bristling with antennae. "I came to within five miles of it, Chief. I was heading east on the 412 when the storm became very HP-ish. That means there was high precipitation, including hail, on the rear flank downdraft. I turned up Wichita Avenue and was trying to reach the nearest flank when I crested a hill and saw this nice stovepipe drifting toward the northeast."

"Then what?"

"It lifted back into the clouds and dissipated. So I continued heading east on the interstate, through Cleo Springs and Ringwood, where I tried to intercept another one before dark. But the RFD surge looked pretty bad, so I turned tail and called it a night." He cocked his head. "You were disappointed when I picked up the phone today, weren't you?"

Charlie smiled but said nothing.

They eyed one another uneasily.

"She'll be sorry she missed this." Rick shuffled through the remaining photographs. "Okay, this blue Mustang belongs to a weekend chaser, a woman named Becky Callahan. Ah . . . Conrad Holzman. He's from Tulsa. He's an okay guy, a regular chaser, very knowledgeable. These, I have no idea. This one's an engineer, he might be from Utah." He drummed his fingers on the top photograph, the only one left in the stack—a blurry image of a white van speeding toward the distant funnel cloud. "Okay, Jonah Gustafson. You wanna pay close attention to him."

"G-u-s-t-a-f-s-o-n?" Charlie wrote it down on his yellow legal pad.

"Foul temper. Doesn't watch his speed. Very competitive. Likes to divert other chasers away from a good storm." He leaned back and folded his arms across his chest. "Scary-looking dude. I don't know what he does for a living or where he's from. There's nothing blatantly wrong with him, Chief, I just don't like him. Nobody does. He keeps to himself mostly. A real loner."

Charlie nodded. "Describe him for me."

"Six one, six two. Thin. Emaciated, actually . . . like a shirt hanging on a fence post. Always wears the same greasy-looking 'Night Train' baseball cap."

Charlie jotted it all down.

"And he's hardly ever sober."

"Any scars or tattoos?"

"I never get that close."

"And you have no idea where he's from?"

Rick shook his head, then set the photographs aside. "Can I ask you something? Do you honestly think that a storm-chaser has time to stop and commit murder?"

"You're the expert. You tell me."

He rubbed his jaw thoughtfully. "It's conceivable, I suppose." He drew a sharp breath through his teeth. "It'd be totally freaky if one of the guys I knew was a cold-blooded killer . . . except for Jonah Gustafson. That would make a weird kind of sense."

Charlie folded his hands on the desktop. "What do you think of Boone Pritchett?"

Rick shrugged. "He likes to core-punch. He goes chasing at night. That's fucked-up, but it takes a certain amount of skill."

"How are you at this prediction thing?"

"Me?" Rick shrugged. "Better than most."

"Have you ever predicted with any accuracy when and where a tornado was gonna drop down?"

He snorted. "Yeah, sure. It's hard on the morning of the same day to predict the mesoscale influences that're gonna arise later on, but I've seen a few guys do it thirty-six hours ahead of time. They're either clairvoyant or geniuses."

"Which guys?"

"The only people I know who're that good on a consistent basis are Jonah Gustafson, Conrad Holzman and Willa."

The skin around Charlie's mouth puckered. "Willa?"

Their eyes met. "She's got it all, doesn't she, Chief? Brains. Beauty. Balls."

He tried to decipher the message between the lines: *I was here first. She's mine. Beat it.*

"Next time we're out in the field, we'd be glad to take you along."

"Can I go, too?" Sophie begged from the doorway, her smile a little too eager for Charlie's comfort. "Can I? Please?"

"Okay, Holly Golightly," he said, getting up. "Let's get those dishes done."

12

JAKE WHEATON was doing 50 in a 35-mph zone, just driving around in his Chevy pickup truck, waiting for ten o'clock to roll around. He had an appointment with an ounce of marijuana. Now he spotted Lester Deere's Chevy Blazer in the rearview mirror as it roared up the road behind him. "Yeah, yeah, I see you, Ossifer Stupido."

Hitting his flasher, Lester edged into the empty lane, then drove parallel to Jake's truck and gestured for him to pull over.

Jake raised his beer can. "Cheers, motherfucker."

Lester eyeballed him through the window.

"What?" Jake said. "I can't hear you!"

Lester sped ahead and fishtailed directly in front of him.

"Shit!" Jake slammed on the brakes and felt his nose collapsing as his face hit the steering wheel. The tires of his pickup truck slid over the road as he swerved to a stop. He sat for a dazed instant, ankle-deep in beer cans, when suddenly Lester opened the door, reached inside the cab and plucked Jake out by his flannel shirt.

"You fucked her?" he screamed, punching Jake in the gut, and he curled double with a *whoosh* of air. "You fucked her, you lying son of a bitch?"

Jake wanted to vomit from the pain.

"What's that, cocksucker? You say something?" Lester's fist moved like a whip.

Jake rocked back on his heels, a searing pain registering across his jaw. He cupped his chin and swayed on unsteady legs. "No, no, no . . ."

"Don't you lie to me, Jake!" Lester stood panting, his eyes crazed. "Did you fuck her? Did you? Because it's all over the station house."

"No!"

"Don't lie to me, boy." He bunched Jake's collar in his meaty fists and squeezed. "Are you lying to me?"

Jake was afraid to look into that face, something raw and wild flickering behind those beady eyes. "Yeah, okay," he admitted, cringing. "Just that once, though, Lester, I swear to God . . ."

The older man let out a terrible roar and cracked Jake's jaw with a solid left hook.

The boy went flying across the road and landed on his back, all the breath leaving his lungs with a guttural hiss. When he woke up, he was staring at the night sky with its millions of stars. Dazed and wondering.

Lester kicked him in the ribs. "Don't you dare breathe a word of this, understand? Not one word," he screamed. "You hear me, loser? Huh?"

Jake groaned and spit blood. He rolled over and tried to crawl away, but a heavy foot came down on the back of his neck, forcing his face into the dirt.

"Not one word," he screamed again. "You hear me?"

"Yes."

"What's that?"

His chest felt as knotted as old rope as he tried to breathe. "Yes, sir," he gasped. "I won't."

"You won't what?"

"Breathe a word. I swear."

Lester rolled him over and got right in his face, eyes ticking back and forth like a stenographer's fingers. "Don't you even think about ratting me out," he hissed. "That would be a very dangerous thing for you to do."

"I won't," he promised, his fear and loathing deepening.

"You and me? We don't know each other." Lester hocked a wad of spit in Jake's face, then got back in his truck and drove off in a cloud of dust.

13

THE FOLLOWING night, Charlie got a call from Sheriff Jimmy L'Amoureux. "We're exhuming the bodies tonight," he said, "just in case you're interested."

"Tonight?" He glanced at the ceiling in the general direction of Sophie's room. "Can't it wait until tomorrow?"

"It's now or never, Chief. You interested? Or should I call the relatives and tell them it's off?"

"No, I'm interested. I'm heading out the door."

It was a long drive back to the dreary little town of Wink, Texas, with its ghost roads and cracked sidewalks. Charlie fiddled with the radio dial, trying to find a station loud enough to mask the rumble of the burned-out valve, while the cones of his headlights poked into the night and lightning flickered in the distant mesquite-flecked hills. He took the Drury exit off the four-lane onto a road that ran straight as a ruler. After a few more monotonous miles, he pulled up in front of a cemetery on the under-populated side of town, its rusty wrought-iron gate spelling out REST HAVEN PARK. It didn't look like a park. You could see emergency lights glowing through the headstones.

Sheriff L'Amoureux met him at the gate. His uniform was faded from repeated washings, and he wore a thick leather belt with a solid silver buckle inlaid with Montana agate. "You a whiskey man?" he asked.

"I don't drink hard liquor," Charlie said, getting out.

"Well, I do, but I hate myself in the morning."

"I figured, so long as we're digging up dead people, we might as well have some coffee and whiskey waiting for us back at the coroner's office."

"Sounds like a plan."

Rest Haven Park was a tangle of blackjack and pitted turn-of-the-century headstones. A cold dampness tickled the back of Charlie's throat as they stumbled over countless unmown ditches clogged with ground cherry and discarded beer bottles. Their dueling flashlight beams slashed through the cemetery, illuminating limestone angels whose wing tips had been broken off by vandals and solemn declarations etched in granite: "Fear of the Lord is the beginning of wisdom."

"Next of kin lives across county lines," L'Amoureux said, daubing at his slick upper lip with his forefinger and thumb. "They didn't want to attend. Can't say as I blame them."

They stumbled down an incline onto a paved road, where the asphalt was crisscrossed with skid marks from local kids doing wheelies and doughnuts. They crossed the road into the newer part of the cemetery, where the Keels had been buried over a year ago, and found their modest headstones after a few minutes of confusion.

No grass grew on or near the graves, as if out of deference to the dead. Both stones held the same death date—March 31. The grave sites had been sadly neglected. An old funeral wreath lay on its side in front of

Matthew Keel's headstone, and a damp pink teddy bear was collecting mold in front of Audra's. Two dried brown roses stuck out of the dirt in front of each granite slab.

Now an arc of light swung crazily through the air, and Charlie spun around. A bulldozer was driving up the road toward them, its headlights piercing the darkness, a cloud of diesel smoke blowing back from the engine.

"Ed Olson, the contractor," L'Amoureux said.

Ed had the kind of slack-jawed face that was made for drooling. He parked the bulldozer by the side of the road and stepped down from the cab. The bulldozer's bucket teeth were the size of a man's fist. Short and stooped with thick iron-gray hair, Ed spent the next few minutes going over his instructions with L'Amoureux before he hopped back in the cab and ground the gears.

Charlie stepped back while the engine burped and the bulldozer rolled methodically back and forth in its tracks like a hesitant bull elephant. Illuminated by two bars of fluorescent light, the push-arm swung like a giant feeler and the bright yellow blade bit into the earth.

Light flared as two more vehicles approached the scene from a distance over the rain-washed streets, headlights barreling toward them and playing across their faces. First came a dirty white pickup truck, driven by a middle-aged woman with orange bubble hair. She hit the brakes and fishtailed to a stop, mist rising from her tires.

"I brought the shovels, Jimmy," said the woman, getting out of the truck and slamming the stubborn door hard.

"Bonnie's our caretaker," L'Amoureux explained.

She came ambling toward them on spiky heels, carrying two heavy-looking shovels, while a black Mustang pulled up the rear. The driver hit the horn and started the wild dogs barking.

"Then there's Hodge, our town coroner."

An obese man wearing Big Boy jeans got out of the Mustang and lumbered toward them. He had a round face with owlish eyes and a handshake so full of good intentions it required two hands to execute. "Hey, Jimmy, how ya doin'?"

"Can't complain, Hodge. This is Charlie Grover, the one I was telling you about. Hodge Rogers, our town coroner."

"Nice to meet you."

Big hearty handshake. "Pretty bleak night for this sort of thing, huh? Hey, Bonnie! Hey, Ed!"

"Hey, Hodge," came the uniform response.

Hodge drew himself up proud, double chin tripling. "Gosh, Jimmy, you got me tossing and turning. What's all this about missing teeth and flying debris?"

"Chief Grover's the man with the questions."

Hodge turned to Charlie and used his coarse, powerful voice to assert himself. "I didn't miss a thing last year, honest injun. You won't find any stray teeth inside those mouths or any other weirdness. Mark my words."

"You've gotta play the long shots," Charlie told him.

"Sure, why not? Everybody's got their own agenda. Forget about the trauma inflicted on the family, right?"

"They aren't even here, Hodge," L'Amoureux said.

Hodge made a gesture of dismissal.

A big yellow moon like a saucer of milk suddenly broke through the clouds, and Charlie tried to ease the growing soreness in his left arm by rotating his shoulder cuff. That sometimes happened, fresh pain shooting out of the old scars.

L'Amoureux had a powerfully built body, like a small bus, and he, Charlie and Ed did most of the heavy lifting.

Even with the winch, it took them several hours to get the two coffins out of their graves and over to the morgue.

It was a short ride back into downtown Wink. Charlie pulled up in front of an ancient wind-battered building and parked behind the sheriff's corroded radio car, its blue beacon casting spooky, leaping shadows. The gate gave with a rubbery squeak. He crossed a lawn where the grass was packed like a mat, as if a lot of people had traipsed through recently. In the distance, you could hear the shrieks of local kids playing pickup games of baseball. He checked his watch. Nine o'clock on a Friday night. Sophie was out with her girlfriends. She had a midnight curfew, and he hoped to be home by then. He turned down a dark alleyway bracketed by heavy scrub, where a row of bur oaks grew above the fence line. In the breaks between clouds, he could see hopeful pockets of glittering stars.

Around back, a posted sign read KEEP OUT OR YOU MAY BE SHOT. The gray frame exterior needed a new coat of paint. The curtains in the downstairs windows were drawn shut. A bead of sweat trickled down Charlie's neck as he scaled the back porch and knocked on the rusty screen door.

"C'mon in," L'Amoureux said in a hushed voice, as if they were entering a library.

In the narrow hallway, a dank refrigerated smell assaulted Charlie's nostrils. Austere portraits of long-dead county officials lined the walls, and the naked overhead bulb burned dustily. They took a narrow set of stairs down into a dimly lit basement, where the stand-alone fan moved the foul-smelling air from corner to corner. Down here in the morgue, it stank of something soft and decaying in the walls.

The sealed caskets were stained with red clay and had to be pried open. Soon the room reeked of decomposition. The bodies were dressed in their funeral finest and seemed to be remarkably well preserved. Audra Keel wore tiny gold studs in her ears and clutched a bouquet of withered daisies. Her skin was covered with a fine sprinkling of powdery white mold. A tall, big-boned woman, she wore a pink skirt and white blouse with a Peter Pan collar. Matthew Keel was three inches shorter than his wife, his blue suit neat as a pin, his black hair shaved close to his scalp.

Hodge spent the next thirty minutes going over the Keels' dental charts. Breathing huskily as if he were exerting himself, he pried each victim's jaws open and traced the fillings along the gum lines, ran dental tools over eroded tooth surfaces. He judiciously charted the victims' teeth with trembling hands, then finally turned to L'Amoureux and said, "Nobody's missing any molars or premolars, except for their wisdom teeth. These mouths are in the same condition as their records indicate prior to death."

"Thanks, Hodge," L'Amoureux said, pouring himself a cup of coffee and lacing it liberally with whiskey.

"You're welcome." He looked at Charlie hard. "You still want to re-autopsy?"

Charlie could feel his body slumping under the weight of this revelation. No replacement teeth meant no murders had been committed. "No, let's call it a night," he said.

The three of them gathered around Matthew Keel to lift him back into the coffin when Charlie felt a rough texture on the back of the corpse's hand. "Wait," he said, turning it over. There were yellow abrasions with a parchmentlike translucence raking across Matthew's knuckles. "What's this?"

"Hm," Hodge said, bending close. "Those look like scrape marks to me. They're usually produced postmortem."

"What do you mean?" L'Amoureux said.

"These type of scrape marks occur after a victim is dead, when a body is dragged across a floor."

They eyed one another uneasily, and then Hodge logrolled Matthew onto his side. After working the jacket and shirt away from the body, he found similar-looking scrape marks on the corpse's back.

A long silence followed.

"I think we should re-autopsy," Charlie said.

Hodge turned to L'Amoureux. "Your call, Jimmy."

"Yeah, let's do it."

The atmosphere inside the morgue grew more oppressive as the victims were undressed and re-autopsied. Hodge opened up each corpse like a dissected frog, snipping sutures and poking around inside plastic bags full of internal organs. He probed old wounds and reexamined X rays, while the sharp fumes rising from the chest cavities made their eyes water. "If you theorize that this was a homicide—*if*, I said—then you've got multiple stab wounds to the chest and abdomen. Autopsy report says impalement with two chair legs, a baluster and a fence strut. There's a picture of the debris sticking out of the bodies . . . I don't know, hard to tell. We'd have to examine the originals, but I believe they're all gone. Isn't that right, Jimmy?"

"I didn't see any need to keep them."

"I had my hands full with the dead and injured," Hodge said defensively. "We lost the town clerk and his wife, my church organist, three young people. Three beautiful members of the next generation. Heck . . . these look like defensive wounds to the hands and arms. How'd we miss that, Jimmy?"

"Damned if I know."

"It could've been caused by flying debris." He continued with the internal exams.

Charlie picked up the old autopsy reports and studied the pictures: The injury to Audra Keel with the strut of a picket fence was particularly obscene. The penetrating end had been driven into the victim's chest wall, pushing the shirt fabric into her flesh and tearing through muscle and body cavity.

"These are Matthew's X rays." Hodge held one up to the light. "Impact abrasion over the right supraorbital ridge. Also a hematoma, a large focal collection of blood on the right cheek. Scalp bruises visible." He tossed the X rays down on the countertop and snapped off his latex gloves. "Blunt trauma to the head, multiple stab wounds. I don't know, chalk it up to a house falling down around their heads." He crossed his arms. "And you've still got no so-called replacement teeth."

The seed of an idea took root. "Maybe the tornado caught him by surprise," Charlie said. "It was a direct hit on the house, right?"

L'Amoureux blinked.

"Maybe his forecast was a little off that day. Maybe the tornado interrupted him right in the middle of the ritual and he couldn't complete the task at hand. The ritual with the teeth? What if he had to get out of the house before the tornado hit?"

"That still leaves us with no definitive proof."

Charlie rubbed his forehead, trying to think.

"I say we call it a night," Hodge grumbled.

"I agree," L'Amoureux said. "The relatives gave their permission to re-autopsy, and that was it. We've gotta put these bodies back where they belong."

"Okay, wait." Charlie bit his lower lip. "What would you do if you got interrupted in the middle of something?"

"I dunno. Go back and finish the job later?"

"Exactly."

"So?"

"Got any sieves?"

It was half past eleven by the time Bonnie the caretaker returned with a box of assorted sieves—a flour sifter, two colanders, a strainer, a sugar shaker and a deep-fry basket. They sifted through the graveyard dirt, searching for any object smaller than a marble. Any bicuspid, eye-tooth, molar, premolar, incisor or milk tooth would do. The theory was that the killer had visited the cemetery one bleak night after the funeral and planted a tooth in the soil above each grave. Another long shot, but you had to play the long shots.

Around midnight, it stopped spitting rain, but the sky still quivered with lightning. L'Amoureux drank from a bottle of Black Jack while Charlie and the pinch-mouthed contractor went to work, loosening dirt clods with their shovels, sifting through shifting heaps of dirt. They created first one pile, then another. Before long, Charlie began to feel a tingling sensation at the base of his spine. Deeply located, it began as a painless spasm, then the muscles around it started to stretch and pull.

"Pass the bottle," he said.

"If I could choose how I was born," L'Amoureux said, "I'd choose erupting out of the deep ocean floor in a hiss of molten rock . . ."

Charlie looked at him. "You're drunk."

"Not yet. But almost."

"Gimme that." Charlie suddenly wanted to catch up. He took several greedy gulps, the pain only getting worse, like a razor cut or an open blister, radiating from groin to knee. Just his old scars acting up. The pain progressed down his left leg with a dry-ice feeling.

Hodge went home around midnight and took Bonnie with him. She left her truck with its winch behind, and Charlie and L'Amoureux continued to get steadily drunker, working at it in earnest as if it were part of the job. Their duty as patriotic citizens. By the time Ed the contractor finally gave up, around one in the morning, Charlie was feeling no pain, no pain at all. He could hear his own hot blood whispering in his ears. When his hands began to throb from all that digging, he redoubled his efforts, muscles engorged with adrenaline. The air above the graves smelled like wet stone, and the wind carried with it the nervous barking of dogs.

"This is a great big goose egg, my friend," L'Amoureux said. "The only reason I'm out here now is because I refuse to go home sober. I have this recurring nightmare. It goes like this. My mother waves a knife over the family jewels. The blade sweeps down just as she shrieks, 'You don't need those, do you?' That's when I wake up."

Charlie laughed. The sky had cleared, and the stars were too numerous to count. The planet Venus glowed like a blown coal. His skin was filmed with grit, and he coughed from too much dust in the air.

"I gotta admit," L'Amoureux said, "you've got tenacity, my friend."

"I'll tell you what I've got. I got a whole lotta nothin'."

The cemetery was full of the sounds of their breathing, of two lonely shovels scraping the earth. Too many headstones, too much polished granite stretching out into darkness on either side of them. Moths swarmed in the headlights' glow, and Charlie's hands grew blistered and aching. Anxiety gripped his heart as he exhaled the smell of death from his nose. A large bead of sweat broke out on his temple and rolled down one side of his face, making him feel lopsided. In the silences between all that breathing and scraping, he could sense the dead watching them. Legions of the dead. One split second was all it took—one wrong move, and you'd be out there among them, horizontal instead of vertical, the soil gradually leaching your carcass of color.

"Give up?"

"Not yet," Charlie said.

"'Cause I've got a cheeseburger waiting for me at Ruby's."

"At two in the morning?"

"Ruby's is always open. I'm buying. They've got so many flies their cheeseburgers sprout wings."

The wind picked up, kicking last autumn's leaves around, and Charlie stopped digging. It felt as if someone had poured hot lead on his arms. Pain and burning sensations extended up his neck and into his shoulders, becoming most pronounced where the shoulder blades winged out. "Bottle," he gasped, and L'Amoureux handed it over.

"We're all tapped out, buddy," the sheriff said. "Time to throw in the towel, pal. You and me gotta lower these caskets."

They left the truck running and unwound the heavy chain from the winch, secured the chain to the hooks on Audra's casket and slowly lowered it back into the ground. The winch strained loudly as the truck's diesel engine growled, and then the casket hit bottom.

Charlie had to crawl down into the hole to unhook the chains. The coarse witchgrass sighed and crackled underfoot as he approached the lip of Audra Keel's grave and switched on his flashlight. A pungent excavated-earth smell filled his nostrils as he peered over the edge, shadows jumping and realigning themselves. He leaped into the hole, feeling all swallowed up, and unhooked the chain. The hairs rose on the back of his neck as he hoisted himself out again, Audra's shadow chasing up his spine.

They lowered the other casket, then filled in the holes. By the time they were done, Charlie's left side was stiff and on fire.

"That's all she wrote," L'Amoureux said, clapping the dirt off his hands. "You joinin' me?"

"For flying cheeseburgers?"

"Smoke-covered ceilings. Six different kinds of pie. Real mashed potatoes. Mmm-mm."

In the smoky play of light, a loose bundle of doubts nagged at him. The two cases were almost identical except for the replacement teeth. It wasn't uncommon for sociopaths to leave taunting bits of evidence for the police to find. Some of them subconsciously wanted to be caught; others enjoyed outsmarting the authorities.

He let his flashlight play up the side of Audra Keel's headstone. *Beloved wife and mother.* Shit. *Sophie.* He'd forgotten all about her. What time was it? Then something glinted in the dirt.

Of course. The withered roses.

He dropped to his knees and started digging.

"What're you doing?"

"Getting the roses."

"Roses? What roses?"

His fingers touched glass, and the first withered rose came out, its cut stem tucked inside a floral tube. Florists cut roses when they were tightly closed so that the bees couldn't get to them. The stem was held in place by a rubber stopper at the neck of the tube so the flowers would stay fresh for at least a week.

"Oh," L'Amoureux said, "*those* roses."

Hands trembling, Charlie aimed his flashlight at the glass tube, and there it was, clinking around inside the filmy bottom. A human tooth. A harmless-looking lump of enamel, dentin and pulp. "Look," he said, holding it out like a prize. "There's your proof right there."

14

Charlie got home around three in the morning and found the house empty. "Sophie?" She wasn't in her room. She wasn't in the living room or the kitchen or the rec room. He noticed that the light was still burning in his study and found an ugly array of crime scene photos scattered across his desktop. "Shit." He hadn't left them out like that. He never left crime scene evidence out where she might see it.

Pushing through the back screen door, a heavy-duty flashlight clenched in his fist, Charlie strode across the yard with its garbage cans and vegetable garden, traipsed through sprigs of beans and corn and tomatoes and squash. His flashlight beam danced ahead of him, highlighting the purple aster and Indian paintbrush in jiggling sweeps as he headed into the back fields where she probably was. Years ago, when Maddie was alive, they'd picnic in these fields, the sea of grass practically swallowing them whole. His daughter's favorite tree was out here, the place she used to come to be alone and cry after her mother had passed away. He strode past the bushy box elders, beyond which stretched a gentle swell of unbroken prairie. As soon as he spotted the cottonwood and the small figure crouched beneath it, he began to relax.

"Sophie?" he said softly, so as not to alarm her.

She turned with a blurred face. "Dad?" She was huddled at the base of the tree, knees raised, her skinny arms wrapped protectively around them. The old cottonwood was massive, nearly four feet in diameter, and the bark's dark ridges teemed with aphids and mites. Its stout trunk grew into a wide-spreading crown where thousands of sharp-pointed leaves wagged gently on their flattened stems. Whenever the wind blew, the crown sparkled and beckoned from a distance, and if you closed your eyes, the sound of crashing leaves mimicked the waves of the ocean.

He sat down next to her, the seat of his pants growing instantly damp from the grass. Once his breathing had resumed its regular pattern, he said, "Do you know what time it is?" He had the luxury of his anger now. "You scared me half to death. Is that what you wanted? To give your old man a heart attack?"

"Yeah, my evil plan is working." She winced. "God, your breath stinks! Have you been drinking?"

He turned his face toward the darkness.

"You drove home drunk, and you're worried about *me*?"

"You shouldn't be out here in the middle of the night," he said. "I'm serious, Sophie. What the hell were you thinking?"

"Don't change the subject."

"Oh? What subject is that?"

"That you're drunk. You lied to me. You said you'd be home by midnight. You're a drunken liar."

It hit him all at once. He rubbed his tired face.

"You forgot to turn on your cell phone again. There was no way I could reach you."

He looked at her. "Why didn't you call Peg?"

"Because I didn't want to bother her. I just wanted you home."

"Don't be mad at me, honey. I did something really unpleasant tonight."

Dismay rose in her eyes. "Like what?"

"I can't tell you that."

"Why not?" She was looking really scared now.

"There are some things I can't share with you, Sophie." A whole panoply of images flashed through his brain, eviscerating images that mostly visited him in the middle of the night when he was least able to protect himself from them.

"Still . . . Mom would be furious."

"I know." He hung his head.

"I love you, Dad, but you test my patience."

He couldn't help it. He smiled. He bit it back, but she'd already seen it, and now she observed him with thinly veiled contempt, her mouth twisting slightly open.

"You think this is funny?"

"No. Not at all."

She dismissed him with feigned disgust.

He felt her reproach like a thump in the chest and watched her sullen face. She smelled of department store perfume, those sample bottles they handed out. "Hey," he said. "Forgive me."

"Mom wouldn't let you get away with it."

"I know." The words slipped off his tongue and into the wind like smoke. "You're right. No more excuses."

In the moonlight, the fertile fields squirmed with new life, little green leaves unfurling like curled paws.

"I came out here, and it was beautiful for a while," she said, "but then things started to move in the shadows."

"It's okay. I'm here now."

She buried her face in her hands.

"It won't happen again. I promise, sweetie." He smoothed his hand over her shiny hair. "The last thing in the world your mother would ever want is for you to be unhappy."

"Remember the picnics we used to have back here?" she said, wiping her eyes and putting up a brave front. "We never do stuff like that anymore."

He could feel a piercing ache around his heart. "I guess I haven't been much of a father lately, have I?"

She curled herself into a compact ball of hurt, and they didn't speak for a while. A patch of mud at the root of the tree kept sucking at the heels of his shoes. He could hear a chorus of crickets nearby, their mating calls discordant and rhythmic. He switched off his flashlight and the night slowly revealed itself to them, the air shimmery clear beneath a full moon. He could pinpoint downtown Promise by the twinkling beer-colored lights in the distance. So this was what the world was like when it finally caught its breath.

"You wanna know what I hate the most?" she said in a scratchy voice.

"What's that?"

"That I couldn't be with her the day she died."

"Your mother was in really rough shape toward the end."

She brushed away a quick tear. "I used to dream about her all the time, but I don't dream about her anymore, Dad."

He nodded in silent agreement. Neither did he. He

thought about Maddie a lot, but his dreams evaporated with the morning mist. Only the nightmares lingered.

She looked at him, her mouth set. "Grandpa says we're all just worm food, anyway."

"Your grandfather's a fool. Don't listen to him."

She glanced skyward, her earnest eyes reflecting two miniature moons, two sparkling orbs. Tears spilled over her lashes and rolled down her cheeks. "I forgot to tell her something," she admitted.

"What's that?"

"I forgot to tell her what a great mom she was."

"So? Tell her now."

Goose bumps rose on his arms as he watched her sending out her sad, loving thoughts into the air. He couldn't look anymore and turned away, a lump forming in his throat. The grass broke before the wind in channels and rivers at their feet. He could hear the activity of the night creatures all around them—the flapping bats and rustling raccoons, the sly, shuffling skunks. His throat was parched, and suddenly he could see the fire with crystal clarity, cinders drifting down like snowflakes. He remembered his father's blue-veined fury, the belt and fist his weapons of choice. It occurred to him that he'd been so brutalized as a boy he could sometimes be indifferent to his own child's pain.

"Think she heard me?" she whispered.

"Of course," he said, wondering himself. He wrapped his arms around her, and she grew docile inside his hug; when he wouldn't let go, she finally relaxed against him and burst into tears, each heartfelt sob as bright as a bell.

ROUGH WINDS DO SHAKE
THE DARLING BUDS OF MAY

1

ALL THE boards in the house screeched at once, like a thousand nails being pried loose from the walls. Then came a terrible *thump,* and fifty-four-year-old Birdie Rideout worried about her Swedish modern furniture, the low-slung canvas chairs in the living room, Sailor's Stratolounger, the dining room set, the bedroom with its pink and persimmon wallpaper. Her house, her beautiful house, was coming apart at the seams. The tornado must be very close.

"Are we going to be okay?" she asked her husband for the hundredth time. It was past midnight on a cold May 10, and the storm had come up suddenly and unexpectedly. They'd only had ten minutes of warning from the town siren before the power had gone out.

Sailor Rideout pinched the bridge of his nose with his forefinger and thumb. He was irritated with her, his features fixed like granite in an effort to project some kind of churlish male courage. They were huddled together inside the hallway closet, seated on the narrow padded bench that lined the wall, and she was holding the flashlight. Sailor's face, when lit from below, reminded her of a Halloween pumpkin, theatrically spooky. "It's gonna be okay, old girl," he said.

"We're gonna get hit. I just know it."

"God's protected us so far, hasn't He?" His hand felt cool against her skin. Sailor hadn't seen his belt buckle in many years, but her heart still quickened whenever she caught sight of him in an unguarded moment, smoothing his gray hair or surveying his chickens, his potbelly rising doughlike over the waistband of his jeans.

Now something hammered on the roof like it wanted to get in, and for a spine-tingling moment, she imagined the two of them blowing away like dandelion seeds.

Thunk, thwunk . . . crash!

She hugged Sailor tight. Forty minutes ago, she'd been curled up safe on the living room couch, watching old movies on their ancient Zenith set. Her husband could sleep like the dead, but not Birdie. She needed to be eased into that dark place with mugs of warm milk, extra pillows on the couch and plenty of late night TV. Now here they were, cowering inside their hallway closet like two scared kids, waiting for the tornado to chew them up and spit them out over the plains.

She could hear the living room windows jumping in their jambs, *whump-whump-whump,* like unruly guests. Noises exploded throughout the house, and she felt each impact in her skeleton. The tornado was a jet plane bearing down on them. Beyond the crack of light, Sailor's body arched with fatigue, and when she rested her palm on his arm, she discovered that he was shaking uncontrollably.

"Sailor?" She dropped the flashlight and took his hand, then felt the next *thunk* in her pelvic bones. The bench they were sitting on was vibrating. The roof beams screeched far above them. She didn't want to die. There was still so much left to do.

"Look at that!" she said, irresistibly drawn to a pale oval of light strobing underneath the crack in the door.

Sailor wiped his shiny forehead on his sleeve. "It's just lightning."

"No, it isn't!" Before he could stop her, she got up and opened the door, her long gray hair whipping back in her face. She thought she saw a figure moving around inside the dark, chaotic house and chased the phantom with her eyes, but there was nobody there.

She felt a shiver of memory . . . party dresses . . . Christmas barbecues . . . her first lipstick, her first bra . . . the excitement of boys . . . the births of their sons. Birdie had lived in Dogtooth, Texas, all her life; her two older sisters had fled to Houston. One married a doctor, the other a lawyer, whereas she had married her high school sweetheart.

She shuddered and pushed the door shut against the wind, then went to him. "I love you," she shouted above the howling wind. "You know that?"

"Don't be silly," he hollered back. "We're gonna be just fine."

2

Down in the bowels of the Wind Function Facility, the missile launcher chamber was thick with the silence of concentration. Wouldn't you know it, Willa Bellman's stomach kept rumbling. She'd only had a few bites of toast that morning and too much coffee. Couldn't eat. It was this weather. It had her all stirred up. *Be still, my stomach.*

Rick was screwing a plastic sabot into the end of the fifteen-pound wooden stud. He was all business today, all frowning exactitude. *Come on, Rick, be spontaneous for once.* The two of them worked well together and knew how to anticipate one another's moves like clockwork. Like an intricate dance.

"Ready," he said, and together they muzzle-loaded the six-foot-long wooden stud into the barrel of the air cannon, a number two southern pine with a fourteen-inch radius at the impact end.

"How many more tests have we got left?" Willa asked with a mental wringing of the hands.

"Impact and cyclic-fatigue."

"Oh my God. We're gonna be here all day."

"That's the plan, babe."

"Three or four more hours, at least." She glanced at her watch. It was ten o'clock on an overcast Monday morning in the middle of prime tornado season, and she could feel the sweat beginning to collect under her arms, her expensive comfrey deodorant having failed her once again. She was such a mess today. Hastily dressed in painter's pants and big hoop earrings, her greasy, coconut-smelling hair falling like a wet mop down her back. She snatched a rubber band and made a quick ponytail to get it off her face, then gazed longingly at the Apple laptop on the cluttered machine table. The downloaded surface data were showing a powerful dynamic system ripping through Texas and parts of Oklahoma today, a lovely swirling pattern of red. Oh God. Radar images so breathtaking she was practically drooling. She'd been out storm-chasing all weekend long and was yearning for more. More, more, more. Couldn't get enough of the stuff. Heroin for the heartland.

"The SPC has issued a tornado watch for East Texas, north-central and northwest Oklahoma," she told Rick. The SPC was the Storm Prediction Center in Norman, Oklahoma. "Gordo just called about another tower popping north of Texola . . ."

"Welcome to my worst nightmare," he said. "Getting stuck inside on a day like today."

"KXDI radio just reported another warning for the Panhandle, but the Weather Channel radar loops don't even show an echo there."

"That's the problem. Their information's old."

"Will you look at that rotation?" She let out a low whistle. The bird's-eye satellite view showed a gorgeous rotating cloud pattern, a big red cell moving southwest to northeast. "Let's go after it, huh? Huh, Rick?" She gave him her patented cutesy-pie look, batting her eyelashes.

"What," he said with a touch of irritation, "now?"

"Yes, now. Why not now? You wanna miss all the fun?"

He smiled, a bundle of contradictory emotions. But then, pain in the ass that he was, stickler for details that he was, he shook his head. "Shut up, temptress. Jacobs wanted these missile stats yesterday. He'll have our frigging heads."

"Yeah, well . . . as the Queen of Soul would say, I ain't too proud to beg."

Her partner in crime wore that serious, calculating expression she loved poking fun at, shirttails tucked neatly into his waistband like a little boy. *Pint-sized science geek, bet the kids used to make fun of you, put tacks on your chair and slap notes on your back, because they'd sure done it to her. Oh boy . . . when you're poor, it's pitiful. Secondhand clothes, ill fitting and out of fashion. Two older sisters, and she got all the hand-me-downs. Not enough water in the well, so she couldn't wash her hair more than once a week, and when puberty hit, she got acne and dandruff . . . dandruff on her shoulders, and the other girls were nasty because she was so poor and smart, a double curse . . . too smart for her own britches. . . . They made fun of her mercilessly the way girls do sometimes, picking on the weakest one . . . her curly dark hair growing oilier toward the end of the week . . .*

Willa's father had introduced her to a whole new world, the storm-chaser community. He'd rescued her from her girlish misery, and she'd gotten to know good people, smart people, people with great senses of humor.

When you chased the wind, the ground fell away from under your feet and you were transported someplace else . . . someplace special. Her dad was so smart and funny, always quoting William Shakespeare: "Shall I compare thee to a summer's day? Thou art more lovely and more temperate: Rough winds do shake the darling buds of May, And summer's lease hath all too short a date." He used to swear at the other storm-chasers in made-up Shakespearean sonnets: "Thou art a douche bag, surely thou art! Hath thou no blinkers, fool?" He was funny, but he could also be stern, and he expected her to get straight As, even though girls weren't supposed to be smart where Willa grew up.

"You don't think I'd beg Jacobs to let us go chasing this afternoon?" she said. "You don't think I'd get down on my hands and knees?" She pointed at the computer screen. "Look! Mucho activity!"

"I am raising a doubtful eyebrow here."

"It's twister weather, baby. A sure thing."

"Can we focus? Can we please stay focused on the task at hand?"

"Fine. Your funeral, buddy."

The missile launcher chamber consisted of an air-actuated cannon capable of propelling timber at speeds in excess of 120 miles per hour into a test panel, thereby testing its resistance to flying debris. The chamber was forty feet long by fifteen feet high, and they were used to hearing their own voices echo back at them. These drab four walls had been painted tangerine in an attempt to brighten up the place, but the false cheer only made it feel more oppressive. After a few hours down here, you went a little stir-crazy. They'd been at it since 7:00 A.M.

Now Willa initiated the electronic timer, a calibrated

timing device that measured the missile's speed before impact. Next she moved down to the breech end of the air cannon and selected the operational air pressure. The barrel was twenty feet long, a PVC pipe painted orange and held in place by two metal supports at either end. The cannon was braced against recoil by three angle struts that ran along the floor at the back of the chamber, where several sandbags anchored the barrel supports. Today, they were testing a batch of "foamcrete" door panels for their resistance to flying debris, but the material wasn't performing up to standards. The company, KeepSafe, specialized in aboveground tornado shelters, also called safe rooms. KeepSafe was hoping to get its new foamcrete material certified by the WFF, but that wasn't going to happen. Not if Willa Bellman had anything to say about it.

"How come we can't put 'this sucks' on the form?" she asked, and Rick lost his constipated look and smiled. "Ah-ha! A crack in the facade! Two smiles in one hour!"

"You're hopeless."

"Will you look at that?" She pointed at the radar loop. "Colliding air masses! Big bad storms likely!"

He loped methodically along, checking everything twice and getting his data straight, but she could tell that his resolve was weakening.

"You want it," she cooed in his ear. "You want it bad."

"Enough."

"Come on, admit it."

From the radio came the beautiful low voice of Lou Reed in his Velvet Underground period.

"Let's try it at a lower speed this time," he said.

"Lower? How much lower? Why don't we hurl turtles at it? It's obvious this crap isn't going to meet FEMA standards. Those last two panels definitely do not qualify, *muchacho*."

"Humor me."

She sighed, ready to die of frustration. She wanted the cloudy day on her face, the wind in her hair. Her father would grab his camera and her, and they'd take off in his beat-up Rambler, just the two of them heading into the wild blue yonder. He could make his ears wiggle. He could smell lightning. She'd roll down her window and hold her face to the sky, fat raindrops kissing her lips and eyelashes. A clap of thunder meant another stop to set up the tripod. *"Kiss of death,"* he told her. *"Setting up a camera for a lightning photo is the kiss of death. The second you open your shutter . . . fizz. No more lightning."*

At the far end of the chamber, beneath the ceiling's soggy acoustical tiles, was a test panel marked "KeepSafe," clamped to a reaction frame by eight yellow C-clamps. The reaction frame had two functions: first, to support the test panel, and second, to stop the missile from penetrating the back wall. Willa waited impatiently for air pressure to build inside the sixty-gallon water tank in the room next door. The water tank room was no bigger than a closet, separated from the missile launcher chamber by a long, narrow plate-glass window. The water tank was linked to the air cannon through a solid-core ball valve, which could be operated remotely.

"There's high risk in our forecast area," she said. "Isolated supercells are expected to become tornadic by this afternoon."

"Stop." He carefully aimed the PVC barrel at the center of the test panel. "You're killing me."

"C'mon, you coward."

"You are in the strangest mood."

"Thunderboomers."

"Get ahold of yourself, woman."

"Do you really want me to drop it?"

He looked at her for a troubled moment. "Truth?"

"Truth."

"No."

"Oh wow, that's great! Hurry, hurry. The weather gods are smiling on us."

"Let's finish this test first, okay?"

"Okay." She blew several long wild strands of hair out of her eyes. "Waiting for pressure to build," she said, checking her watch, then glancing over at the laptop again. As the convection brewed, she could imagine all sorts of watches and warnings popping up across two states. Good news for a few, bad news for many. The loss of all one's possessions in the blink of an eye was not a pretty thing. Put twenty tons of pressure on a small house, and it reached its limit of resistance pretty quickly. She had witnessed again and again the awesome power of these beasts. Yet the statistics were clear: Tornadoes took only eighty American lives a year; swimming pools took four thousand; automobiles took forty thousand.

"I've set the impact speed at a hundred this time," she said.

"That's low enough." He switched on the video feed and picked up the remote control. "Brace for impact."

She slipped on her orange rescue headphones, which muffled all sound, then inhaled sharply as Rick pressed the remote. Almost instantaneously the ball valve released the compressed air from the water tank with a sick *snap*, and the test missile shot out of the air cannon with a *thwunk*.

The cannon fired its fifteen-pound wooden stud at a blistering speed. Quicker than the eye could calculate, the stud impacted the test panel, and the shoddy KeepSafe material splintered all to pieces.

Willa exhaled sharply.

"Wouldja look at that," Rick said as he scribbled something on his clipboard. "Total perforation of the test panel."

She swept off her headphones, smoothed her hair and crossed the room toward the ruined test panel, where wisps of smoke curled up from the debris on the floor. The wooden stud had sustained little damage. She removed the C-clamps and lowered the shattered panel. "It's pierced the skin and penetrated the insulation," she said. "Material is scabbed on the back side."

"Yeah, thought so. I clocked it at one hundred two point eight miles per hour. Another unsuccessful test."

"It's back to the ol' drawing board for these guys," she said, slipping off her safety glasses and massaging the bridge of her nose. She picked up her clipboard and carefully jotted down her notes. In order for a client to qualify for certification, the walls, roof and doors of any given shelter had to be able to resist penetration by windborne missiles. If the material didn't meet the Standard for Windborne Debris Impact Tests, SSDT 11-93, then it wouldn't pass muster. No certification from the WFF meant no sales. "I, Willa Bellman," she read aloud from the certification form, "an employee of yadda, yadda, being duly sworn, et cetera, depose and say that, to the best of my knowledge, the impact tests on these panels did not meet the requirements . . . Underline *not*."

"It's a box kite. Tie a string to it."

"Stamp a big fat 'F' on this baby." She glanced at her watch again. "I'm gonna go see Jacobs now. Would you mind signing off on the rest of these for me, Rick? I wanna leave by one or we'll miss all the action."

He had a cynical laugh. "My, aren't we confident."

"Relax. Herr Professor is putty in my hands." She paused for a moment, hands on hips. "So what d'you think? Should I invite Charlie along?"

He shot her a patronizing look. "Charlie?" He grinned at her through narrowed eyes. "You've got the hots for him, don't you?"

She could feel the tips of her ears going pink.

"Don'tcha? C'mon, admit it. You're among friends."

"I've got four words for you—shut the fuck up."

"My, aren't we touchy."

"What? I offered to take him chasing. He said it would help with the investigation. What's wrong with that? Today's as good a day as any, *n'est-ce pas?*"

"Absolutely." He lowered his head and continued filling out his report.

She stood watching him as if she needed his approval. She felt a bit giddy. Butterflies in her stomach. "Hm . . . lemme think about this a minute and procrastinate some more."

Rick glanced up. "You're driving me nuts. What're you waiting for?"

"I don't know. What am I waiting for?" She absently played with her ponytail, pulling out the rubber band and letting all that coarse black hair collapse around her shoulders. "Maybe this isn't such a good idea."

"Why wouldn't it be?"

"I don't know."

"Look at you, you're adorable."

She winced. "I have a big round face like a porridge bowl. And my ears stick out."

"Quit boasting. You're making me sick." He tossed her his cell phone. "Here. Go crazy."

She walked over to the laptop, where the downloaded radar image kept repeating its seductive loop—*chase me, chase me.* That roiling mass of clouds sweeping across two states. Rick pretended not to be listening as she dialed the number of the station house.

"Hello?" she said, feeling the blood rush from her head. *Whoosh.* She had to sit down. "Charlie? It's me, Willa Bellman . . . Listen, would you like to go chasing today?"

Charlie hesitated. "Now?" The line was staticky.

"Now's as good a time as any, yeah. Sky looks ripe. How's one o'clock sound?"

There was a long pause.

"Look, the satellite images are terrific." She could feel her heart thumping in her chest. "Dew point's risen from mid-forties to mid-sixties. We're expecting a T-box in western Oklahoma this afternoon due to an easterly component of surface winds north of the frontal boundary . . ."

He laughed. "What'd you just say?"

"It was English."

"Plains English maybe."

"You're pretty funny for a cop."

"You're pretty funny for a wind-whatever-you-are."

"Wind engineer." She smiled happily. "So . . . okay? One o'clock? I'll pick you up?"

"Sounds good." He gave her the directions and she wrote them down, fingers cramping around her pencil.

"Okay," she said, hanging up and looking around. Feeling slightly absurd. Had she just promised him a chase ride before she'd even consulted with Jacobs? Was she losing her mind?

Rick pushed his wire-rim glasses back up the bridge of his nose. "So? He joining us?"

"Yeah. Okay. So here's the plan. I've gotta go plead my case with Jacobs. You prep the ratmobile." She fished out her keys and tossed them.

Rick caught them one-handed.

"Okay, Ricky?"

"I'm right behind you, Lucy."

She couldn't help grinning as she headed for the door.

3

MIKE ROSENGARD stood in the doorway in his neatly pressed suit, his moist eyes drooping at the corners. "Good news?" he asked, noticing Charlie's lingering smile.

"Looks like I'm going storm-chasing this afternoon."

His best friend and conscience glanced out the windows. "Mama Nature's in a dark mood today. You don't want to cross her."

"I figure I'd snag a few more license plates. Talk to some chasers. Get the lay of the land." He pinched at his lip, then eyed the manila envelope in Mike's ink-stained hands. "Good news, I hope?"

"We finally got those lab reports back, Chief. Blood's been verified as the victims' ABO."

"Including the drains?"

"Drains and traps, blood spatter, smears and stains."

That wasn't helpful. "What about fingerprints?"

Mike slid a stack of paperwork out of the envelope and took a seat. "Of the ninety-three latent prints we pulled from the scene, eighteen were ID'd as belonging to Rob Pepper, twenty-one to Jenna, twelve to Danielle, and several dozen others attributed to friends, relatives and detectives at the scene. They weren't able to lift any latents off the wooden implements."

"So he never took his gloves off?"

"Looks like it."

Charlie glanced around his corner office, everything reminding him of the weeks he'd spent combing through the tedious details of the case. Witness reports, crime scene photos, empty coffee cups, stuffed-to-the-gills memo baskets. You had to have great powers of patience to live with a case like this. What they needed was more of everything—more manpower, more funds for overtime, more resources, more luck. "What about hair evidence?" he asked.

"We got tentative matches for Jenna, Rob and Danielle," Mike said. "Plus one blond unknown and seven brown unknowns of varying lengths."

Charlie shook his head. "Even if we matched them to the perp, it wouldn't hold up in court. Tornado could've deposited the trace inside the house, blowing it in from other areas."

Mike scanned the rest of the report. "No hair roots. So a DNA match is out."

Charlie knew that, as far as hair evidence was concerned, no forensic examiner could determine with complete certainty whether or not a specific hair came from the head of one individual to the exclusion of all others without DNA evidence, and the only way to obtain DNA evidence was from a hair root or adhering follicular tissue. "So lemme get this straight. We've got no blood, no prints and no suspects." He searched the ceiling for answers. "I'm tempted to run it by a psychic."

"How come most psychics never suspect you're a cop?"

He smiled thinly. The miniblinds rattled in a strong gust of wind. Through his office window, Charlie had a lovely view of the patched parking lot and a hand-painted billboard for Bernie's septic tanks. Nestled in the granite bowels of the courthouse, the police station consisted of four cramped holding pens, a squad room that doubled as a lunchroom and a dispatcher's desk cornered into the roll-call room. Charlie's office on the first floor was jammed to the rafters with cardboard boxes and dusty duty rosters. The wastebaskets were emptied only once a week due to budget cuts.

"Okay, then there's this." Mike handed him a photograph of a partial shoe impression—pale purple in color from being treated with diaminobenzidine.

"Where'd you get this?"

"Those guys at the state crime lab are relentless," Mike said. "You know that pile of shattered glass in the kitchen? They pieced it all together like a jigsaw puzzle—it's called fracture matching—and found this partial print. Pretty nifty, huh? Turns out to be a popular brand of jogging sneaker, left foot. The lab techs couldn't come to an agreement about the size, though."

Charlie nodded. "There's no consensus?"

"They're guessing it's between size ten and eleven, male. They'd have to compare it to a suspect item to be absolutely sure, though. That's the only way they can get an accurate read."

"You mean the suspect item we don't have?"

"Yeah, that's the one." He laughed ruefully, then took his handkerchief out of his pocket and mopped his brow. His face was florid and porous. "How come this case makes me sweat more and you sweat less?"

Charlie smiled. "Did you get any sleep last night?"

"Are you kidding? I toss and turn all night long, and then, just as I'm about to nod off, the pounding begins."

Charlie knew what he meant. Mornings began with the sound of pounding hammers. Bright and early, before the birds were up, the growl of bulldozers announced the arrival of the roofers, plumbers, builders and remodelers. A third of the town looked like a war zone with its bonfires and stripped trees, its piles of debris spray-painted FOR SALE—FIXER-UPPER. There were so many yard signs you would've thought it was an election year. People were fleeing the area in droves as the damage estimates continued to climb. The Federal Emergency Management Agency had released grim county-wide figures: 137 single-family homes had been destroyed, another 420 homes had experienced some form of damage; 65 out of 760 farms were in ruins. In Promise, the water tower, crushed like a beer can, had fallen across the road and washed away an entire chicken farm. Damage was estimated to be $40 million and rising, and every day was Casual Day at the loan adjustment department.

"I left the city," Mike said, "because in Boston, all you could see was your neighbor's back door. Out here, you get to see clear to the horizon. But now that same horizon scares the shit out of me."

"Just don't head for the hills like the rest of them."

"Are you kidding? We're gonna tough it out. We're Rosengards."

Charlie smiled as he handed the photograph back. "What else you got for me, Mike?"

"You're gonna like this one, boss. Fibers found on the victims' clothes." He pulled another lab report out of the envelope. "Numerous blue-black wool fibers cross-transferred between all three victims."

"Jump-start my heart." Quickly but intently Charlie perused the report. "So we're looking for a blue-black woolen item of clothing? Gloves, sweater, scarf . . . a ski mask, maybe?"

Mike frowned. "Kind of warm out to be wearing wool, don't you think?"

"It wasn't all that warm on April fifteenth. Before the storm hit, it was fairly muggy out, but then it dropped precipitously."

"Still, who's gonna be wearing wool with those kinds of temperature swings?"

Charlie could feel the day's tension pinching the back of his neck and rubbed his knotted muscles, his skin slipping too easily over the bones. *He should've known something was wrong before Maddie fell ill. All the signs were there — headaches, nausea, confusion, nightmares, insomnia. Signs of a brain tumor. "It's the flu," she'd insisted. "I've been under a lot of stress lately. It'll pass." But it hadn't passed. Bad news came like that, accompanied by signs. And all the while, he'd felt a creepy sense of foreboding he shouldn't have ignored.*

"We door-to-doored within a three-mile radius and tapped out." Mike's eyelids fluttered like moth wings. "No stranger sightings. No suspicious vehicles."

"What about Conrad Holzman?"

"He's got a rock-solid alibi, Chief."

"Jonah Gustafson?"

Mike rubbed his eye and studied the tip of his finger. "He's got a couple of DUIs, an attempted rape charge going back to '81. We got a phone number, but he isn't returning our calls."

Charlie's fingers twitched on the blotter. "Keep on it. I wanna talk to him."

"I saved the best for last." Mike plucked another lab report out of the pile and scanned its coffee-stained pages. "They found semen inside Jenna Pepper's vagina, and it wasn't Rob's. It was somebody else's. A secretor. AB-positive."

Charlie caught his jaw in his hand and ran his fingers over his beard bristle. "What about the girl?"

He scanned another sheet of paper. "It says, 'No tears or bruising. No vaginal penetrating wounds. No seminal fluids in or on the body. No sperm detected underneath the microscope.' Her hymen was intact. I'm glad for that." Mike shrugged off his uneasiness; nobody liked thinking about the dead girl. "Regarding Jenna, they should have the DNA results soon."

"Lemme see."

He handed it over.

Charlie studied the report. He'd initially expected both female victims to show signs of rape, since overkill-type injuries such as these—multiple stabbings or cuttings to the body—were suggestive of sexual motivation. "No tears or bruising with Jenna, either. No evidence of sexual injury or sexual mutilation. Just seminal fluids in the body." He shrugged. "How soon can we expect to get DNA results?"

"About a week."

"Can you put a rush on it?"

"Lemme talk to Art Danbury." He grinned. "I got something else for you, boss."

Charlie glanced up. "You're full of surprises today."

"Guess who's in the interview room?"

"What is this, Twenty Questions?"

"Jake Wheaton."

He scowled. "He came in voluntarily?"

"Arrested for possession. Got a minute?"

"Are you kidding?" Charlie stood up. "Let's go see to his discomfort."

4

JAKE WHEATON sat staring at his hands. He wore a hooded sweatshirt, jeans and a cheap pair of walking shoes.

"What's your shoe size?" Charlie asked him.

"Huh?"

"Shoe size. Come on."

Jake shrugged. "Ten and a half. Why?"

Charlie took the seat opposite, while Mike stood over by the window and drew the blinds shut. The room was small and unpleasant. Just a table and chairs, an overhead bulb and a hardwood floor. That was it.

"I wanna call my dad," Jake said. Some of his long dark hair stood up in individual strands, thick with gel, and there were dark circles under his eyes.

Charlie nodded. "First let's talk for a minute."

"I don't think so."

"Listen to me, Jake. You got busted for possession. We can make that go away."

He looked up, whirling slivers of doubt in his eyes.

"You interested?"

"In what . . . some kind of a deal?"

"Maybe." Mike nodded. "If you're nice and cooperative, we could make it go away."

"Nobody's taken any statements yet," Charlie said.

The boy tugged on his hoodie, pulling the fabric out and wiping his greasy chin with it. "I should talk to my dad first," he said. "Don't I get a phone call or something?"

"We're offering you an opportunity."

"Listen to him," Mike said. "He's treating you fairly."

"Think about it," Charlie said. "This is your future we're talking about."

The room swelled with silence.

Jake studied Charlie critically, as if he were a mirror. "What do you want me to do?"

"Tell us about Jenna Pepper."

His eyes grew remote. After a pause, he said, "Yeah, okay."

"You're willing to tell us everything? Who she was involved with? Times? Dates? Details?"

The boy hung his head. "Yeah, I'll narc on my friend."

Charlie and Mike exchanged a glance. "What friend?"

5

SOPHIE GROVER sat on the low retaining wall behind the high school and took another swig of diet cola.

Boone Pritchett was looking at her with eyes so blue they seemed stolen from a bag of marbles. His motorcycle boots were dyed white, and he kept his wallet on a chain. "Come storm-chasing with me, Sofe," he pleaded.

She felt a bubble of laughter in her throat. The backs of her red high-tops tapped out an erratic rhythm against the cement blocks of the retaining wall while she listened to an old jazz tune playing on Boone's ugly plastic boom box. "My father doesn't want me hanging out with you," she said. "He thinks you're a bad influence."

"Maybe I am."

She eyed him sideways.

"I like to buck the system. What's wrong with that?"

There were spiderwebs all over the retaining wall, gossamer webs littered with bits of leaves and dead insects.

"C'mon," he said. "Be adventurous for once."

"I can't."

"Why not?"

"Because I've never cut school in my life."

"Ha. They won't even miss you."

She smiled nervously at him. Across the street, a bobbing line of sparrows sat on a phone wire, and beyond the phone wire was the western skyline. There were dark streaks in the clouds. It was going to rain.

"See that high cirrostratus?" he said. "That's the air we want. It's gonna be an outbreak day, I can feel it."

"Yeah?"

"Everything's in place. You've got heat, humidity and colliding air masses, that's all you need. Time to grab some cash from the ATM and gas up."

"Seriously, Boone. My father would kill me."

"How's he gonna find out?"

She looked at him. "I'd be reported absent."

"Nah. I know every trick in the book. What's your next class?"

She laughed. "Will you stop?"

His teeth were slightly crooked in front like a little kid's, and whenever he smiled, his whole face lit up—eyes and everything—and he became a different person. Not so tough. "You can play by the rules all your life and be miserable," he said. "Or you can follow your dreams and come with me."

It was tempting. The sun peeked out from behind the clouds for a moment, and Sophie tilted her head to absorb its fleeting warmth. She could hear lockers slamming shut behind them, lunchtime almost over.

"Hey," he said, putting out his third cigarette, "your dad just pulled up."

She opened her eyes. Her father was parked in the lot next to Boone's casino-pink pickup truck. He got out and headed toward them, his face stern beneath the brim of his police hat. He had worry wrinkles on his forehead, one wrinkle for every year Sophie had been a teenager, he liked to joke. She hated his habit of hiding his scarred left arm around behind his back; it made her feel overly protective of him.

"Dad?" she said, standing up.

"Hi, honey." He gave Boone a hard look but continued to speak to her. "You off to class now?"

"Yeah, I was just leaving."

He glanced at the cigarette butts at their feet. Boone started to back away from them.

"Hold on there, partner," her father said. "We need to talk. Got a minute?"

"Yes, sir."

"See you later, Sophie."

"Okay, Dad. I'm going to class now. Bye." She slipped inside the shadowy building, then stood watching them through the glass doors. Her father gestured toward the parking lot, and he and Boone strode across the asphalt to Boone's truck, where he rested his hand protectively on the hood. She watched them for a long puzzled moment, wondering if anyone else in school could hear her heartbeat. So thunderous now.

6

During an interview, you weren't supposed to show any outward tension. You were supposed to keep your reactions as flat as possible and ask five misleading questions for every serious one. You weren't supposed to rush; the truth would gradually leak out. But Charlie's heart was enflamed. His daughter was infatuated with a boy who'd had sex with a woman twice his age. God only knew what other horror stories lurked behind that innocent-looking brow. "You had sex with Jenna Pepper," he said flatly. "You and Jake Wheaton."

Boone glanced around indifferently as he contemplated what'd just happened.

"Care to elaborate?" Charlie swallowed his saliva and ran his hand roughly through his hair, then put his hat back on. "Tell me about it. Tell me about you and Jenna doing the nasty in the back of her Pontiac."

Boone's eyes remained neutral as he sparked a cigarette, then glanced back at the school building as if he longed to be there—pretty amusing, considering that Boone Pritchett was Truant of the Year. Spanish moss hung in elegant clumps from the oak trees arching over the entranceway, students trailing back inside in groups of threes and fours. Charlie had known Boone ever since he was a scrawny little kid with perfect choirboy features. Even at a tender age, he'd shown sociopathic tendencies, always a touch of fire around the eyes. Charlie had worked hard to set him straight. He'd signed him up for the school lunch program, had gotten him a paper route and forced his mother into rehab several times. A whole lot of good it'd done. Boone was the last person in the world you'd want your daughter hanging out with—smugly arrogant, sometimes charming, always untrustworthy. If Charlie concentrated hard enough, he could burn a hole right through this punk's skull.

"So tell me about the fifteenth," he said. "Where were you on April fifteenth?"

"Me?" Boone grew defensive. "Out storm-chasing."

"Here in Promise?"

"No, man. I was way down south."

"Where, exactly?"

"Is this gonna take long? 'Cause I've got math class."

"I promise to take only seven and a half minutes of your time," Charlie said sarcastically. "Now, enlighten me. Please. Where were you on April fifteenth? C'mon. Gimme details."

Boone jammed his hands into his pockets. "There was this boffo storm system brewing, this big juicy squall line down around Burns Flat and Roll and Reydon. Down around there."

"Did you take anybody with you?"

"No, man."

"Okay, now, that's another thing. I'm not 'man' to you, see? I'm your worst nightmare. Whenever you address me, you say 'sir.'"

"Yes, sir," he muttered.

"Did you gas up?"

He smoothed his hair with a grubby-knuckled fist. "Yeah, probably."

"Yes or no?"

Boone eyed him with hostile boredom.

"Hey, am I a brick wall over here? Am I boring you, Pritchett? Or were you just thinking? Oh, you must be thinking. I can smell something burning. *Did you gas up?*"

His eyes grew menacing. "Yes, I said."

"How many times?"

"Twice, I think."

"How'd you pay for it?"

"What?"

"Welcome to the twenty-first century. I stick my credit card into the slot, insert the nozzle and fill 'er up. What do *you* do?"

"I paid cash."

"Okay, so we've narrowed it down. Now we're getting somewhere. Next question, Einstein. Which gas stations did you stop at?"

The boy shrugged. "I dunno. Shell, I think."

"Both times?"

"I think so."

"You'd better be straight with me."

Boone muttered something under his breath.

"What was that?"

He gave a small defiant smile, and Charlie arrived in his face with such force that he stumbled backward. Charlie could see the carotid artery ticking away in his neck and wanted to rip it out. Standing before him was just another drug-addled kid from a splintered home who treated girls like Sophie with utter disrespect. Use 'em and abuse 'em.

"I got this passion for severe weather," Boone snarled. "So sue me! And keep your grubby hands off me!"

Charlie could feel the old skin grafts tightening. He wanted to squeeze the boy's throat until he turned various satisfactory colors. "Stay away from my daughter," he said softly. "Do you hear what I'm saying?"

"Yeah, I hear you."

"You hear, but do you understand?" His eyes narrowed. "She doesn't need you messing up her life. She's a serious person. I won't let it happen."

An audible swallow.

"And remember. I asked you nicely." Just then his cell phone rang, and Charlie turned his back on the boy. "Yeah?" he answered irritably.

"Chief?"

He recognized Lester Deere's voice immediately, that tortured white-boy grunt. "What is it, Lester? I'm in the middle of something."

"Oh God, I got something really important to tell you."

"What is it, Lester?"

"My gun's in my lap and I'm facing the door."

7

CHARLIE WALKED into the bar, then paused to let his eyes adjust to the appropriate level of dimness. Lester was seated at a table in a far corner of the Howling Dog Saloon; his chair was turned sideways, and his gun was tucked into the waistband of his pants. That wasn't so unusual. Most cops sat facing the door, since you never knew who or what was going to come charging through it. "Two coffees," Charlie told the waitress, a leggy redhead with an attitude problem.

When Lester saw him coming, he pressed his hands tightly to his head and said, "Careful, careful, don't go losing it in front of the chief."

Charlie sat across from him and frowned. "What seems to be the problem?"

"I'm in a very liquid state," Lester admitted.

"So I noticed."

"You Chief." He pointed at his chest. "Me eighty percent Scotch."

"Okay, I'm buying. Clearly I need to work my way down to your level of stupidity." He settled his elbows against the checkered oilcloth, figuring they'd probably speak elaborately for a while about nothing. Lester was holding his cigarette in that upside-down way preferred by most bad actors. The round table was small enough to hold hands across. The scarred, blistered bar was empty except for the waitress and the short, bearded bartender over by the cash register. There was a coral reef behind the bar—a lame attempt at a tropical motif, in conflict with all that dusty cowboy memorabilia.

Lester gazed at Charlie for an excruciating moment. He'd once been good-looking, but then something had happened, and within a relatively short span of time he'd gone all paunchy and soft and unkempt. Two-day beard growth. Squinty, bloodshot eyes. "I liked being a football player. I really did, Chief. I loved the challenge, you know? The game, the uniform, the attention, the girls. So what do you do for an encore? What do you do afterwards?"

"I dunno, Lester. You wanna hand me the gun?"

When he didn't respond, Charlie turned toward the waitress and, raising his voice above the punishing level of the Lynyrd Skynyrd playing on the jukebox, reminded her, "Two coffees, miss?"

She gave a curt, disinterested nod.

"*Near* Miss," Lester corrected him.

"What's that?"

"She was just telling me how she nearly lost her life in the storm, so I'm calling her Near Miss."

"Yeah, I get it." Drinking. He didn't like it. It reminded him of the leather belt with the metal buckle. He snatched the rest of Lester's drink and knocked it back— Scotch, short, no ice. It burned going down. *Yum. Ah. Now I really hate myself.* "All gone." He set the empty glass back on the table in front of Lester's amazed eyes.

"Hey . . . you made my drink disappear."

"Gimme the gun."

Lester stared at him.

"You're a good cop, Lester. Go home, sober up and get your fanny back on the job."

"I wanna ask you something." Deep squint lines radiated from the corners of his eyes due to years of walking the beat under a hot sun, just like the rest of them. His medium-length blond hair was shiny. He sprayed it with shiny stuff. Such desperate measures to regain his lost youth—gel, hair spray. What was next? Mascara? A tummy tuck? On the table between them was an unlit candle in a red glass globe and a silver cardboard dish of peanuts—the greasy, salty kind Maddie always used to say were bad for him. Charlie popped a forbidden peanut into his mouth; it tasted crunchy and oily going down.

Lester thumped on the table with his fist, making the peanuts jump in their cardboard dish. "Fuck, Chief. I'm tryin' to tell you something, but you aren't even listening."

"Are you gonna be nice and cooperative now?"

He sat poised as if ready to spring, his eyes rheumy from too much lonely contemplation. "I had all the advantages and now I'm miserable. I lost everything I ever wanted. You think your life is gonna be a certain way, Chief . . . you believe it'll always be that way, you don't imagine it could ever change. But then, years later, you find yourself in a totally different place from where you'd started." He signaled the waitress. "Hey, another Scotch over here! Chop-chop!"

"Chop-chop yourself." She glowered at them.

"Just the coffees," Charlie said.

". . . Near Miss."

"Give it a rest, Lester."

It was quarter to one in the afternoon. Charlie wondered if he should call Willa and tell her he was going to be a little late. The bar smelled last-Christmas stale. The fish tank didn't have any fish in it. It was a Howling Dog tradition—if you were too drunk to scoop your car keys out of the murky water, then you were too drunk to drive home. A couple of piranhas might raise the bar a little, Charlie mused.

The waitress brought their coffees over on a tray, white ceramic cups chattering on their wafer-thin saucers. "Three-fifty," she said, hand on hip.

"Oh, nurse! I'll have the ziti with vodka sauce . . ."

"Just ignore him," Charlie said, sliding out his wallet and handing her a five. "Keep the change."

Her attitude softened a bit. She set Lester's empty glasses delicately down on her lacquered tray and walked away.

"Is it true?" Lester was listing to the right now.

"Is what true?" Charlie asked, losing patience fast.

"The rumor."

"What rumor?"

"The rumor you jumped out a three-story window when you were a kid. Because, I mean, anything over twenty-five feet, Chief, you've got maybe a fifty-fifty chance of surviving. Anything over twenty-five feet is like . . . suicidal."

Charlie wiped his hands on a cocktail napkin. "I'd stay out of the deep end of the bar if I were you, my friend."

Lester poked his finger threateningly in Charlie's face. "I'm just curious. What's the big deal?"

He felt a sickly anger brewing in his brain. "We never had this conversation."

"Just answer the question, Chief. C'mon . . . didja jump from that high a height? Huh? What is it, a national secret or something?"

Charlie sat there observing the sluggish tick of Lester's pulse, like two unborn animals behind the paper-thin skin of his temples. Lester was a natural-born loser, a coward, one of those towel-snappers who grew booze-brave after three or four drinks. He didn't seem to understand that Charlie didn't give a damn who he was related to.

"How come we never talk?" Lester said, rising up on unsteady legs. "How come you don't like me?"

A stale liquor smell wafted toward Charlie, and all the horrible memories along with it. Macho posturing, incoherent ramblings. He focused on Lester's twitching mouth.

"Give me something, Chief."

"Sit the fuck down."

"So?" Lester sat hard in his chair, his shadow growing taller on the wall behind him. "Didja? Huh?"

Charlie sat very still.

"Didja or didn't you jump, you dumb motherfucker?"

Charlie grabbed him by the collar to stabilize him, then punched him squarely in the nose.

Lester flew backward, blood spurting everywhere, and pressed his hands to his face. *"Oh my God . . . oh God, what'd you do that for?"* He stared at Charlie in disbelief.

Charlie examined his hands wrapped around the delicate porcelain coffee cup, his knuckles beginning to swell.

"Christ, I'm bleeding!"

Charlie handed him a handkerchief. "Do you know what a full-thickness burn is, Lester?"

The younger man stared at him with moist, unblinking eyes as he pressed the handkerchief to his nose.

"It's dead skin all the way down to the subcutaneous fat layer. When I arrived at the hospital that night, my skin was burnt to a crisp. I was leaking fluids all over the bed. They had to give me fourteen IV bags just to keep me alive. You could easily pull the hairs out of my burnt flesh. My left arm was stretched so tight they had to make a foot-long incision in the skin in order to keep the blood flowing properly. Any minor infection could've killed me, if the pain didn't get to me first. Then came debridement. That's just a fancy term for scraping, cutting and peeling away the dead skin."

"I'm gonna be sick." Lester teetered over and vomited onto the floor, and Charlie forgot to move his feet in time.

"Aw shit." He fetched a couple of cocktail napkins from the table and daubed at his ruined shoes. Some of the pinkish vomit pooled down between the laces and into the eyelets, where he'd probably never find it again.

Lester sat rocking back and forth, clutching his stomach, while the bartender came over and sprinkled green sawdust on the floor.

Charlie glanced at his watch. It was closing in on one o'clock. He had an appointment he didn't want to miss. "Give me the gun, Lester."

"I don't even want it. Here." He handed it over, and Charlie made sure that the safety was on. "I had an affair with Jenna Pepper," he said.

"What?"

"I had an affair with Jenna Pepper."

Charlie could feel the shudder all the way down to his toes. It was so unexpected he was speechless.

Lester looked as if he were bleeding internally. "Rob

never suspected a thing. She'd find some excuse to sneak out of the house. She was gonna leave him. He was emotionally abusive, you know. Played mind games. They stopped having sex. She called him the Dufus. She felt like a prisoner in her own home."

"Lester . . ."

"I could tell she was trouble with a capital *T* almost the instant I set eyes on her. I should've stayed away, but she made me feel so goddamn good about myself, you know? I could be strong around her. I could be brave. All those things."

It came in a rush: Lester was the first officer at the scene; he'd had blood on his hands; he was right-handed; he was an avid storm-chaser; now there was motive. Shoe size? Looked like tens maybe.

Charlie stood up. "Get your hat."

"What for?"

"Stand up. I'm doing you a favor."

Lester faltered to his feet. "You were gonna find out about it, anyway," he slurred. "Mike says they're doing a DNA test. I had sex with her the night before. That's my sperm inside her."

"Anything you say I could end up using against you. Do you understand?" Charlie grabbed him by the arm. "Come on."

"Where we goin'?"

"I'm taking you home."

"Yeah, but . . . what am I supposed to do now?"

"Go home," Charlie told him firmly. "Sober up and get yourself a good lawyer."

8

After nearly twenty minutes of chasing turkey towers and transverse rolls, those slowly spinning horizontal tubes of air, they veered off the highway and turned down a bad state road, where the car made plenty of noise and smoke, each new jounce setting Charlie's teeth on edge. The butt of his gun kept poking into his rib cage, and his eyes stung from staring too long and too hard at the sky. The front seat was littered with road maps and laminated phone lists, a first-aid kit and a laptop computer. The backseat was a jumble of packing quilts, flashlights, duct tape, binoculars, photography equipment and bug repellent.

"So how come we got stuck with this jalopy?" he asked Willa, whose shoulder-length black hair was tucked behind her ears, those beautiful pearly white ears of hers.

"Are you kidding?" she said, eyeing him sideways. "You want a vehicle you can run into the ground."

"Is this thing capable of warp speed?"

"You know, Charlie, your *Star Trek* jokes are starting to get a little tired." She grinned at him.

"Cut me some slack. I don't get out much."

"Engine's fine, it just needs a whole new car wrapped around it." She scanned the sky. "Hm. Broken strato-cu. Hazy. Mushy tops. Nothing to write home about."

The '82 Ford station wagon with its mismatched doors was roomy inside, if a bit musty-smelling, and had about 175,000 miles on it. Pings pimpled the veneer, and the beige body was covered with contagious-looking rust spots. All sorts of expensive-looking equipment was mounted on the dash—radios, scanners, GPS receivers, a video camera on a Morganti mount.

She followed his gaze. "My wallet hurts whenever I think about the money I've spent on this stuff. But I come from a long line of gadget lovers."

"So this is your car? Not the lab's?"

"Hey, don't knock it. I've had six chase-mobiles in the past seven years, Charlie. They last me about a season." She slid him a look. "Guess that's longer than some marriages."

"You divorced?"

She shrugged. "He was my meteorology professor. I was young and stupid. Looking back, I realize I was more impressed with him than in love with him."

"Still friends?"

"Ha. Next question." She pointed with a manicured nail painted purply red. "Look over there, Charlie. See that cap, that very strong cap? See how the linear cloud base curls into a cumulus tower with a rounded end?"

"Yeah." They hit another rut, and the top of his head grazed the disintegrating roof padding. "Ow."

"This could get fairly interesting."

They took off in a belch of exhaust. The sky was the color of wet cement, and the dew point was in the upper fifties—a good thing, she kept telling him. The NOAA weather radio had promised explosive development somewhere in central and northwestern Oklahoma today, but so far this chase ride consisted of following a bunch of clouds, watching them pinch off and dissipate, and then following another bunch of clouds. During their occasional pit stops, Willa would call up computer readouts and radar reports inside the accompanying Doppler van that Rick was driving—a brown Doppler van with ENVIRONMENTAL SCIENCES LAB stenciled on one side. They'd lost track of him five minutes ago.

Now the weather radio interrupted with another update: "A tornado warning has just been issued," said the tired male voice over the crackling speaker, "for north-central and northwest Oklahoma this afternoon . . ."

"Ah. Sounds good and bleak." She tossed him the rumpled road map. "Okay, Charlie, you're the navigator. We need to avoid all the dirt roads and dead ends, keep our escape routes open."

"Escape routes? You never said anything about escape routes."

She glanced at him. "Don't worry, I'll protect you. I'm really good at this. Sit back and relax." She wore ivory-colored overalls and a black pullover sweater, and her wool clogs kept slipping off the brake pedal.

"What do we need escape routes for?"

"Hey, a lot can go wrong out here. Flash floods, hail-storms, downed power lines, that sort of thing. What's the quickest route to Lawton?"

He squinted at the map. "You wanna take . . . um . . . your next right."

She stomped on the accelerator. At the cloverleaf entrance ramp, they hydroplaned back onto the highway and sped past trucks with their air brakes roaring in a swirl of diesel fumes. The car felt sluggish against the wind. He didn't know what to think about Lester's revelation. It put him squarely in the category of "persons of interest." They'd have to have him in for an official interview now, and he should probably take a polygraph in order to eliminate himself as a suspect. Charlie didn't think Lester Deere—foolish as he was, lost as he was—was capable of anything like murder. Then again, half an hour ago, he would've laughed at the very thought of Lester and Jenna Pepper having an affair. You thought you knew your friends, but you didn't know everything about them.

"We're following a slow-moving storm front ten miles to our southwest," Willa said. "Seventy dew points, moving north by northeast. I'm plotting an intercept course. We've got to find a southern road to get behind the storm." She cast him a sidelong glance. "You okay?"

"Yeah."

"No regrets?"

"Are you kidding? I'm loving this."

She smiled and said, "So tell me about Maddie."

He glanced at her, decided she was serious. "She was honest and unpretentious." Like you, he thought. "One day without warning, she fainted. I thought it might be heatstroke and drove her to the hospital. On the way over there, she started to nod her head. 'Yeah, yeah, yeah,' she said, over and over, to lots of different questions. It scared the hell out of me. I pulled over and called an ambulance. I thought she might be having a stroke and needed a paramedic quick. She couldn't remember her name. She kept fumbling with her purse and wallet, looking for her ID."

The sky was full of chaos and contrast, but he wasn't

seeing it; instead, he saw Maddie fumbling with the clasp of her purse, everything tumbling out onto her lap.

"She couldn't remember her name," he repeated, feeling the echo of his former shock. "I followed the ambulance, and as they wheeled her inside, she said, 'How nice of you to take the day off from work and bring me here.'"

"I'm sorry." Willa's voice was rich with sympathy. "I lost my mom when I was twelve, and it looms so large in my head . . . but that's nothing compared to what some people have had to endure. I feel a little selfish bringing it up, like I'm the only person on the planet who's ever known trouble. Hey, I survived. It toughened me up. In a way it helped, you know?"

They drove along in silence for a while; then, through a break in the clouds, Charlie caught a glimpse of the towers. A dramatic cloudscape loomed before them, spanning the entire 180 degrees of horizon. The towering cumulus clouds rose up like the dust from an exploded A-bomb and gave him pause. He felt humbled. It started spitting rain. In a matter of seconds, a thick driving rain pummeled the car, obscuring their view.

"I can't see shit," Willa said in a tense voice. "We need a southern route. Charlie?"

"Oh. Right." He unfolded the road map and tried to pinpoint their position. "Hold on a sec . . ."

"Anything?"

"Wait . . ."

"Charlie?"

"Take your next . . . left," he guessed.

What the map indicated to be a paved road turned out to be a poorly maintained dirt road where the slopes had washed out in winding gullies. Willa slammed on the brakes, and they skidded until they hit something hard, the Ford bouncing back several feet upon impact. They sat for a stunned instant while the rain beat down around them and fog wafted in through the windows, curling up in their faces like cigarette smoke.

He half expected her to curse him out for leading her the wrong way, but instead, she just laughed and said, "You okay?"

"Yeah, I think so." He rubbed his sore jaw. He'd bitten his tongue hard enough to draw blood. The rain was blowing in sheets against the car. "Whatever we hit wasn't on the map."

"This is Oklahoma, Charlie. Plenty of things aren't on the map." She snatched a rain slicker out of the backseat and drew it on, then shot out of the car and did a quick inspection of the vehicle, while the rain held them in its chill, silvery embrace. Bright shimmery raindrops spiraled down in the headlights' glare, as if the sky were shedding all its elements. She opened the door and said, "My muffler's come loose. Lemme fix it real quick."

He got out to help. "What'd we plow into?"

"Tree stump." She looked into his face the way a woman sometimes looks at a man. "No biggie. My tailpipe gets knocked off at least twice a year. You should know that about me, Charlie."

He laughed and said, "This road is soup."

The front bumper was crumpled like an aluminum can. She grabbed a roll of duct tape out of the back, and he stood around helplessly while she taped the muffler to the undercarriage of the car. The mud kept sucking the clogs off her feet. When she was done, he helped her up.

"Like my father used to say, ain't nothing that a little sandpaper can't fix. Whatever that means."

He kissed her.

She seemed surprised, rain streaking down her face. "What was that?" she asked.

"Presumption. Sorry."

"Don't be. I'm very selective about who I take on a storm intercept with me." She threw her arms around him and kissed him back, her lips sweet and soft and needy.

A stroke of lightning snapped to the ground less than a mile away, and he drew back with his hand still on her shoulder. "Phew, that was close."

"We'd better get moving."

They shot back into the car, and she quickly turned it around. They took a paved road as straight as a paper cut, where the trees were dark and wet, their leaves waxy green in the relentless driving rain. Through a small hole in the cloud cover, Charlie could see compact bubbles and aquamarine interstices lacing up through the cauli-flower tops. He glanced at the gas gauge—half-empty.

"Tornado on the ground!" the radio sputtered.

He searched the sky but saw nothing.

"Lots of nice structure, no confirmed tornadoes," Willa said. "Do you see anything, Charlie?"

"No."

"This must be the Invisible Vortex, then, 'cause there ain't no tornadoes around here."

The cloud towers that had been so visible for miles abruptly collapsed into an overcast haze. Willa checked the frequency indicator on her ham radio and scooped up the mike.

"Rick?" she said. "You still with us? I sense we're really getting into something."

"Make sure you stay on the south side as it intensi-fies," he answered in a burst of static.

She keyed the mike. "Inflow winds are strong.

Lightning's getting closer. They've been under warning for two hours now."

"I've got a wall cloud sitting right in front of my face. Keep heading south. Doppler radar in Amarillo detects a vortex signature at a range of about sixty miles. You've got another terrific upper-level system with winds packing one hundred and fifty knots approaching from behind. Looks like we got a twofer, Bellman."

A warning signal broke the squelch of the NOAA radio. She dunked the mike back in its retainer and turned the vehicle around again, the tall grass bending underneath the front bumper and springing back up as they sped over it. "This time we'll approach the storm from the clear air mass behind the dry line," she said. "Better visibility that way. Okay with you?"

"Like I'm gonna disagree."

She smiled. "You can disagree with me anytime you like, Charlie. I don't mind."

He grinned at her, and they drove through the center of another benign little prairie town, past a dreary stretch of dilapidated buildings that harbored the kinds of country stores you could buy just about anything in, from snuff to beer to hunting licenses. Beyond the jagged rooftops, the gunmetal-gray sky bubbled like something simmering on a back burner.

"See that right-flank overhang to our southwest?"

He gave a hesitant nod.

"The rear-flank convection's beginning to mask the Cb tops."

"Cb?"

"Cumulonimbus. Clouds showing strong vertical growth in the form of mountains or huge towers topped by an anvil. What's generally known as a 'thunderhead.'"

She bit her lower lip. "I don't know which one to pick. Looks like the second storm further south has mesocyclones in it. We'd better get back on the 277." She waited a beat, then said, "Charlie?"

"Oh, that's my job." He picked up the map, its surface tacky to the touch. The car was making that weird rattling sound again. "You sure this thing is safe?"

"About as safe as any chase-mobile can be."

He looked at her. "What's that supposed to mean?"

"Considering that the most dangerous place to be during a tornado is inside your car?" She shot him an amused glance. "Not safe enough."

"Jesus, that's reassuring."

"Welcome to my world."

"Remind me to take you on a ride-along one of these days."

Darkening clouds dripped down into showers, and the sky took on a ragged look. The heady sweetness of fresh damp dirt filled the car. Fat cumulus clouds towered higher and higher, pools of warm and cold air colliding, and a saucer-shaped overcast hung suspended along the horizon like a glorious threat. Soon they entered another dense curtain of rain and were instantly enveloped in humid, buoyant air. They hydroplaned past a highway sign that said "Welcome to Splitback, Oklahoma, Pop. 2,830." On the outskirts of this mustard seed of an outpost, they spotted a weak funnel cloud dangling beneath the ominous-looking rotating cloud base. It snaked its way down into the ground and drew up a curtain of red into the air—the legendary red dust of Oklahoma.

Now a local radio station transmitted a warning. "Take shelter immediately! A tornado is reported to be on the ground."

Hovering over the green fields less than three miles away, the ropelike tornado crossed the long straight road ahead, then gracefully lifted up into the air, becoming just a "funnel" again. Charlie held his breath. The air sizzled with energy. Illusion was a real risk—which way was it headed?

The radio meteorologist said, "Believe me, folks, you should take shelter now! These storms can kill."

Charlie glanced at Willa, who was doing sixty. The wind roared in his ears. Scattered hailstones hit the hood of the car, and the tumbleweeds were flying about three feet off the ground. The sides of the road were lined with storm-chasers, all watching the wall cloud put down numerous filaments. These filament funnels made strange, eerily graceful turns around the main funnel, then quickly dissipated. The main funnel muscled its way earthward and touched down again, ripping up dirt, plants and shrubs—basically anything in its path.

"I'd give that an F-1 on the Fujita scale," Willa said. "Definitely not bad for May eleventh."

There was a party atmosphere—cars filled with wide-eyed kids, cameras hanging out the windows. They all watched the stiletto shadow as it skipped gracefully across the flattened landscape, changing direction on a whim. The sky had turned so dark that Charlie could see the dash lights inside the car. Very faintly, he felt the concrete beneath their tires beginning to rumble like a slowly approaching train. Moments later, the F-1 lifted up into the rain and disappeared for good.

"That was amazing."

"Look over there between the breaks in the strato-cu," Willa said, pointing to their southwest. "You can see the sharp knuckles of that other tower continuing to develop.

See how the rain wraps around the wall cloud? And there's a distinct hail shaft north of the tail. We want to avoid that."

She hit the gas and they zoomed southward, where an even larger rotating cloud in the shape of a beaver's tail churned darkly along the horizon.

"These storms are killing people as we speak," the local meteorologist said anxiously.

They veered down a bumpy two-lane road, where Charlie noticed a pair of headlights dogging them at a distance. He remembered the camera in his hand and turned around to take some pictures. A blue Mazda pickup truck and a vintage Buick Electra converged on the road behind them, along with a burnt-umber Chevy Caprice Classic and another pickup truck. *Casino pink.* Boone Pritchett's truck. The little prick had lied to him.

"Too many yahoos on the road today," Willa complained, glancing in her rearview mirror. "Go hang gliding, you idiots! Go bungee jumping and leave the rest of us alone!" She stomped on the gas and they roared toward the second wall cloud, where dust whirls and short-lived condensation tubes bubbled to life beneath it. The top of the tower ballooned well beyond the anvil cirrus, while chunks of clouds under the storm base tore loose and pushed southward. The remaining low-hanging clouds located further east moved rapidly northward. Immense bolts of platinum lightning arced across the sky, then shot straight down the wall cloud toward the earth. Charlie's adrenaline surged as he watched a violently whirling debris cloud suddenly form on the ground, chewing at the earth like an electric mixer.

The funnel shot up amazingly fast. It was five miles away but plainly visible. It narrowed and tightened, then needled its way into the ground, producing a classic elephant trunk. Debris rose from the flattened fields as it ripped a path through.

"Bingo. We got the tornado of the day," Willa said, a mix of raw fascination and professional respect in her voice. She hit the brakes, and Charlie shot forward in his seat. "Move, you weather weenies!" she screamed.

A line of cars had developed in front of them as several slowpoke chasers went podunking up the road ahead, gawking at the tornado and paying scant attention to those behind them.

"Maybe he's afraid of hydroplaning at twenty fucking miles an hour," Willa said as she blasted her horn.

Two chase cars ahead of them pulled around the rank amateurs, and Willa followed suit. "Sit on this and rotate!" She flashed the slowpokes her middle finger.

Charlie just stared at her.

"What?" she said, mildly agitated, her cheeks a lovely rustic color.

He couldn't help grinning from ear to ear. "You're something else."

"Yeah, well. I've been called worse."

The air grew electric between them. His hair crackled with static. The car made sick chugging sounds as they sped past abandoned pastures where swaths of box elder and cottonwood scruff whirled in the wind, everything illuminated by stunning bursts of near-constant lightning. Khaki-colored leaves, torn off their stems, spun wildly through the air. The circulation intensified as they edged ever closer to the beast.

Charlie gritted his teeth as the tornado rapidly widened, gathering strength. He could see why it was so addictive. All around them, brilliant streaks of lightning slapped out of the clouds, and enormous droplets hit the windshield at an angle. Then it began to hail.

"Hold on to your hat," Willa said as hail pellets peppered the ground around them, stones of ice banging off the roof and popping off the hood. "When a hailstone the size of an egg hits you on the head, it hurts," she said. "But don't worry, one-inch-diameter hail is just below the damage threshold for most metals and windshields. Anything bigger, and we'd be in serious trouble."

"Thanks for sharing." He clutched the dog-eared gas station map, trying to stay ahead of the curve. He tore his gaze away from the tornado long enough to search for street signs, but it turned out that the road they were on was misprinted on the map. The Ford's engine whined and wheezed, the temp gauge rising as they sliced through the hailstorm into a broad shaft of light. On the far side of this light, they could see the cone-shaped tornado very clearly now, dark with pink edges against a charcoal-colored sky. The racket was incredible. The wind bent the grass completely over in the field, and the air was filled with leaf debris.

"Major chaser convergence," Willa said, glancing in her rearview at the string of cars behind them, hurrying to catch up.

Charlie turned in his seat to snap a few more pictures, his palms oozing sweat. His hair felt as if it'd been whipped by an eggbeater. They took a left onto Eyebright Road, where they had a sweeping panorama of the grasslands splashed with purple and yellow wildflowers. When the sun burst from between the clouds, the dark vortex turned suddenly milky white. The sun briefly struck their faces before disappearing again, and the sound of the wind grew thunderous as they moved parallel to the tornado, now just a few miles away. It took Charlie's breath away, how close they'd come.

"I can hear its voice clearly," Willa said. "Hear it talking to us?"

He listened. He heard. Gurgling and cascading. Like water. There was a cold, heavy odor to the air. The tornado cut a swath across the plains, slicing through dead weeds and sagebrush, everything spinning up into the air like a plague of locusts. It was wrapped in a shawl of torrential rains and screaming upper-level winds, and within the northeastern edge of this mesocyclone, great swirls of clouds dove for the ground and then dissipated.

Willa's hands grew white-knuckled on the wheel as she maintained a constant right angle to the line of movement. "Oh fuck," she said, suddenly losing control.

The vehicle spun out, skidding across the rain-slick road. Charlie's arm rose automatically to protect her as she hit the brakes and they both slammed forward in their seats. Through the windshield, he could see the tornado shrinking before his startled eyes. It stretched out like taffy, grew skinny as a rope and then lifted up into the clouds, where it abruptly evaporated.

Her cheeks were flushed. Her eyes were glazed. "I can't believe I spun out," she said.

"Are you kidding? You were amazing."

She squeezed the steering wheel while lightning rippled across the slowly retreating wall of thunderheads, the spider-egg mammatus clouds glowing silver and gold in the afternoon sun, the storm gradually tapering off into calmness.

"Now what?" he asked, his heart slowly regaining its regular rhythm.

"Now we stop at some grease palace and analyze the

data." She looked at him and smiled in all her awkward beauty.

He edged forward in his seat, thinking he might kiss her again, when all of a sudden a screaming emergency vehicle tore past them in the opposite direction. Without hesitation, Willa shifted gears, and they made a U-turn in the middle of the road.

They dogged the flashing beacon down one lone country lane after another, until somewhere south of town, the emergency vehicle pulled over to the side of a poorly paved road and Charlie shot forward in his seat. Boone's pickup truck was wrapped around a denuded oak, suction spots in the grass around the base of the tree where the tornado had left its devastating impact.

They rocketed out of the car and jogged toward the scene, where two EMS personnel were already immobilizing Boone on a back board. He lay flat on his back with a dazed look in his eyes. The cowboy hat was gone, and his short black hair was laced with insulation dust. He appeared to be choking on the blood in his mouth. The male EMT performed a quick finger sweep, while the female EMT applied a rigid cervical collar.

"Stabilize the head . . ."

"No loose teeth . . . Let's suction his throat . . ."

Charlie's shirt was soaked with sweat. The sky was full of quick-moving, low-level scud clouds. The tornado had left a trench of braided prairie grass in its wake, four-foot-long cordgrass leaves impossibly twisted around broken milkweed stems. Several nearby oak trees had been completely denuded, and the wheat fields held swirl patterns. The wind must've lifted the truck up like a toy and slammed it into the massive oak, which clutched the mangled chassis in its sagging limbs. The truck was riddled with bullet-shaped holes from flying debris, and all the windows were busted in.

"Sinus bradycardia at fifty beats per minute . . ."

"Let's load and go."

The wind was making the grass gallop. Above the whistling sound, Charlie could hear something else—a cry, almost human. *Clara, howling with indignation at having been abandoned, the tips of her teeth like glistening barnacles breaking through the pink and healthy gums.*

"Daddy?!"

The fields were yanked into sharp focus as he recognized Sophie's voice.

He spun around, heart hammering dangerously in his chest. His daughter staggered out of a stand of trees, covered in mud and blood, the wheat around her braiding and streaming in the wind. He could taste the tang of his own panic as he tried to swallow. "Sophie?" He ran across the road and swept her up in his arms. He hugged her so tightly she squealed in his ear. "You okay?" He inhaled sharply. "Are you hurt?"

"Is he dead?" she wailed, looking beyond her father's shoulder, her eyes staring wide with helpless terror.

He thought he was going crazy. His heart kept booming in his ears. What was she doing here? She was cut up pretty badly. He checked her scalp beneath her wet, windtossed hair. "Did you hit your head?"

Her eyebrows rose with mild surprise. "Is he dead?" she asked. "Did he die?"

"No." His blood went cold. "He's unconscious."

"Is he going to die, Daddy?"

"Shh. Calm down, sweetie." He stomped hard on his anger.

"We were in the truck. It got so dark, it was raining really hard. We were getting closer to the tornado," she said, "when a tree branch flew into us head-on and smashed the windshield. Boone tried to keep the truck upright, but then the tornado got us." She burst into tears, and he held her in his arms, wanting to shield her forever from the wind, the bogeyman, all bad things. "I was wearing my seat belt," she said with a shiver. "But Boone wasn't wearing his. He got thrown from the truck, but I was wearing my seat belt, Daddy . . . so I was okay. I unhooked it and climbed down."

"Thank God."

She struggled to keep her footing. "Is he gonna be okay?"

"Shh."

"Is he?" She sobbed against his shoulder.

"Did you hit your head? How's your head? Are you dizzy?" He checked her scalp with a lingering sense of unreality. "Over here!" he yelled at the paramedics, and the female EMT came right over.

"Does it hurt anywhere?" she asked before calmly listening to Sophie's heart with a stethoscope. "Can you breathe okay?"

"Take her in," Charlie told the EMT. "We'll follow."

"Daddy?"

"We're right behind you, sweetie."

9

CHARLIE FOLLOWED the EMTs into the emergency room, where Sophie thrashed around on the gurney, hair plastered to her face with sweat. "What's going on?" she said. "Where's Boone?"

He caught her hand and held it, while half a dozen doctors and nurses swarmed around them, ordering CAT scans and X rays and blood tests. Then a nurse began to cut away her clothes.

"Daddy?" she cried, overwrought with emotion and shock.

"Quiet, sweetie." He was sweating bullets now. "Everything's going to be all right."

"What are they doing?"

"Helping you."

He didn't let go of her hand until one of the nurses took over. "I've got her now," she said. "You can go wait outside."

Back in the corridor, Willa kept pressing on her wind-whipped hair as if she were trying to calm it down. "Charlie? She okay?"

"I think so. I hope so. Christ, I'm shaking."

She rested her hand lightly on his arm. The waiting room smelled of dead flowers and was virtually identical to the one he'd grown to despise so many years ago—that robin's-egg blue waiting room outside the ICU. There'd been no burn units back then, and he'd spent weeks recuperating in the ICU before being transferred to the pediatrics ward on the sixth floor. *Waiting room.* Even the name was grim. A place where time crawled, where every chair was unforgiving. Better to pace up and down the halls, dragging your IV caddy around behind you.

"I'll kill him," Charlie said now, his pants and shirt stained with his daughter's blood.

Willa held his eye. "She'll be all right."

"This can never happen again."

"Charlie," she said, squeezing his hand, "she's going to be just fine. She was wearing her seat belt. She's conscious, coherent, moving around."

"I lost my sister. My mother. Maddie. No way am I losing my daughter to that little prick." He stared straight ahead in deep shock. After a few minutes, he got up and talked to the receptionist, a steely-eyed brunet who told him that a doctor would be with him momentarily.

Momentarily. He knew what that meant.

He sat back down on the beaten green couch and stared at the dirty white walls and glazed tiles in earth tones. Willa waited with him in silence while the steady drip of the TV set provided a constant background hum, like rain on the roof. His mouth was bone-dry. He formulated a plan at the water cooler. He would ground her for a month, send her off to private school, lock her in a castle tower and throw away the key. He tried to cool his overheated imagination as he sat back down and pushed the hair off his forehead. *Waiting room.*

How many operations had he had altogether? Twenty? Twenty-five? As a young burn patient, he used to curse the nurses who forced him to flex his aching limbs. He cursed the dressings, the antibiotic cream, the daily wound cleansing. Twice a day, one big-boned nurse in particular—a beefy Swede, tough as a drill sergeant—made him do his ROM exercises in a whirlpool that reeked of disinfectant. Not moving his limbs meant fibrosis of the joints. Nurse Natalie, with eyes the color of unripe pears, had made his short life miserable. She'd pushed him harder than he'd ever been pushed before, but now, every day, he silently thanked her.

"Chief Grover?"

A movement at the top of his vision made him look up. A frowning doctor, very young, crossed the room toward them. His ID tag said "Russ Pressler, M.D."

Charlie got to his feet. "How is she?"

Pressler had small, deep-seated eyes and a buzzed haircut. "You were lucky." He kept his voice professionally detached. "No broken bones, no concussion. We treated her for minor injuries and gave her a tetanus shot. She'll be feeling it tomorrow. I'd recommend bed rest and plenty of Tylenol."

"What about those cuts on her face and arms?"

"Tempered glass is designed to shatter into little cubes upon impact. Those marks on her skin are linear, right-angled and very superficial."

"So she'll be okay?"

He nodded curtly. "They'll heal. We're waiting on the CAT scan, but she'll be released once that checks out. She's with the other patient now. He's in a coma but stabilized. He's vented and we're monitoring his life signs."

Charlie darkened. "Where are they?"

The doctor walked him toward the ICU, then pointed at the daffodil-yellow curtain in the corner.

Boone Pritchett lay motionless on his motorized bed, an endotracheal tube taped to his mouth. His eyes were slightly open but unseeing. His ventilator worked noisily up and down, adding a sibilant hiss to the air.

Sophie stood next to the bed, dressed in orderly scrubs. Her hair was combed off her face, and she clutched a plastic bag full of her own bloody clothes. "It was leaking cold air through the floorboards," she said without looking up. "My feet were freezing from the blasts of cold air."

Charlie stood for a moment, quietly observing her baby-smooth complexion and expressionless face.

"It happened so fast." She wiped away a tear. "It got dark, and then the rain came. I could feel the whole truck lifting up into the air. I kept my eyes closed . . ."

"He placed you at great risk," Charlie told her. "I'll never forgive him for that."

She turned around, so frail-looking he wanted to whisk her away from here and never let her out of his sight. "He's not as bad as you think," she said.

"Sophie . . . this guy embodies every shade of shadiness."

He could detect the panic in her eyes. "He's smarter than most people give him credit for. . . . Just because his dad's a Neanderthal . . ."

"Sweetie, you can't see him anymore."

Her eyes brimmed with angry tears. "That is so bigoted," she cried. "How can you say such a bigoted thing?"

"Your mother wouldn't want it. I don't want it."

She crossed her arms and rocked back and forth, biting back the tears.

"This can never happen again."

"Why are you doing this to me?" she said in a high, reedy voice, failing to comprehend the significance of what had just happened, how close she'd come to dying.

"You lied to me," he said. "You said you were going back to class."

"So?"

Shock waves. Still in shock. Count to ten and take a deep breath. "Excuse me?"

"Revelation, Dad. I'm not perfect."

He resisted the urge to overreact. "We shouldn't be talking about this right now. We'll talk about it later."

Her head sank lower. "You don't have any right to tell me who I can or can't see," she said, fingering the locket at her throat, those tiny silver links. "It's a free country."

"Do you understand what I'm saying at all?"

"You're the one who doesn't understand!"

His pager beeped, and he snapped it off his belt. It was Mike. "Honey," he said to her, "I've gotta take this."

"Don't touch me!" She jerked away. "Go make your stupid phone call."

He activated his cell phone. "What is it, Mike?"

"There's been a double homicide, Chief. Last night in Texas. A middle-aged couple, unusual circumstances. A tornado touched down about three hundred yards from the house."

He felt the news like a feather tickling the back of his neck. "How soon can you get here?" he said.

10

IT WAS dark by the time they arrived at the crime scene, red and blue beacons from the local radio cars greeting them with an eerie, strobing silence. Power was out all over Dogtooth, Texas, due to downed electrical lines, and the house was veiled in a gray haze. Charlie could feel his pulse ticking in his throat as he and Mike climbed the porch steps together, their shadows jumping away from their flashlight beams.

The interior of the house was pitch-black. Charlie's body gave an involuntary twitch as he shone his light over the once-bright wallpaper in the front hall, with its muddy boots and coat hooks strung with limp rain ponchos. He got a whiff of the '70s in the daisy decals covering the cellar door and the purple-painted handrail leading up to the second floor, a string of lights from last Christmas wrapped around the banister, all that fun and color ending in blackness at the top of the stairs. He noticed that a couple of balusters were missing, like the grotesque gaps in a jack-o'-lantern's smile. When the wind slapped the screen door shut behind them, they both jumped.

"Holy shit." Mike looked at him and grinned foolishly.

A gruff voice sounded in the dark. "Don't touch anything." It was coming from the open doorway at the end of the front hall. They walked through a narrow vestibule and turned a corner into a rather large living room, where none of the furniture matched. The woodwork was all mahogany and oak with fluted pilasters, and the air smelled stale and slightly humid, and of something vaguely familiar. Something that stood Charlie's hair on end.

"You Grover?" Sheriff Chester McNeese was on the delicate side, a little man with something big working around inside of him. His pale hair was shaved close to his scalp, and he had a vividly pockmarked face and a nasty habit of sucking on his front teeth.

"Sheriff." Shaking hands in the dark felt oddly intimate. "This is Detective Rosengard."

"How do." McNeese shook Mike's hand. "Rosengard, is that Jewish?"

"Yeah," Mike said, going through his little ritual. "I'm the only Jew in Oklahoma."

"Well, hey. I ain't no Bible-slappin' man myself. I have great respect for all religions."

Mike smiled thinly. "Amen to that, brother."

"Behind you," McNeese said, and they swung around.

Charlie fell silent as he stared at the grisly scene. Two lifeless bodies were propped side by side on a worn rawhide sofa, their mouths ajar, their eyes suspicious. The man wore flannel pajamas and a George Hamilton tan that made his lips look almost white. The woman had her legs curled underneath her wide hips, so that she tilted slightly toward the man. She wore green stretch pants and little white shoes, and both of them appeared to be in their mid-fifties. He had a half-smoked stogie in one hand, and she looked like a freeze-dried apricot. Some of the impalement injuries were partial-body thickness; others were full-body thickness, with both an entry and an exit wound. Miscellaneous pieces of wood stuck out of them at odd angles, to freakish effect.

Charlie winced, his scars prickling with sympathy pain.

"I figure it's your guy, right?" McNeese said, the tremolo in his voice betraying the fear he failed to mask. He kept one hand on his holstered gun. "The one in all the papers?"

Charlie nodded grimly. It hit him in the solar plexus. The killer wasn't trying to disguise the murders anymore. The victims were just sitting there on the sofa. He was taunting them openly now.

"Twister touched down three hundred yards north of here," McNeese told them. "The damage path was seven miles long. It hit a trailer park. That's where we've been focusing most of our attention since last night. Three dead, countless injured. Broken bones, head injuries. People walking around just wailing, their clothes torn to shreds. We didn't find these two until late this afternoon, when a concerned neighbor came calling." He paused to scratch his head, and you could hear the sound of fingernails on dry scalp. "If this ain't the craziest damn thing . . ."

"Not a lot of blood spatter in the living room," Charlie said. "No disarray or overturned furniture."

Mike glanced at him in silent acknowledgment.

"Nobody thought to look here," McNeese went on. "The house wasn't hit. We were up all night fighting fires and digging out survivors. My cousin's dead. I'm still in shock about it."

Charlie tracked a trail of blood droplets and sliding marks across the Oriental carpet into the kitchen, where all the refrigerator magnets and recipe cards had slid off the door and landed in a puddle of blood. The teakettle was cool to the touch. A mug of tea, now at room temperature, sat on the oak table. The telephone notepad had doodles all over it. On the floor, walls and ceiling was an inordinate amount of blood spatter.

And then something different. A small parade of kitchen appliances was lined up on the pink Formica countertop—a food processor, blender, electric can opener, a coffeemaker and an electric mixer. Each appliance was plugged into a wall outlet, and inside the blender, food processor and electric mixing bowl were dozens of pieces of silverware—forks, knives, spoons.

Charlie took a puzzled breath, then lowered his flashlight beam. The blood on the floor had been cleaned up in places—he detected wipe marks on the linoleum. He found the mop standing upright in a metal bucket in the pantry. If they sprayed the floor with luminol, he predicted, a circular pattern of blood would emerge on the linoleum, left there by the bottom of the bucket.

Back in the living room, three sheriff's deputies were milling around in the dark, processing the scene by flashlight. The mood was sober. Charlie swept his light over the bloodstained rawhide sofa. "What's the deal with the silverware?" he asked McNeese.

"You got me." The little man shrugged. "Forks and spoons in a blender? What d'you think that's supposed to mean?"

Charlie eyed the woman's rhinestone-framed eyeglasses, now bloodied and cockeyed. "Who were the victims?"

"Birdie and Sailor Rideout." McNeese sucked noisily on his front teeth. "They're farmers and he's also a bricklayer. He's the quietest man in town, and she bakes a mean pecan pie. They raised four kids, all solid citizens. My little girl goes to school with one of their grandchildren. Sailor and me are distantly related. Great-great-whoever-he-was."

A cat leaped at the window screen, clawing desperately for a pawhold, and Charlie felt the fright at the base of his spine.

"Shoo," McNeese said, going to chase it away.

Seized by a grotesque feeling of complicity, Charlie moved closer to the staging area and studied the tautly stuffed cushions, the box of tissues on the coffee table, the roller shades that didn't quite roll up all the way. Several clocks disagreed about the time. The windowsills were covered with the kind of ancient stone tools you might pick up in the back fields—broken pottery and arrowheads. Remnants of past civilizations. Sailor's arm muscles appeared to flex for an instant, making the gooseflesh burn across Charlie's scalp. An illusion created by crisscrossing flashlight beams. He leaned in close and could detect a suspect redness around Sailor's mouth. Birdie's jaw was slightly swollen.

"Tell your coroner to check the victims' teeth," he told the sheriff. "And you'll want to seal your findings. I'd like a copy of your autopsy report, if that's okay."

"Sure, partner. I have no ego."

The TV set was positioned directly in front of the victims. You could tell by the rug impressions that it had been moved recently. A few feet behind the Zenith was an upright vacuum cleaner, plugged into the same wall outlet. Charlie aimed his flashlight beam over the dusty set with its assorted collectibles on top—ceramic cows and cheery-looking toadstools with blissful, hand-painted smiles. The vacuum cleaner was a large brown Hoover, standing upright on the Oriental rug. Punched into the opposite corner was a pine bookcase clutching a large collection of vinyl record albums. At the center of the bookcase was a Pioneer stereo system with two medium-size speakers pointed out into the room.

Charlie ignored the pieces of talk floating around him as he focused on the scene. The homicides were blatantly obvious this time, which meant that the killer's M.O. was changing. A scary thought. He was becoming bolder. Charlie looked at the vacuum cleaner. Had the perp caught Birdie Rideout in the middle of her vacuuming? He doubted it. Most of the blood evidence was back in the kitchen, where the initial attack had taken place. So why stage the scene like this? Because he was playing God. Because the victims were his dolls, his playthings. He could do anything he liked with them.

Charlie sensed the killer was calm, methodical. He had all the time in the world. He wasn't afraid of severe weather. He was in his element. He was taunting the police. Bad guys watched TV, too. Bad guys read the papers. As he went over the details in his head, he felt separated from the others by a film of heightened awareness as thin and trembling as the membrane of a bubble.

Suddenly there was a loud *bang,* and full power was restored to the neighborhood, every lightbulb and electronic appliance in the house kicking on at once. Charlie yanked his .38 from its holster and held it tight against his trouser leg, while competing mechanical screams assaulted his ears: the blender grinding away in the kitchen; the silverware dancing around inside the electric mixer like a train wreck; the food processor whistling like shrapnel; canned laughter swelling and crashing from the TV set; the vacuum cleaner whining and careening across the rug. And throughout all the noise and confusion, Charlie thought he could hear a low, sweet song playing on the turntable.

Gooseflesh stood up on his arms. He held his gun loosely, trying to stem the awful tide of fear that rose like bile in his throat. His clothes absorbed his terrorized sweat as he glanced around at the others, frozen like a herd of deer in the proverbial headlights. The speaker volume was turned down low, as if the killer had wanted to whisper in their ears this 1950s rendition of "Smoke Gets in Your Eyes" by the Platters. The moment burned inside Charlie's gut like a hot coal. He toyed with the trigger. The entire house was vibrating like a lung. Even the dead couple looked sharp and alert.

Wet with sweat, he turned to Mike and said, "Okay, now. That's exactly the reaction he wanted."

11

Sophie WORE an oversize football jersey to bed. Her face was bruised and covered with little nicks, and her arms were wrapped in bandages. It broke his heart. "She's nice," she said, looking up at him with narrowed eyes, as if she were peering at him from the bottom of a well. "Ms. Mysterioso."

He smiled and nodded. Long strands of damp hair clung to her forehead, and he smoothed them away with his thumb. "Get some sleep," he said.

She turned to face the wall, and he could tell she was still nursing a sullen grievance against him.

"Want the door open?"

"Nope. G'night."

He closed the door and walked through the empty house, then draped his jacket over the arm of the sofa and went into the kitchen for a beer. The refrigerator whined and rumbled. It would probably break down one of these days. If it did, he wouldn't be able to fix it. He was happily ignorant of all things mechanical—electrical wiring, mechanical tinkering. A great disappointment to his father, whose only response to Charlie's announced intention of becoming a cop was a blank, fixed gaze.

Now he worked two beers out of the cardboard container and joined Willa on the back porch, where the air was cool and dense, the stars twinkly bright. Today's clouds were mostly gone. They sat on the creaky wooden swing in the faint glow of the bug zapper, and he felt both weightless and heavy at once.

"You okay?" she asked. "You look all squeezed out."

"I was accused of being a bigot today." He rubbed his face hard, then leaned forward on his elbows. "Thanks for looking after her."

"No problem. She's a great kid."

"She takes after her mother."

"Oh, I can see a little bit of her father in her, too." She kicked off her mud-covered clogs and rested her bare feet against the painted wooden floor.

He smiled. "She's her own person, that one."

"At Sophie's age, I had zits, no boobs and a skateboard that I worshiped. I was the weird girl in school. I used to draw penises in the margins of my English assignments, then spend the rest of class erasing them before we handed our papers in."

He leaned back in the swing, making it rock just a little. It felt good to be smiling. Her long black hair shimmered in the purple light of the bug zapper, and he could make out the outline of her breasts beneath the bulky pullover sweater.

She put the beer bottle to her lips and tilted her head, revealing the sandy underside of her chin. He could see the swallowing mechanism of her throat, her Adam's apple bobbing up and down. She waited an appropriate beat before she said, "So what happened today?"

"A double homicide in Texas." The corners of his mouth grew pinched. "Nice people. Not an enemy in the world."

"How old?"

"A couple in their fifties." He could hear the honking of the wild geese, a haunting sound. A magnificent sound. He loved the wildness of the Oklahoma night. He loved how it embraced them—surrounded by darkness, the porch light stopping at the edges of the driveway.

"Were they killed the same way as the others?" she asked in a tremulous voice.

"Yes."

He could see her struggling to keep her emotions in check.

"It could be somebody you know," he said.

She was peeling the label off her beer bottle. "One of the storm-chasers I know?"

"I'm going to FedEx you some pictures in the morning. I'd like you to look at them and tell me if you recognize any of the vehicles we haven't been able to identify yet. Would you do that for me?"

"Sure."

He could feel the beer's coolness passing through the glass into his fingertips. "I'm not trying to scare you."

She looked into the darkness and shivered. "Most of the chasers I know . . . they're a very passionate bunch. They love severe weather. They'd drive thousands of miles for maybe five minutes' worth of tornado-watching, and they'd do it in a heartbeat."

He gazed beyond the reaches of the porch light into the great mystery of the night. Somewhere out there, in the vast landscape of the plains, was a man who defined himself by the deaths of others. "The tornado came to within three hundred yards of the house this time. How can he be so accurate?"

She thought for a moment. "He must be playing at a whole other level. He's mastered it, Charlie. He's a dozen moves ahead of everybody else."

"What would he have to have in his head?"

She shrugged. "Either an unusually sophisticated understanding of radar principles, Doppler velocity interpretation and pre-storm environment, or else . . ."

"Or else what?"

"A brilliant instinct. He's plugged in."

He glanced at her. They didn't speak. He could hear the wind playing through the trees, the gentle shush of the leaves. She traced her finger in the hollow of his palm, and it stirred him. He tried to imagine the place where she grew up and pictured a red-dirt town, a run-down house and a bunch of unruly kids; she was the Texas tomboy in pigtails, waiting for it to rain. Always with one eye on the sky.

"It's such a cliché," she said. "The Butterfly Effect. You've heard of it, right?"

"A butterfly flaps its wings in China, and the next day there's a tornado in Oklahoma."

She nodded. "The world's weather is extraordinarily sensitive. One region influences another. You can't control it. You can't predict it in a global sense. I hope to visit China one of these days and watch that butterfly flap its wings. I want to see the genesis of our tornadoes." Her hand grew warm in his. "It's a real mystery, how something so subtle and beautiful can lead to so much devastation."

Charlie assessed the lovely structure and economy of her features as they sat together, gently swinging.

Her eyelids drooped sleepily. She glanced at her watch. When she let go of his hand, he felt naked. She slipped her feet back into her clogs and stood up. "I really should be going, Charlie."

He tried to keep the disappointment out of his voice. "Been a long day."

She put down her half-finished beer and absently jiggled her keys in her hand. "Maybe we could have dinner sometime?"

"Great."

"Yeah?"

"I'll call you." He leaned in for a kiss.

They kissed for a long time, until finally she pulled away. She drew a deep breath and smiled. "You will call me," she decided.

He laughed. "Come on, Hiawatha. Lemme walk you to your car."

12

THREE DAYS later, Sophie went to visit Boone at the hospital. He lay in bed with his eyes closed, and whenever his ventilator paused, she would hold her breath and count the seconds before he resumed breathing again. "Brain-dead" meant no gag reflex, no blink reflex. Nurse talk. They said a lot of things. *"It's best to be realistic in these instances. The odds are against him, statistically speaking."* They flitted from bed to bed, ministering to the sick, checking patients' charts and making scary pronouncements. She didn't want to hear it. She would think only positive thoughts today. *He will open his eyes and smile at me . . .*

Her grief came and went in little bursts. The bright sunshine streaming in through the slatted blinds gave her hope. She sat curled in a chair she'd pulled up to the bed and clutched Boone's moist, limp hand. She remembered when her mother was in the hospital. Sophie had missed her like crazy, but when she came home two weeks later, Sophie couldn't help feeling awkward and distant. Almost angry. It was only later that she realized her reluctance to get close to her mother was because she didn't want to have to say good-bye to her.

But she'd had to say good-bye, anyway. And then everything changed. The world got darker. Nobody seemed to care. Nobody understood what she was going through. Not even her best friend, Katlin, who could only talk about Sophie's grief for so long before she started to fidget or change the subject. *"You have to get over it. You've gotta move on."* That was Sophie's hardest lesson—that people didn't like to wallow in other people's misery, no matter how much they loved you.

But Boone was different. He listened to her talk about her mother for hours. He was the only person in the world who seemed to understand what she was going through, and because of their friendship, Sophie was disappointing people right and left. Her father had grounded her for two weeks; her girlfriends were acting narrow-minded. They didn't like anyone who wasn't on a college track, even though America was supposed to be a classless society.

Supporting her chin on her forearm, Sophie watched Boone as he slept. He had the complexion of a child—rosy and wrinkle-free—and a head of exquisitely combed hair. Usually his hair stuck up like a bunch of middle fingers, but his mother had been to the hospital that morning and combed his hair like that—slicked back, smoothed behind his ears like a little boy's. She'd also left a box of his possessions at the foot of the bed—his Game Boy and skateboard, a bunch of video games with ominous-sounding names like *Doom* and *Resident Evil*. As if he needed toys more than his mother's love. She was probably in some bar right now, getting plastered. Sophie's heart went out to him. He'd had to learn to live in a motherless world, just like her.

Now a freckle-faced nurse came into the room and

snapped the blinds open, sunlight knocking against Sophie's eyelids.

"How is he?" Sophie asked, blinking away the glare.

"No change yet," the nurse said, reading his chart and adjusting his IV line. "But the pressure on his brain has started to drop."

"Is that good?"

"Maybe. Don't get your hopes up." She checked his heart rate, fluffed his pillows and left.

Sophie's stomach muscles tensed, and she fell weakly back against her chair. Maybe death wasn't as bad as people thought it was. Maybe death was like falling asleep in the middle of the day. Maybe you melted slowly in the sun, like an icicle, all your molecules dispersing into the sun-warmed, buoyant air. Maybe death was a feeling of completeness and fullness. She sat staring blandly ahead, lost in thought, when Boone's hand suddenly stirred in hers.

She shot forward in her chair. "Boone?"

He responded by fluttering his eyelids.

"Nurse!" she screamed. She squeezed his hand and could feel the bones underneath the skin, tendons and muscle. She waited in the ticking silence for him to react. "Boone?"

He wiggled his fingers, and she suppressed a giggle.

"I love you," she said.

His face lurched into something like laughter.

She felt it twist inside her.

He opened his electric-blue eyes.

13

—————

W HERE THE hell is Lester?" Charlie said, storming out of his office.

Sergeant Hunter Byrd glanced up from his desk. "No idea, Chief." Beneath the fluorescent light, his curly red hair was looking coppery, as if it might have chemicals in it.

"How many messages have you left on his machine?"

"Three."

"Do me a favor and leave another one, okay? Tell him to get his butt in here for a friendly interview."

"Friendly?"

"You don't like that word, 'friendly'?"

Hunter shrugged and picked up the phone. "No, boss. Friendly's fine."

"I've got the Rideouts' autopsy results," Mike interrupted.

"My office."

They went into his office, where Charlie sat behind his desk and rattled the ice in his plastic cup. He could feel a nagging tension deep within him. They hadn't seen or heard from Lester in three days, and Charlie was worried that an affair wasn't the only thing his assistant chief might be hiding.

"I've been meaning to ask you," Mike said as he sat with his legs crossed, red tie dangling from his jacket pocket. "How come 'Smoke Gets in Your Eyes'? The song playing on the Rideouts' stereo?"

Charlie shook his head. "I have no idea."

"Think about it, Chief. The killer could've chosen any song out of hundreds. I went through their rather extensive album collection. Why not 'Little Things Mean a Lot' by Kitty Kallen or 'Wake Up Little Susie' by the Everly Brothers?"

Charlie put his cup of ice down. His desk was a confusion of paperwork. They'd collected enough material on the triple homicide to fill over a dozen binders. An electric fan rotated noiselessly on the ceiling, stirring the papers below. It was a beautiful day out, strong afternoon sunlight streaming through the slatted blinds, but nothing could ease the disquiet he was feeling. "What're you getting at, Mike?"

"I think it means something. That record, those lyrics. 'Smoke Gets in Your Eyes.' Think about it, Chief."

The soft hairs on the nape of his neck prickled, all his random fears crowding in on him at once.

"This is a brilliant, in-your-face sociopath. He's trying to see how much he can reveal about himself without getting caught. I think it's all part of his sick game plan."

"So you think the perp knows me? Is that what you're saying?"

Mike shrugged. "'Smoke Gets in Your Eyes.' Who else could that be directed at?"

Charlie tugged at this unpleasant thought. *Lester Deere, Boone Pritchett, Jake Wheaton, Jonah Gustafson.*

Not a good list. They must have interviewed over a hundred storm-chasers who'd been photographed near the scene of the crime that day, but so far they were drawing blanks. Most of the interviewees had alibied out. The public, the press, his superiors, were all demanding immediate action, but Charlie had nothing to offer them. Nothing at all. On his desk was an autopsy photograph of Danielle, and he turned the picture over so he wouldn't have to look at it.

"Maybe he knows *of* you, boss," Mike mused. "Maybe he saw your picture in the paper and decided to send you a message. I dunno. I just have this sinking-in-the-gut feeling that he chose that record on purpose." His face was slick with sweat. "There's a reason for everything. A twisted one, but a reason nonetheless."

Charlie lifted a brooding glance out the window. The parking lot was jammed with cars, heat rising off the asphalt. He and his men had meticulously matched the Peppers' injuries to the bloodstains they'd found inside their house and had deduced beyond a shadow of a doubt that the killer was right-handed. They'd been able to piece together a scenario from the lab reports, photographs and blood spatter trajectories. The killer had first attacked Rob Pepper in the front hallway, clubbing him in the chest, forearms, abdomen and head. A second blow to the head knocked him unconscious. The killer then attacked Jenna Pepper with the same weapon—a knotted log they'd found on the property—landing vicious blows to her head, chest and forearms, and finally rendering her unconscious. Both victims left matted sliding marks on the hallway walls and the red-and-green-patterned hallway rug from where they'd tried to crawl away.

In the meantime, Danielle fled into the kitchen, where

the killer followed her, delivering one tremendous blow to the back of her skull. Severely injured, she somehow managed to scramble out into the living room and hide behind the piano (they later found dust balls in her hair). He plucked her out of her hiding place and landed a paralyzing blow to her forehead, then dragged all three victims upstairs to the master bedroom, where, with unimaginable ferocity and savagery, he did his worst work. The perpetrator had to be relatively strong, Charlie thought, completely fearless and absolutely lacking in any conscience or remorse. It was a monstrous act of madness, full of risk and defiance, and it made no sense whatsoever.

Mike opened the folder. "Birdie and Sailor Rideout, ages fifty-four and fifty-six respectively. Bloodstains match the victims' ABO. Defensive cuts on the arms and hands, blunt trauma to the head. Impalement injuries were both full-body and partial-body thickness, fixed in place . . ." He glanced up. "It goes on. I'll just give you the broad strokes." He skim-read the next few pages. "Says here they picked up some interesting soils and botanicals from the scene. Insulation fibers, asbestos fibers and minute traces of plaster. The trace is very old, about a century. Nothing matches with the house, though."

"That's no good. It could've blown in from other areas."

Mike's pinstriped shirt stretched across his chest as he tipped his chair back. "No blue-black wool fibers, Chief. Just some white cotton ones."

Charlie shrugged. "That's so common it's useless."

"All the hairs they recovered from the drains leading into the main sewer line belonged to the victims, but there were several unknowns on the premises. Two strands of medium-length brown Caucasian hair, one short blond Caucasian, one short black Caucasian and one medium-length white Caucasian."

Charlie frowned. It made him think of his father, for some reason. Medium white hair.

"Also several black rabbit hairs."

"Rabbit?"

"According to the state lab."

"Did the Rideouts own any rabbits?"

"Not that I know of. That's why it piques my interest." He paused to turn the page. "They found a single green carpet fiber in Birdie Rideout's hair, and blue jean fibers underneath her fingernails."

"That won't give us anything. Blue jean fibers are as common as white cotton. Useless to the case."

"Now we come to the teeth," Mike said, clutching at the report with his short fat fingers. "Female vic's upper right canine was extracted and replaced with an as-yet-unidentified tooth. Male vic's lower left incisor was replaced in a similar manner."

"The teeth," Charlie said, rattling the ice in his plastic cup. "That's our link. That's what's gonna bring us and the killer together."

"I agree."

"Do me a favor. Ask McNeese if he'd loan us those teeth for a little while, would you?"

"Sure." Mike flipped through the rest of the report. "No sexual assault. No semen. No rearranged clothes that might indicate rape. No eyewitnesses. No reports of any suspicious activity. No incriminating latents. That about wraps it up."

Charlie could feel a slow, steady pulse in his neck. "What about the Peppers? Anything new on that front?"

"Besides a million nut calls?" Mike cracked a smile.

"Everybody's got a theory. Everybody's developed extrasensory perception all of a sudden."

"Any word on Gustafson?"

"Yeah, we got an address." He clunked his chair forward, the soft underbelly of his chin vibrating. "I was gonna go over there and talk to him in person, since he refuses to acknowledge our phone calls."

Charlie stood up. "What're we waiting for?"

On their way out, Hunter stopped them. "Chief? There's some lady on the phone . . . insists on talking to you personally. Says it's about the case."

"Meet you outside," Charlie told Mike, then took the phone from Hunter. "Hello?"

"Chief Grover?"

The line made a clicking sound.

"How can I help you, ma'am?"

"I wanted to report something about those murders that happened last month."

"Yes? I'm listening."

"Well," she said in a thick Texas drawl, "when I was a little girl, we had a tornado here in Dime Box, Texas. An F-2. Oh, it was bad. Mama, Dickie and me hid in the closet. It was right under the stairs, so we thought we'd be safe. That was a terrible day, I don't know if you remember . . . but half the town got blown away."

Charlie furrowed his brow. "Yes?"

"So there we were, huddled inside the closet, scared out of our wits, when I peeked out the door and saw this little person moving around inside our house. I thought it was an elf . . . I thought we had an elf in the house . . . but now I think it must've been a little boy. He wandered through the front hallway. A little boy of about . . . oh, I don't know. Five or six years old?"

Charlie frowned. It didn't make any sense.

"After the tornado roped out, there were no elves or little boys to be found, of course. I figured I must've been dreaming. But we discovered to our amazement that our silverware was gone. Our TV set was gone. The radio was gone. I mean, you understand, we were close to the damage path, but the house was still standing, and those items were missing as if by magic. As if someone or something had come into the house and plucked them out of existence. I just wanted you to know . . ."

"Well, ma'am. I appreciate the call. I sincerely do."

"I don't know. Maybe the wind blew everything away. But I can't seem to get that day out of my head."

"I'll take it under advisement. Thanks for calling."

"No, thank you, Chief Grover," she said. "Thank you and your men for doing such a wonderful job."

"I wish I deserved that," he said, and hung up.

14

JONAH GUSTAFSON lived between two freeway ramps somewhere east of Tulsa. He had medium-length brown hair, big knotty joints and a slightly manic look in his eyes. He sat on a plastic-covered couch while the setting sun streamed in through the old-fashioned windowpanes. He wore jeans, a leather vest and no shoes on his dirty feet, which Charlie guessed were size elevens. There was a framed moonscape on the wall behind him, and Charlie noticed that his hands shook as he hand-rolled himself another cigarette.

"Thanks for agreeing to talk to us," Charlie said.

"Yeah, no problem."

Out in the driveway sat a gleaming white van polished so spick-and-span it might've burned a hole in your eyes if you stared at it for too long. Charlie could hear children playing in the back bedrooms.

"You got kids?" he asked.

"Three boys. Three hellions." Jonah wouldn't look at him directly. He was working on a tall bourbon and soda and could barely lift the glass to drink.

Charlie gave a disengaged nod. The boys were yelling

at one another, the sound of their voices looping drowsily toward him like bees. "We've been talking to other storm-chasers who were in the vicinity of Promise on the fifteenth. Anything you could tell us would be much appreciated."

"Just routine, huh?"

"Strictly routine."

Jonah had thick white scar tissue where a right eyebrow should be. "What d'you wanna know?"

"Where were you that day?"

"I started out in Ponca City."

"Kansas?"

He nodded. "Local Skywarn nets were heating up, so I signed in, flipped on the portable and saw two tornado warnings shooting up southwest of me. The Nexrad summary and local Doppler radar confirmed this. So I swung around, and before I knew it, there was this ting and tang off the hood. And I'm thinking to myself, so far so bad."

"By bad, you mean good?"

"Yeah, good." He grinned. He drank. He blew out a thin ribbon of smoke. "Bad always means good."

Charlie glanced around the living room. The place was plain and simple. No plants, no curtains, no amenities. Just crumbling roller shades, squat discount furniture and lots of handmade cabinets and bookshelves. "You do your own woodworking?" he asked.

"Hell, yeah. I built that kitchen table out of particleboard. See my CD holder? I made that. See the entertainment center over there? I could make you one for fifty bucks plus material. *Hey, what's going on back there?*" he barked over his shoulder. He picked up the glass in his right hand and smiled apologetically. "My wife stranded me. Three kids, and one of 'em ain't even mine."

Charlie gave a calculated nod. *The perp was right-handed. Unknown brown hairs had been found at two of the crime scenes. Size eleven shoe, that was in the ball-park.*

"She used to come chasing with me all the time, my wife. We met during a hailstorm. We ran around like a couple of kids and took a bunch of hailstones home with us. Popped 'em in the freezer. Six months later, my wife served hailstone cocktails at our wedding." He took a drag of his hand-rolled cigarette, inhaling the unfiltered smoke deep into his lungs. "First thing she ever said to me was, 'A white van? Why white?' White gets dirty as shit. But hey, that ain't nothing a little core-punching won't fix, you know? A good driving rain is better than any car wash. Fucking gorgeous, my wife. She had some ass on her."

"What happened?"

"The bitch ran off with a grease monkey."

"No, I mean . . . on the fifteenth?" Charlie said.

"Oh. Right." His narrow triangular face made him seem both crafty and stupid at once. "So I headed back to Oklahoma, where the storm appeared to be back-building. Dome and anvil were really crisp. The northern flank had a nice tower to it, and the northwestern flank was punching through to the stratosphere . . . incredible explosion."

"So you were in Promise that day?" Mike said.

He nodded. "South of downtown. Next thing I know, I'm in heavy rain and the concrete is rumbling beneath my wheels. Rumbling like an earthquake. I figure I'm about to get eaten alive. Things can change so damn quick, you know? I saw it surge across the highway. It blew over a semi. Then all of a sudden, this moderately large piece of house falls from the sky directly in front of me." He leaned forward, his whole body tensing. "I abandoned my position. That debris was starting to track towards me."

"You left the area?"

"Hell, yeah. I floored it out of there, no kidding."

"Where'd you go?"

"There was another tornado warning down around Burns Flat and Reydon, down around there. Did you know they have a Twister Park in Burns Flat? Now, that's a sad fact."

"Were you anywhere near Shepherd Street on the fifteenth?" Charlie asked, and Jonah gave him a bloodless look.

"Absolutely not."

"You didn't happen to drive by the Pepper residence that day?" he said in an emotionless voice.

Jonah's eyes narrowed suspiciously. "I don't like where this is leading. These insinuendos."

"Would you mind if I took a look around?"

"Yes, I would." He sounded affronted.

Footsteps. "Dad?" A small boy stood in the doorway, two of his front teeth missing. That got Charlie's attention.

"C'mere, you." Jonah drew the boy close, his boxer shorts showing above the waistband of his jeans as he hugged his son tight.

The boy turned to stare with deep hostility at Charlie. He glared at his shiny badge. "What's your name?" he asked.

"Chief Grover. What's yours?"

Jonah's eyes lit with sudden recognition. "Grover? Any relation to Izzy Grover?"

Charlie nodded. "Yeah, that's my father."

"Man, there goes one hard-driving dude." Jonah had a cackling laugh. "That guy can be criminally dangerous, you know? Tailgating and bullying little Japanese imports out of the way. Who cares who's at fault? The dude needs a hug desperately. Him and his mangy old jacket."

The hairs on the back of Charlie's neck bristled like a cold morning. He pictured his father pulling that old pea-coat of his out of mothballs. "We're talking about Isaac Grover, right? Sixty-two years old? White hair?"

"Yeah, yeah. Make a mistake and he'll gleefully flatten you into a pancake under that sorry-ass pickup truck of his."

Charlie felt an uneasiness floating in his stomach. His father took that old navy-blue peacoat out of mothballs in the fall and wore it as late as June sometimes. *The dark blue peacoat.* Something registered. *Blue-black wool fibers.*

"Izzy Grover, man, and his piece-of-shit Loadmaster. Last time we pulled out the engine, he'd blown out a rod bearing and ruined the crank. That thing has a gazillion miles on it. He'd better get it rebuilt one of these days. One of these days soon."

Charlie could sense his own shifting consciousness like a change in air pressure. "Thanks for your time," he said, and stood up.

15

MUD SPATTERED the wheel wells of his police car as he took the snaking curves past the First Baptist Church and the dead pecan grove toward his father's house. He pulled into the long driveway and parked, then sat in his car with the engine ticking and stared at the recently mown lawn, the black-limbed trees. The house in the moonlight frightened him. Instead of comfort and warmth, he saw danger. He saw pain.

He stepped out of the car, heart leaping to his throat, and shot up the porch steps. "Hello?" He knocked on the front door. When nobody answered, he went over to one of the porch windows and peered inside.

His father was planted on the living room sofa, dozing in the flickering blue light of the TV set. He slept like a still life. Charlie rapped sharply on the windowpane, and the old man jerked awake.

"Pop? We need to talk."

He got up from the sofa with a sleepwalker's groping gait. "Charlie?" he said. "Is that you?"

After a moment, the screen door squealed on its hinges. "What're you doing here?" he asked groggily.

Charlie studied the way the porch light hit his father's head, outlining the skeletal shape of his skull—that broad brow, the gaunt cheeks, those miserly lips sinking over the toothless gums—and suddenly realized what it was he'd been avoiding all this time. His father was right-handed; he wore a size eleven shoe; he was an avid storm-chaser; he was a temperamental man with a violent past. His Loadmaster pickup truck had been photographed in the vicinity of the crime scene on April 15, and a single white hair—medium-length, Caucasian—had been found at the Rideout residence. And now there was the peacoat. Blue-black wool. *His father? Ridiculous.*

"Don't just stand there," Isaac said. "C'mon in."

Charlie stepped inside the house, its walls enveloping him in a musty cloak of oldness. He couldn't enter his father's house without clenching into a defensive posture. He had dozens of pale scars on his back, scars shaped like blades of grass made years ago by a leather strap. The body remembered everything, even when the mind forgot.

"Something to drink?"

"No thanks."

The living room was neat and tidy, with little islands of furniture grouped together. The molding was plain, the woodwork dark, the rooms small and boxy. There were no comforting touches—no flowers, no pictures, no books. Just a bucketful of pennies and stacks of old magazines, some scanner equipment and a TV set that turned people's faces purple.

Charlie paused. The CD player was new. So was the laptop. "Where'd you get those?" he asked.

"Down at Dirty Ed's. They're used. That okay with you?"

The laptop was open on the coffee table. On screen was a satellite picture of a rotating cloud mass. Charlie froze with a look of sniffing suspicion. "Since when do you go on-line?" he asked. "I thought you hated all the bells and whistles?"

"Shows how much you know," Isaac snorted. "That's basic chaser gear . . . laptop, GPS, cell phone. I also bought some brand-new tires for my truck. Is that okay with you?"

There were miles between himself and his father. Epochs of misunderstanding. "We need to talk, Pop."

"What about?"

"Where'd you get the watch?"

His mouth grew defiant. "I already told you."

"Yeah, right. How about the truth this time?"

Isaac slid the metal watchband up his wrist, hiding it underneath the sleeve of his orange sweatshirt. "Like I said, this nice couple . . ."

"Gave it to you, I know. What are their names?"

His father stared at him fiercely.

"Dad . . . I know you stole it."

His mouth grew hard. "Get out of my house."

"Look, I've heard some real horror stories about off-duty cops and paramedics stealing from disaster sites, which is just about the lowest thing a man can do. The victims' loved ones never have the balls to ask, 'Okay, who took the jewelry and the wallet?' So tell me, Pop. Did you steal the watch? Or did you find it in the mud? Please tell me you found it in the mud."

"You want the truth? I'll give you the truth." His father glared at him, then plopped down on the ugly floral sofa that curled around the mosaic coffee table. "Look at you, coming home late every night and expecting her to be waiting up for you in that big old empty house all by her lonesome. What d'you think? You think she likes growing up without any parents?"

It was the kind of low blow he was not expecting at all.

"She's still grieving and you're hardly ever home. She needs her dad to comfort her and listen to her. According to what she tells me, you were hardly ever there when Maddie was alive, either. She used to hear her poor mama cry herself to sleep at night, only Maddie refused to blame you. She said that's what being a cop's wife was all about. She said—"

"Shut up!" He silenced the old man with a look of pure murderous hatred. "Don't you dare say another word." He pointed at that sneering face.

"I thought you wanted the truth," his father said with such smug indifference it made his stomach ache.

"How can you sit there and lecture me, Pop? You, of all people? Jesus Christ . . . you used to beat the crap out of me on a regular basis."

"I haven't hit you in years," Isaac whispered fiercely. "Not since the fire."

"Oh, so all is forgiven? So it's okay now?" Charlie's nostrils bubbled with fury. "I wouldn't treat a dog the way you used to treat me. You once called me a particle of dirt. Do you remember that?"

Isaac sucked in air through his dentures.

"The truth this time. Let's get it all out in the open. Tell me about the fire, Pop. The fire that killed Mama and Clara. You started it, didn't you? Or were you too drunk to recall the particulars of that night?"

Isaac's gaze locked tight on Charlie's face.

"C'mon. Let's talk about the fire, Pop." He realized he was clutching something sharp and cold in his hand. His car keys. "Did you start it? Did you set the house on fire?"

He looked away. "That fire was an accident."

"Go ahead and deny everything. You're good at that."

"You don't know what the hell you're talking about."

"Oh, right," he said sarcastically. "I wasn't there, how would I know? After you hit Mom? After you used to beat the crap out of her? You know what I'd do, Pop? I'd go sit on the edge of her bed and hold her hand mirror for her so that she could see herself. Then I'd watch as she applied rouge and foundation to cover the bruises. She had all these tiny brushes and little lacquered makeup boxes. And once, after a particularly brutal display of what can happen when you mix testosterone, alcohol and my father . . . I heard her weeping in her room . . . and you know what I did? I went and hid under the bed. She kept calling my name, but I hid in my room, pretending I lived about a thousand miles away . . . I'm really proud of that one."

Isaac lowered his head and pounded the couch cushions with his fists. "Please stop . . ."

"Daddy?" a small voice broke in.

Charlie could feel the pinkness in his cheeks spreading to the area beneath his eyes as he spun around.

Sophie stood in the doorway, her face bloated with sleep. She had her cotton pajamas on. "What time's it?" she asked, her hair haphazard from her pillow.

He blinked, not quite believing his eyes. "What are you doing here?"

"I came to see Grandpa. You weren't home, so—"

"Get your jacket," he snapped. "Put some shoes on."

"Why? Where're we going?"

"Home," he said. "I'm taking you home."

"What's wrong?"

He grabbed her by the arm and pulled her out into the hallway. He tried to still his furiously beating heart. He opened the closet door and rummaged through the coats and slickers and musty-smelling sweaters.

"I didn't bring any jacket," she protested. "Dad?"

The peacoat wasn't there.

"C'mon," he said.

"My shoes!"

"You've got plenty of shoes at home."

"Daddy!"

He yanked her out the door.

16

W HAT WAS that all about?" Sophie demanded to know on the ride home, her eyes bright with criticism.

"Nothing."

"Nothing? You guys were, like, screaming at each other."

"We weren't screaming."

On the road ahead, a giant white 1960 Polara station wagon was weaving all over the road, four teenagers crammed in the front seat together. The driver was a frazzle-haired idiot with a cell phone glued to her ear who kept screaming at her friends to shut up. He should hit his take-down lights and pull her over, but he and Sophie were in the middle of an argument, and for once he didn't give a damn.

"What were you fighting about?" she asked.

"Do you not understand the word 'grounded'?"

"I was lonely! Peg has a life, you know. She can't be with me every single second of the day. What else am I supposed to do? You're never home."

The station wagon suddenly fishtailed in front of them, and Charlie slammed on his brakes. "Jesus, lady!"

"She has no concept of what a dangerous driver she is," Sophie said softly.

He hit the horn in a short burst, and the station wagon took a right down a dirt road and sped off in a cloud of dust.

"Dad . . . aren't you going to arrest them?"

"No."

They drove along in stony silence, the car's droning engine giving him a migraine. He would have to invent some excuse to go back and rummage around in his father's house, find the peacoat and take some fiber samples to send off to the state lab for testing. If the fibers didn't match, that would eliminate the problem quickly. He wanted to forget about this crazy notion and get back to the business of solving the case.

"So," she said, "aren't you going to tell me?"

"Tell you what?"

"What's this thing between you and Grandpa? This thing that's always been there?"

He felt the color draining from his face. Minutes ago, he'd demanded that his father face up to the truth about their past, and yet he'd spent his entire life hiding the same truth from Sophie. "It's never been right between us," he admitted.

"Duh." She watched him with unwavering eyes.

"Your grandfather wasn't always such a nice guy."

"What d'you mean?"

"We're all three-dimensional people, Sophie. We're all complicated." His neck muscles stiffened. "Your grandfather was a vicious drunk at one point in his life."

She didn't speak; she seemed caught on a barb of disbelief.

"This was before the fire," he told her. "The fire sobered him up. But before then, he was a brutal man."

She was staring at him, her tall forehead nibbled with worry. "Did he hurt you?"

There was a cold spot in the pit of his stomach. *Broken nose. Fractured bones. The belt. Yeah, he hurt me.* "He used excessive punishment," he said. "He punished me excessively."

"Why didn't you tell me sooner?"

"Because. I didn't want you to hate him."

She sat rooted in fear. Huddled and shivering.

"I learned three things from my father," he told her. "Don't talk, don't trust, don't feel. I had to work very hard to overcome those early lessons. I felt a lot of deep-seated shame, as if I were to blame for his misery. I thought it was all my fault. I believed I wasn't lovable."

She gave him a strange look full of pity.

"Living with an alcoholic is a lot like living with a wild animal," he said, trying to explain it to her. "You never know when they're going to turn on you. I was in a perpetual state of anxiety whenever he was home."

She edged closer to him.

"I love you very much, sweetie. I didn't tell you about it because it's ugly."

She rested her head against his shoulder, and he thought about her mother. He'd been faithful to Maddie for seventeen years; not that their relationship hadn't been rocky at times. They'd had their ups and downs, just like anybody else, but he'd loved her with all his heart. She'd accepted him, scars and all, warts and all. He was a head case when they first met—twenty-one years old, drinking and carousing. A fool. She helped him grow up. She helped him become a man.

"I know Grandpa has his faults," Sophie said, "but this makes me sick to my stomach."

"Don't hate him," he told her.

"Why not?"

"Because . . . he needs somebody good in his life."

"Still . . ."

"It's ancient history. He hasn't had a drink in thirty years. But you asked. And I don't want to lie to you." He tried to slow his breathing. "Look," he said, "I'm sorry I overreacted tonight. I had no right to lose my temper like that."

"It's okay."

"No, it's not okay. And I'm sorry I can't be home with you every night."

"Sometimes it feels like you're mad at me."

"No. Never. Just overworked."

She smiled, her arms elegantly poised in her lap. "You know what's weird?"

"What's that, sweetie?"

Her breathing came and went in little pauses. "Last month, during the tornado . . . all the roses in Mom's rose garden blew around, and they were so beautiful. They shook in the wind, and the petals swirled up into the sky. It was beautiful and scary, all at once . . . like she was in the garden . . . watching over me."

He smiled, but then his cell phone rang, spoiling the mood. "Sorry," he said.

She gave him a forgiving look. "Go ahead and answer it."

The phone felt cool in his hand. "Hello?"

"Charlie," Roger Duff said, "I need you to come down to the morgue right away."

"What's up, Doc?"

"You're gonna want to see this for yourself. Trust me."

She rolled her eyes. "Go," she said.

"You sure?" He pocketed his phone. "I won't be long."

17

I THOUGHT you'd want to see this right away, Charlie."
He could detect a pulse of fear in Duff's tone. "Dr.
Robles over at the state lab is an expert on this sort of
thing. I was on the phone with him for over an hour."

Charlie stood on the opposite side of the stainless-
steel table, where five human teeth, each in its own plastic envelope, were splayed like a winning poker hand.

"Two incisors, one cuspid, one bicuspid and one
molar." Duff used his ballpoint pen to point them out.
"That's what we've got so far. Five calling cards."

"The replacement teeth?"

Duff wiped his moist brow, then straightened his
shoulders importantly. "We're each born with two sets of
teeth, Charlie. A set of milk teeth and a set of permanent.
Most of us have all our milk teeth by the age of three, but
then, between the ages of three and six, our permanent
teeth start to erupt. By the time we're thirteen, we've
pretty much got all our permanent teeth. You with me so
far?"

Charlie nodded.

"Okay. Everyone's teeth are unique," he continued.

"Their shape, their juxtaposition inside the mouth, et cetera. Now, through analysis and comparison, and without destroying any of the teeth for verification, Dr. Robles has concluded that, within a reasonable degree of certainty, all five of these teeth came from the same mouth."

Charlie's heart leaped, a new fear gripping him.

"But . . . ," Duff said. "But . . ." He pointed at the various plastic envelopes. "Each one was extracted during a different stage of development within the victim's lifetime."

Charlie glanced up, sweat collecting on his brow.

"Two are milk teeth, three are permanent. The three permanent teeth are no older than preteens."

"And you know this how?"

"Dr. Robles compared the imperfections on the biting surfaces—microscopic pits, broken edges, wear patterns. He also reconstructed their alignment inside the jaw."

Charlie stared at the teeth, each one indistinguishable from the next to his unpracticed eye. "How does he know some of these are milk teeth and others aren't?"

"The roots of the baby teeth are designed to dissolve as the permanent teeth develop." He pulled a lab sheet out of the stack on the countertop. "Using something called panoramic radiography, he was able to measure the secondary dentin inside the pulp. There's a correlation between the reduction of the coronal pulp cavity and the victim's chronological age, but apparently this method is only accurate to within five years. The most common method of age detection relies on microscopic examination of the structural changes inside the tooth. There are chemical tests as well, but unfortunately each of these methods would require the complete destruction of the tooth. And we're not ready to go there yet, are we, Charlie?"

"Am I hearing you correctly?" he said angrily. "Some poor kid's been getting his teeth yanked out year after year?"

Duff tugged on his silver-stubbled face. "Dr. Robles found pliers impressions on some of the enamel surfaces, yes. Now, listen to me. He's not a hundred percent sure all five teeth came from the same mouth. It's just a theory at this point. For him to be absolutely certain, he'd have to perform mitochondrial-DNA testing, which again would require the complete destruction of the teeth."

"So it's possible they might've come from several different victims?"

"That's still a possibility, Charlie." He put down the report. "It's also possible that the victim or victims are dead."

Charlie pictured Jonah Gustafson clutching his son. "I just interviewed a suspect whose kid is missing a few teeth."

"How old?"

"Seven or eight. By his own admission, the guy was out chasing on the fifteenth. I've been told he's quite capable of predicting when and where a tornado will drop. He's got three sons altogether. I don't know their ages . . . I only met one of them."

"Okay. Look. Your main concern is for those kids," Duff said. "If they're being abused, I want them out of there."

Charlie nodded. "I'll contact the local law."

Duff slid his ballpoint pen back into his breast pocket.

"I promised I'd get these back to the lab as soon as possible."

Charlie crossed his arms. "So we have another victim to worry about? The kid or kids whose teeth these are?"

The overhead fluorescent tubes cast a stark, incandescent glow.

"In all my years as county medical examiner, I've never seen anything like it, Charlie. And I've witnessed plenty of viciousness, cruelty and rage. But this . . . I can't even begin to understand it. Where's the sense?"

"There is no sense, Duff," he said, wondering how long the killer sat beside his victims, looking into their faces. "No sense at all."

18

THE NEXT day, Social Services took Jonah Gustafson's sons away from him. The official reason was neglect. The house was neat but the cupboards were bare. Four six-packs in the refrigerator and no milk. Plenty of bourbon, no Flintstones vitamins. A heavyset woman from Social Services tossed the kids' clothing into a gym bag, while several police officers held Jonah at bay. He stood moaning in the wild weeds as the county van drove off, three stunned little faces pasted to the rear window like pale decals.

Jonah clutched himself as if he'd been punched in the gut, then looked into Charlie's eyes. *"What've you done to me?"* he screamed.

It pricked Charlie's conscience; he knew exactly how he would feel if anyone tried to take his daughter away from him. It would rip a huge hole in his heart. There was a brief period after Maddie had died when he'd been careless and irresponsible, no kind of father at all. He'd gone on a drinking binge that'd lasted several weeks, se-cretly hoping to drown himself in a bottle of whiskey, tequila, whatever. For three weeks, Mike had followed him around from bar to bar, patiently explaining, "Okay, Chief. Time to go." Reminding him, "Sophie's waiting for you." His best friend and conscience had sobered him up and driven him home on more than one occasion. He'd listened patiently to Charlie's drunken ramblings. He'd stood by him. *Nobody's innocent. We're all guilty of something.*

"My boys." Jonah's voice rose heatedly. *"What've you done to me?"*

"You did this to yourself," Charlie answered, all sympathy gone. The moment had passed. Jonah had a full-page rap sheet for assault and battery, several DUIs, possession with intent to distribute. Although he was a widely known drug dealer, the Tulsa Police Department's investigative unit didn't have enough on him yet to make the charges stick. And since Charlie couldn't connect him to the homicides yet, there would be no arrest warrant forthcoming. The important thing was that the kids were safe.

Charlie visited the Gustafson boys at a local children's shelter. Three little towheaded boys, all under the age of ten, sat on the same bed together, staring down at their tapping feet.

"How're you guys doing?"

"Fine," they murmured.

Charlie knew from firsthand experience that living with an alcoholic was like playing hopscotch in a minefield. He wanted to tell them they'd be better off without their abusive father, but said nothing. It wasn't his job. The unpacked gym bag slouched on the floor at the foot of the bed, and he noticed there was a yellow chalklike substance on the blue nylon handles. "What's that yellow stuff?" he asked, pointing at the bag.

They looked. Shrugged. The oldest one was nine. The

others were seven and five. All three were missing some of their teeth, and their smiles were riddled with decay.

"Does your dad ever hurt you?" he asked the oldest boy. "Does he ever spank you?"

"Yeah," he admitted. He had light blond hair and blue eyes, was pretty as a girl, but whenever he opened his mouth, you could see the rot.

"Does he use his hand or a belt?"

The boy shrugged. "Both, I guess."

Charlie eyed them with tremendous sympathy, wanting to protect them from harm. They wore baggy corduroy pants, dark blue hoodies and baseball caps that kept their unruly hair in check. "Mind if I took a look at your back?" he asked the nine-year-old, then caught the others' furtive glances. "Just a peek?"

The boy's mouth grew pinched. He got off the bed and walked over to Charlie, then turned and raised his hoodie and T-shirt. There were old scars on his back—pale pink, about the size of two fingers making a peace sign.

"Where'd you get these?"

"We were just foolin' around. I fell on a fence or something."

"Or something? You're not sure?" It was exactly the kind of lie Charlie used to tell. "Okay, siddown."

He went back to his brothers. "Can we go home now?" he asked plaintively.

Charlie took a patient breath. "You guys are gonna have to stay here for a while."

"How come?"

"It's better this way."

The seven-year-old rolled his tongue around inside his cheek. "How'd you get them?" he asked, pointing at Charlie's scarred left arm.

Charlie glanced down. "Those are second- and third-degree burns from a fire."

"Did it hurt?"

"The second-degree burns were extremely painful. The third-degree burns didn't hurt because the nerves'd been destroyed. So your father never pulled any teeth out of your head?"

The boys looked at one another and seemed confused by his question. "No," the nine-year-old said.

"He never helped your teeth come out? Any of you?"

"Yep, he did," the littlest one admitted.

"Shut up," his older brother said, "if you ever wanna see Dad again."

Charlie held the five-year-old's eye and said, "How'd he help your teeth come out?"

He pointed inside his mouth. "Pulled 'em wiff a pair of pliers."

A shiver crawled up Charlie's spine.

"He was just helping you because that tooth was hanging on for dear life," the nine-year-old said. "And I don't think we should talk about this anymore."

"One more question . . ."

"Dad says we don't have to talk to the police," he said angrily. He turned to his brothers. "If you say another word, I'm gonna make sure Dad finds out, understand?"

Charlie let it go, and they talked sports for a while. The boys liked baseball best. They liked the Sooners and Greg Dobbs. They said their mother had left them one fine spring day and had never come back.

"And you haven't seen her since?" Charlie asked.

They shook their heads.

"Not even a phone call?"

The nine-year-old's eyes suddenly filled with tears. "I think she must've forgotten all about us by now."

They hadn't been able to locate Gustafson's wife. By all accounts, she'd disappeared several years ago, vanished without a trace. Jonah hadn't been charged, since there was no body. No evidence of foul play. But it raised suspicions. The whole thing stank, and Charlie decided he was going to work very hard to find out exactly what'd happened.

He drove back to the house to talk to Jonah, but he was busy on the phone, trying to get his kids back. Jonah's criminal defense attorney met Charlie out in the front yard. They stepped gingerly over broken toys as they approached one another.

The lawyer, Andrew Findale, had so many hair plugs his scalp looked like a doll's head. He wore a tweed jacket and horn-rimmed glasses, and his eyes had the edgy, irritable look of a midlife-crisis male. "Jonah doesn't want to talk to you right now," he said, enunciating each syllable. "Jonah feels betrayed."

"The guy's a piece-of-shit drug dealer and God knows what else," Charlie told him angrily. "You tell him I'm gonna make sure his kids stay safe."

He drove into the dying sun, so tired he could barely think straight. Then his cell phone rang. "Hello?"

"Dad?" It was Sophie. "You're late."

19

WILLA BELLMAN lived three towns over. Thirty-five minutes away. She'd given him the directions—past the Rocket Roadside Diner, straight through the heart of town, take your first left down a winding country road.

The house was like something out of a storybook—picket fence, flower garden, cats curled up on the porch. The barbecue was in the backyard—paper lanterns, smoke rising from the grill, chunks of red meat slathered in barbecue sauce. Charlie was surprised to find Rick Kripner standing in front of the grill with a beer in one hand and a spatula in the other. He wore baggy shorts and a T-shirt that said "Dryden Tech Rules!"

"Hey, Chief." They shook hands. "How's it going with the case? Any progress?"

"We're moving forward," Charlie said, unwilling to share his uneasiness, his deepening suspicion that they just might have the killer in their sights.

"Beer?" Willa was looking painfully sexy in a red halter top and prewashed jeans, those dangly silver earrings drawing his focus back to her face.

"What?" she said, laughing.

"Just enjoying the view."

"You don't have a clue what you're getting yourself in for, do you?" she said with a teasing smile.

"You made it!" Sophie galloped over like a colt and wrapped her skinny arms around him. She was looking better, the cuts on her face and neck almost healed, her arms still speckled with little scabs. "Rick was telling us these great stories . . . something about chickens . . . you tell it!" she said, turning to Rick.

"Some chickens get so stressed out when a tornado touches down," he explained, "that their feathers come loose and blow away. It's called flight molt."

Sophie wrinkled her nose. "What about the other thing, the thing with the frogs?"

"Tornadoes have been known to pick up hundreds of frogs and carry them off. Bullfrogs. Fish. Once in Colorado, thousands of dead ducks dropped out of the sky. It was literally raining ducks. During that same tornado, a tie rack with seven ties was carried forty miles by the wind, and all the ties stayed on the rack."

Awe was set in Sophie's face like a flower pressed between two pages. She nibbled on her lower lip, and some of her rose-colored lipstick stuck to her front teeth. Charlie understood why she'd been so preoccupied with bad weather lately. Two words—Boone Pritchett. Boone was recovering nicely from his coma, and Charlie suspected that he and his daughter had been carrying on a secret dialogue via the phone and Internet. Several times he'd walked in on Sophie, and she'd instantly cupped her hand over the mouthpiece and waited for him to leave. He decided to let it go. He sensed that the more he forbade this friendship, the more likely she was to fling herself into Boone's tattooed arms.

"Remind her how dangerous a tornado can be, would you please?" Charlie said.

"Dad," she groaned. "Would you quit worrying?"

"I need help with the cooler, handsome," Willa said, and they went inside together. The kitchen held the rich aroma of blueberry pies steaming on the countertop. Charlie helped her move the cooler of beer and sodas back outside, then they sat at the picnic table together, while Sophie and Rick attended to the charcoal grill.

"I want to apologize for all the obnoxious things I may do in the future," Willa said, sucking on a beer.

"What d'you mean?"

"I'm one of those overachievers who can really grate on people's nerves. I can't help it. So I like to say my sorries up front."

Charlie smiled. "Let me get this straight. You're such an overachiever you even stockpile your apologies?"

"Now you're getting the picture."

He laughed, then glanced at Sophie and Rick, deep in conversation. "You invited him?" he asked, trying to phrase the question as innocuously as possible.

"Not me," she said. "Sophie."

His eyebrows lifted in surprise. "Sophie invited him?"

"Yep."

He grinned.

"Why?"

"Nothing. It's just . . . I always sense something edgy between Rick and me whenever it comes to the subject of you."

She laughed. "Aw, c'mon. He's like a brother to me."

"Does he know that?"

She leaned in for a quick kiss. They seemed a bit shy around one another tonight. The sun had fallen beneath the rim of the world, and he was enjoying the way the sunset's amber light glinted off her wet lips. She looked so beautiful he didn't know where to rest his gaze.

His cell phone rang just then, killing the moment. It lay on the picnic table between them.

"Aren't you going to answer that?" she asked.

"Not important."

She snatched it up. "Hello? Just a second." She handed it over. "For you."

He rolled his eyes and took it.

"Something's up." It was Mike.

"I do actually have a life, you realize."

"Yeah, right. You and me both. Lester's gone missing."

"What?"

"I've been on the phone with his parents. They're very concerned. The mayor is concerned."

"Jesus . . ."

"Nobody's seen him in three or four days. Parents, uncles, cousins. They've been calling all around. They're in a panic. What d'you want me to do?"

Glancing skyward, Charlie spotted the start of the evening, the planet Venus. Stars twinkled, planets didn't. "Send somebody over to his house to check it out."

"Tyler just got back. The house was in slight disarray, but that's nothing unusual for Lester. Plus his truck is gone."

"All right, put out a BOLO to all county sheriffs' units and highway patrol. I doubt it's serious. Let's see what happens tomorrow."

20

THE FOLLOWING morning, Charlie and Mike took a ride over to Lester Deere's property to have a look around. He lived way out in the boonies, where you could hear the metal roofs of the barns ticking in the heat of the day. On this cloudless May morning, Charlie's eyes watered from staring at the shiny skin of the police car and the ribbon of hot asphalt beyond. It was the kind of gorgeous spring day that winnowed the wind and left the sky cloudless, the prairie grasses stirring and undulating on either side of the road.

They pulled into a bumpy driveway, clumps of tall grass brushing underneath the fenders of the cage car. No trees grew around the white frame two-story house. There was a satellite dish on the roof and speakers set out in the front yard. Swallows dipped and glided from a nearby barn, and the walkway was terraced with flagstones.

They climbed the rough wooden porch planks past a trio of webbed aluminum chairs arranged to face the rising sun. "Lester?" Charlie thumped on the door with his fist. "Hello? Anybody home?"

No answer. They went inside.

The house was dense with the stench of stale beer, and a warm wind blew the lacy curtains out. They walked past a mountain of empties in the living room, scattered pizza boxes and dirty laundry.

"Must've been some party," Charlie said, kicking an aluminum can out of his way.

They checked the lower floor for signs of a struggle. The kitchen walls were painted as blue as a summer's day. They found no evidence of foul play—no blood spatter on the walls or bloodstains on the floor, no overturned furniture.

The living room had a comfy lived-in feel. There was a videotape in the VCR, all played out. Charlie ejected it. Pirates vs. Tigers. Lester liked to replay his glorious football moments. He could be both smug and self-effacing at the same time, the kind of guy who constantly lived in the past—high school jock, senior vice president, ladies' man. Just like all the other towel-snappers Charlie had butted heads with over the years. Just like Hoyt Bledlin . . .

As he wound his way through the house, Charlie tried not to think about good ol' Hoyt, his primary tormentor in elementary school, junior high and high school. Right after the fire, Charlie's hair had fallen out, and it took a long time for it to grow back. Sitting in his third-grade classroom had been particularly tough. *"Hey, Mount Baldy! Hey, Telly Savalas!"* Sitting there feeling the contractions in his leg because the scarred skin didn't grow as fast as the rest of his body did. Hearing those taunting whispers. *"Contaminated. He's contaminated, don't go near him."* Hard to ignore when you were eight years old. And then in high school, Hoyt's favorite trick had been to

toss lit matches in Charlie's face. He also enjoyed light-
ing firecrackers behind his back to see just how high he'd
jump. *"Hey, Burned-All-Over! This remind you of something?"* Hoyt would crinkle cellophane in Charlie's ear,
making him think of the fire. Good ol' Hoyt, dead and
gone, stuck a vacuum cleaner hose in his mouth five
years ago after a final drinking binge. But the pain he'd
caused still lingered.

Upstairs, they moved quickly through each room. The
bureau drawers in Lester's bedroom had been yanked
open, clothes strewn about. His wallet, service weapon,
off-duty gun and watch appeared to be missing. Lester
never went anywhere without that watch, a two-hundred-
meter, depth-tested, impact-resistant, digital-drive water-
proof Eagleton.

"I got a bad feeling about this," Charlie said. "He was
supposed to come in for an interview. I wanted to for-
mally eliminate him as a suspect."

Mike squinted in disbelief. "You think he fled?"

"Maybe."

"What's there to hide? So he had an affair with one
of the vics, so what? That doesn't make him guilty of
murder."

"Let's subpoena the phone records."

Mike's eyes grew intense. "Why would that idiot go
and do a thing like that?"

"I don't know."

He let out a sigh. "What're we gonna tell the mayor?"

Charlie shook his head. It wasn't his day.

KNEE-DEEP IN JUNE

1

Sıxteen-year-old Toby Lake shoved the dirty laundry into the washing machine, sprinkled in soap, snapped the lid shut and switched it on. His mother was out buying groceries, and the day was getting strange. First cold, then muggy, now these dark streaks along the horizon. He shivered and put on the sweater his mother had knitted him last fall during her Mrs. Brady phase. The washing machine began to tremble like it always did, and he thumped on the ka-chunking lid with his fist.

He slipped on his headphones and went back into the living room, where he flopped down on the sofa. A sudden gust of wind stirred the gauzy white curtains, and he sat up and raised his headphones again. "Duke?" he said, looking around for the dog. "Here, boy!"

That clumsy, nearsighted black Lab was probably out back chasing prairie dogs. He pulled the brim of his Texas Rangers cap down low over his eyes and tapped his foot to the beat of an Eminem song. On TV, a news anchorman in a power suit was yacking about the impending storm. Everything was always the Tragedy of the Century with those guys. He raised his headphones and listened for a second. "Here to tell us more about tornadoes and the kind of damage they can cause, we turn to . . ."

Just then the power went off.

"Yow," he breathed, getting up from the sofa and going over to the window, where the curtains billowed against his face. It was raining hard. The glass held the steam from his breath, and he wiped it clean with his hand. He could see strokes of lightning on the edges of the cattle pasture. At the end of all the big farms in Wolf Pass, Texas, was their lonely little farmstead, where the highway ended and the back roads turned to gravel. No way did he want to become a farmer like his old man. He wanted to go into broadcasting.

Now the front door blew open, and Toby ran across the room to close it. The door kept flapping open in the wind, and he became obsessed with pushing it shut. Finally the latch connected with a *click*, and he leaned against the door, breathing hard. "Duke?" He stood hugging himself. The house was too dark for midafternoon. He caught a sudden movement out of the corner of his eye and turned, then stood looking around uncertainly. Hadn't he just seen someone walking into the kitchen? *Shit.* He must've been hallucinating.

Toby picked up his aluminum baseball bat. "Hello?" He gripped the bat and walked slowly toward the kitchen doorway. "Anybody in here?" He stood for a puzzled moment in the doorway, but all he could see were the table and chairs, the refrigerator, the pine china cabinet. "Wuss," he muttered, shaking it off. He could be such a pussy sometimes.

He felt the blow against his head, swift and furious, then stood in total shock. "Oh God . . ." Blood ran down his face as he staggered backward into the living room, where, in a blind panic, he dove behind the sofa. He crouched there for endless seconds, shivering in terror, while outside a fistful of hailstones peppered the roof and the wind made an unbearable whistling sound. He crouched among Duke's chew toys, inhaling dust balls, then heard the dog yelping outside.

"Duke?" he screamed.

Something struck the back of his head, and the bat went flying out of his hands. Now a fist was dragging him kicking and screaming out of his hiding place, dragging him by the roots of his hair. He thrashed and screamed and finally broke loose; but then another blow impacted his forehead and his eyes filled with blood. He screamed and flailed at shadows. Whirled around. Staggered out the door, into the back field, where the blue alfalfa grew and those fleshy, fawn-colored mushrooms burst in bunches from the tangled ditches.

"Duke!" he screamed, blinking the blood out of his eyes. He stumbled over the busted fence and stood in the cow pasture. In the distance, he could see a shopping cart inching its way up the road in fits and starts. All the tall blond wheat seemed to be whistling one note. The birds were clumped under the trees, and his hair blew practically sideways in the wind. He looked up at the blackened sky and saw white prairie blossoms shaking down like snow.

"Duke? Where are you, boy?"

No dog came panting through the curtain of gray. Instead, a thick fog came up in a nearby field and began to swirl. Then the most incredible thing happened—a large cone-shaped funnel shot up from the fogbank and moved slowly toward him, like something out of a dream.

Toby's shoulders lifted as he took a stunned breath. Debris flew out of the base of the tornado, whipping up into the air, and he could see something tracking toward him. It hurtled through the air at maybe forty miles an hour. He couldn't move. He couldn't think. His final scream died in his throat as a flying piece of sheet metal sliced through his neck.

2

CHARLIE PULLED over to the side of the road and parked, in a foul mood. The mailbox said LAKE. A teenage boy was dead. It hit him once again with dull shock. The dispersing storm clouds looked like gray brains, and the late afternoon sun sent crepuscular rays shooting down— Jesus rays, some people called them. A midnight-blue Buick was rolled over onto its side in the driveway. Yesterday's F-2 had circumvented the house, coming to within eighty yards and littering the landscape with debris.

The farmhouse looked old and run-down—peeling paint, rusty window screens. Charlie got out and climbed the porch steps. The doorknob was jiggly loose. He walked through a dark vestibule and stood in the living room doorway.

The living room had a plank floor and a potbellied stove, and a cautious sun poked intermittently between the gauzy curtains. The victim reclined on an old plaid sofa, positioned in the center of the room but facing away from the door. Charlie could see the back of the boy's head resting on a pillow. He wore a Texas Rangers baseball cap and a pair of headphones. The sofa faced a blood-spattered television set.

"Chief Grover?"

He turned.

Compact and muscular, with wrinkled brown skin and frosty eyes, Sheriff Dorsey stood in the kitchen doorway. "We've been piecing together a scenario from the blood evidence," he said. "We think he was standing right here when he received the first blow."

There was blood spatter on the walls and "flyers" on the ceiling—blood and tissue flung from a weapon being raised and lowered with each successive blow.

"Was the scene staged?"

"See for yourself."

As he moved toward the sofa, Charlie became rooted in revulsion and shock. The boy's torso was missing. His severed head was propped against an embroidered pillow, and a fence post was stuck like a stake in the bloody stump of his neck. There was a look of mild surprise on the boy's face, as if he'd been caught with his hand in the cookie jar. His hair was shoulder-length and pale blond, like the wheat in late summer, and his eyes were brown and long-lashed.

Charlie swallowed hard. "What's his name?"

"Toby."

"Where's the rest of him?"

"Kitchen," Sheriff Dorsey said. "When his mother came home and found him like that, she just lost it."

Charlie turned the corner. Three grocery bags had coughed up their contents on the speckled linoleum floor. The dog food in its plastic doggie dish still held the shape of the can. There were drag marks from the back door to the kitchen table, and seated at the table was the headless boy, his elbows propped on either side of a straw-colored place mat. A computer had been set up in front of him, and someone had downloaded forecasting information. The website displayed raw satellite data, a hook echo rotating across the screen.

Charlie tried to rein in his revulsion. Usually when somebody committed serial murder, the M.O. would change from scene to scene but remain consistent in other ways. This was very different, this beheading; the killer was becoming bolder, taking chances. The cut was too clean to have been made with an ax or even a saw. Behind him, Sheriff Dorsey said, "We found a piece of sheet metal out back . . . looks like he got decapitated by the tornado."

Charlie lingered on the horror. The decapitation probably fed into the killer's sick fantasy of himself. He and the wind were both murderers now; they were one and the same.

"They call this guy the Debris Killer, you believe that?" Sheriff Dorsey shook his head. "Sick bastard gets a nickname."

"Debris Killer, Tornado Killer, Plains Slasher," Charlie said, putting on a pair of latex gloves. "They got a lot of names for this guy. Mind?"

"No, go right ahead."

He went back into the living room and, very gingerly, held the boy's head. His pale mouth was at the beginning stages of rigor. Charlie peeled back the lips and examined the teeth. "There." A lower incisor was missing, and in its place was a bloody replacement tooth.

Sheriff Dorsey squinted. "What is it?"

"This tooth has been replaced."

The sheriff gave a low whistle.

"Have your coroner send it to the state lab for processing. They've got the rest of them."

He looked up. "The rest?"

"Yeah. We've managed to keep it from the press. Make sure to seal your findings."

They heard a dog barking outside, and Sheriff Dorsey went to the door. "Hey, fellah," he said, kneeling down to pat the dog. "Sorry you can't come in, buddy."

Charlie had a sudden thought. The killer had spared the dog. What if there'd been a time when he'd spared the human being and killed the dog?

W E'VE BEEN collecting death and injury statistics for about six years now, yeah." Rick hunched over his computer keyboard. "Total tornado deaths, livestock losses, that sort of thing."

Charlie drummed his fingers on the desktop. Rick's office was located in a corner of the underground facility, the brains of the operation, he jokingly called it. There was a fake plastic traffic sign on the wall that said GENIUS AT WORK, a multitude of yellow stickies posted everywhere you looked and plenty of state-of-the-art equipment. Tacked to the cluttered bulletin board was a handwritten note that said "Gone Chasing" in black Magic Marker and a computer-printed note that said "Recipe for a Slow-Moving Wedge: Blend the following ingredients—Meso-slow dryline bulge + 700 mb winds exceeding 20 knots + CAPE (greater than 4000); stir in 500 mb winds & wait 3 hours."

"Let's see . . . horses, cattle, pigs." Rick punched in a command, and the data scrolled on screen. "Sometimes there are so many carcasses afterwards they have to plow the fields and bury them in a mass grave."

Charlie glanced at the TV set, where a spiraling, comma-shaped cloud pattern arced across the screen.

"Those radar signatures are from another planet, huh?"

"I wouldn't know."

Rick grinned. "Don't worry, Chief. You'll get the hang of it. Willa says you're a natural."

Charlie just looked at him.

"What?"

"What is it with you and me?"

"Nothing. Don't worry about it."

"Because I kind of get the feeling it's more than that."

"Nah. Willa and I are just friends."

"Nothing more? Because maybe it's something we should talk about."

"C'mon, Chief. She's like a sister to me."

"Okay," Charlie said uneasily. "Good."

"Look, I'm a little grumpy today. I've been up all night working on these algorithms. Hand cramps and eyestrain, that's all I've got to show for it."

"Appreciate the help."

"Okay, here we go. House pets. Cats and dogs. Check this out. Somebody lost a pet llama once . . . impalement with a fence strut . . . had to be euthanized."

"I'd like a list of all family pets that were killed by flying debris going back six years."

"For the whole USA, or just Tornado Alley?"

"Within a five-hundred-mile radius of Promise. Print it out for me, would you?"

"Sure." His fingers spidered across the keyboard. He hit the command for print, then turned to Charlie, his wrinkled nose holding up his glasses. "You're looking for patterns, right? Because that's what we do here. We search for weather patterns the way you search for crime patterns. Science is all about patterns."

"I figure he started with animals first. Most serial killers start with animals, then progress to human beings."

Rick gave an involuntary shudder. "So you're tracking his apprenticeship, so to speak?"

Charlie shrugged. "You follow as many leads as you can and hope that something sticks."

The printer spat out several pages, and Charlie scooped them up. He studied the data for a moment, then frowned.

"What is it, Chief?"

"Lots of dog deaths starting around three years ago. Now all I have to do is convince someone to let me exhume their pet."

4

THIRTEEN PEOPLE on the list refused to cooperate, but five said yes, and Charlie spent the rest of the week driving to various parts of Texas, Oklahoma and Nebraska, digging up people's backyards and checking out their dead pets' teeth. At four o'clock on a Friday afternoon, he found himself in the kind of mom-and-apple-pie Kansas town that had more letters in its name than residents. The Cavitts had lost their golden retriever four years ago, and the family farm was overrun with chickens, goats, boys on bicycles and girls on skateboards.

Mr. Cavitt had deep-seated eyes, slick gray hair and a protruding Adam's apple. He greeted Charlie with a firm handshake and a rusty shovel. "C'mon around back," he said with quiet dignity. They cornered the house and walked into a shady backyard, where the large handsome elm cast a wide shadow.

"When it comes to kids, you need to be straight with them," Mr. Cavitt said as he approached the grave marker, a large pink slab of stone. "Don't sugarcoat it. If you tell them the dog got 'put to sleep,' they might stop closing their eyes at night. So you tell them flat out . . . your poor ol' doggy's dead."

Charlie helped him remove the stone, and then Mr. Cavitt stepped on the shovel and broke the earth.

"Salem was a good boy," he said as he dug. "Whenever I got home from work, soon as I opened the door, there he'd be." He paused for breath, resting his callused hands on his hips. "I must be getting sentimental in my old age," he said, tears resting on the rims of his pale eyes. "This is harder than I'd expected."

"Here, let me." Charlie took the shovel and dug up the dog's skeletal remains in the cool shade of the old-growth tree. There were fly pupal cases among the bones. He picked up the skull, pried open the jaws, and there it was—a human-looking tooth, much smaller than the one it had replaced.

5

THAT NIGHT, Sophie went to a party where kids her age were drinking beer and making out to heavy-metal music. She followed Boone into the darkened backyard, where the trees were beginning to grow their leaves back, a green mist settling over everything. They sat in matching lawn chairs, and Boone dropped his crutches in the grass.

"I'm on diazepam and Skelaxin," he told her. "I am feeling no pain." He drew thoughtfully on his cigarette as if he were participating in a national taste test. He wore a pair of unlaced sneakers, a black ribbed undershirt and denim jeans slit up the leg so that his cast would fit. "Oh man, wouldja look at that sky?"

"No good, huh?"

"Sucks."

She caught sight of the evening star rising above the plains and the moon popping out from behind a scud of clouds. "You can't go chasing, anyway," she told him. "Not with your leg in a cast and your truck totaled."

"Maybe you'll take me, Sofe?"

She laughed, secretly relieved that tornado season was

almost over. She didn't want there to be any more deaths. The wind pushing through the trees made her stomach hurt. "The bust is in, huh?" she said.

He leaned over and kissed her.

She tasted salt on his lips and felt an odd elation, like being underwater for an extended period of time. She drew back. Wrapped around her heart were confusion and anxiety.

"Wanna go upstairs?"

Looking deeply into his eyes, she said, "Okay."

The house belonged to a friend of Boone's whose parents were away for the weekend. Upstairs, they found an unoccupied room with a large bed, a TV set and an orange chair over by the window. Sophie went to use the bathroom and tried to catch her breath. The light was harsh in here. The sink was white, shiny as an eyeball.

She didn't understand the changes her body was going through, despite all the sex education classes she'd taken. Real life was somehow different than any book. She'd read somewhere that the average woman would sleep with twenty men before she got married, but Sophie refused to believe it. She'd never slept with a boy before and only wanted to sleep with one.

Back in the bedroom, Boone stood naked in front of the TV set, the bluish light playing over his skin like an aura. "I got the condom," he said.

She nodded and crossed the room.

"Can I undress you?" he asked thickly, and she let him unzip her jeans.

At first, it hurt, him going inside her; but then a space opened up, and she could feel his heartbeat overlapping hers. He rocked against her, his breath shooting out in hisses and grunts, and then Sophie started to shake and couldn't stop shaking. She squeezed her eyes against this unexpected pleasure.

Afterward, he lay behind her, tracing words on her bare back. She couldn't guess a single one.

"What're you thinking?" he said.

She shrugged, feeling calm and peaceful.

"You think your dad's a good guy, don't you?"

"What?" She turned to face him.

"You think all cops are good guys."

"What are you talking about?"

He withdrew into himself.

Shivering, she pulled the sheets up around her neck. There was a soreness between her legs that wouldn't go away. "Boone? What's the matter?"

"There are things I wish I could tell you, but I can't."

"What kind of things?"

"Forget it."

She stroked his cheek with her finger.

"We belong together, you and me."

"I know," she whispered, wrapping her arms around him and pressing her body close.

An hour later, Sophie was running across the yard toward her house. Moths swarmed around the porch bulb, and the air was thick with the scent of lilacs. The house was the same, but she was somehow different. Inside, she paused in the wide arched doorway to the living room, where her father sat reading on the sofa. He closed his book and looked at her.

"Hi, Dad," she said, mouth going dry. "I'm going to bed now. G'night."

"You weren't over Katlin's tonight," he said in a hostile monotone.

She could feel her shoulders sagging.

He stared at her an angry beat.

"Dad, I'm sorry."

"I called Katlin. She said you were with Boone Pritchett at some party. I won't tolerate deception, Sophie. You're better than that."

It was so quiet in here she could hear the white noise in each room. "It was just a party, Dad," she said. "No biggie."

"Just a party?"

Her laughter was false. The place between her legs still hurt, and her underpants were spotted with blood.

"You lied to me," he said, infuriated. "You snuck around behind my back. I've been sitting here listening to every car that drives past, thinking it's you. Hoping it's you." He stared at her. "Christ, are you drunk?"

She leaned against the wall. "A little . . . I'm just . . . I'm a little drunk. I had a beer."

He strode across the room. "That's it, young lady. You're grounded for a month."

Her thoughts grew like arms, arms with fists, thrashing, whaling away. "I hate you!" she cried.

"Every car that drives past, and I'm listening for the sirens," he said. "Don't you ever do this to me again."

"Do this to *you*?"

"You can't see him anymore. I forbid it."

"I hate you!"

"Fine. Hate me, I don't care. I'm not about to let you ruin your life."

"It's mine to ruin!" She ran upstairs and collapsed on her unmade bed, so heartbroken and exhausted she couldn't summon the energy to cry.

6

CHARLIE DROVE past strip malls and welding shops out into open countryside, where a chorus of crickets repeated its lulling refrain. He came to a fork in the road and threw the car into the turn, hitting a pothole so hard he almost sprained an ankle. These little county roads got practically no traffic. They weren't high-priority, so they got run-down and stayed run-down.

Boone lived with his parents on the bad side of town, where dire poverty had a tendency to turn family member against family member, where most of the calls they got were either domestic or drug-related. Charlie told himself to remain calm. Steady, steady. It was, after all, his fault. He'd raised too innocent a daughter. She didn't judge. She was open and honest and trusting. Nowhere near cynical enough. Boone Pritchett was as transparent as glass to everyone else but her. She'd been raised in rarefied air. *All his fault.*

Now he parked his car on the side of the road and got out. Beyond the barbed-wire fence with its No Entry sign was something too wild to be called a meadow. Amid the tall grass and flapping trash was Boone's wrecked pickup truck, a casino-pink accordion. Parked in the driveway behind it was the full-size rust-red pickup belonging to his dad. Charlie had pulled Eddie Pritchett over a number of times for various misdemeanors and DUIs.

Now he opened the creaking gate and crossed the wild, overgrown yard toward the one-story house, where he knocked on the door. "Police! Open up!"

The boy answered, something mocking and malicious going on behind his eyes. "What do you want?" he snarled.

Charlie crooked a finger. "Step outside."

"What for?"

"We need to talk."

"Are you arresting me?"

"Not yet."

Staring at him with fixed blue eyes, Boone said, "Then I don't have anything to say to you."

Charlie chopped his fist vertically into Boone's nose, and he dropped like a sack of grain. Grabbing the boy by his hooded sweatshirt, Charlie dragged him out the door and across the weed-choked lawn.

Boone howled and clutched his nose, blood leaking through his fingers. He stomped his feet in an effort to slow Charlie down, but that only deepened Charlie's resolve.

"Looks like you need more dancing lessons there, partner." Charlie stood him upright. They were illuminated by the sweep of passing headlights and a gossamer glow cast by the corner streetlamp. Bunching up the hoodie in his fists, Charlie said, "If you see my daughter again, you're a dead man."

The boy's teeth were flecked with blood. "So I'm not supposed to mess with you because you're some big bad dude? Throwing sucker punches? *Pfft* . . . get real."

Charlie grabbed him by the ears and snarled with perfect concentration: "This is real simple. You won't be seeing Sophie anymore. Got it?"

The boy's voice grew shrill. "What'd I ever do to you?"

"It's not what you did to me, you worthless jag-off. It's what you plan on doing to my daughter."

"I'm not gonna do anything to her, you pervert."

A big man loomed in the doorway, blotting out the light. "What the fuck is going on in my front yard?" Eddie Pritchett's voice had the town in it; you could tell he was used to addressing the world in a belligerent drawl.

"I'm talking to your son," Charlie said, sitting on his rage. "Stay back."

"You can't speak to a minor without the parent's consent," Eddie yelled from the doorway. His stringy hair looked like it should have leaves in it, and he tucked a few unruly strands behind his ears. He wore tight jeans, no shirt and a pair of fingerless gloves, and there were tattoos of skulls running up and down his body. "Either you arrest him, or get the hell off my property."

Charlie's eyes searched the inner recesses of Boone's narrow skull. After a moment's hesitation, he released him.

"Get your ass back inside, fool," Boone's father told him.

The wind riffled gently through the weeds as the boy retreated. Before stepping inside, he turned to Charlie and said, "I wouldn't hurt a hair on her head."

"I'm warning you." Charlie pointed his finger for emphasis. "Go anywhere near her again, and I'll come down on you like a ton of shit."

"Those are intimidation tactics," the big man said from the doorway. "You'll be hearing from our lawyer!"

"Shut up."

"Police brutality! We're gonna sue!"

"Yeah, yeah," Charlie muttered. "You got off light, you mutt."

7

THE BALL of Charlie's thumb itched and his eyelids drooped sleepily. The caffeine wasn't doing it for him anymore. Maybe if he injected it? He had a way of posing so that no one would suspect he was drifting off to sleep. He looked down at the paperwork on his desktop, one hand covering his forehead as if he were deep in thought. That way, he could close his eyes and nod off, just as long as he didn't collapse in a heap on his desk.

"Knock, knock."

Charlie jolted upright.

"You asleep at the switch again?" Mike asked with a laugh.

"Cut me some slack, Mike. I get less rest than a shark."

"Join the club. So guess which song was playing on Toby Lake's Walkman?"

Charlie shook his head.

" 'I'm on Fire' by Bruce Springsteen."

He made a gesture of dismissal, but it disturbed him deeply. "Coincidence," he said. Outside his office window, heat shimmered off the asphalt, and the cottonwoods released a large flock of birds into the clear blue sky. "What's the word on Lester?"

"We put out a BOLO on the Blazer. We've searched the area extensively around his house. We've shown his picture around the county and interviewed over a hundred friends and relatives. Still no clue as to his whereabouts."

"He must be out there somewhere."

"Now what do we do?"

Charlie gave a grunt of annoyance. They were overwhelmed with routine June stuff—sexual assaults, DUIs, burglaries, drug killings and now this. Lester had gone missing. It bothered him that the rest of the world wouldn't cooperate and do nothing while they tried to solve their most important case. "What about the phone records?" he asked.

"Nick's still working on it. Credit cards, too."

"Okay. Let's wait and see what he comes up with." He wanted the familiar pattern of time back. A beer, a newspaper, his feet up on the coffee table. What a luxury that would be. "Is that Toby Lake's autopsy report?"

"Injuries fit the pattern." Mike took a seat and opened the file folder on his lap. "Blunt trauma to the head, defensive lacerations to both arms, impalement with a three-foot fence post . . ."

Charlie listened with a tight expectancy.

"Three smooth glove prints," Mike went on. "No blood besides the victim's ABO. No semen. No toolmark evidence on either door. Just like a goddamn rerun."

"Any trace?"

"We're in luck." He plucked out a page. "They found some microscopic dots on the victim's socks and pant cuffs."

"Microscopic dots?"

"A common plastic. Polyvinyl chloride, used in numerous products, from garden hoses to various household items. It says here, yellow microscopic dots."

Charlie's back stiffened. "Tiny yellow specks?"

Mike shrugged. "Says here, dots."

"Around the ankles?"

"Socks and pant cuffs."

The casters of Charlie's chair squealed across the carpet as he reached for his phone. "Hunter? Get me the Tulsa P.D."

8

Sᴇʀɢᴇᴀɴᴛ Dᴡɪɢʜᴛ D. Harbuck of the Tulsa Police Department's investigative unit had once been Charlie's beat partner back in the bad old days. Since the Debris Killer case was multijurisdictional, they'd joined forces and were about to issue an arrest warrant together. Charlie's friend D.D. was an order-loving man. He kept his uniform pristine and his thoughts pure. "I hope they fry his ass," he told Charlie as they took a hard right into Jonah Gustafson's driveway. "I'll throw the switch myself, I don't shiv-a-git. I've got no more patience for the slimy bottom of life's barrel."

A radio car pulled up behind them, and a pair of officers got out with their weapons drawn.

"You two go around back," Harbuck told his men.

The suspect's white van was parked in front of the house. Charlie patted his breast pocket where the arrest warrant was, then dropped his .38 down against his trouser leg, shielding it from view. He followed the sergeant up the rough porch steps, and Harbuck thumped on the door with his fist.

"Police, open up!" He didn't wait for an answer, just

kicked the door open and led the way inside with cocky vigor.

Sunlight poured in through the generous living room windows, painting everything a golden Vermeer hue. Harbuck moved swiftly down the hallway, making broad, dangerous sweeps with his .38 snub-nose. "Police! We've got you surrounded!"

Charlie's weapon felt as cold as fog in his hands. He trailed Harbuck into the kitchen, where the teakettle was screaming and the other officers had the suspect surrounded.

Jonah Gustafson stood in front of the stove with his arms raised, a chipped Grateful Dead coffee mug clutched in one hand. "What the fuck?" he said, dumbfounded.

"How y'all doin' this afternoon?" Harbuck holstered his weapon and twisted Jonah's arms around behind his back. "You're under arrest. Will somebody turn off the teakettle, please?"

One of his men reached for the stove.

"What am I being charged with?" Jonah asked with wide, annoyed eyes.

"Show him the warrant."

Charlie dropped the target copy on the kitchen table, then removed the arrestee's greasy "Night Train" baseball cap. Jonah was extremely thin and had medium-length brown hair. *Brown hair, Caucasian.* Charlie conducted a pat-down search and found cash dispersed throughout his pockets, an electronic pager and an Opus X Pyramid cigar from the Dominican Republic.

"You like this brand?" Harbuck said, pocketing the cigar.

"What the hell am I being arrested for?" Jonah cried. "You haven't even told me yet."

"A boy was killed on June ninth," Charlie said. "In Wolf Pass, Texas. We found trace evidence linking you to the crime scene."

"Me?" He looked deeply shaken.

"That yellow stuff on your gym bag."

"Yellow stuff? What yellow stuff?"

"It's called PVC. Polyvinyl chloride, a common household plastic. The state lab came up with a match for the trace. We found the same material on the victim's socks and ankles from where the body was dragged."

"Wait a minute, wait a minute. June ninth? I was home all day." His brown hair was carefully parted down the middle and oiled flat, and he made a tremendous effort to come across as soft-spoken and cooperative.

"Can anybody corroborate your story?"

Jonah shook his head. "Look, I just wanna get my kids back. I've enrolled in a twelve-step program. I'm cleaning up my act . . . I'm cooperating here."

"You think you're pretty smart, don't you?" Harbuck said.

"No," Jonah admitted. "I'm a dumb motherfucker." His face looked like it was about to hatch. "Look, I didn't kill nobody . . . C'mon, guys, this is ridiculous!"

"That's funny, because you're under arrest for first-degree murder." Harbuck slapped on the handcuffs, ratcheting down tight.

Jonah squeezed his eyes shut. "Oh man . . . okay, look. I used to own a pair of yellow work gloves," he said. "They were pretty old. White fabric . . . well, they aren't so white anymore . . . with yellow plastic palms. But the plastic dried out and started to flake off, okay? I guess some of it must've come off on my gym bag. But I swear to God . . . I lost those stupid gloves months ago."

"Lost them?" Charlie repeated.

"Yeah, two or three months ago, I swear to God. You know what? Fuck it. I wanna talk to my lawyer."

Harbuck thrust his gnarled finger in Jonah's face. "You piece of shit. Come out in the backyard with me."

"That's right, give me some excuse to sue the city!"

That was it; it was over. They searched the premises and gathered up the evidence—white powder residue on a triple beam scale, empty plastic Baggies, over a thousand in cash. Charlie rummaged through the closets and bureau drawers, looking for a blue-black item of clothing, but nothing fit the description. There were no detectable bloodstains inside the house. No green carpet fibers. The Chevy's floor pads were maroon. They looked for the white gloves with the yellow palms, but couldn't find those, either. Jonah wore size eleven sneakers, both Nike and Adidas. They bagged those. They bagged the woodworking equipment. They bagged as much as they could, then they hauled the suspect outside and negotiated him into the cage car.

Jonah started to rock back and forth inside the cage as if his brains were on fire. "This is bogus! I didn't kill nobody!"

Harbuck popped the car into neutral and swung around. "Shut the hell up."

"I ain't no freaking murderer!" he screamed, the veins in his neck pumped up with blood. "You mindless shitbirds! Go ahead, take me downtown and arrest me! Ruin my whole life!"

Charlie's cell phone rang. "Hello?"

"Chief?" It was Mike, shouting in his ear through a bad connection. "They found Lester's vehicle . . ."

9

TWENTY MILES west of the Oklahoma-Texas border, a state trooper found Lester Deere's bruise-colored Chevy Blazer parked behind an abandoned farmhouse, its windows broken down to the frames, its cut-stone walls crumbling to dust. Charlie navigated the grasslands toward the site, riding over a ridge and then edging back down, his police car tilting precariously before the front wheels slammed into a cattle trail. He parked and got out, then stood scanning the horizon. Vaporous cirrus clouds threw their soft shadows across the grasslands—lacy shadows moving swiftly over swell after swell of distant plains. The wind was so hot it felt like the gust from a blow-dryer. This land looked the way it always had, the way the buffalo and the rain and the wind had made it look—worn to a polished smoothness, like a stone at the bottom of a riverbed. You could drive a locomotive through the loneliness.

Now Mike came wading through the tall grass toward him. "I checked the immediate vicinity, boss. No extraneous tire tracks or footprints. You can see where he pulled off the road and parked in the weeds, but then the trail goes cold."

"Let's check it out."

They descended a short rise together, then climbed again, flights of grasshoppers escaping from the weeds at their feet. They stepped gingerly down another incline before stumbling out onto a dirt road, where tangled vines of wild grape grew alongside the soft shoulders. Together they studied the tire tracks leading up to the site and found Lester's Blazer angle-parked behind an ancient ruin, crests of bleached grass swelling against the crumbling foundation.

"No body damage," Charlie said as they circled the vehicle together. "Doors unlocked. Keys are still in the ignition."

"Which means he can't be far, right?" Mike cupped his hands over the window. "Trip odometer's set at three-thirteen."

"It's only a hundred miles from here to Promise."

"No visible bloodstains on the seats or floor."

Charlie stepped back, his uniform pants flapping around his ankles in the stiff breeze, and scanned the sagebrush ridges and distant rock outcroppings. He could almost picture dinosaurs wading through the ancient marshlands and getting stuck in the mud, their bones gradually turning to rock over millions of years. This land had originally taken its shape from the movement of the sea—the stacked trapezoid hills, the rolling restless prairie. Modern fossil hunters still found plenty of sea creatures trapped in the limestone—brachiopods and trilobites, the grain-sized fusulinids.

Now Charlie caught sight of a circling bird. In order to fool their prey, the local hawks had evolved to look like vultures, except that a vulture's legs were gray, not yellow. Squinting hard, he watched the gray-legged bird swoop down and disappear behind a ridge. *Vultures.*

He took off in a dead run, grass tassels hitting his kneecaps, and tried not to acknowledge the uncomfortable swelling in his gut that knew before he did what this meant. He couldn't get enough oxygen into his lungs as he stopped at the crumbling edge of the cliffside and looked down at the sun-baked ground below.

"What is it?" Mike called after him.

Charlie felt a visceral fear in his gut. Two corpses lay facedown in the grass below. He scrambled down the slope, toes digging into the soft dirt, then slid the rest of the way, kicking up rocks and dust. He stumbled out into the clearing, where the vulture was busy plucking at the bloody pulp of a head.

"Git!" He waved his hands, and the vulture reluctantly hopped off the carcass and flew away, stirring the nearby grass with its wingbeats.

Mike stood above him on the cliff. Tight-lipped. Eyes grim. "Is that Lester?"

Charlie felt as if he'd been hit by a soft train. He knelt down next to the blond-haired corpse, the foul air around it smelling faintly of cordite. The back of the victim's head was matted with blood and brain matter from where a bullet had plowed through, and a service revolver lay in the dirt next to his right hand. Nike sneakers, black leather belt, alligator shirt tucked into the waistband of a pair of brand-new-looking jeans. The Eagleton watch was still ticking. Charlie could feel his skull constricting around his brain, squeezing it like a grapefruit. With a shaky breath, he rolled the body over.

The sight of Lester Deere's ruined face sent the horizon careening for a moment. Rigor mortis had come and gone; the flies had laid their eggs. *Dead a few days, at least.* He wiped his hand nervously across his mouth and tried not to gag, while a raw space opened up inside of him. He let the body fall gently back to its original position, then frisked the corpse for ID. He found Lester's wallet in his back pocket, license and credit cards accounted for.

Mike stumbled down the incline toward him, kicking up puffs of Texas dust, then stooped to retrieve a dirty bill from the ground. He opened it up. "Look a that. A hundred-dollar bill."

A knot of nausea rose in Charlie's throat as he loosened his tie, then turned to gaze glassy-eyed into the distance. The prairie stretched for miles around them, with just an occasional set of tractor tires scoring the earth. He could see other bills scattered about, fluttering in the wind. A scissor-tailed flycatcher trilled nearby, and high overhead, the vulture worked its wings to catch the next gust of wind.

Charlie got a dreamy, suffocating feeling as he went to roll the other body over.

"Who's that?" Mike asked.

"Jake Wheaton." He stared down at the boy with a hooded expression. Jake's face was fiercely doll-like, and he wore a T-shirt that said "Don't Ask Me 4 Shit." There was blood spiked across it. His eyes were open and his hands were fisted shut due to cadaveric spasming.

Charlie could feel the familiar tightening of his facial muscles, a physical reaction that occurred whenever he got upset or excited, blood rushing to the place where the scarring was heaviest from his undershirt catching fire thirty years ago. "Let's cordon off the site and start a dialogue with the local law."

"You think they killed each other over the money?" Mike asked, picking up hundred-dollar bills.

"I don't know what the fuck I think anymore," Charlie said, prairie dust gritting between his teeth.

10

LATER THAT day, Charlie found himself standing in the front hallway of his father's house and caught sight of his reflection in the marbled mirror. Charlie's scars itched. His brain itched from too much exhausted speculation. He used to think that he looked like a freak and tried to convince himself that the "real" him lived somewhere underneath the deformity. Underneath the melted-cheese skin.

The house was empty. His father was out working the back fields. Charlie opened the hallway closet and hunted through the coats and jackets, sliding the hangers from one end of the pole to the other. *No peacoat. No lucky jacket.*

He closed the door and could hear the twittering of countless birds. The late afternoon threw a leafy pattern of sunlight across the far wall. He took the stairs to the second floor and ducked into his father's room, a forbidden place. So still. His gaze slid over toiletries on the bureau top, slippers underneath the bed, a water glass on the bedside table for his father's false teeth.

False teeth. Replacement teeth.

Charlie let it drop. They had their killer. Jonah Gustafson's bail hearing was set for tomorrow. His bail would be high. He'd stay in jail. Charlie could relax. They had their man. Except that . . . he'd been trained never to lock in on a suspect. *Turn over any rock, and you'll find a whole network of squiggling, pulsating life underneath. Secret life . . . an underworld.*

He poked through his father's closet—shirts, pants, a tie rack with a dozen dark-colored ties he never wore anymore. The leather belt with its metal buckle. He could taste the tang of his own panic; he hadn't seen that belt in many years, but he could still feel its bite.

No peacoat. No lucky jacket.

He faced the room again and realized the peacoat was probably out in his father's truck, which was parked in front of the barn, where the old man kept his woodworking tools. The muscles of Charlie's back twitched. He should go out there and look around, but he was afraid. The thought of his father catching him made him feel seven years old again.

He noticed the dusty steamer trunk at the foot of the bed, where all the winter clothes were stored. He opened the trunk and mauled through stacks of sweaters and mittens and scarves, eyes tearing from the scent of mothballs. Old army blankets. *No peacoat.*

There was a rumpled paper bag at the bottom of the trunk. Curious, he opened it up. Inside were dozens of withered balloons—red, green, blue, yellow. That was odd. Why would his father keep a bag of withered balloons? It didn't make any sense.

He dropped the bag back and closed the lid, then heard a sound and cocked his head. Barely able to breathe.

His father downstairs, walking around inside the

house. The floorboards creaking under his feet. Charlie pinched his mouth shut. How would he explain his presence here?

The refrigerator door opened and shut.

The footsteps retreated.

Ka-thunk. The back door slammed shut.

Charlie caught his breath and headed for the stairs, heart thundering in his ears as he practically tripped over himself getting the hell out of there.

11

THE TWO corpses were down in the morgue, packed in dry ice. "We found high levels of ethyl alcohol in their blood and vitreous," Duff said, "indicating that they were both drunk when they shot each other."

Charlie looked up. "You know this for a fact?"

"Both victims' fingerprints were on the gun. The nitric acid washings on their hands tested positive." Duff examined the interior of Lester's scalp, the exposed cranium fractured like an egg. "Lester shot Jake twice in the stomach while they struggled for the gun. Then Jake grabbed the gun away and shot Lester once in the head. The mouth is the most effective way to end it. Powder burns on the tongue. Gunshot residue is fan-shaped."

Trying not to picture it too vividly in his mind's eye, Charlie leaned against the sink and folded his arms across his chest. Jake's body was laid out on the autopsy table next to Lester's, two round neat holes in his abdomen, a gray ring around each one. The ragged exit wounds were in back, where profuse bleeding had occurred. "What's your TOD estimate?"

"There's greenish discoloration of the lower quadrants

of the abdomen, swelling of the face, marbling. I'd guess he was three days dead when you found him. Same with the boy."

Charlie put down the death certificates. "So Lester shot Jake first, then Jake shot and killed Lester . . . and then Jake died of his own injuries shortly afterwards?"

"Due to rapid blood loss, yes." After removing the rubbery brain, Duff stripped the dura away from the cranial cavity and examined the fractured interior of the skull, tracking the bullet's trajectory. "Skull is shattered where the bullet entered here," he said, pointing with his scalpel, "creating projectiles of bone fragments which caused additional tissue destruction. The exit wound is large and ragged at the back of the head, where all this impacted tissue pushed its way through. How many bullet casings did you find?"

"Four."

"All from Lester's service weapon?"

Charlie nodded.

"Two shots to the stomach, one to the head and one misfire." Duff smoothed Lester's face back up. "Defense wounds to the body. Bite marks on the arm. The shots came from very close range. There's blood and tissue spatter on Jake's hands." Duff paused to rub his neck. "There's no doubt in my mind, Charlie. These two fools killed one another."

"We found over fifteen hundred dollars scattered nearby, along with the pot and cocaine in Lester's truck." Charlie pinched the bridge of his nose. "Am I blind? One of my officers is dealing drugs right underneath my nose, and I don't see it?"

"Relax." Duff peeled off his gloves and snapped them into the trash. "Nobody has that much power, Charlie."

An old-time band, Jimmy Dorsey, was playing on the radio. If you bumped into Duff outside the morgue, you'd notice right away that he reeked of formaldehyde, the sour smell of death clinging to him like cheap cigar smoke.

"Jenna Pepper was involved. And Boone Pritchett. I've been trying to locate him all morning." He had warned Sophie repeatedly to stay away from Boone, and it worried him now that he hadn't stated it clearly enough.

Duff slipped a sheet over Lester's body and started to carefully stack his pathologist's tools. "Looks like you've solved two big cases within the last forty-eight hours, Charlie. Congratulations."

His indignation rose at Duff's missing the whole point. He should've known about Lester. He should've been able to prevent this fiasco. Lester had wanted to talk to him, but all Charlie could think about was proper procedure—lawyers, polygraphs, alibis. Stroking his jaw, he gazed off into some middle distance.

"Charlie?"

"Hm?"

"Jonah Gustafson. The Debris Killer."

"Oh. Yeah."

Duff crossed his arms. "What's eating you?"

He shrugged. "Just a hunch."

"C'mon. Spill it."

"We couldn't find the gloves anywhere. Gustafson claims he lost them months ago."

"Is he credible?"

Charlie shook his head. "Some of these guys have been lying their whole lives. It's hard to tell."

Yellow dots, blue-black fibers, black rabbit fur, a single green carpet fiber, size ten to eleven shoe. Bits and pieces of evidence lay on top of one another in his mind, forming a confusing grid. He sucked in his next breath. "I dunno, Duff. Maybe I'm just tired."

The older man tapped the table lightly with his knuckles. "Follow your nose, Charlie."

"My nose? My nose tells me we have an overabundance of trace. Yellow dots, blue-black wool fibers, rabbit fur, unknown hairs, a single green carpet fiber . . ."

Duff nodded. "And?"

"And it doesn't add up. The perp knows enough about crime scene procedure to realize we'd find those microscopic yellow dots, right? His methodology is meticulous. If Gustafson's guilty, then why the slipup?"

"The perp does seem awfully careful not to leave any trace behind. He wears gloves, mops up his own footprints . . ."

"So I'm thinking . . . what if he stole Gustafson's gloves in order to implicate him and confuse us? I mean, how hard would it be to steal from a storm-chaser? There are plenty of places these guys hang out . . . truck stops, diners, motels. How hard would it be to swipe a pair of yellow work gloves? He steals the incriminating evidence and plants it later on at the scene. What if Gustafson's telling us the truth, Duff? What if he's innocent?"

In the silence of the morgue, Charlie could hear Duff's breath whistling through his nose like the wind through the witchgrass. "Remember Locard's principle?" Duff said.

"Every contact leaves a trace. Nobody, no matter how clever he thinks he is, can eliminate every last bit of trace from his person."

"So the criminal will always leave something of himself behind at a crime scene, and take something with him. It's up to you to discover which trace is significant."

"The trace that was left behind by accident?" Charlie said.

"Exactly."

White hair. Blue-black wool fibers. His father?

The medical examiner's face softened imperceptibly. "You know what, Charlie? You should lighten up," he said. "Go home and hug your daughter."

He swallowed his bitter confusion.

"Go on." Duff turned out the overhead light. "Don't argue with me."

Charlie swiped his jacket off the back of the chair. "What about you, Duff? Where're you going?"

"Home to blow bubbles for my cat."

12

Sophie WAS upstairs in her room, doing her homework. She sat cross-legged on her neatly made bed and chewed on the nub of a pencil.

"Hey, honey," Charlie said from the doorway.

"Hi," she answered without looking up. Her face was serious and intent, and he could tell by the set of her mouth that she was carrying a long-term grudge against him.

"What're you doing?"

"Studying."

"Studying what?"

"I have a history test."

"How'd you do on that English paper?"

"Good."

"Yeah?"

"I got an A."

"Great. Good for you." He tried to see what she was reading. "So you've got a test tomorrow?"

"Mm."

Her socks were thick and ugly pink, the same color as her sweatshirt. He glanced around the room. A clutch of teddy bears conspired together in a forgotten corner, their fur rubbed off in places from a child's possessive fondling. Computer, TV, CD player. Kids never had to leave their rooms nowadays.

"Everything else okay?" he asked.

She wiggled her foot impatiently. "What do you want?"

"Gee, I dunno. Do you want to stop being mad at me?"

She shot him a withering glance. So like her mother. Down to the molecules.

"It's okay to forgive people, you know," he said.

"Willa called three times. I let the machine pick up. Is your cell phone broken?"

He patted his pockets. "Forgot where I left it."

An indignant energy animated her limbs, her arms flopping lightly with exasperation. "Don't you ever check your messages? You're worse than Grandpa, for Pete's sake."

"I've been busting my butt lately, in case you hadn't noticed. What'd she say?"

"What am I, your phone maid now?"

"I thought you had forgiven me."

She stared at him with unforgiving eyes. "Don't you see how mature I'm being? I'm supporting *your* choices, even though you're not supporting mine."

"Listen." He softened his tone. "Promise me you won't see Boone anymore."

"Dad! That is so unfair!"

"This isn't about fairness, okay? I can't be fair when it comes to you."

"Boone had nothing to do with any of that stuff."

"You have to trust me, Sophie."

She rolled her eyes. "Awesome vote of confidence, Dad."

"I have all the confidence in the world in you."

She looked at him obstinately. "Are you going to let Willa drift out of your life, too? Go call her back." She picked up her book, anger simmering in the corners of her face.

He lingered in the doorway, thinking he'd blown it again. That he'd only escalated the hurt between them.

"Stop lurking," she said.

"Open or closed?"

"Closed."

He shut her bedroom door and went downstairs to listen to Willa's three messages.

Half an hour later, Charlie foolishly blew a stop sign, then drummed his hands on the wheel through every traffic light, mentally urging the reds to turn green. The deep night sky loomed overhead like a sheet of black ice, with just the glint of a moon wrapped in mist. He shot through the heart of town, then took a left down an unlit country road, where scattered fireflies winked in the darkness.

He pulled into the circular driveway at the end of the street, then hesitated a moment while the pale moon slipped behind a thin cloud layer. He got out, loosened his tie and stared at the peach-colored house with the mint-green trim, at the flower beds brimming with color. Pansies, tulips, wild iris.

"Hello," she said, opening the screen door. She wore a front-button Hanes undershirt, sweatpants and two-dollar shower shoes. There was a sneaky strength to the set of her mouth. "You're an expert in avoidance, you know."

He slipped his arms around her waist and kissed her. He held on tight, glad to be back to the complicated reality of her. "I missed you," he said.

Two cats sprang over the railing and made braiding turns around her ankles.

"My fan club," she said. "All two of them."

Moths fluttered into the porch bulb, and the cats begged for attention.

"I'm the world's biggest jerk," he said.

"You want something? Beer? Iced tea?" She squeezed his hand and laughed. "I don't know what cops like."

"I like you."

She grinned. "Let's sit outside. Too many books in there."

"Books?"

"A whole lotta books and no place to put them."

They sat in the creaking love seat on the back porch and listened to the bullfrogs fluting down by the water—a stream or a creek. The sky momentarily cleared, and whole constellations of stars opened up like flowers above their heads. Charlie inhaled the haunting smell of the earth and the grass, then stared at the flexible pink curves of her mouth. She smelled faintly of crushed sage rose. Her hands were a delicate mystery.

"Does this hurt?" she whispered, touching his scarred arm.

"No."

She ran her finger up the left side of his neck. "How many surgeries have you had?"

"I don't remember. Lots."

She gave a sympathetic shiver.

"They threw in a chin implant."

Her laughter was lovely, her mouth so soft and sweet that he just had to kiss it. With desperate longing, he sank to his knees and wrapped his arms around her thighs and buried his head in her lap. Forgiven.

13

THE FOLLOWING day, Charlie shuffled his feet restlessly over the carpet and stared at the photograph on his desktop—a picture of his father's gray Loadmaster pickup truck speeding past the damage site. It was one of those humid, overcast days where your hair kept sticking to the back of your neck and you had a rubbery grip on things. He felt hunched. Tense. This was the question: After the old man quit drinking thirty years ago, where had he placed all his pent-up rage?

Mike came to the doorway. "About the evidence we collected from Lester's house," he said. "Cocaine residue, an unregistered gun. We're tracking his whereabouts this past month, reviewing phone records and ATM withdrawals ... Before April fifteenth, he made numerous calls to Jenna Pepper. After April fifteenth, he called Jake Wheaton and Boone Pritchett on several occasions."

Charlie tugged on his lower lip. "We've gotta find Pritchett."

Mike nodded. "So I'm assuming Lester got his drugs from local dealers in exchange for his silence. Then Jake and Boone distributed it throughout the high school." He shifted uncomfortably in the doorway. "I would've trusted Lester with my life. Shows you just how much I know."

Charlie nodded miserably. "What d'you got there?"

Mike tapped the folder in his hand. "They found some unaccounted-for tire impressions in the Lakes' driveway and sent them to the state lab for analysis. Sheriff Dorsey just sent us the results. They've narrowed it down to a full-size pickup truck riding on a set of brand-new Michelin tires."

Charlie took a careful breath. His father drove a full-size pickup truck. He was a Michelin kind of guy. He'd just purchased a brand-new set of tires. A pixel of anxiety formed in the pit of his stomach. "That would eliminate Gustafson," he said.

Mike glanced up.

"Gustafson drives a van . . . riding on a set of Goodyear tires." A cold certainty rose in his gut. "What if he's telling the truth, Mike? What if the Debris Killer stole Gustafson's gloves and planted the evidence just to throw us off?"

Mike paused a beat, then said, "Anything's possible."

His shoulders sagged. He rubbed his tired eyes. "My father owns a full-size **pic**kup truck," he said, holding up the blurred shot. "He **just** bought a set of Michelin tires."

Mike's nostrils quivered. "Yeah? So?"

"We were poor as dirt when I was growing up. Mama was a real pack rat. Our house was so knee-deep in garbage even the social workers were afraid to come in. The fire marshal figured that the fire started down in the basement, where all the rags and newspapers and kerosene lanterns were . . ."

Mike was stopped like a clock.

"But I've been thinking . . . what if it wasn't an accident? What if my father started the fire?"

"This is just mental exhaustion talking, Chief."

"He wears a peacoat every chase season. Blue-black wool. He's right-handed. He's a storm-chaser." He slumped way down on his spine. "There's a history of violence, Mike. He wears a size eleven shoe, that's in the ballpark. A medium-length white hair was found at the Rideout residence. Those teeth . . . did you know my father wore dentures?"

"Listen, Chief, it's a sad fact." Mike stood solid and unsmiling in the doorway. "Your dad was a real motherfucker. He may even have done something criminal in the past, but you don't want to overreact."

The wind picked up, toying with the miniblinds. It was going to rain this afternoon and spoil Lester's funeral.

"He keeps a bunch of woodworking tools out in the barn," Charlie went on, looking down at the blurred shot of the Loadmaster. "If you only knew what I know about him . . ."

Mike couldn't mask his skepticism. "Listen, it should be easy enough to verify. We'll compare the tire treads, see if they match up. We can compare hairs and fibers, too. Relax, boss. It won't be the first time we barked up the wrong tree."

"Yeah," Charlie said. "A crazy thought."

"You should talk to him, though. Sounds like you need to get a few things off your chest."

Charlie checked his watch. "Funeral's in one hour," he said. "We'd better get moving."

14

SEVERAL HUNDRED people showed up for Lester Deere's funeral. His parents were pillars of the community, and nobody wanted to believe the worst about their son just yet. After the eulogy, a long train of cars drove across town to the cemetery, where Charlie and his father followed the other mourners through the graveyard. Isaac wore an ash-gray Stetson and a shapeless brown raincoat over his cheap black suit. "When I die, Charlie, feel free to dispense with the formalities and just scatter my ashes into the eye of a storm."

"You don't want a funeral, Pop?"

Scowling, he looked around the cemetery at the other mourners. "*Pfft.* I can do without all the good intentions and bad hairdos."

A black king snake was coiled on one of the gravestones, enjoying the last few rays of afternoon light before the sun slipped behind the clouds. It was starting to look serious out, the cumulonimbus piled along the horizon for miles, a bilious force rolling in from the southwest.

Charlie removed his hat and let the wind play with his thinning hair. "We need to talk, Pop."

"Talk?" His father eyed him skeptically. "What about?"

"A few things that need clarifying."

The old man was sucking on something—a cough drop or a piece of hard candy—holding it in his mouth like a sour secret. "I've got this theory about you," he said. "Wanna hear it?"

Here it comes. "It's a free country."

"Remember that snot-nosed kid who used to torment you all the time?" Isaac said. "All those names he called you? Burned-All-Over Grover, Charbroiled Charlie . . . I wanted to shoot the little redneck son of a bitch."

It was a startling admission coming from him, the closest thing to warmth Charlie had felt in years. He could smell the sulfur in the oncoming storm. Lightning flared, and an indigo cumulus tower emitted a low rumble of thunder.

"My theory goes like this. You've been waiting your entire life to get even." He tapped Charlie's chest with hostile insistence. "Now's your chance to get even for all those years of torment . . . all those years of feeling so out of control. Look at you, Charlie, you're the goddamn chief of police. As the guy in charge, you get to be the moral arbiter of the whole damn town. You get to push people around, throw people in jail, harass anybody you want to . . . including your old man."

Charlie shoved his hands angrily in his pockets. "And why would I harass you, Pop?"

His leathery face caught the last burnished rays of light before the sun disappeared permanently behind the clouds. "For things I may or may not have done in the past."

"Like what? Like beating Mama senseless?"

"I'm no monster, Charlie. Don't make me out to be one." He turned his cold, wet eyes toward the crowd. "You have no idea what your mother and I went through. You don't even have a clue . . ."

Years of anger rippled through him. Muscle memory. A violent image unfurled before his mind's eye with sickening clarity—his father's spit-flecked face and that shriek of a mouth. "Service is starting," he said flatly.

They joined the other mourners at the grave site. Sam Deere wore a lively tie and a bitter smile; Tammy Deere looked so outraged, so heartbroken, Charlie wanted to fold her in his arms like a wounded bird.

"We gather in this restful place to honor a good cop and a loving son," Reverend Cavenaugh began. "Lester Deere walked like a man, and we were all proud of him . . ."

The clouds broke just then, and dozens of black umbrellas mushroomed in the rain. Fifteen minutes later, after they'd lowered the casket into the ground and said their final farewells, Lester's parents approached Charlie with bruised faces, their eyebrows arcing out in bewilderment. He groped for something inspiring to say, all the tired old clichés exploding inside his head at once. Lester's favorite topic had always been himself, and yet, right when he needed it the most, Charlie couldn't dredge up a single anecdote upon which to base a few consoling words. "We were proud of him," he said, taking their hands. "He was a good cop and a good friend."

"You'll clear him of these charges, won't you, Chief?"

He uttered a few false words of consolation, and they accepted these crumbs with immense gratitude, which was more than Charlie deserved. He walked away, sick of himself. Sick and tired of the heartache. Grief flattened you like a freight train, and sometimes the only answer was a tall bottle and a short glass. He knew from experience that, just as the pain was about to heal over, something else would come along and trigger another memory—the rainwater smell of your mother's hair, a stranger's hiccup reminding you of your baby sister's laughter—and the bounce would leak right out of your step again.

The air was dripping with rain. He took off his hat, lifted his face to the sky and let the rain come down on him. He could feel himself drifting momentarily out of his own skin . . . but then he heard the chirp of rubber on asphalt and turned in time to see the back of his father's Loadmaster pickup truck disappearing into the mist.

Charlie jogged across the ruddy, blooming clover, past an uprooted flower bed and into the cemetery parking lot, where he hopped into the only undercover car the department owned—a squeezed-lime Chevy Cavalier—and put it into gear. He shot out of the lot after the old man, dogging those cardinal-red taillights through the driving rain. He caught up with the Loadmaster on a long ribbon of blacktop, windshield wipers flapping furiously. This was crazy. *His father, guilty of murder?* Absurd. Raindrops flurried out of the mist like a thousand doubts. Isaac had been a bad man once, yes; but hadn't he repented? Hadn't he suffered? Charlie was wrong to doubt him. Wrong to suspect him of anything worse than petty theft. *The watch.* Then again, what better alibi than that you were at the scene of the crime that day, along with dozens of other storm-chasers? And what better way to avoid your son's questions than to put him on the defensive? *I have this theory about you . . .*

The road dipped gently, then climbed in imperceptible increments past rolling green fields of grazing Angus into the vast open areas south of town, where so little appeared to exist. Was his father right? Was his entire career about getting even? Why hadn't he stayed in Tulsa? Why join the police force in the first place? *Because he wanted to find out the truth . . . the truth about what'd happened that night . . . the night of the fire . . . wondering his whole life . . . burying his doubts year after year . . .*

Charlie chased the wink of taillights, careful to keep at least thirty yards between himself and his father at all times in order to avoid detection. He sped past feedstores and tractor agencies, his deepest fears mounting as he spotted an oily black trash bag in the back of the flatbed. As the trash bag fluttered in the wind, he couldn't help thinking about the killer's M.O. He'd brought the pieces of flying debris with him to each of the crime scenes— chair legs, balusters, splintered fence struts. How? In a trash bag in the back of his pickup truck?

The Loadmaster slowed to a crawl, then turned down a winding road leading to the town dump. Charlie could feel the heat of his body as he tapped his foot on the brakes and followed suit. They passed a chain-link fence, beyond which mounds of ash grew at a glacial pace on either side of the road, and the air grew fetid with the smell of rotting fruit and smoldering furniture. They came to a large clearing, where the Loadmaster pulled over and parked with a squeak of rubber. Charlie watched from a safe distance as his father got out of the truck, snagged the trash bag, carried it down an embankment and disappeared from view.

He cut the engine and got out. A cold stinging rain hit him in the face and streaked down his neck. He grabbed a rain slicker from the backseat and headed after Isaac, the heat of his body steaming off his clothes. Beyond the low smoldering hills, he could see the wheat fields pitching in the wind. The wheat moved like water, rumpling and crumpling before each great marching sheet of rain.

A haze of burning rubbish stung his eyes as he approached the truck. A cursory glance revealed nothing. The fenders and hood were peppered with hail dents; the Michelin tires were brand-new. A stack of wet newspapers sagged against a plastic picnic cooler in the back of the flatbed beside a toolbox and a rusty shovel. Charlie had no legal authority to search the truck, since his reasons fell short of the legal requirements of probable cause. Without a search-and-seizure warrant, you couldn't search a vehicle or take anything from it without the owner's consent. Motor vehicle searches traditionally caused serious problems in court, so you had to limit your search to whatever you could see through a window.

There was nothing in the front seat but storm-chaser gear. No bloodstains, wipe marks or weapons, as far as he could tell. A bolt of lightning crashed and burned away the shadows as he crested the embankment and looked down at the top of his father's Stetson. The old man seemed to hesitate a moment before he dropped the trash bag down the sloping hillside. Charlie watched as the oily black bag tumbled down the incline, then came to a sluggish halt, trapped in the legs of an old piano stool. Now that it was officially abandoned property, anybody could pick it up and look through it.

"Dad?"

His father turned with great surprise.

"What's in the bag?"

The old man squinted up at him, rain spattering his face and making him blink. "None of your damn business!"

"Pop?" Charlie's eyes narrowed as he proceeded down the slippery hillside. "I don't need a warrant to look in the bag."

"What'd you do," he barked, *"follow me here?"*

15

CHARLIE'S ACCELERATING heart rate primed his body to the peak of alertness as he trekked down the slope, slipping over potato peelings and coffee grounds and ignoring the dark thoughts crawling around inside his skull. "What's in the bag?" he repeated.

"None of your damn business."

"Step aside, Pop."

His father's eyes grew raw and wild. "You go to hell!"

Charlie edged past him down the incline, then kicked the bag open with the toe of his boot, and out spilled dozens of bottles — vodka, whiskey — stinking of fermented grains. They tumbled slowly downhill, clinking into one another. Charlie turned with an anguished stare. "Since when did you start drinking again?"

Isaac looked away, a deep flush crawling up his neck. "I never stopped."

A mosslike silence followed as they stared at one another the way two children do sometimes. Then the old man glared malevolently and shook him off. Charlie could smell the storm coming, a metallic odor like wet copper. There was a strange hurricane-like warmth to the air.

"I'm going to ask you something," he said slowly, "and I want a straight answer."

His father's face was laminated with sweat.

"What happened on April fifteenth?"

He looked visibly affronted. "You know damn well where I was that day. I already told you."

Charlie nodded. "What about May eleventh?"

"That storm front produced four tornadoes over three states, if you'll recall. I didn't get any further south than Ardmore and Durant. I was chasing junk all night long."

"Can you prove you weren't in Texas that night?"

"How am I supposed to prove a thing like that?"

"Did you stop for gas, food or lodging? Talk to any other storm-chasers?"

"What you mean is . . ." His father held his eye. "Am I a cold-blooded killer? That's the real question, isn't it?"

It sounded absurd, coming from his lips. Charlie had an urge to grab him, hug him, hang on tight. He was afraid of his next question. A lump formed in his throat, while all around them, low fires glowed in the distant mounds of ash. "Well?" He swallowed hard. "Are you?"

Isaac's eyes narrowed to slits. "I've been called plenty of things in my life, Charlie. I may be one sorry son of a bitch, but I sure as hell don't have enough ice in my veins for that sort of hobby."

"I want to believe you, Pop."

A mist of wrinkles crept across his face as he frowned. "Screw you." He wrapped his musty old raincoat around him and started back up the incline, but Charlie hooked him by the arm, spun him around.

"What happened the night our house burned down?"

Isaac's stubborn face closed like a fist. "You don't wanna go there."

Charlie squeezed the deep muscles of Isaac's arms until he flinched, until he sucked in air through his false teeth. "You're not leaving until you tell me what happened."

Isaac jerked away and straightened his rumpled raincoat, then settled his hat more squarely on his head. "I had my dreams," he said angrily. "Big dreams, Charlie. I was gonna see the world. Join the Coast Guard. Boats, the ocean . . . that's what got my juices flowing. But in a fit of bad timing, Adelaide got herself pregnant."

Charlie could feel his pulse ticking in the thin skin of his temples, while bits of trash spun in snaky gusts of wind and the sound of the rain deepened in tone.

"We got caught in the act. It was a shotgun type of thing. I honestly did love her, but marriage? Now, there's a commitment." The skin around his eyes screwed tight as he focused on his son. "You remember your mother's condition, don't you?"

Charlie drew back. "What condition?"

"Nerves, they called it. A nervous condition. Remember how insufferable she could be? How awful full of herself? There'd be days when she wouldn't get out of bed to boil water. Then other times, she'd be bouncing off the walls, juggling a hundred different things at once."

Charlie felt a frantic activity going on inside his head, like a million flies trapped in a jar.

"When she hit those heights or sank to those lows, you couldn't reason with her." He rubbed his jaw. "Times like that, I'd make my getaway. Let her wallow in her own misery, I figured. I didn't realize just how sick she was. That's the way it is with mental illness. You think a person's trying to needle you on purpose. You think they're in control of their emotions . . ."

Charlie's clothes grew clammy, while the rain brought with it the cold down their necks.

"It became a vicious cycle," his father said with absent, haunted eyes. "She'd get depressed, I'd go out drinking. I'd go out drinking, and she'd get depressed. Then one day, I don't remember why . . ." He licked his lips, his wet pink tongue sliding along the withered skin. "I'm ashamed of this part. One day, I believe I may have pushed her over the edge."

Raped her, you mean, you deluded bastard. Charlie tried to swallow, but there wasn't enough spit in his mouth to go around. The old man's eyes seemed very far away, lost in the milky fog of memory.

"Your mama achieved an awful sort of vengeance that night. Self-destructive and terrible. I never cried. It was too awesome. The authorities never suspected arson. They said it was due to faulty wiring and too much junk down in the basement. Kerosene lanterns and overburdened outlets. I never corrected them. Why should I? We needed the insurance money. Why should we be punished for what that poor, tormented soul did?"

"Liar!" Charlie lunged at him, and they did a slow pirouette to the ground, where they tumbled over the trash, a scramble of arms and legs. They rolled downhill over pockets of smoldering rubbish until they hit bottom, where bluebonnets sprouted from the ash. Grabbing his father by the collar, he screamed, "You fucking liar!"

The old man's Stetson blew away in the wind, and he gazed up at Charlie with desperate eyes. "The last thing I knew, I'd fallen asleep on top of her. And when I woke up . . . all this smoke was pouring into the room. So thick you could hardly breathe. I got out of bed and ran to the door, and there she was . . . hair sticking to her cheeks.

Flames shooting up the stairs behind her. Awful. There was nothing in her eyes . . . not a hint of recognition, Charlie. She just looked at me and walked away, and that's the last I ever saw of her."

Charlie could smell lemons and a faint whiff of booze on the old man's breath, and it sickened him. Oldest trick in the book. Why hadn't he noticed it before? He wrapped his hands around his father's neck and squeezed, his heart drubbing with hatred.

"Charlie . . ."

He choked the words off at the back of the old man's throat, arms pulsing with fury. He drew his breath in hitches, while Isaac tried desperately to break his grasp. His lips turned blue. He wriggled around beneath Charlie—so weak and insignificant. That hideous, twisted face. Those dilated nostrils. A quick thought: Charlie could snap his neck. He could choke the breath right out of him. *What's the sound of nothing? What's the sound of nothing, you little bed wetter?* His hands ached as he squeezed tighter.

Stop it, you're killing him . . .

Charlie gave a sudden leap inside and stumbled to his feet. Humiliated. Furious. Hands trembling with this newfound knowledge. How terrible to discover your own basest instincts. Horrible, horrible. He looked at the sky ribbed with clouds, at the nearby hills where the mesquite and blackjack had been scorched from the burning trash. *Self-control. Hold on.*

"Charlie?" his father gasped, some massive struggle going on behind his eyes. The cowboy hat was gone, white tongues of hair licking at his withered cheeks. "Help me up."

Charlie pulled him to his feet. "Why didn't you tell me

this before?" he said in a husky whisper. "You stupid bastard, why didn't you tell me?"

"Charlie, seriously . . . would it've helped?"

They stood wrapped in tangled strings of air, a dark knowledge passing between them. A halting strangeness to the air.

When his cell phone rang, Charlie felt the pain in his head like a bundle of knife points. "Hello?" he barked into the receiver.

"Charlie?" came a hesitant female voice. "It's me, Peg. Listen, I'm at your place now . . ." She sounded vaguely out of breath, and he could picture her leaning against the kitchen counter in her blue and yellow jogging suit, even though she'd never gone jogging a day in her life.

"What is it, Peg? I'm right in the middle of something."

"Sophie isn't here. She's supposed to be, but she isn't."

A nervous shiver straightened his spine.

"We were supposed to go shopping this afternoon. It was all arranged."

He avoided his father's eyes. "You checked out back?"

"Out back, upstairs, downstairs. I found a note."

"What kind of note?"

"It says she went storm-chasing."

"Storm-chasing?" he almost shouted. "All by herself?"

"It just says she went storm-chasing. Period."

He could feel the heaviest kind of apprehension, the kind that only visits you when something totally unexpected happens. "Did she take the car?"

"No, it's still parked in the driveway," Peg said irritably. "And I gave up a bridge game for this."

Fear trilled like an alarm bell inside his head. *Boone Pritchett.* She must've gone storm-chasing with Boone Pritchett. His leg was broken, so he wouldn't be the one driving. Sophie had left the Civic parked at home. Boone's casino-pink pickup truck was totaled, but his father owned a full-size rust-red pickup truck that Charlie had pulled over many times. Sophie knew how to drive a stick. Would she honestly do that? He knew she was mad at him, but would she disobey him like that and leave a note? Was she that completely lost to him?

"Stay put," he told Peg. "Call you right back." He hung up and dialed Willa's number at the wind facility but got the machine instead. Impatiently he tried her on her cell phone.

Isaac hovered restlessly nearby. "What is it, Charlie? What's going on?"

He got Willa's voice mail and left a message. "Hey, it's me. Call me on my cell soon as you get this." Then he dialed Rick Kripner's cell phone with clumsy fingers.

"Yello?"

"Rick? It's Charlie Grover."

"Hey," Rick said warmly. "What's up?"

"I think my daughter's in a bit of trouble. She went out storm-chasing without my permission, she was grounded . . . I think she might've gone off with Boone Pritchett," he said with the faintest tremor in his voice. "I need to find her right away."

"Hm. They're probably headed west," Rick said.

"West?"

"A red box just went up for East Texas this afternoon."

"What's a red box?"

"Tornado watch. It means conditions are favorable."

He squeezed his eyes shut. "Where's Willa?"

"Inside the boundary-layer tunnel doing wind inversions."

"Would you tell her I called?"

"Yeah, sure. Is there anything I can do?"

"Maybe. Are you going storm-chasing this afternoon?"

"Actually I'm on the road right now. Why?"

"Okay, good. Could you keep an eye out for her?"

"Sure, what's the vehicle?"

"A rust-red Ford pickup truck with Oklahoma plates."

"Gotcha. I'll keep an eye out."

"Call me if you spot it?"

"Absolutely."

He hung up. Eyes frantic.

"Is Sophie in trouble?" Isaac stood blinking the rainwater out of his eyes. "Are you gonna let me in on this thing, or what?"

He pocketed his cell phone. "Come on." He grabbed the old man by his musty-smelling raincoat and hauled him back up the hill.

"Where in the blazes are we going now?"

"You're taking me storm-chasing, Pop."

16

C<small>OLD</small>?"

Sophie shivered. "A little."

"Want my jacket?"

"No thanks," she said politely. "Who was that on the phone?"

"Just a chaser buddy." Rick Kripner looked at her with intense interest, his eyes both intelligent and caring behind his wire-rim glasses. "Sure you don't want my jacket?"

"No thanks, I'm fine." She tried to keep from shivering.

His flannel shirt was tucked neatly inside the waistband of his jeans, and his hair was disheveled from the wind blowing in through the open windows. He took off his glasses and pinched the bridge of his nose, fingers circling the reddish bands of skin on either side. He was better-looking without his glasses on, she thought, with his big brown eyes and nice smile, and that surprisingly muscular body beneath the L.L. Bean outfits. Just good-looking enough, in fact, to make Boone blow his top.

He'd broken up with her three days ago and hadn't

bothered to explain why. Just told her it was over. She'd been going crazy trying to figure it out. She hadn't cried this much since her mother had died. He wouldn't return her phone calls and refused to talk to her at school, and she suspected that her father might have something to do with it. When Boone hadn't shown up for school today, she figured he'd gone chasing with one of his buddies. So when Rick dropped by the house and invited her to go storm-chasing with him, she'd practically leaped at the chance. If they ran into Boone and he saw her with Rick, he'd really freak out. Then maybe he'd realize how much he loved her.

Sophie couldn't stop shivering. It was spitting rain on the interstate, and in all the excitement back at the house, she'd forgotten to bring her sweater. Now the cold air whistling into the truck was giving her goose bumps. They were in Rick's GMC Sierra, a black all-wheel-drive pickup truck virtually bristling with antennae, and already she was having regrets. Her father would be furious. But then she remembered it was all his fault to begin with. *Good, let him think the worst. Let him suffer the way she'd been suffering lately.*

"So what's with all this equipment?" she said.

Rick's chest puffed with pride. "This here's what you'd call your basic weather-weenie-mobile, fully loaded and ready to roll. You've got your C-band Doppler radar with three hundred fifty thousand watts . . . you've got your ham radio . . . this Icom 2100's great. It's got tone encode/decode/scan and plenty of memories, alphanumeric memories. Great performance. There's an in-motion satellite tracking system, a Nokia cell phone with laptop link for real-time Nexrad, a satellite phone for remote weather data access from anywhere in Tornado

Alley that doesn't have cellular coverage. Eggbeater antenna for omnidirectional polarity at the horizon. A mini-DV camcorder on a Morganti mount that allows for steady video recording during the chase . . . Let's see, what else? A GPS satellite downlink navigation system so you can find your way through any unfamiliar territory. A Cassiopeia PDA for wireless Internet access, a fifteen-inch flat LCD and"—he took a deep breath—"plenty of nifty software."

"Wow," she said with a laugh. "You really are a nerd."

"That's 'severe weather aficionado' to you, kiddo."

She giggled. "Okay, Mr. Aficionado."

"See those transverse rolls?"

She squinted at the sky beyond the blurry, rain-washed windshield, where the clouds had a feeling of whispered density.

"You're witnessing . . . right over there . . . the birth of a megatornadic supercell."

"A mega what?"

"Megatornadic supercell."

"Gesundheit."

He looked at her and smiled. "Wise guy. See that string of mammatus clouds trailing behind the super-cell?"

"Platypus clouds?"

"Mammatus." He shot her a crooked grin. "Did you know that weaknesses in upper-level flow allow a storm to recycle precipitation particles, thereby turning into what's known as an HP blob?"

She rolled her eyes. "That's a scientific term? *Blob?*"

"So shoot me."

"You really are a geek." She gave him an apologetic glance. "But don't worry. I'm a geek, too."

"So I'm in good company, huh? Hey," Rick said, "you're shaking like a leaf. Take my jacket. No more arguments."

"But then *you'd* be cold," she protested.

"Never look a gift horse in the mouth." He removed the navy wool peacoat while keeping one hand on the wheel, shrugged his other arm out of the sleeve and handed it over. "Go on," he said.

"My grandfather's got one just like this."

"Great minds think alike."

The jacket's cool blue lining wasn't itchy at all, and the sleeves smelled faintly of pinecones. As she drew it on, she could feel the silver chain of her necklace catch on the fabric. She reached for her locket, but to her surprise, it came off in her hand. "Oh, no," she gasped.

"What's up?"

"The clasp just broke."

"I can fix that."

"You can?"

He nodded. "We're headed there now."

"Headed where?"

"To the wind facility." He held out his hand. "I'll duck inside and fix it real quick. You can wait in the truck. Only take a second."

She gave him a small worried look. "I've never taken it off before," she said. "Not since Mom died. I don't know what I'd do if I ever lost it. So thanks."

"No problem."

She handed him the necklace and could feel her whole body beginning to relax to the quiet hum of the engine, while the rain streamed out of the sky in vertical pen strokes.

TWISTED

1

CRADLING HIS cell phone in the crook of his neck, Charlie sped west on the I-40, doing eighty. The storm clouds were gunmetal blue, scorched bronze along the horizon. He couldn't read the sky. As a cop, he could read body language and faces, but not skies. It was muggy out, an awful kind of mugginess that made your clothes stick to your skin. A black curtain of rain dimmed the distant air like a flurry of gnats. He was on the phone with Mike, trying to sound rational. "Boone Pritchett took off with my daughter after I explicitly told him not to. They both disregarded my feelings."

"You want us to pick them up?"

"Yeah, ruin this guy's day."

"I'm all over it."

Charlie hung up and drove along in worried silence.

Isaac took a swig from his Thirst Buster travel mug. "She's with Boone Pritchett?"

He glanced over. "You know him?"

"Smart-ass punk." Isaac scowled. "Sophie told me about the accident. Nowadays, any yahoo with a set of wheels can become a chaser. There's no licensing or certification, and some of these amateurs think they own the road." He glanced at Charlie as if he had something else he wanted to say, something pressing he needed to confess, but Charlie wasn't in the mood. He was consumed with thoughts of his little girl. "That first night at the hospital, they wouldn't let me see you until I'd washed up good."

Charlie watched the road, not wanting to hear it.

"I had to wash my hands and face, put on a paper gown. They said your chances of survival were about fifty-fifty. I remember going into the ICU, and lying there on the bed was this unrecognizable little person. Skin peeling away. Tubes going in and out. Noisy equipment. And all I could think was, 'fifty-fifty . . . fifty-fifty . . .'

"I sat glued to your bedside, holding your hand . . . the hand that wasn't burned." He cocked an eyebrow at him. "Do you remember any of this?"

Charlie shook his head.

"They wouldn't allow anything inside the room because of the risk of infection. No flowers, no toys, no food. There was one exception. Balloons. Don't ask me why, but balloons were allowed." He smiled faintly at the memory. "So I went out and bought you a whole bunch of 'em. Every color of the rainbow."

He eyed his father, remembering the trunk, the withered balloons. You learned to live with the scars, but not the grief you harbored in your heart.

"I'm sorry for all those years I can't take back," Isaac said hoarsely. "And I'm sorry I hid the truth from you."

Charlie's cell phone rang just then, interrupting this remarkable confession. "Mike?" he said, picking up. His hand tightening on the phone. "Is she okay?"

"I just talked to Boone Pritchett, Chief. I called over to

the house, and he swears up and down he hasn't seen your daughter today."

"He's lying."

"I sent Tyler over to check it out."

"No, send Hunter with backup. And tell them to be extremely careful. This is my daughter we're talking about. And call me the second it goes down." He hung up, feeling a cold rush of air against his face.

"What was that about?" Isaac asked as Charlie hit the brakes. "What're you doing?"

"Turning around."

"What for?"

"She didn't go storm-chasing. It was a ruse."

"A ruse?"

"She's still in town." He dialed Rick's number.

"Yello?"

"Hey, it's me again. Looks like Sophie didn't go storm-chasing after all, just so you know."

"She didn't?"

"No. So don't worry about it."

"Okay, big guy. If you say so."

"Thanks, Rick." He hung up.

"Who was that?" Isaac asked.

"Rick Kripner."

"You mean, Miracle Boy?"

Charlie glanced at him. "What?"

"That's his handle. Miracle Boy."

"What're you talking about?"

"Seventeen, eighteen years ago in Wewoka, this kid survives an F-5 . . . so they called him Miracle Boy in all the papers."

"In Wewoka? Don't you mean Pixley?"

Isaac shook his head. "I used to buy horses from a

rancher down in Wewoka, that's how come I remember the name of the town. It was in all the papers. A hundred houses were destroyed that day. Thirty-six people died, including Rick's father." He cracked a perplexed smile. "Rick went flying out of a house and landed unhurt in a field."

Charlie stiffened. "That's not what he told me."

"Yeah, well . . . he's probably ashamed to admit that his father was a thief."

"What? Wait a minute. Back up. Run it by me again."

"Rick Kripner's father was a house burglar, it turns out. Back in the seventies and early eighties, all across Tornado Alley, he'd ride the storm track in search of homes to rip off. He'd waltz right in, brazen as could be, since most folks would be huddled in their basements or holed up in their closets or what-have-you, too scared of the impending storm to do anything but hide. He'd take off with the silverware and whatnot. I guess he took the boy along with him, too, because one day, while he was robbing this house in Wewoka, the tornado struck dead-on. Six people were killed, only the boy survived. Press always gives them a moniker," Isaac said. "Miracle Boy. Not that anyone remembers." He tapped his head. "I keep a lot of trivia up here."

Breathing shallow and fast, Charlie activated his cell phone and dialed Rick's number again, but all he got was the voice mail. Mind racing, he called Peg Morris back.

"Charlie?" she complained. "I've been sitting here on my keister waiting for you to call me back again."

"Read me the note, Peg," he interrupted.

"What?"

"The note. Read it."

He could hear her fumbling for her glasses. "It says . . . 'Gone chasing.'"

Fear gripped him. "That's it?"

"Just two words. 'Gone chasing.'"

He remembered the clutter in Rick's office, the handwritten note that said "Gone Chasing" in black Magic Marker.

"Do me a favor and stay put, Peg."

"Charlie, you sound upset. Is she all right?"

"Just sit tight." He hung up and called Mike back. "Listen, something's come up. I need you to put out a BOLO on a black GMC Sierra, full-size pickup truck. Owner's name is Rick Kripner. You can get his plates from the DMV, or else maybe the Wind Function Facility at Dryden Tech . . ."

"What's up, Chief? What's going on?"

"I think she might've gone storm-chasing with him instead."

There was a puzzled pause at the other end of the line. "Did she go voluntarily?"

"Look, if this is what I think it is . . . then he came to my house uninvited." The thought pulled taut as piano wire inside of him. "I don't know where they went. I don't know what's going on. I need to locate her ASAP. The guy's like thirty years old . . . what business does he have hooking up with a teenage girl?"

"Okay, Chief. Not to worry. I'm on it."

"Follow both leads and call me back." Charlie pocketed his cell phone.

His father shot him a sidelong glance. "Is she gonna be okay?"

"I don't know, Pop. Quit asking me that." With growing apprehension, he dialed Rick's cell phone again, but all he got was the digital recording.

He stared straight ahead at the silvery, slanted lines of

rain and started adding it up in his head: Rick had superior storm-chasing capabilities; he was right-handed; he had medium-length brown hair . . . what about shoe size? Charlie wasn't sure. He was exceptionally neat and well organized, scientifically precise, kept lists of all tornadic-related activity and elaborate death statistics. He was a devoted chaser, and most damning of all, he'd been the one to finger Gustafson. Fingered him and then planted the evidence against him.

Charlie had a thought. "Pop? Where's your lucky jacket?"

"Oh, that. I must've lost it somewhere, dammit," he said. "Been out of luck ever since."

His vision spun; unfocused, swirling. "Do you remember seeing Rick Kripner around that time? Did you talk to him or see him in passing?"

Isaac frowned. "We've crossed paths on occasion. Why?"

"Around the same time you lost your jacket?"

"What's this all about, Charlie?"

He reined in his rising dread and shook his head. "Smoke Gets in Your Eyes" had been a deliberate choice. "I'm on Fire." *A message to Charlie. Hey, Chief, I know you. I'm on to you. I'm watching your every move.* That stiffened gait and those buttoned-up shirts. That hitch in his step that suggested a greater pain he'd never mention. At his father's knee, little Rick Kripner had learned to intercept tornadoes and raid people's houses during the occupants' moment of greatest vulnerability.

He remembered the call he'd gotten from Dime Box, Texas. *"So there we were, huddled inside the closet, scared out of our wits, when I peeked out the door and saw this little person moving around inside our house. I thought it was an elf . . . I thought we had an elf in the house . . . but now I think it must've been a little boy."*

Little Rick and his dad, chasing tornadoes, invading people's homes and robbing them blind while the town siren wailed and the threat of devastation loomed . . . but then one day, the elder Kripner had overplayed his hand. A monster F-5 made a direct hit on the house, and Rick and his old man got flung like debris into the surrounding fields. *Miracle Boy.* The trauma of his father's death must have pushed him over the edge. He'd already made a deal with the devil. He was out there helping his father rob defenseless citizens . . . How easy would it have been to escalate to violence? How easy to turn from burglary to animal cruelty? From killing dogs to killing human beings? *Gone chasing.* Who else said that? Rick Kripner. *Gone chasing.* Shit, and now his daughter . . . unthinkable.

No, ridiculous. Another wild-goose chase. Not Rick. He needed verification. He needed further evidence. Proof that this was possible. He took the next exit.

"Where the hell are we going now?" Isaac grumbled.

"Pixley."

"Pixley? What's in Pixley?"

"Maybe an answer," Charlie said.

2

CHARLIE SWERVED onto a poorly paved country lane that bumped over a pair of railroad tracks and passed through a winding draw full of purple wildflowers. It was raining hard now, a blustery downpour by the time they pulled up in front of Rick Kripner's house. He stared past rivulets of rain at the sad little farmstead with its broken-down smokehouse and saddleback barn. The rambling gray Victorian stood in splendid isolation on several hundred acres of fallow fields. The copper oriel windows were relieved against a high mansard roof of green slate, topped off by a weather vane. The stained-glass bay windows repeated an azalea pattern, and the porch bulb glowed like a blurry beacon in the inclement weather.

"Stay here," he told his father.

"Where're you going?"

"Be right back." He stepped out of the truck, the rain making pitter-pat sounds against his hat. The big old house formed a monstrous face in the gloom—the porch was its unhappy mouth, the front door its nose, the windows its beady eyes. He shot up the wooden steps, then paused to listen to the rainwater collecting in the aluminum gutters. A strange tinkling sound rose above the sibilance, and he looked up. Dozens of wind chimes dangled from the porch beams, jingle-jangling in the wind, their dissonant notes sending anticipatory shivers up his spine.

The front door was massive, flanked on either side by leaded fogged-glass windows. He hammered on the door with his fist, and when nobody answered, went to a nearby window and cupped his hands over the cold glass. What he saw next made his heart flutter: bite-sized chunks were missing out of the windowsill, as if somebody'd taken a hatchet to it. One of the load-bearing walls in the small rectangular room beyond the window-pane was completely exposed; in places you could see through the yellow insulation to the veins and guts of the house—exposed wires, leaking pipes.

He hammered on the oak panel with his fist. "Police! Open up!" When no response was forthcoming, he tried the door and found it wasn't locked, then hesitated on the threshold. *Fuck probable cause.* He stepped inside.

"Sophie?" he hollered into the immense front hallway. "You in here?"

He paused to listen to an echoing silence. The front hallway's twelve-foot ceilings were topped off with crown moldings, and the hardwood floors still had their original quarter-sawn boards. A sudden flash of feathers gave Charlie a start as a pigeon flew up the central staircase. Some of the balusters were missing from the oak railing, as if they'd been yanked out, leaving just the splintered ends.

A kernel of fear took root as, unfastening the safety strap on his holster, Charlie approached the small dark room he'd seen through the porch window and stood in the doorway. Somebody had gone mad in here. The molding was gouged; in places there were holes in the plaster so deep the lath was exposed. The skeletal frame of an entire wall could be seen—diagonal braces, jack studs, joists, lintels. There wasn't a stick of furniture, just a stepladder leaning against a wall and a trail of carpenter ants cascading out of the cellulose insulation.

He moved back into the dark-wood entryway with his weapon drawn. The drafty old house came alive with sound. The wind whistled through the rafters and the ping of dripping water echoed. Plenty of plaster had been knocked out of the hallway walls as well, leaving bald patches of exposed plank in stark contrast with the prim Victorian wallpaper. To his right was a parlor full of plain, simple furniture and tall spires of books, precisely stacked newspapers and videotapes. The old single-thickness windows still had their original frames and sashes, ripples of rain trailing down the panes. Beyond these ripples, he could see other wind chimes, and beyond the dangling wind chimes was a curtain of gray.

Charlie passed through a narrow vestibule into an austere-looking living room. The old fieldstone fireplace had recently been used—he found bits of burned paper among the ashes. There was a rich wool carpet and floor-to-ceiling windows with fringed valances over mauve curtains. The furniture was a hodgepodge of heirlooms—an art deco pole lamp, a cumbersome sideboard, a grandfather clock, matching straight-back chairs. The computer was missing from the antique desk in the corner, cables snaking across the polished walnut. Unpaid bills were scattered over the floor, and the desk drawers were askew. Charlie examined the long, low table crowded with all sorts of equipment—a GPS receiver, an anemometer, some barometric pressure instruments. He ran his finger over the polished wood—not a speck of dust anywhere.

As he entered the kitchen, he squinted, then opened his eyes wide. Lists everywhere. If you didn't write it down, it didn't exist. There was a built-in Hoosier-style hutch, several glass-front display cupboards and a farm-style sink. The canned goods were stacked with the labels facing out so you could read them lightning-quick. Charlie opened the refrigerator, empty except for a few six-packs and some cold cuts. The freezer compartment was chock-full of hail balls, each one carefully labeled inside its own plastic bag. *Marble-sized, golfball-sized, softball-sized, spiky, smooth.* Dates and locations. Out back was a porch that was literally falling down.

Upstairs was an eye-opener. On the second floor at the top of the stairs was a sloped ceiling you had to duck under to get by. All the small, colorless rooms were crammed to the rafters, each pile neatly stacked and labeled. This was orderly chaos. In one room, Charlie found a bundle of twisted tree branches, a stack of tattered pictures from old Sunday School quarterlies, at least twenty Tupperware bowls either torn in half or twisted by the wind, and a mound of snapped black cables. Rick had studiously labeled every item—date, town, F-scale. And then . . . chair legs and balusters stacked like kindling. Plastic bags full of refrigerator magnets—the Pillsbury Dough Boy, Felix the Cat, My Little Pony. His flesh crept. If you ate dinner with this guy, you'd notice midbite that your fork was labeled "fork."

In the next room, Charlie found a building-block tower of concrete chunks, each one more progressively deteriorated than the last; a collection of glass "genie" bottles; a heap of watches and clocks, their hands stopped at the exact moment the tornado had struck. There were bundles of shredded clothes and pages torn from books. Dog and cat collars. Twisted highway signs. Turntables and radios from the seventies and eighties. Unbroken china and pewter. A Mickey Mantle baseball card that was probably worth something. A receipt for somebody's 1984 class ring.

In the bathroom, painted avocado green with a mosaic tile floor, he found little plastic bags of obsessively trimmed fingernails. The hairs rose on the back of his neck. What a sick, twisted fuck. Everything had to have its place. At least fifty rolls of toilet paper were stacked beneath the vanity. There were two of everything: two toothbrushes, two razors, two soap dishes. All the items in the medicine cabinet had been arranged in alphabetical order, aspirin first. Charlie glanced at the original cast-iron Kohler fixtures, everything spotless and gleaming. Would the world come to an end because there was a speck of toothpaste in the bathroom sink? Somehow, yes.

Only the modest room at the far end of the hallway looked lived-in. It held an unexpected innocence, its pine shelves lined with the kind of plastic action figures you might purchase with your Happy Meal. A large window let in a square of dirty light. There was an original stone fireplace and hearthstone. Above the driving rain, you could hear the wind pushing in through cracks in the rafters. The bed was neatly made. The bureau drawers stored whites and colors. The walls were painted an odd chemical blue. On the old RCA turntable, Gloria Swanson's 1932 recording of "I Love You So Much I Hate You." On the bedside table, a half-empty glass of

clear liquid. Charlie picked it up and sniffed. Water. He
set it back down.

He opened the steamer trunk at the foot of the bed and
found stacks of desiccated newspaper clippings that
spanned decades. He leafed through yellowing articles
about old killer tornadoes and the recent spate of murders. He dropped everything back inside the trunk, a ringing in his ears. He took a deep breath, let it out cautiously.
Stood up. The closet door was closed. He crossed the
room and opened it.

Clothes on plastic hangers, spaced evenly to keep
them from getting wrinkled; shoes in perfect rows at the
bottom of the closet. Four pairs of identical-looking Nike
sneakers—white and champagne shelltops. With the tip
of a ballpoint pen, he inspected one of the sneakers. Size
eleven, wads of cotton stuffed in the toes. All the other
shoes in the closet were size nine.

Feeling a palpable heartbeat in his throat, he stepped
out into the hallway. *No probable cause. Illegal search.*
He feared his own impulses, his transgressions. The last
thing in the world he wanted was to blow the case due to
some legal loophole, but his daughter was missing. *His
daughter.* Nothing else mattered. He stood staring at the
ceiling. "Sophie?" he hollered. "You up there?"

He lowered the hinged jaw of the attic staircase and
mounted the steps two at a time. The attic smelled of
mothballs. Old, old. Ancient grievances. Pain. Tears.
Heart-pine wood floors and a transom window. Old exposed posts and beams. A single bare bulb that cast sickly
shadows down the roof-sloped ceiling.

Charlie ducked his head. To the right of the stairwell
was a pile of dusty whiskey bottles, each one containing
the residue of some ancient amber liquid. Each one with

its own bizarre label, "1981, upper right canine." He took a sharp breath, then let it out slowly. He could feel the seething atmosphere inside the house. To his left was a player piano that looked like it hadn't been played in decades, a thick bed of dust coating the mahogany fall board. The discordant sound of many wind chimes could be heard, like a tickle at the back of your throat. The wind chimes were feelers, he imagined, delicately testing the air for weather patterns. The entire house shivered like a bell; or more accurately, like a living creature alert to the shifting winds.

At the western end of the attic, a narrow window overlooked the back fields, the horizon stretching infinitely into the distance. Angled in front of this window was a large straight-back chair made of some dark sturdy wood. Two old leather belts were strapped to the chair's back splat—leather straps grotesquely misshapen and rigored with age. Time slowed to a crawl as Charlie circled around it. A trickle of ice water hit him on the back of the neck and he looked up, goose bumps rising everywhere on his body. It was only rainwater, leaking in through a crack in the weatherboarding and providing a constant *drip-drip*.

On the floor around the base of the chair were blood spatters, like the concentric echoes of a fading scream. The chair's spindles were covered with a green mold and clotted with dried blood. A nearby wooden table held a collection of old-fashioned dental tools—forceps, a mirror, an elevator and chisel, needles and suturing material, and two glass mason jars. One of the jars held a wad of gauze pads, now ivory with age. And the other . . .

Charlie's hair stood on end as he picked it up and gently shook it. He couldn't quite believe his eyes. Inside the old-fashioned mason jar were dozens of extracted human teeth, mixed with animal teeth. Canine, bovine. As hard as he tried, as much as he pretended to maintain a professional distance, he couldn't keep his hands from shaking or his mind from reeling at this ultimate proof of evil.

He took a pained step backward, the souls of the dead swirling around him. He knew their outrage. He felt an almost intolerable pain begin to grow inside his head. He stood transfixed while he tried to regain his composure and realized, at that moment, just how deep the wounds were, how far back this most inhuman crime went.

3

CHARLIE TOOK a detour in order to bypass a bad traffic jam and ended up on this sorry stretch of road way out in the middle of Mayberry, slowing to a crawl due to heavy rains. Hydroplaning through long drizzling threads of rain, his windshield wipers dragging across the glass.

"East Texas looks promising." Isaac had his laptop computer propped open on his lap.

"Promising? Can't you do any better than that, Pop?" Charlie rubbed his face with hard, angry gestures. *Out of breath. Out of breath.* The horror of that house. The chilling revelation. Rick was the Debris Killer. There was no doubt in his mind. "We don't even have a target storm yet," he said angrily. "We don't know where the hell we're going!"

"I'm trying to figure out where a tornado is likely to form, which direction it's likely to move in. We've gotta know where to be and where not to be. The Texas mesonet is showing the highest dew points. I believe a storm's gonna form around Matador and become tornadic around Aberdeen or thereabouts, but I need to get a confirmation." He swiped the CB mike from its metal retainer and, cupping it close to his lips, said, "This is Poppa Vein, can I get a break?" He fiddled with the volume and wattage controls while multiple voices channeled out of the speaker. "Break one-oh?"

Charlie pressed the pedal to the metal, willing the Loadmaster to go faster than it was probably capable of. The scalloped cumuli were blowing in a brisk northeasterly wind that enveloped the truck in warm buoyant air. It was closing in on 5:30 P.M. He stepped hard on his panic and had a sudden tender memory of Sophie as a baby, kicking at the world from her crib, her eyes deep blue wells of love and curiosity. He could barely grasp the significance of what he'd just seen. He was still in shock. His hands were shaking.

"Does the driver of the eastbound red Wilson have his ears on?" his father said, adjusting the squelch and volume levels. "Break one-oh. Can I get a break one-oh?"

"Who's that breaker out there?" came the laconic response.

"Poppa Vein," Isaac said, using his handle.

"Hey, Poppa, this is Cloudy. Watch your back, we got a real bunch of cowboys on the road today."

"How's it looking in Texas? You got a target storm for me, Cloudy?"

"What's your twenty?"

"I'm passing through Hardeman County, heading west."

"I got thunderboomers in Childress . . ."

"I'm looking for that special one percent . . . a terawatt supercell that'll spawn a tornado in its updraft. What's your feeling about Aberdeen?"

"Aberdeen's lookin' real sweet," he responded. "We got a large circular-shaped storm with tops to fifty thousand feet moving northeast at about thirty-five miles an hour."

"Sounds juicy."

"That's your best bet."

"Catch you on the flip-flop." Isaac dunked the mike back in its metal retainer. "That's our target storm," he said, sweat beading on the sides of his nose and rivering down the deep grooves of his mouth. "We've got maybe an hour to get there before we miss the whole show."

"One hour? That's it?"

His eyes narrowed to slits, as if this were a trick question. "Aberdeen's the place we wanna be, son."

Charlie stared gloomily ahead, the road winnowing before him like the wrong end of a telescope. Unless the state police or highway patrol could locate Rick's black GMC Sierra soon, Charlie had no better plan than to chase down the nearest tornado and hopefully intercept Rick's truck before Sophie got hurt. Everything rested on the forlorn hope that the killer wouldn't kill until he'd found a tornado to his liking, and that they could somehow intervene before he'd succeeded. Charlie didn't feel like dwelling on the absurdity of those odds.

He absently shot past the highway entranceway, then hit the brakes and sluiced all over the road, peanut butter in the brake lines. Swearing angrily, he jammed the truck into reverse and zigzagged backward across the road. Raindrops swarmed in the sweep of their headlights as they edged down an embankment, the front of the Loadmaster tilting precariously skyward.

"What the hell are you doing?" Isaac put his hands on the ceiling of the cab in order to keep from cracking his skull as they skidded backward down the wet slope.

"Getting back on the I-40," Charlie said as he leveled

it out and stomped on the gas, but then the radiator hose exploded with a loud hiss. "Shit!" He jerked the wheel as the temp gauge dipped toward zero. "What the fuck . . . ?"

"I got it, I got it." His father was out of the vehicle, rummaging around in the flatbed in the rain. He snatched a roll of duct tape and jury-rigged the radiator hose, then hopped back in and slammed the door. "Okay, go!"

Charlie mashed his foot on the accelerator and could feel the Loadmaster's wheels tiptoeing along the edges of a rut as they veered back onto the road. They sped toward the entrance, scenery flying past in a green blur. "It's about time for some new brake pads, don't you think? And maybe a new transmission?"

"She's a little hard to keep running at a stoplight, but once you get her rolling, she does all right."

"I can't see shit," Charlie said, squinting past his flapping wipers. "Ray Charles might as well be at the wheel."

"Just drive us straight into Texas, son."

"I sure hope you're right, Pop," he said with a paralyzing sense of disbelief.

"I'll keep honing my forecast."

Moments later, they were back on the I-40, heading west, streetlights floating toward them in a static of rain. Charlie's cell phone rang, and he answered it with a pulsating anxiety. "Mike?"

"We've issued a statewide BOLO, Chief. I've got everybody and their uncle out trying to locate the vehicle."

"Listen, we were wrong about Gustafson. I was just inside Rick Kripner's house. I found the replacement teeth."

"Jesus Christ . . . you went in there without a warrant?"

"Goddammit, he's got my daughter!"

"Chief . . ."

"I'm telling you, Rick Kripner's the Debris Killer."

"Are you sure about this?"

Charlie took a deep breath, so dazed he could barely think straight. Sitting on his panic. "Mike? You need to trust me right now."

"Yeah . . . of course."

"My best guess is he's headed for Aberdeen."

"Hold on. That's my other line."

"Call me right back." Charlie cradled the phone in his lap and gripped the wheel. There was a handprint in the dust of the dashboard, small and delicate. Sophie's handprint, left there the last time she was in her grandpa's truck. "You were right about me," Charlie said, his gaze sweeping across the haze of blowing rain. "If only I'd been home more often . . . then maybe none of this would've happened."

"Sure." His father slid him a forgiving look. "And I'm Father of the Year. We all make mistakes, Charlie. I was a fool to try to tell you how to run your life."

The clutch of his throat muscles choked off all sound. He felt raw and exposed, like the map spread open on the seat between them.

"I'll find us a tornado," his father said. "I'll find us a whopper. We'll get her back, I can promise you that."

It reminded Charlie of all the comforting lies he'd told Sophie over the years. *Your mother's going to be just fine . . .*

The ringing phone made them both jump.

"Chief? They just spotted a black GMC Sierra in Montoya," Mike said, "heading eastbound on the I-40. They lost track of it five minutes ago, but I figure he's headed for—"

"The wind facility," Charlie finished the thought.

"Exactly."

He checked the rearview, his adrenaline shooting through the roof. There was nobody behind him, so he hit the brakes.

His father's startled eyes resembled the crinkling clouds. "What on God's green earth are you doing now?"

"Turning around."

"What for?"

"He's in Montoya."

"Montoya? But I thought you just said . . ."

They bounced over the median strip. Charlie waited for a Mack truck to blow past, rattling the doors, before he swung the lumbering vehicle around and pulled into the eastbound lane again. He could hear Mike's voice buzzing in his ear. "Chief? Should I notify the local law?"

"No, don't make that call just yet. This needs to happen softly."

"You don't want any backup, boss?"

"What I don't want is some trigger-happy cop putting my daughter's life at risk. Notify campus security and have somebody meet me in the parking lot."

"Got it."

"And get a chopper on the freeway." He hung up, then checked to make sure that his gun was loaded. He could hear his father's worried breathing beside him. "Been a change in plans," he said.

"So I gathered."

"Hang on, Pop," he said as he stepped on the gas.

It was 5:45 p.m. by the time they pulled into the parking lot of the Environmental Sciences Laboratories, the Loadmaster's motor racing before cutoff, its new tires edging forward over the asphalt. Charlie spotted Rick's GMC Sierra parked crookedly in front of the building's entranceway. "Sit tight," he told his father, a sick fury propelling him out of the vehicle. He took three steps before a glaring light stopped him dead in his tracks.

"Chief Grover?"

"What the . . . ?" He shielded his eyes with his hands. "Get that fucking light out of my face."

The campus security guard lowered his flashlight. "I was told to meet you here, sir." He was squat and stoop-shouldered inside his beige uniform, sallow-skinned from years of working the night shift. "They said I should—"

"Listen to me very carefully," Charlie interrupted. "We've got a hostage situation inside the building. You with me so far?"

He nodded blankly.

"You're going to accompany me inside. You will not

use your own initiative. You will not veer from my instructions. Is that understood?"

The guard stiffened. "Yes, sir."

"Just follow me and do exactly as I say."

He gave a tight, shocked smile.

It was spitting rain. Charlie drew his weapon and moved swiftly across the parking lot toward the GMC Sierra. The engine idled lazily, keys in the ignition. He spotted the lucky rabbit's foot dangling from the key chain and felt a tightening in his jaw. *Black rabbit fur.* With a roaring sound in his ears, he swung his light over the interior of the cab. The floor pads were green. *Green carpet fiber.*

Locard's principle . . .

He switched the motor off, pocketed the keys and headed for the horseshoe-shaped entryway of the enormous concrete building, "Environmental Sciences" etched in pink marble over the front door. Skipping up the marble steps, he pushed on the double glass doors, but they were locked for the night. "Open it," he told the guard.

"Shouldn't we call for backup first?" The young man stared at him nervously. They stood beneath a cone of yellow light, so close together Charlie could count the individual pores on his pasty face.

"Open the *door,*" he said, coming down hard on the last word.

Obediently the guard stooped over the access panel, punched in a security code and slid his plastic key-card through the magnetic trough. Then he threw the bolt with a sharp *click* and swung the door open.

"Not you." Charlie blocked his father's path. He had appeared out of nowhere, out of the darkness. "Go wait in the truck."

"I'm coming with you." His jaw was set.

"We can't afford any fuckups, Pop."

"She's my granddaughter," he said stubbornly.

Charlie had learned not to go head-to-head with the old man a long time ago. A dozen razor straps across the back could be pretty persuasive.

"I'll keep out of your way," Isaac promised.

Charlie glanced at his watch. They were all out of time. He entered the cavernous yellow lobby with the two other men in tow, the heavy glass doors thwumping shut behind them. Their footsteps echoed throughout the brightly lit building.

"This way," the guard said, but Charlie brushed past him and led the way down a forking corridor toward a bank of freight elevators, past dark-wood walls and simple-framed pictures of proud scientists and their machines. He stood punching the Down button over and over again.

"Come on," he hissed through clenched teeth.

"Yeah. That'll make it go faster," Isaac said sarcastically.

"Shut up, Pop." He pointed a finger. "You wait here."

"I'm coming with you, Charlie."

"We aren't having a debate here."

One of the freight elevators stopped at lobby level, its metal doors rocking open, and the three of them stepped inside. It seemed to take forever for the doors to jostle shut again, and then, shoulder-to-shoulder, they descended into the bowels of the building. Charlie gave his father a grim look, but the old man simply averted his gaze, while the security guard kept one hand on his holstered handgun.

"You ever use that thing?" Charlie asked him.

"Yes, sir. I was in the ROTC."

"Good. You're my backup."

"What're we looking for, sir?"

"White male in his early thirties, average height and build, brown hair, brown eyes, wire-rim glasses. He's got a girl with him . . . she's my daughter." The elevator landed with a jolt and a mechanical whir, and Charlie held the guard's eye. "If you hurt her . . . if you cause any injury to her person . . . I'll shoot you dead."

Beads of sweat collected on the guard's upper lip. "I . . . I'll be careful."

"You'd better be."

The elevator doors shimmied open, and Charlie ventured out into the corridor alone. Icy fingers of light stabbed through the overhead gantries, and the walls emitted a maddening hum, like a broken chord on a player piano. He made a ninety-degree turn into a higher-ceilinged corridor, where he carefully scanned his surroundings before motioning the others forward.

The test facilities were locked up tight for the night. Charlie tried each door, while the security guard fumbled with his overcrowded key chain. They hurried past one dark, unoccupied space after another, little bronze plaques beside each door identifying the tow tank facility, the signal-light structure, the wind tunnels.

"Try this one." Charlie waited impatiently while the guard unlocked the door and switched on the lights. They stood in the sodium glare of the hangar-sized wind-tunnel section when something caught his eye—a wisp of smoke curling up from the back of the facility.

He shot through the maze of cubicles, refrigeration pipes and electrical cables lining the walls, until he reached the eighty-foot-long boundary-layer tunnel. He could see white smoke wafting against the observation windows of the test section. "Get a fire extinguisher!" he shouted at the guard as he clambered up the ladder.

"That isn't smoke," the guard hollered back. "It's some kind of chemical they use to make the wind visible . . . the same stuff they use in skywriting."

The door wouldn't budge. Charlie noticed a pencil wedged in between the handle and the metal plate, jammed in there good. He worked it back and forth, and all of a sudden, it snapped off in his hand.

The brittle spring made a loud squawk as the door shot open, and a thick white mist spilled out, nearly choking him to death. Gagging and coughing, he hung back a beat. "Willa?" He felt a sudden shyness around the edges of his feelings for her. A certain tenderness or fear. Fear of losing her. It made him hesitate to move forward.

The white toxic substance had filled the entire test chamber. He shot inside and lost himself in the dissipating mist; he stumbled around, trying to clear the air by waving his arms, but it didn't do much good. He knew enough to turn on the fans. "Willa?" he said, then coughed as if his lungs might explode. "You in here?"

He bumped into a pair of legs sprawled across the floor, and he dropped to his knees. She wasn't wearing any protective gear. She lay very still in her jeans and lab coat with its pockets full of keys and pens and those little notebooks she was always scribbling in. He took her by the arms and dragged her toward the exit, but her face was so pale—skim-milk pale—that he bent to feel for a pulse. Fear pounding through his fingertips.

She wasn't conscious. She was barely breathing. Her eyes were shut. Her lips were blue. "Breathe," he said, pinching her nose shut, tilting her head back and blowing a single breath into her lungs.

No response.

"Hey." He gently slapped her face. "Willa?" Frantic. Terrified. *We just fell in love, and already you're leaving me?* "Willa!" His voice rebounded off the tiled walls as the white stuff continued to exit out the doorway in ropy twists and gusts. He leaned over and blew another breath into her lungs.

She coughed. Sputtered. Sat up. "Charlie?"

He almost laughed with relief. "You okay?"

"No, I'm . . . yes." She looked dazed.

He turned to the guard. "Call an ambulance!"

The guard got on his portable.

"My respirator stopped working," she said, "and I couldn't breathe. I tried the door, but it was stuck."

Shaken and enraged, he rocked her in his arms. "I need to find Rick. Do you know where he is?"

She shook her head, then threw her arms around his neck and held on tight, seeming to understand the implication of his question but unwilling to face it just yet. "He took the keys to the Doppler van," she said.

"The Doppler van?" He turned to the guard. "Is the Doppler van missing from the parking lot?"

The guard's confused eyes pulled closer together. "It wasn't registered to be checked out tonight, but I noticed it was gone."

"When did this happen?"

"About fifteen minutes ago. They do that sometimes, borrow the van without telling anyone. They always bring it back, though." His voice rose defensively. "I made a note of it on my rounds roster."

Just then a piercing cry came from out in the corridor. *"Charlie?"* It was his father.

"Be right back," he told Willa.

"Yeah, go." She smiled bravely at him. "I'm fine."

"Stay with her," he told the guard, then clambered down the ladder and ran back into the main hallway. "Pop?"

"Down here."

Around the next corner, he found his father standing near an open door, creamy white light spilling out into the corridor. The bronze plaque read "Missile Launcher Chamber."

Isaac's eyes were wide with fright. "It was open."

"Stay back." Aiming his gun, Charlie approached the doorway with extreme caution, like a man walking into a den of rattlers. Breathing through his mouth, he took a single step into the room and swept his gun around. "Police!"

The missile launcher chamber appeared to be empty. A long orange pipe, held in place by two metal supports, occupied the center of the rectangular room. Charlie felt his heart in his throat, right up near his gag reflex, as he crossed the chamber toward the long plate-glass window at the back of the room, his footsteps echoing off the tiled walls. Through beads of condensation on the glass, he could see a large water tank inside the closet-sized space and nothing else.

He lowered his weapon. "All clear," he said, and his father cautiously entered the room.

Just then Charlie caught something out of the corner of his eye—a glint of light. At the far end of the chamber, in the center of a plyboard panel, dangled an object that was startlingly familiar to him. Sophie's silver locket was the one piece of jewelry she would never take off. The necklace dangled from a penny nail and made a soft clinking sound. A wild sweat broke out on his face. "Jesus Christ . . ."

His father stepped directly in front of the panel.

"No!"

Isaac turned and eyed him questioningly.

A *snap* of compressed air, and the air cannon exploded, an eight-foot-long wooden stud flying out of the barrel and hitting his father center-mass with a thundering crunch. A small wavering sound of protest passed from Isaac's lips as it pierced him through and blew him backward into the wall.

Charlie sank to his knees, everything turning prickly for an instant. Heart pounding crazily. He couldn't catch his breath. From a tunneling darkness, he could hear faraway screams. *"Oh my God . . . oh my God . . ."*

Then he realized those screams were coming from him. He blinked away the dazzling red spots floating in his field of vision and looked down. Blood spiked his uniform front. He stumbled to his feet and crossed the room to where his father was pinned like a bug to the wall.

"Pop?" He checked for a pulse. *"Pop?"* The lurid light revealed too much. The missile had penetrated Isaac's chest cavity, his heart visible and pulsating weakly through the entry wound, an adjacent collapsed lung exposed. There was blood everywhere. Pooling down around his ankles.

"Pop?" Charlie stared into the meat of his father's face. His lips were so gray they looked like pipe smoke. Isaac tried to speak, then went completely still.

Charlie attempted to remove the wooden stud from the

wall, grunting and tugging, but it wouldn't budge. Cradling his father upright in his arms, he applied pressure to the wound, but there was a tremendous amount of give. The torn heart had stopped beating; he could count the broken ribs. *"Pop?"*

The old man's pupils were of differing sizes, and there was no reactive movement when Charlie touched one of the lenses with a tentative fingertip. Fixed and dilated. His hair reminded him of milkweed fluff. He paused to comb a few stray strands from that frozen face with trembling fingers, then heard a voice inside his head. His father's voice.

Never mind about me. Go save our little girl.

5

THE SNAP of feet over asphalt. Heart pounding, legs pumping, Charlie sprinted across the parking lot and tugged on the pickup truck door. *This is not how it's going to end,* he thought furiously as he crawled back inside the cold cab. He stabbed his key in the ignition, put the truck into gear and tore out of the lot, all the while groping for a sense of calm. *Take it on the chin. Breathe deep. Be a man.* His father, talking to him at the hospital, holding his hand. Talking him through the pain.

The air was speckled with blowing rain. He activated his cell phone and dialed the station house. "Mike?"

"What's going on, Chief?"

"It isn't good." He could feel his lips quivering around each word. "My father's dead."

"What?" came the incredulous reply.

"Rick Kripner rigged an air cannon with a trip wire. He used Sophie's locket as bait. She'd never go anywhere without it." He could feel his throat closing around this unspeakable thought. "I don't know what he did with her, but I can't believe he'd hurt her. He knows her. How could he hurt her?"

"Chief, calm down."

"I'm following the storm track to Aberdeen . . ."

"Wait a second, boss. What happened? What went down?"

"Rick was at the wind facility. We just missed him. He ditched the Sierra and took the Doppler van. He sabotaged the facility. Willa Bellman almost died. My father's dead. I couldn't find Sophie. I think he took her with him. My hunch is . . . Jesus Christ, I knew his M.O. was changing, but *this*." Fear clung like a net. "She can't be dead."

"Calm down, Chief."

"My hunch is he's wants to find a tornado before he . . . does anything to any more victims."

"The department's behind you. All our resources."

"There's a tornado warning down around Aberdeen. He's probably halfway there by now. I've got maybe forty minutes to catch up . . . I've really gotta book it, Mike . . . make up for lost time. Notify local law, tell them I'm on my way." The exhaustion hit him. There was no weight to him, no weight at all. "My guess is he's on his way to Aberdeen . . . looking for a tornado. Put out a BOLO for a brown Doppler van with 'Environmental Sciences Lab' on the side. And get some choppers in the air. Apprise everybody as to the level of danger. Tell them he's got a hostage with him. She's sixteen years old, five-foot-seven, brown hair, blue eyes . . . Jesus, Mike. Are you getting all this?"

"Yeah, I got it, boss."

"You'll be where I can reach you?"

"I'm right here, buddy. We're working the phones like crazy. We'll find this nut job, never fear."

"Tell them to be careful, this is my daughter we're talking about."

"Not to worry."

He hung up and stared at the sky. *Supercell. Find a supercell.* He had to get to Aberdeen as soon as possible. Once he got to East Texas, he'd look for one of those rotating clouds that resembled a nuclear explosion. A bead of sweat slid down his forehead as he squinted at the sky through the rain-spattered windshield, his gaze drifting toward a distant curl of cumulus, its underbelly like mauve-colored wool. He had maybe an hour of daylight left. He picked up the road map. Twitchy. Nervous.

Forget it. Forget the map.

He dropped the map on the seat, while the seconds boomed inside his head. *Tick, tick, tick.* He couldn't keep his teeth from chattering. The world was vast and blurry and all out of reach. In the distance, beyond the hills' crooked fence line, he could see a truck inching along a country road. Sophie couldn't be dead. He was convinced she was still alive, out there somewhere beyond the alfalfa fields and cattle ranches. When darkness came, when somebody you loved was out there all by herself . . . it shut you down. It beat you up. *No more losses. No more grief.* The smell of his own cowardly fear was making him gag.

Snagging his cell phone, he tried Rick's number again, fingers fumbling. Not expecting an answer.

"Yello?" came the toneless response.

Charlie stared at his own sweaty face with its questioning smile in the rearview mirror. His eyes looked back at him, reflecting a watery horror. "Rick?"

After a suspicious beat, he said, "Yes?"

"This is Charlie Grover."

A strangled laugh. "Oh . . . hello."

His heart pounded crazily. "Could I speak to Sophie, please?"

Short pause. "Well," Rick finally answered, "I took one look at those clouds last night and couldn't pass it up."

Charlie stiffened. Rick's evasiveness meant that Sophie was still alive—and that she was listening. Otherwise he wouldn't have bothered to evade the question. "Let me talk to her."

"I don't think so."

"Is she okay?"

"Right as rain."

Rick was clever. He hadn't mentioned Charlie's name yet, which meant that if Sophie was listening, she wouldn't know it was her father on the other end of the line. Charlie could deduce two things from this: one, that his daughter wasn't aware of the danger she was in, and two, that she wasn't bound and gagged. If Rick had tied her up, he wouldn't bother hiding Charlie's identity from her.

Charlie had been trained—ever so briefly and long ago—in hostage negotiations. The person he was dealing with was a sociopath who would be loyal to no one but himself. His relationship to others was manipulative and self-serving. He wanted what he wanted, when he wanted it. He blamed others for his behavior and didn't feel guilt or remorse the way most human beings did. He could be extremely cool. *Be careful. He may end up interviewing you.* Threats of punishment would not alter his unacceptable behavior. The solution must be face-saving, otherwise you were looking at a shoot-out. Tactical solutions were best. *Be calm. Be patient.*

"What're you doing?" Charlie asked in a level voice. "I thought we were friends."

"Yeah, sure. Good buddies."

Allow him to vent his feelings.

"What's this all about? Did I piss you off somehow?"

"Oh, hey. Don't get all philosophical on me now."

"I want to know what's bothering you. Tell me how I can help you, Rick."

"There's really nothing you can do."

Convince him that the safe release of the hostage is to his advantage. Do not try to bullshit this guy. He responds to authority figures; therefore, introducing a non-police negotiator might make the situation worse. Keep him busy. Offer something in return for a concession.

"If you let her go," Charlie said, "I'll back off the case. I won't pursue it."

That strangled laugh again.

"I won't follow you. You can go wherever you want to, just let her go. Please. I'm begging you."

"Well, now . . . *that's* believable."

Charlie's hands went stiff on the wheel as he drove past a filling station, while the rain poured down from the sky and dimpled the hood of the truck. He caught sight of his own pathetic face in the rearview mirror again and couldn't meet his desperate gaze. "Please . . . look. Let's negotiate."

"Nothin' doing."

He gripped the steering wheel, held on and felt himself dissolving, unraveling. *Don't get irritated. Don't interrupt.* "I know where you're headed," he said. "I'm coming after you."

"Oh, I doubt that very much."

"I'm right behind you."

"Uh-huh."

Don't use trigger words . . .

"You sick bastard, I'm right on your ass. You'll be seeing my face in your rearview mirror very shortly, you crack-headed piece of shit. It's the gray Loadmaster pickup truck, just so you know."

"What, those antiquated wheels? That heap leaks like a waterfall. I'm talking Third World antiquated. No, wait. The Third World would laugh at you."

Don't get mad . . . don't be argumentative . . .

"I'll track you down and rip out your heart with my teeth, you sorry-ass son of a bitch."

"Hm. You think?"

Don't be tough, don't be defensive . . .

"I'm coming after you, you demented freak . . . you sick fuck . . . I'll kill you, make no mistake about it."

"Listen," Rick said coolly. "Because you're such a nice guy, here's what I'll do. I'll let you in on a trade secret. Don't let the models do the forecasting for you. Use them selectively. They've burned many. I mean, yeah . . . you can look at them and get a basic idea. Like today, for instance. Everybody's got a hard-on for Aberdeen. Check it out yourself. See if the previous twelve-hour forecasts match your current analysis, but I'd advise you to listen to your gut. This is where fate steps in."

Charlie pressed his fingers to his eyelids and blinked away the tears. ". . . wait a second."

"Good luck."

A scream of static disconnected them.

"Hello? Motherfucker!!!" Charlie tossed the cell phone and reached for the old analog controls of the CB radio, multiple voices sputtering out of the speaker. He scooped up the mike and, working to keep his voice under control, said, "Can I get a break? Break one-oh? How's it looking in Texas? How's it looking in Aberdeen? Anybody out there with an update?"

He listened to sporadic reports through the crackling

static: ". . . we're on the boulevard, driver, let's do it to it . . . watch your back, it's spitting hail balls . . . slow down, you got a bunch of Boy Scouts past the next rest area . . ."

Charlie searched the darkening sky, then pounded his fist on the steering wheel, pounded until it was sore. He slumped over the wheel in a daze. This was hopeless, like looking for a needle in a haystack. His mind went stubbornly blank. His body felt brutalized. Time rivered away like raindrops on a windshield. Exhausted and shaken, he thought about the brown Doppler van and had a flash of Rick Kripner behind the wheel. In this vision, he pulled up alongside the van, aimed his loaded gun at Rick's head and pulled the trigger . . . blew his fucking brains out. *Just find her. Shut up and find her.*

His father's voice.

A renewed fury tore at his limbs. He jabbed the horn and raced toward the yellow light, exhaust echoing. A blue Pontiac slammed on its brakes behind him as he shot through the red light and went tearing off down the interstate.

6

SOPHIE TOUCHED the naked-feeling spot at the base of her throat where her locket used to be. Rick had told her to wait in the Doppler van, that he'd fix it real quick; but when he came back out of the wind facility, he didn't have the necklace with him. "We'll pick it up on the way back," he'd promised her. That was twenty minutes ago.

Now they were heading west on the I-40, and Rick was going on and on about tornadoes—blah, blah, blah—and the only thing she could think about was her missing necklace. She never should've given it to him in the first place. "What?" she said distractedly.

"Catastrophic." He wiped a spot on the windshield with his thumb. "Cataclysmic."

"You really like those cata words."

He laughed.

"You've gotta admit," she said while an echoey thunder rolled across the plains, "storm-chasing's a pretty weird hobby."

He shot her a glance. "They're all heroes in my book."

"You've got a book?"

"Yeah, I've got a book. And a motto. *Cogito, ergo zoom.*"

" 'I think, therefore I chase.' See? I'm no slouch myself, you know. I almost got killed chasing an F-2 the other day."

"I know. You told me. And the reason you almost got killed is because your friend Boone Pritchett doesn't know his ass from helicity. You hungry?"

"No thanks."

"Because there's a candy bar in the glove compartment. Go on," he said. "Help yourself."

"No thanks."

"Really. Don't be shy."

She clicked open the glove compartment and fished around for the candy bar, mostly out of politeness. She wasn't that hungry, but she peeled off the wrapper and took a bite, anyway. "It's getting kind of late," she said. "Don't you think?"

"Nah. Best part of the day. Besides, these are dream conditions. You don't want to pass up an opportunity like this, do you?"

She shrugged. "Guess not."

"Go on. Eat up. You'll need your strength."

She took another bite and was beginning to have serious doubts about the whole thing. Regrets. Rick had been so persuasive back at the house. He'd promised to call her father; he'd even written the note himself. "I dunno," she said, thinking about her father and how upset he would be. "Maybe we should just blow it off."

"Are you kidding? We've got another forty minutes left before sunset, and even then —uh-oh. Don't look now, but an eighteen-wheeler's trying to run us over."

In the side-view mirror, she could see a cobalt-colored Mack truck bearing down on them.

"Lucky for him I'm a nice guy," Rick said, easing his foot off the gas. "If I see a big rig gaining on me, I'll reduce my speed by five or ten miles and let him pass. You don't want him just sitting there on your ass."

The Mack truck roared by on the left, honking its horn.

"Like I don't see you, you mesomorph!" He flipped a switch and the flat fifteen-inch LCD screen mounted above Sophie's head lit up. Across the display screen, a repeating radar loop flashed mostly red. "Wow. Look at all those East Texas beasts," he said. "Time to head north."

"North?" She looked at him, confused. "But I thought we were going to Aberdeen."

"Nah, Texas is bush-league. We're taking a different route to paradise."

She rested the candy bar in her lap, no longer hungry.

"See these two storms?" He pointed at the LCD screen. "See the one further north? That's what you'd call a mother-ship storm. Once the cap breaks, it's gonna grow explosively. I predict we'll be playing with this baby very shortly."

"But aren't you supposed to quit when the sun goes down?"

"What're you, chicken?"

She shook her head, feeling light-headed all of a sudden. She looked down at the candy bar. Her brain was numb.

"I thought you wanted to see a tornado up close and personal, kiddo?" he said.

"I did. I mean, I do." Her facial muscles knotted. "I guess."

"You guess?" His eyes dwindled in their frowning sockets. "Didn't you just say to me, 'You ain't no slouch'?"

"I'm not, but . . ."

"But what?" He looked at her sideways. "You're not going soft on me, are you, Sophie?"

"No . . ."

"Because you're the one who begged me to take you storm-chasing in the first place, remember?"

"I know." She shot him a sidelong glance. "But . . ."

"But what? What's all this 'but' crap?" His look was a challenge. "Don't put me in a black mood, kiddo. You don't wanna see me in one of my black moods."

She curled her arms around her chest, feeling dizzy. Something was wrong. The interior of the van was freezing because he had the a/c cranked so high. They passed a deserted gas station, its metal sign swinging to and fro in the wind. She didn't have a clue where they were anymore. The rain was clicking and tapping against the roof like little claws.

He glanced at her, his knuckles going white on the wheel. "Sorry," he said. "I didn't mean to scare you."

"No," she said softly. "That's okay."

There were dots of pink on his cheeks as if, deep down, he were holding himself very tenderly. "Can I trust you?" he whispered. "With a secret?"

She closed her eyes for a second, not wanting to hear any secrets.

"Remember how my father died?"

"Yeah," she said. *The tornado, the wheat, the barn.*

He grinned, coaxing a smile out of her.

"What?"

"I lied."

"What d'you mean?"

"He died in a tornado, but under different circumstances."

She was getting drowsy. The droning engine was making her sleepy, and the rain had turned the air purple. "I don't get it," she heard herself say.

His face showed both discomfort and excitement. "Lemme put it this way." He glanced at her through parted lashes. "My father was a thief."

"What?" That got her attention.

"A house burglar."

"Really?"

"He'd rob houses during a tornado watch or warning. Now, before you go judging me . . . wouldn't you lie, too? If your father was a thief instead of a cop?"

She took a confused breath. She really didn't understand where this conversation was headed. She tucked her hands between her knees, the air inside the van so cold you could see your own breath.

"Doesn't matter how he died," he said. "The fact remains, he got what he deserved."

She eyed him through a haze of drowsiness. "How can you say that?"

"Don't you believe that some people are so evil, Sophie, they deserve to die?"

The silence that followed made her scalp prickle. It was hard to stop watching the horizon. She couldn't help but be mesmerized by the swirling, dangling clouds. All she could hear was the drumbeat of the rain and the steady *clip-clip-clip* of the windshield wipers. Something had turned in him, she didn't know what. She had a vague sense that she might be in danger, but all she wanted to do was close her eyes and fall asleep, worry about it later.

Rick spoke with a slight hesitation. "You should've

seen me back then. I was the nicest kid on the block. The Boy Scout next door. But then over time, I built up a real hatred for the world, you know?"

She drew very quietly into herself and tried to become invisible. Her eyes swept to the street. They were off the I-40 now, sailing past wild prairie and abandoned houses like the bones of ruin, fallen-down corrals and rusting crew-cab pickups. She had no idea where they were on the map. The rain made a steady hammering sound, while all around them, thunder crashed like the boom of the surf.

"I didn't start out that way," he went on. "I started out soft and open, like you. Well, maybe not exactly like you. You fit in, right?"

She didn't answer.

"I never fit in. Oh, I can fake fitting in. I can fake it pretty good. But it's like you're on the outside all your life, looking in." He studied her face as if he were deciding whether or not to go on. He held out his hand. "See that?"

She remembered: The finger was bent at the tip, permanently deformed from flying debris.

"He did that to me." He rolled up the sleeve of his flannel shirt so that she could see several dime-sized scars on his arm. "He'd burn me with his cigarettes whenever I misbehaved. He decided early on that I was incorrigible. I had to ask his permission to use the bathroom. If I forgot to ask permission, he'd burn me with his cigarettes."

Her hands felt as tiny as paws in her lap.

"But that's nothing compared to what happened when I *really* screwed up." He looked at her. "By the time I was your age, I didn't have a single tooth left in my head."

"What?" She sat rigidly upright.

"One tooth for each bad deed." He clacked his teeth together. "Any stupid mistake. Any insubordination, and he'd yank another tooth out of my head."

She stared at his mouth, and it was true—his teeth didn't seem quite real. They were too perfect. Too white.

"All growing up, I'd look in the mirror and think I was dead," he said. "I was small for my age, bowlegged. I got picked on a lot. I wore long sleeves in the summertime so the other kids wouldn't see my scars. I can't remember ever being happy." He stared at her fixedly. "But I wouldn't trade what I've become . . . what I've evolved into . . . for anything in the world."

She could hear her own heart thudding in her ears.

"There was this chair up in the attic, a very special chair reserved just for me." The van's engine droned hypnotically behind his voice. "He'd strap me into that goddamn chair and leave me there. He'd let me wait with my awful fears. I'd wait all by myself, scared out of my wits, imagining the worst. The chair faced a window, and I'd watch the wind stirring the wheat outside. I thought it was God, writing me messages with his finger." He laughed. "I thought He was trying to tell me something."

She idly picked at the peacoat's big navy buttons, trying to blot him out. *Take me home, take me home . . .*

"To this day, I can't stand being confined. I won't fly. And I absolutely refuse to wear a seat belt."

She noticed that he wasn't buckled in.

"I'd sit there staring at new cells developing along the

horizon . . . and back-sheared anvils . . . and sheets of rain flapping across the plains . . ."

Her hair fell loosely, hiding her face.

"Waiting for him to come upstairs and do bad things to me. Up those attic stairs," he said. "He'd come at me with everything he had. If I cried out, he went at it harder . . . he'd pour whiskey over my face and down my neck . . . grab the pliers. I'd be screaming the whole time. After a while, you learn to shut down emotionally. You stare out the window and start to see things." His voice grew hushed. "I remember my first tornado. It was just *rrrr, rrrr, rrrr*. A puny, rope-sized F-1, but to me it was a real beast. I was strapped in that chair, helpless, when suddenly I realized . . . *I wanted to be that thing . . . that breathtaking thing . . .* wanted to rip through the wheat and roar toward the house and kill everything in my way, including my old man. We watched the wheat get completely demolished. Dad started crying. And I said to him, 'Don't worry, Daddy, we'll put it back together.' But inside, I was thinking that I'd destroyed his wheat. *Me.* I'd put that look of torment on his face. And it felt so fucking good."

A large silence.

He turned to her. "Are you mad at me?"

"Why?" she asked with veiled eyes. "Should I be?"

"I dunno. You seem kind of distant."

She was feeling smaller and smaller. "Well, I'm not."

"Did I scare you?"

She hesitated, not knowing what the right answer was.

"I didn't mean to scare you." His expression changed. His eyes grew warmer. "I had this dream last night, Sophie. About the two of us."

She glanced at the door handle. Stared at it. They were doing sixty, and there was nothing around for miles. Literally nothing but grass. Should she jump?

"Sophie?"

She folded herself into silence.

"Buckle up," he said as they swerved full bore around the Mack truck. "You're in for the ride of your life."

7

BARRELING WEST on the I-40, Charlie was forced to slow to a crawl when a TV truck decided to park in the middle of the highway and block the oncoming traffic while the cameraman set up in the passing lane, since they needed a dramatic backdrop for the reporter broadcasting live feed. Charlie jabbed his horn repeatedly, then wove in and out of traffic, saying, "Excuse me! Excuse me!" Finally out of sheer frustration, he veered onto private land and cut across a field doing 40 mph.

When he got back on the highway, he was crying. Pathetic. Tears streaming down his face. Voices whispering inside his head. *Don't let the models do the forecasting for you. Use them selectively. They've burned many.* Why tell him this? Why give him any advice at all? What was Rick trying to do? Was it a miscue? Did he somehow sense that Charlie would fail? That his gut would mislead him? The Panhandle and Aberdeen were hotbeds of activity tonight. Why shouldn't he follow everyone else's lead? Maybe that was exactly what his gut was telling him to do.

Tears of frustration streamed down his face, while the

voices continued to give conflicting advice. *Check it out yourself. Just drive straight into Texas, son. This is where fate steps in.* He tapped the steering wheel with anxious fingers, trying to concentrate. He'd been monitoring spotter reports from as far away as Clarendon, Texas, where a huge storm system was spewing out F-1s and F-2s, weaker tornadoes that touched down harmlessly and dissipated quickly. Every chaser on the planet, it seemed, was tearing a new asshole into East Texas—porcupine trucks, Explorers, Chrysler New Yorkers, a big old Impala with the Road Runner painted on the hood. And what was Charlie doing? He was en route to Aberdeen, just like everybody else. *Aberdeen's the place we wanna be, son.*

I'd advise you to listen to your gut . . .

He cast a feverish glance at the equipment inside the truck—a laptop computer, an Internet-by-satellite service and a ninety-nine-dollar portable clip-on DSS dish used to download information. His father carried basic gear. A regular cellular modem that didn't get any better than 9,600 bps, which meant that if you were out of the coverage area or in heavy radio congestion, you were flat out of luck. A CB radio. Charlie recalled Willa's advice: *CBs aren't used as much these days, but truckers are everywhere and they're better than the weather forecasters as to road conditions and the looks of the sky. Remember to ask questions. They can be your eyes and ears.*

He fumbled one-handed with the laptop and downloaded a weather update from the National Weather Service. The forty-eight-hour satellite imagery showed an impressive air mass approaching from the west near Aberdeen. The radar showed big red splotches moving southwest to northeast, covering all of East Texas and parts of Oklahoma. He could hear thunderboomers way off in the distance.

Follow your gut.

His gut was confusing the hell out of him. He needed an expert, somebody who could walk him through this nightmare. He needed Willa. *Willa.* God, he hoped she was okay; she seemed fine when he'd left her. He groped for the cell phone and hastily dialed her number but got no response. He hung up and tried the station house.

"Mikc? I need you to track down Willa Bellman for me. I think she might be en route to the hospital . . . Mike?"

Through bursts of interference, he heard: ". . . Chief? . . . they had to call off the choppers . . . sky's getting hairy . . ."

"What?"

". . . canceled the choppers . . . we're not . . ."

"I can't hear you!" The phone spit static in his ear. "Mike? You're breaking up," he said, his own sour breath rebounding off the receiver.

". . . called highway patrol . . . don't think . . ."

There was a final spritz of noise as their connection was severed. "Fuck!" He was outside the coverage area. He tossed the useless phone away and searched the sky. Where was he going? Where the hell was he going? He squinted at the overcast. Blanks. He was drawing blanks all over the place. He tried to stem the rising tide of panic, while memories of Sophie came and went like the checkered images of a movie montage, washed in shadow. *Skinny, freckled, walking on the balls of her feet; laughing, crying, shrinking from strangers. Sophie in her Xena costume, trying to look ominous. Her funny little smile. Bubble gum, flip-flops, school plays; Sophie in the spot-*

*light, her small face growing pale onstage as she forgot
her lines. His heart aching for her. Fearing for her.*

Checking his rearview, he noticed a refrigeration truck
bearing steadily down on him. "Look at this lunatic, right
on my ass . . ."

The refrigeration truck clipped his mirror, practically
blowing out his windows and giving him the impression
that he was standing still. The wind rocked the
Loadmaster as the truck roared past, hammer down. Once
it'd cleared his hood, he saw the "Will Have Sex for
Beer!" bumper sticker.

Cranking the CB and scooping up the hand mike,
Charlie said, "Hey, where's the fire?"

The driver of the rogue vehicle came back over the
radio with a simple "What's your handle back there?"

Charlie didn't have a handle.

"Who's that sweeping the leaves behind me?"

"Burned-All-Over," he finally said.

"Come back on that? Somebody walked all over you."

"Burned-All-Over," he repeated angrily.

"Appreciate it, Burned-All-Over. This here is Reefer.
I'm on my way to shaky town via Lubbock. Wolfgang
Puck wants his arugula freshly picked, you know. Watch
out for the picture machine up ahead at mile marker one-
six-oh."

"I need help in locating a vehicle," Charlie said.

He listened to crackling static while gazing at the gentle roll of land beyond the hypnotizing *slush-slush* of his
windshield wipers. There was nothing but grass on either
side of the road, wild grass that ran before the wind in
great strings of air, great flapping sheets. Scuds of rain
crackled against his windshield, creating a tent of sound.
He tried to keep the hitch out of his voice as he keyed the

mike again. "I said I'm looking for a brown Doppler van with 'Environmental Sciences' stenciled on the side."

"Haven't seen any Doppler trucks . . ."

"Van . . . a brown Doppler van . . . This is an emergency."

"Sorry, driver. Gotta shake the leaves. Channel 9 is reserved for emergency use."

"Channel 9?"

The CB clicked and went silent. Charlie watched the refrigeration truck hydroplane into the rain, then he swerved into the breakdown lane and let the truck idle, while other chase cars continued to pass by on the left. *Zoom, zoom, zoom.*

Charlie tapped his holstered handgun, and the fear hit him all over again. It sank like a hot rock in his gut. He didn't want to think about her. If he thought about his daughter, he might lose it completely, and that wouldn't do anybody any good. He sat searching the steel-colored sky to his west, then slowly honed his gaze northward, where darker clouds pulsed with lightning. The sky looked more promising to the northeast, for sure. He didn't get it. Why was everybody and their mother heading for Texas tonight?

He flipped the channel selector on the CB and transmitted a message. "I'm looking for a Doppler van." He gave details. Kept it short. "Anybody? I'm looking for a Doppler van with 'Environmental Sciences' stenciled on the side . . . a brown Doppler van . . . This is an emergency." A few people responded, but no one had seen any Doppler vans in the vicinity.

He dunked the mike back in its metal retainer and lowered his forehead onto his fist. "Whoever said 'No news is good news' is an idiot," he muttered. The sound of his own voice made him angry. He thought about the corpses they'd found with pieces of flying debris sticking out of them at odd angles. Shame burned across his scalp. He wouldn't let Rick harm his daughter. It became a sticking point in his heart. He wasn't about to let anybody hurt a hair on her lovely head.

His brain felt scorched. His eyes were in a permanent squint. He could feel pins and needles in his legs from where his circulation had been compromised. These tiny agricultural communities in northwestern Oklahoma consisted of little more than a farm equipment store and a string of roads reeling out into the grasslands. He scanned the horizon, nothing but prairie and telephone poles for miles around. He drummed his fingers on the steering wheel. On the radio was the chasers' anthem, "Bad Moon Rising."

Trust your gut.

The overcast sky had a sculpted appearance, the horizon turning progressively more ominous toward the north, where the revolver-colored clouds were veined with lightning. Up through the ugly cloud bank, he could see a mass of ivory-white storm clouds shooting up like an A-bomb. You needed three things to make a tornado, he recalled: sufficient moisture, dynamics to lift the air and jet streams to provide wind shear, which would help create rotation. A combination of perfect timing, positioning and good fortune. He had a gut feeling he should be heading northeast, not west; against all expert advice.

Trust your gut.

The very thought made his skin crawl. What if his gut was wrong? *Follow the yellow brick road.* Which way? On a bare-naked hunch, he released the hand brake, looked over his shoulder, put the truck in reverse and took the nearest exit off the interstate. He headed east for several miles before the panic began to set in.

Wrong way, wrong way . . . turn back. Go to Aberdeen, you loser. Don't lose her.

He checked the map on the seat beside him and followed his finger northeast of his current position. He switched channels on the CB again, keyed the mike and said, "Breaker one-oh. I'm looking for a Doppler van in the vicinity of Erick or Texola . . ."

Follow your gut. Take a chance.

A pale blue El Camino whizzed past him in the westbound lane. "Hey, breaker, you lookin' for a tornado?" the driver said.

"Yeah, anything."

"I just got a call from my nowcaster. He says all this hyped-up stuff over Texas is dying out but that something truly awesome is popping to the north of us."

"North?"

"Up around Sweetwater. My nowcaster tells me a tornado warning has just been issued. I'm gonna bug out . . . Good luck!"

Charlie hit the gas, looking for an exit that would take him north to Sweetwater. After a few minutes, darkness seized the sky. It got so dark he needed a flashlight just to read the road map. Several other chase vehicles shot past him in the opposite direction. The direction of Texas. He felt a nagging doubt.

He switched back to channel 9. The first rule of radio courtesy was to listen before you transmitted, but Charlie committed the cardinal sin and interrupted again. "This is Burned-All-Over, I've got an emergency request . . ." He made his announcement again. Listened to scattered voices. ". . . roller skate, greasy side up . . ." CBs used radio frequency waves that traveled from transmitter to receiver in a fairly straight line near the ground. Maximum range was twenty-five to seventy-five miles, depending upon the terrain and the vehicles' antennae. Only one person could transmit on a channel at a time without creating chaos.

Now a deep male voice squelched the static. "Burned-All-Over? This is Spare Wheel. You lookin' for a Doppler van?"

Charlie snagged the mike. "You've seen it?"

"Five minutes ago . . . Let's move to one-two."

In some neighborhoods, channel 9 was used as a calling channel, which meant that after making contact, you were to immediately move to another channel so that everybody in the neighborhood could monitor channel 9 and increase the chances of an emergency call being heard. Charlie switched to channel 12.

"Where?" A spike of static made him jump. Multiple voices crackled competitively over the radio speaker, while he fiddled with the old analog controls. "Hello? Say again, Spare Wheel. Somebody trounced all over you."

". . . heading north . . ."

"Which way?" Fear thickened the words in his throat. "I didn't catch that."

"Heading north on Route 30," the trucker broke in. "I don't run Route 30 very often, it's a real boardwalk. There's a pothole every five inches."

"Route 30?"

"Three miles west of Sweetwater. Those weather weenies from Dryden Tech don't know shit. All the action's in Aberdeen today. He must have his head inserted firmly up his ass."

"Thanks a million." He dunked the mike back, put the

truck into high gear and drove east until he intersected Route 30 at a perfect right angle. Then he drove north . . . north . . . speeding over potholes so large you could go fishing in them. What if he was too late? His heart clenched. *Hope to God . . . hope to God . . . don't let it be too late.*

8

S_{HH}." R_{ICK}'s mouth tensed into white crinkles.

"What?" Sophie whispered, hearing only a glassy silence.

"Just listen."

She stared at him uneasily. She felt like she was in a trance. They were parked by the side of the road, and the world outside had gone all methyl green. She drew her collar close against the chill and held her breath, but all she could hear was the trembling wind, the ceaseless drumbeat of rain on the roof, the van rocking very gently on its axles.

"That cap's gone thermonuclear," Rick said. "I predict we're gonna get blitzed very shortly. Should we go or stay put? Up to you, kiddo."

She eyed him questioningly.

"Towers looming. Incredible punch throughout the sky." He frowned. "We'll stay put and watch it for a while."

She nodded as the sky grew suddenly blacker, a shadow falling over the van, over the road, over them.

"You get nickel- and dime-sized hail as a storm collapses, so obviously you want it bigger than that. The bigger the hail, the stronger the storm." He cocked his head. "Listen."

"To what?"

"Here it comes."

A large hailstone pinged off the windshield, a silver web forming instantly on the black glass. Her heart convulsed. She felt the texture of the seat with her palms, then raised her hands to run them over the wool jacket, its fabric crinkling with electricity.

"Can we go now?" she asked, struggling to keep the fear out of her voice. "Please?"

His face grew strangely taut as he stared at the streaks of silver flashing past their headlight patterns, two alabaster circles in the dark.

"Can we?"

"Not yet."

He was somehow too powerful to contradict.

"It's gonna be a good show. Heavy stones. You don't wanna miss this."

The van shook as a slew of hailstones briefly whacked the right side of the vehicle. She reached for her locket, then remembered it was gone. Tears flooded her eyes and dropped down her cheeks, and it sickened her to think how far away from home she was.

"I like the way this looks," Rick said. "Smooth. Some spiked. We may get hailstones up to three inches."

"Please don't hurt me," she whispered.

He gave her a strange look. "When the weather changes . . ." His eyes never left her face. ". . . you lose control . . . you just lose control and everything changes . . ."

She could feel a small scream rising inside her.

"I won't deny what I've become." He looked out the

window again. "It builds slowly inside you. And then a voice says, 'This house' or 'That one.' I just hate to see it all standing there. I want the wind to blow it all away."

Terrified of the storm, of him, she yanked on the door and was barely able to push it open against the wind. She screamed as a curtain of hail whipped across the van, ice hammering metal.

Bang, bang, bang . . .

Large spiky hailstones battered her pale, shivering flesh, and with a terrified scream, she ducked back inside.

Bang, bang, bang . . .

A damaging volley of hailstones crackled against the windshield, leaving granular fractures in the glass. She screamed as hail thundered down around them—rattling the roof, denting the doors, hammering the hood.

"I wanna go." She shuddered convulsively. "Take me home!"

He gave her a skeptical look. "Do you honestly think it's safer there?"

There followed a weighty pause.

She could feel her face becoming tense as he inched closer. She dragged her nails across his face. "Get away!" She fought him off with an animal fear. "Get away from me!" She reached for the door handle again, but he grabbed her by the wrists and pulled her close—so close she could hear him breathing, could see the stitched white line of his mouth. Could feel his legs tense beside her.

"When lightning is this close, needless to say," he hissed in her face, "remain in the car."

Sophie screamed. She screamed until her lungs were raw, while all around them, thunder boomed and jagged lightning brought the sky terrifyingly close. She bucked from side to side, but he struck a swift blow with his open hand, hitting her in the windpipe.

It messed up her breathing.

She felt the blow in the soft tissue of her throat . . . and trembled all over . . . before everything went black.

9

THE ROAD from hell, Route 30, was as straight as a trail of ants. Charlie hit another pothole and could taste his own blood. "Fuck!" He was jamming through yet another one-light town, bouncing over the deeply rutted road and feeling all twisted and sweaty inside his clothes. An updraft of wind blew a burst of twigs and leaves against the truck, and a few stray hailstones popped off the roof. Glancing in his rearview, he caught sight of the northern edge of a massive storm front—a vast, churning super-cell cruising north by northeast at approximately forty knots, the entire atmosphere in fast-forward. An escalating wind mussed the grass and flung the birds about. It blasted through the trees and spit out leaves and twigs like watermelon seeds.

His eyes burned with fatigue. The defensive shell he'd worked so hard to construct over the past several hours was beginning to crumble, and in its place was nothing but a sheer, unadulterated panic. Crows flapped away from inkblots of roadkill, and lightning leaped between the clouds as Charlie's foot squeezed the gas pedal. The long, straight road sucked him onward, past blighted patches of

dirt and saplings too small to hide behind. The monotony
of the landscape got into your blood like a slow-acting poison. One day you woke up and couldn't live anyplace else.

"Come on, come on . . ." The pickup truck strained up
a gradual rise as he threw it into gear, the flesh of his back
clutching tighter. He tried not to picture his daughter—so
small, so helpless—and groped for some kernel of hope.
She had backbone. She would fight him.

Now he spotted a lone vehicle on the road up ahead
and throttled down. Unholstered his .38 and rested it on
the seat beside him. The vehicle was parked by the side
of the road. Charlie eased his foot off the gas and caught
sight of a satellite dish on the roof.

The brown Doppler van.

A surge of elation spasmed through him. He wanted to
tear out of the truck, but all his years of police training
prevented him from acting on impulse. If he pulled up behind the van now, Rick would have the advantage. He
might hurt her. Charlie had to think. *Don't try to solve
everything at once. Be patient. Achieve safe surrender of
the perpetrator.*

His eyes welled with indignation as he edged past the
Doppler van and caught sight of two figures inside the
cab, the interior light bathing them in a yellow glow.
Don't stop, don't stop. Behind him, a giant striated updraft was slowly churning its way across the plains. They
had somehow arrived at the foot of a massive HP beast;
it looked like a 1950s atomic bomb blast with its rock-
hard tower, cumuliform anvil and great gnarled knuckles.

Fear tearing at his sanity, Charlie inched past the van
and kept going for several mind-numbing minutes more,
until he was certain that the van hadn't followed. The rotating wall cloud suddenly changed shape, going from a

transparent mist to a solid brown mass. It was perfectly backlit, Jesus rays streaming down the western side of the updraft. From this dark mass, a pencil-thin tornado descended from the clouds and jabbed into the ground like an ice pick.

Ignore the hostage. Give her minimal attention. That only makes her more valuable to the hostage-taker.

He switched off his lights and decelerated, slipping into neutral. Taking his foot off the gas, he turned the wheel ninety degrees, and the truck fishtailed across the wet road, tires chirping. The rear end swung around, items in the flatbed banging against one another, metal slamming metal.

The Loadmaster came to a rickety stop. He could hear a high-pitched hum in the air from a nearby transformer, while up ahead, two flags of rain shimmered in the Doppler van's high beams. The air was hazy with dust and debris. Gritting his teeth, he grabbed his gun and stepped out of the truck.

10

THERE WAS silence in the center of her mind, an odd calm. Her lower jaw throbbed dully. The wind was making a harmonica sound, whistling through the van. Another flock of hailstones hit the glass.

Bang, bang, bang . . .

Groggily Sophie opened her eyes. Rick Kripner was hovering over her, his face lit with an odd fascination. She feared him. She did not know him. Screaming, she struck him across the face.

He flinched and caught her arm. "Somebody's awake."

She screamed again, blood filling her mouth.

"Do you think you could work on that attitude of yours?"

"Leggo!" She lashed out, stars strobing in her field of vision. She gasped for breath. "Let go of me!"

Suddenly and indifferently he released her and rested his hands on the steering wheel, fingers curling possessively around it. He tapped his thumbs to the beat of the wipers and looked out at the night as if he were hypnotized by it.

Bang, bang, bang . . .

Another volley of hailstones swept across the vehicle. The driver's side window cracked, a spiderweb forming on the glass. Behind them, she could see a spectacular coffee-can updraft in the lightning flashes. She reached for the door handle and was about to leap out when he jerked her back inside.

"Things don't always go the way we want them to, Sophie," he said. "Life's funny that way."

Choking back her revulsion, she reached for the door again. Spasms in her breathing.

Bang, bang, bang . . .

He yanked her back.

Bang, bang, bang . . .

Then something awful happened. The driver's side window shattered, glass shards exploding into the cab like a thousand icicles, and a fat sweaty fist smashed into Rick's face with a sickening crunch.

His head flew sideways. His neck snapped. His false teeth went flying. The upper plate nicked Sophie in the scalp, and the lower plate landed in her lap. It was pink and wet and disgusting, and she screamed until her voice gave out.

Now an arm reached into the broken window and tried to tear Rick out of the van. Sophie groped for the keys, but Rick stomped on the gas, released the emergency brake, and suddenly they were lurching forward into the blinding storm, while hailstones screamed down out of the sky. The van slid over the road, tires squealing, as Rick bellowed, *"Teef! Teef!"*

"What?"

He held out his hand. *"Teef!"*

She stared in horror at that raw-looking hole.

He scooped up the lower plate and mashed it into his mouth, making the shrill, obscene sound of a castrated bull as they flew into darkness.

11

SHIT!" CHARLIE fired three rounds at the fleeing van, trying to blow out a rear tire. He'd seen his daughter, seen her alive. Rain dripped down his neck, and the wind turned his uniform into a million dancing butterflies. His nose was broken, and his knuckles were bleeding. He'd used the butt of his PR-24 baton to smash through the glass and could still taste the impact of knuckles on jawbone. He stood for a paralyzed instant while hailstones pounded down around him and the van's taillights zigzagged into the mist. Then he holstered his weapon and broke into a sprint, boots sinking into the mud.

Charlie dug in with pounding strides back to the Loadmaster, where he tore open the door and hopped inside, a gust of wind slamming it shut behind him. He held on tight to the steering wheel and stomped on the gas, tires grabbing and spinning forward. The truck slewed sideways—it was like driving on ice cream—but he managed to level it out and floored it down the road.

It took a combination of poor steering, lousy road conditions and weight shifts to turn a vehicle over, and Charlie wasn't about to let that happen. He couldn't see a damn thing through the prismed windshield and knocked out the rest of the safety glass with the butt of his gun. He'd seen his daughter alive—she was wearing her seat belt and shoulder harness. *Good girl.* He'd also seen that Rick wasn't wearing any seat belt. Dumb move. Now Charlie could ram the back of the vehicle at full throttle, jolting it off the road and preventing Rick from fleeing; since Sophie was buckled in, she'd be relatively safe. Safer than if he let them go.

The Doppler van made an abrupt left turn, cutting across the field on an intercept course. Charlie lurched after them, Michelin tires chewing up fist-sized chunks of earth and humping over ruts. He could feel the rear wheels spinning viciously as he veered down yet another poorly paved road, the old engine ripping and grinding.

Visibility cleared as he punched out of the hailstorm, pink whorls of light breaking through the scattered clouds. He could see the van's taillights twinkling on the road up ahead and a terrible sight beyond—electrical discharges the color of marigolds shooting out of the core precipitation, the dark dusty wedge itself whipping around like a cosmic tantrum. A cap of exploding azulene billowed above the band, visible in a vivid background of lightning, with suction spots circling the outer edges. The debris cloud was at least half a mile wide at the base, with two-by-fours and tree limbs flying around the periphery like tiddlywinks. The monster was twice as wide as it was tall, an enormous spinning top rotating at about 250 miles per hour. He figured he should probably get out of the way of that.

The next bolt of lightning crackled the atmosphere, and an icy wind scraped into the cab. Charlie glanced at his speedometer. The needle was inching past sixty, and the fuel tank was nearly empty. *"Don't fail me now, you lovely piece of shit."* He heard a muffled snapping sound as he rammed it into gear and drove the pedal to the floor.

The new tires tore for a grip on the slick asphalt as he steadily gained on the van. He veered into the oncoming lane, the smell of burning rubber hitting his nostrils, and picked a spot on the back bumper. He waited a beat, then wrenched the wheel sharply to the right. Throttle down, he slammed into the van at probably 70 mph. He could feel the flesh of his face rippling over bone as the two vehicles converged and the Loadmaster delivered a disabling crunch.

BAMMMM!!!

The frame pushed straight up. His front bumper, embedded in the van's fender, made a huge squealing sound, in sour harmony with the flogged V-8s and screaming tires. After a few hairy moments, the van tore away and spun off the road, tires spitting out white clouds of smoke.

Charlie slammed his foot on the brake pedal, and all four wheels instantly locked solid to the brake drums. He was out of control, spinning counterclockwise, the heavier front end dragging the rest of the truck around. Equipment flew sideways inside the cabin, chunks of plastic breaking off and exploding like shrapnel. A black toolbox collided with his skull and he saw stars. Time dilated. He was plunged into a chilling silence, into a thick and coiling darkness, as the truck described a lazy arc in midair.

12

SOPHIE PLASTERED herself against her seat as the van went into a deadly skid, slewing sideways across the road. They spun around, *thwunk, thwunk,* crack-thumping over potholes. A disabling fear descended as the vehicle ground to a halt, and then, with a creaking groan, everything went still.

Pain shot up her spine. She licked her lips and could taste the blood on her teeth. Raising her hands to her face, she noticed that some of her purple nail polish was chipped, an incongruous thought. She heard a sound like rapidly flowing water. It got louder. Deeper tones became audible. The windshield was crazed into a thousand fractures, and through the jewel-like glass she thought she saw insects swirling in the sweep of the van's headlights. Only those weren't insects, she soon realized, but chunks of debris caught up in the ferocious updraft.

"Fuck." Rick rubbed his forehead, and she looked at him uncomprehendingly. He gazed back, the corners of his mouth drawing up like curtains.

She became terrified of him all over again. The van shook with pulses of inflow wind, and she could hear the

crisp *snap* of kindling. She turned to look out her window
at the pitch-dark. A transformer exploded nearby, blue
sparks shooting out like fireworks, and for an instant, she
could see the wedge-shaped tornado trundling toward
them, churning up the atmosphere. She got that shaky
feeling in the pit of her stomach, like a bubble that
wouldn't pop. Her hands went numb. There was glass in
her hair. Her heart raced harder than she'd ever imagined
possible. Lightning the color of tiger lilies strobed across
the sky as the tornado hit the first in a long line of telephone poles, blue sparks spitting out horizontally into the
air. One by one, the telephone poles got sucked up into
the gyrating vortex and pitched away.

Rick keyed the ignition, released the emergency brake,
and the engine roared to life with a coarse, deafening
sound. She groped for the door, but he grabbed her by the
arm and wouldn't let go. She tried desperately to break
away, a shriek clawing at her throat.

With a sudden inrush of air, the door flew open, and a
gaunt figure aimed his gun inside. His face was spattered
with blood, his hair was plastered to his skull and his wet
uniform was stuck to his body.

"Daddy?" she screamed.

Rick pressed the accelerator to the floor, and the van
tore out of the ditch. Her father jumped on the rocker
panel and held on tight. Sophie fumbled with her seat
belt, while her father girded himself, every muscle straining against the slapping door. Then he aimed his gun and
squeezed the trigger.

The sound was deafening.

Rick's lower lip blew off.

Sophie's eyes grew glassy with shock.

Blood flew everywhere.

The van danced across the road in a shower of sparks.

Sophie unbuckled her seat belt, but Rick only tightened his grip, the pain making her eyes water.

Another bump, and her father almost lost his balance.

Feeling a cold ache around her heart, she bit down savagely on Rick's arm, sinking her teeth into the sweaty, straining muscles until she could taste a warm gush of blood at the back of her throat.

He wrenched his arm away. Screaming and quivering with outrage. The sight of his mangled face curdled her blood. Those missing teeth, that shattered lip.

Her father hooked her around the middle, held on tight, and together they leaped into chaos. She felt as if she were falling off the planet at a million miles an hour. They hit the ground rolling, her arms clamped tight around his neck. They bumped over the wet grass until the field finally caught them. Sophie sputtered for air in a tangle of wildflowers, a searing pain registering in her lungs. *Try again, try again.* Air scudded into her lungs. She clasped her twitching fingers around her father's neck and gave a faint grateful cry.

He helped her upright, then the two of them staggered in the wind. Green sky, purple lightning. The air around them twisting and screaming. *Which way?* She heard the sound of squealing tires and looked back at the Doppler van. It was caught in the updraft, tires spinning futilely as Rick tried to get away.

Her father wrapped an arm around her. "Don't look back!" he said. "Run!"

13

Rick was caught in a vicious riptide, the howling wedge right in front of him now. The wind was screaming into the updraft at around 80 mph, mud and leaves whipping past like a powerful current. He could hear that classic freight train sound as he downshifted. *Frantic. Perspiring.* The bitch . . . the bitch was playing him like a yo-yo. She was illuminated by a series of exploding transformers, sparks accelerating into her base as a line of telephone poles got sucked into that gigantic vortex of spinning debris.

Gulping at the air like a banked trout, he put the van into reverse, whipped around in his seat and stomped on the gas. *"No, no, no!"* He tried to speed away from the heaving cloud base, where multiple vortices sprouted beneath the indigo-blue wall cloud, each tendril large enough to be called a tornado in its own right. He felt blasted out of his head. This wasn't supposed to happen. A cloud of splinters hit the van, then something cracked overhead—the satellite dish. He could feel his arteries bursting with blood as he tried desperately to get away.

All the windows broke at once with a loud crash. Both

doors were forced outward by the air pressure and jammed shut. He was sprayed with glass fragments, some of the cuts going deep. His world spun. Equipment collided in midair, computer circuitry exploding upon impact. *Thwunk, thwunk, thwunk.*

He stomped on the gas, a muffled roar in his ears, but the wheels spun around uselessly on the wet road. Visibility was bad, traction even worse. Both tires blew out, throwing the van into a crooked skid, and he felt the vibration in his bones as his very worst fears squeezed his lungs. *"No!!!"*

The van was riding on two wheels now, its chassis slowly twisting. Rick's nails split and snapped as he dug his fingers into the steering wheel and tried to level it out. *"Come on, come on . . . you bitch!"* The van blew sideways and slammed into the wedge with a deafening impact. He took a shuddering breath as it inhaled him whole.

The wind lifted the vehicle into the air with a spine-melting moan. Rick's hair snapped like fur touched by static, and air pockets bubbled beneath his skin as the van's frame crunched and buckled. His brain flooded with pain messages. He could hear the roof of the van ripping off, sending up a shower of sparks. Then a great hiss of air suctioned him out of the hole in the roof, and the van fell away like discarded litter.

He was upside down, right side up in a tumult of steam. Limbs flailing slow-motion. Above it all. Gazing into the lightning-dappled darkness. Suspended in a whirl of shattered glass and coiling barbed wire, splintered two-by-fours and dirty hailstones. Arms windmilling. Legs pinwheeling. Time slowed to a crawl in the tingling dark. And then, with horrible clarity, he felt the descent before it happened.

14

THE ENORMOUS wedge was uprooting saplings now, tossing them around like Popsicle sticks. Blinking the dirt from his eyes, Charlie scooped his daughter up in his arms and ran with her through the grass, their breath steaming ahead of them like paper cutouts. Something was wrong. Her right cheek was swollen and bruised, there was blood in her mouth; he wanted to shoot Rick all over again. He waded through the sodden, flapping field for what seemed like an eternity—holding her with bone-white, raw-knuckled resolve—until they finally splashed out onto the road.

The rain was coming down sideways now, streaming across their faces. He set Sophie down and looked around for the truck. Blinking the rain from his eyes, he spotted the cones of its headlights slicing into a furry darkness. "Run!" he shouted.

Sophie didn't want to let go of his hand. She stretched her arm out as they pulled away so that their fingers grazed one another. They leaped inside the truck, slamming the doors, and the cab instantly filled with the sound of their breathing.

"Hurry, Daddy!"

He keyed the ignition and pumped the gas, but the engine stalled out.

"Daddy?"

The air was the color of dirty water. A big piece of weatherboard danced along the ground, then flapped away like an awkward bird. The tops of the trees all bent in one direction—away from the enormous wedge that was corkscrewing across the land.

"Hurry!"

Not far from them stood a lone cottonwood tree, its shiny leaves wagging like a thousand tongues. The trunk was massive and grew into a wildly swaying crown, around which birds flew in roller-coaster formation. Only those weren't birds, he realized, but tractor tires and tree limbs. The very air was being scissored apart.

"Daddy?" Her voice grew plump with tension.

He keyed the ignition, pumped the gas, and the engine finally sparked to life. He shifted into reverse, jammed on the accelerator, and they sped backward down the ruler-straight road.

"Look out!" she shrieked.

Behind them, a telephone pole bent like a pipe cleaner before the wind, then reached its breaking point and snapped in half, sawdust spritzing into the air as it came bounding toward them. Charlie veered out of the way just as the top half of the pole bounced over the road, missing them by a hairbreadth. He turned the truck around, debris banging off the fenders. The engine began to sputter and pop. The ominously rising temp gauge stared back at him.

"Move, you piece of shit . . ."

The gust front nailed the intersection, traffic light

swinging to and fro on its flimsy cables. Near the high-way entrance ramp, scraggly patches of squawbush and hawthorn bowed at a forty-five-degree angle in front of a used-car lot. Lightning zapped all around them, while the rain began to gain in vertical growth. Then it really started going nuts. Definitely hairy. There were lightning flashes inside the funnel cloud, behind it, to either side . . . like a huge spark plug igniting some humongous engine in the sky. The debris cloud whipped up so much dust it was throttle-down turns in the dark. Charlie kept one eye on the monster and the other on a good ditch to jump into.

Then he heard it: the sound of hell clawing for a hand-hold. The sound of space collapsing. Dust billowed past their windows—a series of shapes and flying mirages. The noise became deafening. Something somersaulted directly overhead, then landed in front of them and kept moving. A Mazda from the used-car lot barreled across the street and struck the guardrail in a spray of sparks. Next a Dodge Caravan rose up into the air and slammed earthward, spanking grille-first on the pavement with a terrible pounding thud that Charlie could feel in his skele-ton. Automobiles from the car lot staggered across the road, bounding toward them like broken-down drunks.

BOOM! BOOM! BOOM!

"Holy shit!" He alternately hit the gas and slammed on the brakes while car parts flew at them from the whirling debris cloud, tumbling out of the darkness. Car after car barreled through the air, spinning end over end like kids' blocks and spewing streams of gasoline and brake fluid all over the road. The image was bizarre—luminous and hyperreal. Twisted, torn steel blown scraping across the asphalt like metal fingers. Automobiles raining down from the sky. Half of Detroit gone airborne.

Charlie jammed into reverse, nailed the throttle and backed down the road, while something else pirouetted into the sky—the sweeping headlights of a turning car. He slammed on the brakes, cranked the wheel hard, then skidded sideways just as an apple-green Pontiac came bearing down on them.

Sophie's screams were like paper cuts—sharp, deep and bloodless. The airborne Pontiac hit the ground directly behind them, its shuddering chassis slamming down hard, its cage collapsing with a ringing sound like a cathedral bell. Metal grinding metal, windshield glass exploding, it continued to roll . . . crumpling and folding like an accordion. Alligator treads spitting from the wheel wells as the tires buckled and split.

"Get us out of here!" She covered her eyes.

He braked and swerved, then pushed his daughter down on the floorboards just as the truck began to shudder. Their ears popped from the mounting pressure as the truck lifted up, just the back end. The tornado had ahold of them, and they were going up. *Jesus, they'd come so far, and now this.* The tornado had them. They were going to die.

He could've sworn the floorboards and doors were wobbling back and forth. The air smelled of things hidden underneath a house for a very long time. They were floating in an inky river, so thick and substantial he could almost touch it. Then the truck snap-crackled to life, rearing up and bucking across the road. Debris shot into the flatbed like bullets. They were whirling and vaulting, and then, when they thunked back down onto the ground again, Charlie bit his tongue and drew blood. A flurry of motion, and suddenly . . . unbelievably, everything went still.

They sat in the eerie gathering calm. He waited for a moment, then peered at the sky. The tornado was slowly shrinking, becoming smaller and smaller as it churned uneasily away from them. Then it snaked back into the clouds, leaving a vaporous trail in its wake. A foggy haze, like the exhaust from a racing engine.

Charlie sat motionless for a moment, then lifted Sophie up off the floorboards. "You okay?"

A weak smile. "Yeah."

"Looks like we made it."

She laughed and hugged him tightly.

He would never let go this time.

15

THEY DROVE along in silence. The traffic was tied up in knots due to cars wrapped around light poles and draped over billboards. Charlie let his daughter rest her head against his shoulder. Her inhalations were shallow, and she jumped at the slightest rumble of thunder. Her fingers were torn and bruised. Her jaw was swollen, and her lower bicuspid was missing; the monster had taken her tooth. It disturbed him deeply, how she'd lost her innocence today.

"Are we going home now?" She lifted her drowsy head.

"Shh, sweetie. I'm taking you to the hospital."

Her eyes reflected the sun's last fiery glow. "I'm okay, Dad. I'd rather go home."

"Shh. Sit back and relax."

She gave a reluctant nod and sank back against him. "But we'll go home after the hospital, right?"

"You have my word."

"I love you," she said softly.

"I love you, too, baby." He allowed himself to relax just a bit and was immediately overcome with a draining sense of weariness. He could smell the stink of his own sweat, a raw clay odor. He was covered in mud, battered and bruised, but they'd made it. They were alive. It was a miracle. He'd finally managed to get through to the hospital, and Willa was fine. She was relieved to hear that Sophie was okay. They'd all made it. The sky strobed with gaudy colors, scuds of clouds like freshly raked coals pouring into the retreating thunderstorm. The air smelled sweet as mint, and the evening star had risen above the plains. He was happy to be alive. Humbly grateful, his heart and head synchronous once again.

Then he saw it. The brown Doppler van. He swerved over to the side of the road and hit the brakes.

"What is it?" She stirred, hair matted up on one side.

The Doppler van lay upside down in a muddy field. The radiator shroud was dented, and the tires were in shreds.

She sat forward in her seat. "Dad?"

"Be right back."

"What's wrong?" Her eyes grew wide. Her lashes were wet.

"Everything's gonna be okay." He hugged her one-armed. "Don't worry, sweetie."

"Please don't leave me here."

He drew his gun. "I'll be within earshot."

"Careful," she whispered. "Okay?"

He flew down the slope into the wild-growing grass, drenched pink in the dying light. He approached the overturned vehicle with extreme caution. The tie rod jutted out like a broken bone, and the snarling bumper was pushed up nearly two feet. Above the wreck, a fantastic rainbow filled the sky.

Carefully aiming his .38, Charlie said, "Step out of the vehicle! Now! Put your hands up where I can see them!"

The windows were shattered. The roof was torn off. He swept his gun before him as he slowly circled the wreck, then bent to have a closer look.

The interior of the van appeared to be empty. Charlie straightened up, feeling a chill like wet leaves, and scanned the horizon with its fringe of backlit farms. A languid cloud of monarch butterflies caught the dying light as the sun edged beneath the horizon. In places, the tornado had reduced the grass to stubble, leaving a miles-long damage path through mostly untamed prairie.

He glanced back at the truck, where his daughter was watching him with wide, frightened eyes. The sunset made her face look on fire. The silver locket was tucked inside his shirt pocket; he wouldn't give it back to her until he'd washed the blood off. He wouldn't tell her about her grandfather, either, until everything had settled down.

"Daddy?"

"I'm right here."

She gave him a sad little wave. The moment would remain forever frozen in his mind.

He took one last look around, then holstered his weapon. He'd have to call local law. Let them deal with it. His daughter was waiting. Then he noticed the distant heap of white against the cold, dark earth.

He drew his weapon again and jogged across the field. He jogged over furrows banked with sodden leaves and debris, the sharp odor of freshly plowed earth filling his nostrils. His boots sank into the soft dirt, and his breath came out shallow and fast as he moved further and further away from the road. Away from Sophie. He tiptoed along the edges of a rut, anticipation crackling up his spine, then stooped in the gathering gloom.

The flannel shirt was gone. So were the shoes and socks. The mangled victim wore only a pair of blue jeans, the rest of his outfit having been apparently sucked away in the wind. Charlie let out a quick troubled breath as he crouched for a better look. Stalks of wheat peppered the victim's chest like the needles of a startled porcupine. The battered face was unrecognizable. Most disturbing of all was the severe angulation of the neck and the caved-in appearance of the skull from where the body had been dropped from a great height. The eyes—shiny black as feeding insects—were fixed and dilated. He was dead, all right, whoever he was.

Charlie turned the body over. Old scars crisscrossed the trunk and upper arms, some as thick as fingers. Grim evidence of childhood abuse. He stepped hard on his anger and let the body fall. The broken legs were trapped inside a tangle of barbed wire. They were going to have to cut through the rusty wire to get to the pants pockets, where a wallet or other ID might be found.

Very faintly he could hear sirens off in the distance. Examining the victim's ruined mouth, he parted the lips and found an absence of teeth, then he ran his finger carefully up over the maxillary arch. This had to be Rick. Had to be. Doppler van nearby. Same color hair. Absence of teeth. Small red marks over the bridge of the nose where his glasses had recently rested.

Hair lifting in the breeze, Charlie had a sudden thought. He reached for the corpse's right arm, picked it up, turned it over, and there it was—a perfect bite mark. Sophie's tooth impressions sunk in the chalky white flesh, those lateral incisors distinctive for their slight overlap.

This was Rick Kripner, all right. Of that there could be

no doubt. Charlie released the cold limb and tried to find the still center of himself, but his heart wouldn't stop thundering in his ears. He'd found his killer . . . still he wasn't satisfied. His eyes lingered suspiciously on the broken body before him—the dead eyes, the becalmed face. Nothing made any sense. Nothing would ever make sense to him again. Rick Kripner had been such an ordinary guy.

He stood up, exhaustion welling inside him. The distant sirens were getting louder now. He glanced down at his feet, where a Styrofoam cup was partially buried in the dirt. *Styrofoam, arrowheads.* Greater battles than theirs had been fought on this hallowed ground. History was just another place the wind blew through.

"Daddy?"

"Be right there."

He detected a troubling shift in the atmosphere and felt the sudden uplift, like a tap on the shoulder. A friendly tap. A warning.

He turned, but there was no one there—just a crow that appeared to be watching him. He stood for a moment scanning the horizon, where distant bur oaks flared in the wind. Then a playful breeze slapped his hat off his head, and he caught it one-handed before it blew away.

The wind moved on, unhurried and graceful, disturbing his thinning hair along with his complacency; it eddied and spilled across this broken land, stroking the slumped shoulders of the prairie in an ancient dance. It gave him a start. It gave him the gift of breath, and then it moved on.

ONE WEEK LATER

DIVIDING OKLAHOMA almost in half was an area called the Cross Timbers, an impenetrable swath of blackjack trees and scrub oak that ran down the center of the state. To the east of the Cross Timbers were the woodlands, where the annual rainfall sometimes exceeded fifty inches. To the west was the drier half of Oklahoma, once home to the Plains Indians, a group of warlike nomads who followed the migrating buffalo herds. This was where the Wild West began, in the arid prairie of the Great Plains.

From west to east, the land fell away like the steps of a staircase, the high plains of the Panhandle giving way to descending beds of sedimentary rock. Red sandstone from the canyons of the sandy river valley swept across the plains in great undulating waves. The dirt was red, the wheat was yellow, the sky sometimes green during tornado season; but the heart of Oklahoma beat red, white and blue.

Charlie stood on a rise with Willa and Sophie, facing the southern sky, where the horizon merged into one hazy line and the distant storm, infused with lightning, was in excess of fifty thousand feet. Swirling rain, fog, the constant growling boom of thunder. His father would've approved.

Sophie clutched the canister of her grandfather's ashes in her arms, the grief making her quiet. Her silver locket was clasped securely around her neck. The skies to the north were striated with horsetails, and whenever the sun burst from behind the clouds, they could see shimmering fields where hundreds of wildflowers turned various shades of pink and purple in the flapping wind.

Wearing a white shirt and a wide tie, Charlie helped his daughter open the canister, and together they prepared to release Isaac's ashes into the oncoming wind. She rose up on one foot, the bones of her vertebrae rippling like the segments of a caterpillar, while Willa read aloud from a Christina Rossetti poem. "Who has seen the wind? Neither you nor I: But when the trees bow down their heads, The wind is passing by."

Sophie tensed, nervous wrinkles creasing her face. "You do it," she said, handing her father the canister.

Charlie flung the ashes into the air. "So long, Pop." They filtered up like the ephemeral bodies of swarming insects, while an unearthly light splintered through the clouds. What was strong in him came from his father; what was wrong with him came from his father as well, and he could accept that.

Willa closed the book and eyed them with tremendous empathy. He held her tightly, reminded of the loneliness he felt whenever she got up for work each morning, the warm little concavity she left in bed beside him. She rose on shaky legs to kiss him, a single tear sliding on a curved path down her cheek. The sun rose higher across their faces, and for one trembling moment, all was right with the world. Charlie Grover was a hopeful man.

"There goes Grandpa," Sophie said softly. "There he goes."

Together they stood staring at the spectacle of grass in motion. Coneflowers and blazing stars brightened the grasslands, where enormous herds of buffalo used to graze, herds measuring up to twenty-five miles long and fifty miles deep. The herds were gone. Their grief flooded forward like the wind.

Acknowledgments

Many thanks to Sara Ann Freed, Jamie Raab and Larry Kirshbaum, Carter Blanchard, Helen Fremont, Wendy Weil, Rich Green and Keya Khayatian, Harvey-Jane Kowal, Kristen Weber, Molly Kleinman and Emily Forland, Eric Brown and Mike Rudell; and most especially to my husband, Doug, whose wisdom and insight grace these pages.

About the Author

ALICE BLANCHARD won the Katherine Anne Porter Prize for Fiction for her book of stories, *The Stuntman's Daughter.* She has also received a PEN Syndicated Fiction Award, a New Letters Library Award, and a Centrum Artists in Residence Fellowship. Alice Blanchard lives in Los Angeles with her husband.

More
Alice Blanchard!

Please turn this page
for a
preview of
her new novel.

Coming in hardcover
in August 2005.

Daisy Hubbard caught herself staring at the flight attendant's elegant French knot and wondered why she didn't have the flair some women had with their hair. As a scientist, Daisy had always been hopelessly pragmatic when it came to her looks and seldom wore jewelry, never used perfume or nail polish. She pressed her unpowdered forehead against the cold glass. They were hurtling through the atmosphere, cruising along at six hundred miles per hour under the illusion of stillness. The moon floated in the night sky as if it were tethered to the ground by an invisible line. Daisy gazed at the landmass below. They were flying over scattered American cities—cities she'd never been to, cities whose identities evaded her now, constellations of light blossoming out of the darkness. Clusters of wattage, billions of bulbs.

She caught her troubled reflection in the window and tested her forehead for a fever. A migraine had moved in and unpacked its bags. She had taken the night flight from Boston to Los Angeles and was on her third glass of sour-tasting Chablis, the Boeing 747's turbo engines droning steadily in the background. She tried to process what the detective had told her over the phone: *Your sister stopped paying the rent and disappeared from her apartment without a trace. Her current whereabouts are unknown.*

The plane suddenly began to shake with turbulence, and the "FASTEN SEAT BELT" sign blinked on. She hadn't reviewed the emergency instructions yet—something she traditionally did before each flight—so she picked up the laminated card. The printed instructions reminded her that the seat cushions doubled as flotation devices, the life rafts were stashed inside the overhead compartments, and the nearest exit doors were pretty far away from Row 23, Seat A. As she studied the brightly colored diagrams, she became convinced that, should the plane crash for whatever reason, she and the strange man seated next to her would plummet into some polluted, unknown city and become one with the asphalt.

Daisy shoved the laminated card back in its plastic sleeve and closed her eyes, while the plane bucked and shuddered against the oncoming wind. They were thousands of feet above the cold, silent earth. She wanted an aspirin badly, but she'd packed the bottle inside her checked luggage. The next jolt against the jet stream took her breath away. Fear was shortness of breath. Fear was rapid breathing.

Now the strange man sitting next to her said, "Watch the flight attendants. If they're not scared, don't you be scared."

She smiled gratefully.

He offered her a peanut. "What's your name?"

"Daisy," she said.

"I'm Bram."

"Hello, Bram." They shook hands.

"Are you from Boston, Daisy?"

"Yes," she said, remembering that she wasn't very good at idle conversation. Most people didn't like to talk about the things she wanted to talk about—quantum physics, the Earth's rotation around the sun, the fact that Einstein got his best ideas shaving.

"So, Daisy." Bram seemed to enjoy the sound of her name on his tongue. "What brings you to L.A.?"

"My sister's missing," she told him.

"Missing?"

"She's schizophrenic. She does this sometimes. She runs away. Only this time it's thousands of miles away from home."

He looked at her as if she'd just rattled off a list of fatal plane crashes. They exchanged a few more inanities before he fumbled for a magazine and pretended to read.

After a while, the turbulence eased, and she could swallow normally again. She turned to look out her window at the pitch-black below—the haunting emptiness of the American West. The sun felt all of its 93 million miles away. She could hear Detective Makowski's voice inside her head now, low-pitched and authoritative. *"We checked the Jane Doe's. We've checked all the morgues. Nothing's come up."* She stopped breathing momentarily, unable to absorb the fact that the police were already thinking that her sister might be dead.

After they'd landed safely at LAX, the man named Bram followed her silently off the airplane. The terminal was a blur of activity. She trailed a huge crowd down a long green corridor toward the Baggage Pickup area. There were countless twists and turns, and they had to pass by two metal detectors. Daisy found an ATM machine, but it was broken. She looked around and realized she was lost. "Which way to Baggage Pickup?" she asked a passing stranger.

"Follow me." Bram took her by the elbow.

Daisy didn't trust men who steered you places, since there was no telling when the steering would end. It was only eleven o'clock (2 AM back in Boston) and she'd had too many bravery drinks. Most of the people inside the terminal were dressed for the beach, colorful logos splashed across their jeans and T-shirts, and Daisy was feeling seriously overdressed in her tailored blouse and knife-pleat skirt. These terminals were well air-conditioned. She felt a chill and wished she'd worn a sweater.

They found the Baggage Pickup area and waited for their luggage. The baggage handlers kept hurling people's suitcases through a trapdoor in the ceiling. Bram got his right away, then stood around waiting for hers to arrive.

"It's okay," she said. "I'm fine."

"I'll wait."

"Thank you. Really."

He left looking mildly disappointed.

She didn't like the sickening fluorescent wavelengths and grew dizzy watching people's luggage rotate by. Several other night flights had arrived from the East Coast, and soon this corner of the terminal was noisy and overcrowded. As the suitcases with matching totes came flying through the trapdoor in the ceiling, Daisy instantly recognized her ugly yellow suitcase, the one she'd dragged around with her from college to graduate school to her internship at Berhoffer. She'd always been embarrassed by that cheap, cheese-colored vinyl, which had never failed to give away her lowly status as a scholarship student who knew nothing about cotillions or summers in East Hampton, and who'd never set foot inside a country club. She made the mistake of attending a liberal-arts school for spoiled rich girls whose doting dads bought them Thoroughbred horses to be stabled nearby. Daisy had been brought up on her mother's accounting salary; somehow it'd never occurred to her how poor the Hubbards were until she'd gone away to college.

Now the baggage handlers tossed Daisy's suitcases down the chute as if they were trying to see how far they could throw. The wheeled pullman landed with a crack on the edge of the luggage carousel, its lid popping open, her unmentionables spilling out.

"Idiots," she grumbled, snapping it shut again. She couldn't help feeling small and insignificant as she wheeled her bags over to a plastic bench molded to fit the contours of something—not the human body, that was for sure. She sat in exhausted silence, while people became pinpoints. The airport was so huge and impersonal, she dissolved into apathy. Banks of fluorescent lights made a constant hum, like a dull chorus. So this was how Los Angeles swallowed you whole—right away, before you'd even set foot outside the airport gates.

She leaned against the cement wall until the back of her head began to throb. She swore she could feel the Earth's motion somewhere underneath her breathing. Conflicting noises washed over her like dust disturbed by a fan. *Anna's missing.* She didn't want to think about it. Fear was paralyzing. Fear was immobilizing. She stood up, determined to keep moving, and dragged her luggage across the lobby and through the sliding glass doors, where she was hit by a torrid blast of muggy air.

She swam through this soup down the gritty sidewalk toward the taxi stand. The cabdriver was tall and gaunt and reminded her of an aging character actor. He deposited her luggage into the roomy trunk of the cab, while she slid in the backseat. All around them, concrete terminals stood in beams of washed-out light.

"Where y'all from?" the cabdriver asked in a southern drawl that reminded her of Truett.

"Boston," she said, suddenly nostalgic for everything she'd left behind.

"Beantown, huh? Miracle City?" He glanced at her through the rearview, tires squealing as they swerved away from the curb. He drove past monolithic buildings and dark alleyways—was the city always this desolate? "Remember Dukakis riding around in that tank, looking like an idiot?" he said. "And then his campaign tanked, remember? Miracle City, ha. That was some miracle."

She didn't know what he was talking about. She leaned against the sticky vinyl seat, the pain milling aimlessly around inside her head now. They drove past a series of squat, empty-looking buildings, then took an entrance ramp onto the freeway. The sky was filled with millions of stars struggling to penetrate through the smog layer. It was hard to believe that, thousands of years ago, there had actually been glaciers in Hollywood instead of palm trees.

"I'm from Alabama originally," the cabdriver said, turning around briefly to look at her. His nose began with a broad bridge and grew vigorously from his face before ending abruptly in a pair of deeply grooved nostrils. "Me and the missus moved here twenty-five years ago and never regretted it for a single second. Nossir. There're plenty of advantages to living in the second-largest city in America, you know? Out here, you've got more of everything. Out here, everybody has a different set of wheels. Nobody needs a cab."

And it was true, the driveways were crowded with vehicles of every kind—SUVs, motorcycles, trucks, mini-vans. They were cruising through a residential area now, the gridlike streets stretching for miles past identical-looking bungalows painted pink or persimmon or peppermint. Everything seemed so promising here, so full of hope and opportunity.

"Hey, do you like pie?" he asked.

"Pie?" Daisy blinked. "Um . . . sure. I guess."

"Well okay, then. You've got to try the Pied Piper

down on LaBrea. They make fifty different kinds of pies, I kid you not. You won't find anything like that back East."

He dropped her off at a small, ugly motel in the middle of West Los Angeles. A low-grade fear was making her ill. The sky was deep cobalt, and the closer she looked, the more stars she could see. She paid the driver, who tipped his hat and sped off. Then she dragged her luggage across the asphalt toward the manager's office.

The middle-aged manager had a face like a tight ball. His mouth was slightly open, and he stared at the color TV on his desk. A ballgame was playing.

"Daisy Hubbard," she said. "I made a reservation."

The motel promised low rates, air-conditioning, free parking, and a swimming pool. AAA members received a 10 percent discount.

Inside the privacy of her own cabin, Daisy stretched out on the double bed and tried to find her inner self. The air conditioner hummed noisily and the room reeked of Lysol. She thought she understood what might've drawn her sister to the West Coast. Out here, you could reinvent yourself. You could slip on a whole new personality, and nobody would notice or even care.

She went to the bathroom and splashed cold water on her face, then tugged at her hair with wet fingers, all her motions anxious and hard. The paleness of her skin alarmed her. She had a bad hangover and pinched her cheeks, trying to feel something. Even pain was preferable to this present torpor. She smiled at her reflection, revealing a set of perfectly proportioned teeth. Back in the sixth grade, she'd forgotten to brush her teeth on a regular basis, and when the orthodontist finally took her braces off, there were cavities in her front teeth as random as bullet holes. These days, her porcelain fillings were faintly stained because of all the coffee she drank. But she liked her smile. It was wide and friendly, unafraid to show off its defects.

Daisy collapsed on the motel bed and squeezed her eyes shut, trying to block out the luminous neon glow leaking through cracks in the mini-blinds. She tossed and turned, while outside her window, fragments of light whizzed past. After a while, she fell into an exhausted sleep. Her dreams were shallow and disturbing, like mild stomachaches. She had a dim memory of Anna back home in Vermont, shuffling downstairs like a zombie and squinting into the noontime sun as she entered the kitchen with a cigarette dangling between her lips. Her long red hair was caught up in an elastic band at the base of her neck, her eye makeup was smudged and her face was puffy from too much sleep. Or maybe it was the meds. "Hey, you," she said, trudging over for a lethargic hug and kiss on the cheek. "Finally made your way home, huh?" She smelled of sleep, of the desire for oblivion.

Daisy stirred and opened her eyes. The clock said one AM. She sat up and turned on the TV set, and some kind of plucky banjo music assaulted her ears. A man in a cheap suit was standing on his head. "You won't find a better deal, I guarantee!" he hollered at the camera. He reminded her of Truett, same lanky sex appeal and hard-sell sensibility. In the next shot, he was doing cartwheels.

She wondered how there could possibly be fifty different kinds of pie and added them up in her head. *Apple, pumpkin, lemon meringue, Boston crème . . .* She counted all the way up to fourteen and figured there couldn't be any more than that. Then she remembered. *Pecan.* Of course. *And peach.*

"Sixteen," she said out loud, the unexpected smallness of her own voice sending shivers cascading across her scalp. Great. Instead of curing fatal diseases, she was counting pies. How could Anna have been so careless with her life? Was she trying to ruin everything? *Because congratulations, Anna, you've succeeded.*

Sweating profusely, Daisy got out of bed and decided to take a shower. She peeled out of her damp clothes, balled them up, and tossed them on the bed. Her back was knotted. The bathroom door didn't close all the way. She worked her hands over her tense neck muscles as she stepped into the shower. She unwrapped the bar of complimentary soap and let the cool spray hit her. The shower stall smelled of other people, and the tiled floor was spotted here and there with mold. How well did they clean these places, anyway? She avoided rubbing up against the milky glass doors, while a sharp, tepid spray hit her face. She lathered herself all over, hands circling her skin, and hoped that by the time she was done, things would have magically righted themselves again.

With a gathering sense of optimism, she stepped out of the shower and dried herself off with a terrycloth bath towel, then put on the extra-large T-shirt she used as a nightgown. Constantly aware of Anna all along the edges of herself, Daisy collapsed back in bed, heart racing, and had a hopeful image of her sister taking refuge in some local homeless shelter or halfway house. Once or twice a year back in Edgewater, after she and Lily had had a particularly bad fight, Anna would sometimes freak out and disappear. But they always knew where to look for her—at her best friend Maranda's house, or else the Edgewater Presbyterian church or the local battered women's shelter. Anna always showed up eventually, like a cat.

Soon Daisy was sound asleep, dreaming of the flight out to Los Angeles, of the dark earth below and the man seated next to her. *Bram. Short for Bramwell.* In her dream, he grew horns, and the peanuts he offered her looked like miniature penises.

She woke up in a clammy sweat. It was dark outside, still the middle of the night. She switched on her bedside lamp and stretched, contrasting the paleness of her skin with the dark blue of the motel wall. There was a pattern of miniature gold anchors on the blue background. She'd always envied her sister's close relationship with their mother. Lily and Anna had the biggest case of love-hate Daisy had ever witnessed. She was always getting caught in the middle of their feuds and taking frantic phone calls from one or the other. *She's doing this, she did that, she said blah blah blah.* Still, Daisy envied their bond. Sometimes she felt as if her entire life had been swallowed up by Anna's problems. *How's Anna? What're we going to do about Anna? What's wrong with Anna?* From the time she was eight or nine, *ad nauseam, ad infinitum.* Daisy and Lily rarely had a conversation that didn't revolve around her younger sister.

Suddenly thirsty, she remembered the soda machine in the front office and got out of bed. Pulling on a pair of jeans, she left the security of her cabin for the vastness of the arid hot night. She had once heard that Los Angeles was seventy suburbs in search of a city, and she was somewhere in the middle of that lostness now, surrounded by concrete and glass. Out here, everything was called something-wood: *Brentwood, Hollywood, Inglewood.* And where were these so-called woods? All she could see were two rows of palm trees running along the spine of Santa Monica Boulevard, swaying in the balmy breeze. The palm trees, stamped against the night sky, reminded her of movie props. Back in Boston, it was probably snowing, the New England sky dropping more and more inches, as if it wanted to obliterate spring.

The deserted front office behind the Moorish-style fence and plastic-webbed lawn chairs was brightly lit. "Hello?" Daisy said, but the office was empty. She found the soda machine, inserted a few quarters, and out clunked a can of ginger ale. On her way back to her cabin, the asphalt's warmth surprised her. She padded along in her bare feet, while a Buick Regal drove past, casting a large shadow across the motel's facade. Her own shadow grew like a cornstalk, then slid sideways in the headlights' glare as the car sped on down the boulevard. These shadows were reborn again as another car drove past, detritus stirring and skittering in its wake.

Back inside the false security of her cabin, Daisy took a seat in a moldy-feeling armchair and drank her soda, gripped by an undefined panic. There was nothing to do now but wait. She rubbed her shivering arms. It was too early to call Lily. She had to fix her eyes on something. Anything. Fear was a slippery incline. She turned on the TV set and wrapped her arms around her knees. She had brought the smell of outside in, her molecules mingling with the heavy metals of this polluted city.

ALSO AVAILABLE ON
TIME WARNER AUDIO BOOKS:

THE BREATHTAKER
By Alice Blanchard
Read by Peter Coyote
Unabridged
6 cassettes/ 9 hours
ISBN: 1-58621-696-1